HUDA F ARE YOU?

Huda Fahmy

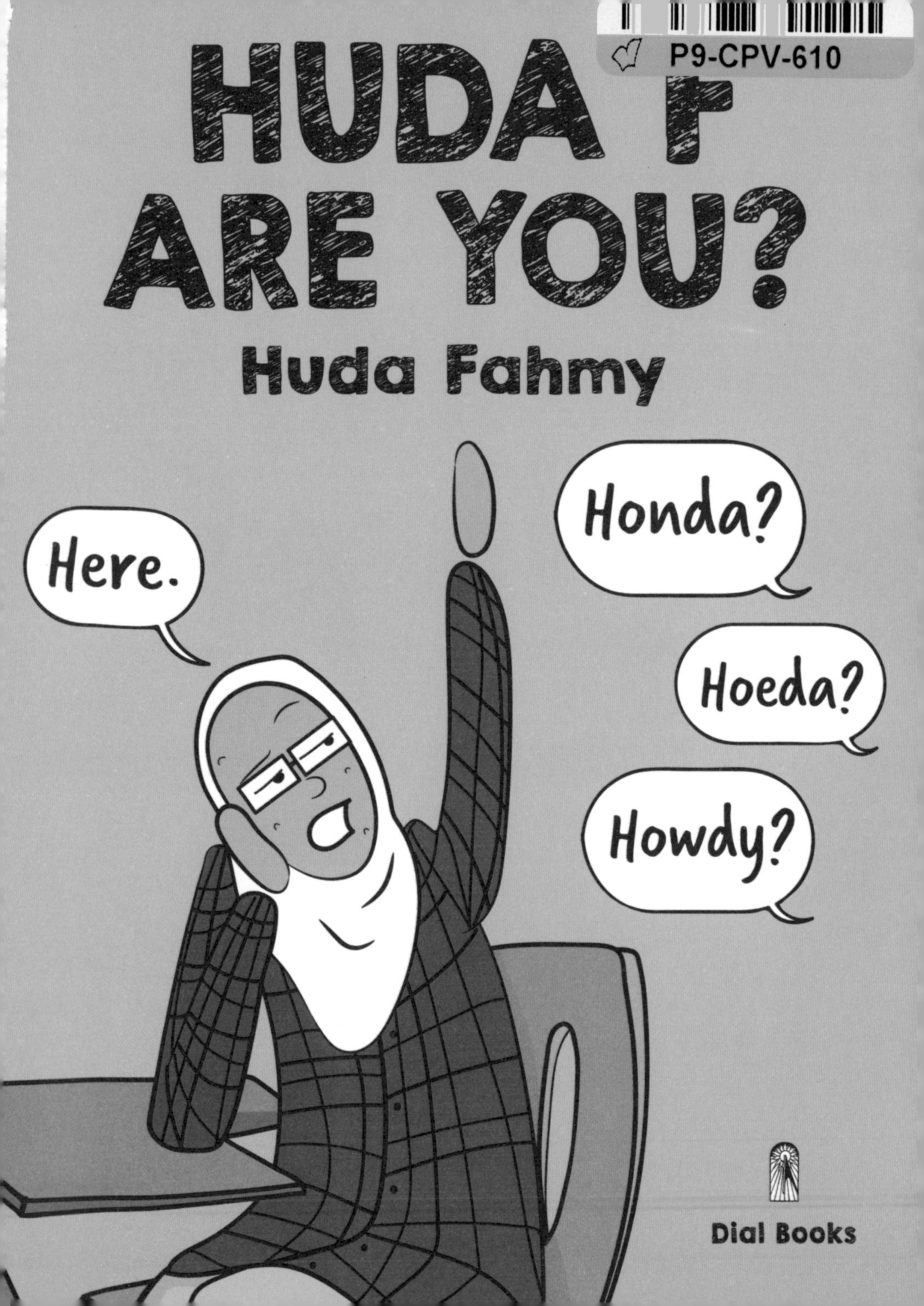
Here.
Honda?
Hoeda?
Howdy?

Dial Books

DEDICATED TO MY MOM

(who wants everyone to know she hates the title)

AND TO MY HUSBAND, GEHAD

I owe you a million weekends.

Dial Books
An imprint of Penguin Random House LLC, New York

First published in the United States of America by Dial Books,
an imprint of Penguin Random House LLC, 2021

Copyright © 2021 by Huda Fahmy

Dial & colophon are registered trademarks of Penguin Random House LLC.
Visit us online at penguinrandomhouse.com.

Library of Congress Cataloging-in-Publication Data is available
Printed in China
ISBN 9780593324318 (pbk) • 10 9 8 7 6 5 4 3 2 1
ISBN 9780593324301 (hc) • 10 9 8 7 6 5 4 3 2 1
TOPL
Design by Mina Chung • Text set in Baskerville MT Pro and Verveine

Dear Reader,

It is a cliche jokingly acknowledged that a Muslim kid who grows up in the United States must eventually experience an identity crisis. This is a story of just such an experience.

While you read, please keep in mind that this story and these characters are not meant to represent all Muslims or all Muslim experiences. In other words, Muslims are not a monolith. Speaking as a hijab-wearing Muslim woman, we are especially complicated, nuanced, and most definitely don't wear our hijabs to bed*.

While much of this story is based on real life, it is not an entirely autobiographical tale. Most names, characters, businesses, and places are either the products of the author's imagination or used in a fictitious manner. Any resemblance to actual persons, living or dead, or actual events is purely coincidental.

Thank you for reading my book! I hope you laugh a little, learn a little, and maybe even meme it a little.

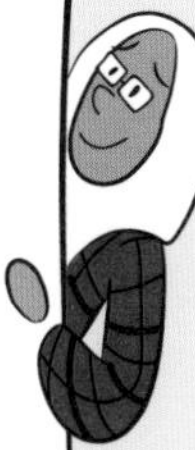

Sincerely,

Huda F.

*Because I consider my character an extension of myself, and I would never de-hijab in public (extenuating circumstances not included), I made the choice to never draw my character without her hijab. This is why, throughout the book, you'll see Huda in bed wearing her hijab. This would never happen in real life (unless I came home like super exhausted and could do nothing but plop face-first onto my mattress, in my outside clothes and all. Don't judge me).

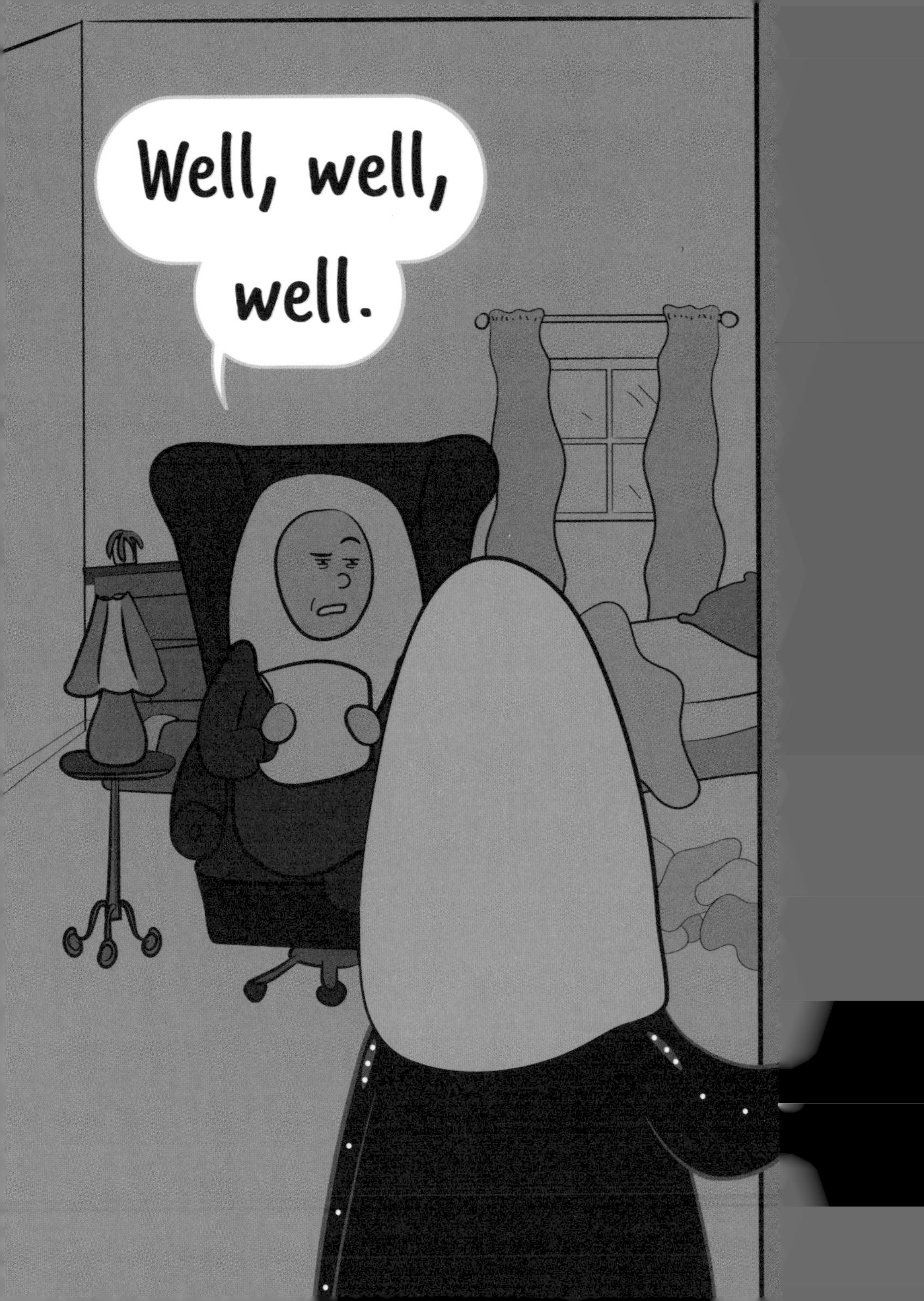
Well, well, well.

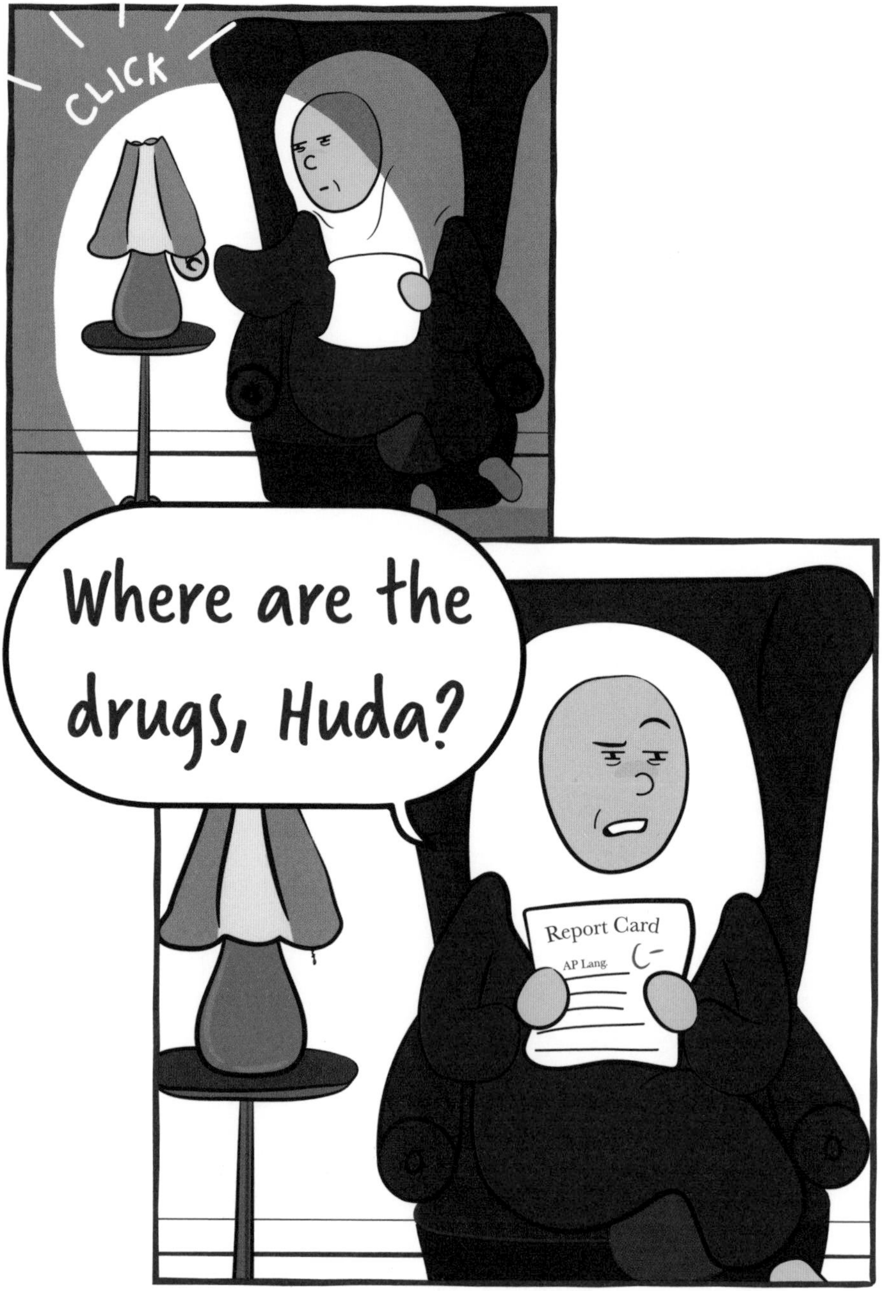
CLICK
Where are the drugs, Huda?
Report Card
AP Lang.
C-

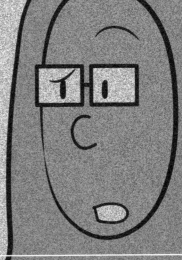

PAUSE II

Yup. That's me.

You're probably wondering how I ended up in this situation.

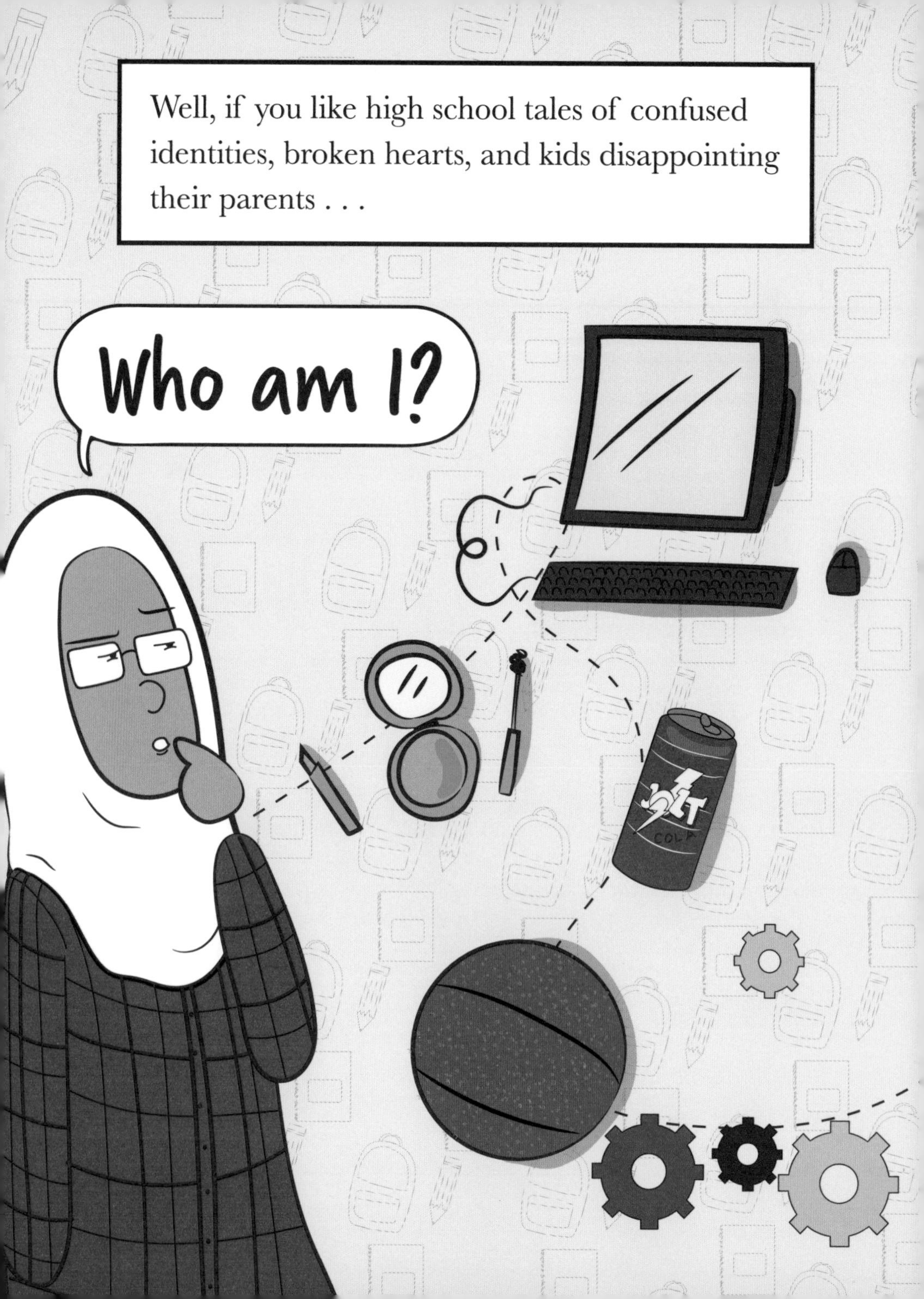
Well, if you like high school tales of confused identities, broken hearts, and kids disappointing their parents . . .
Who am I?

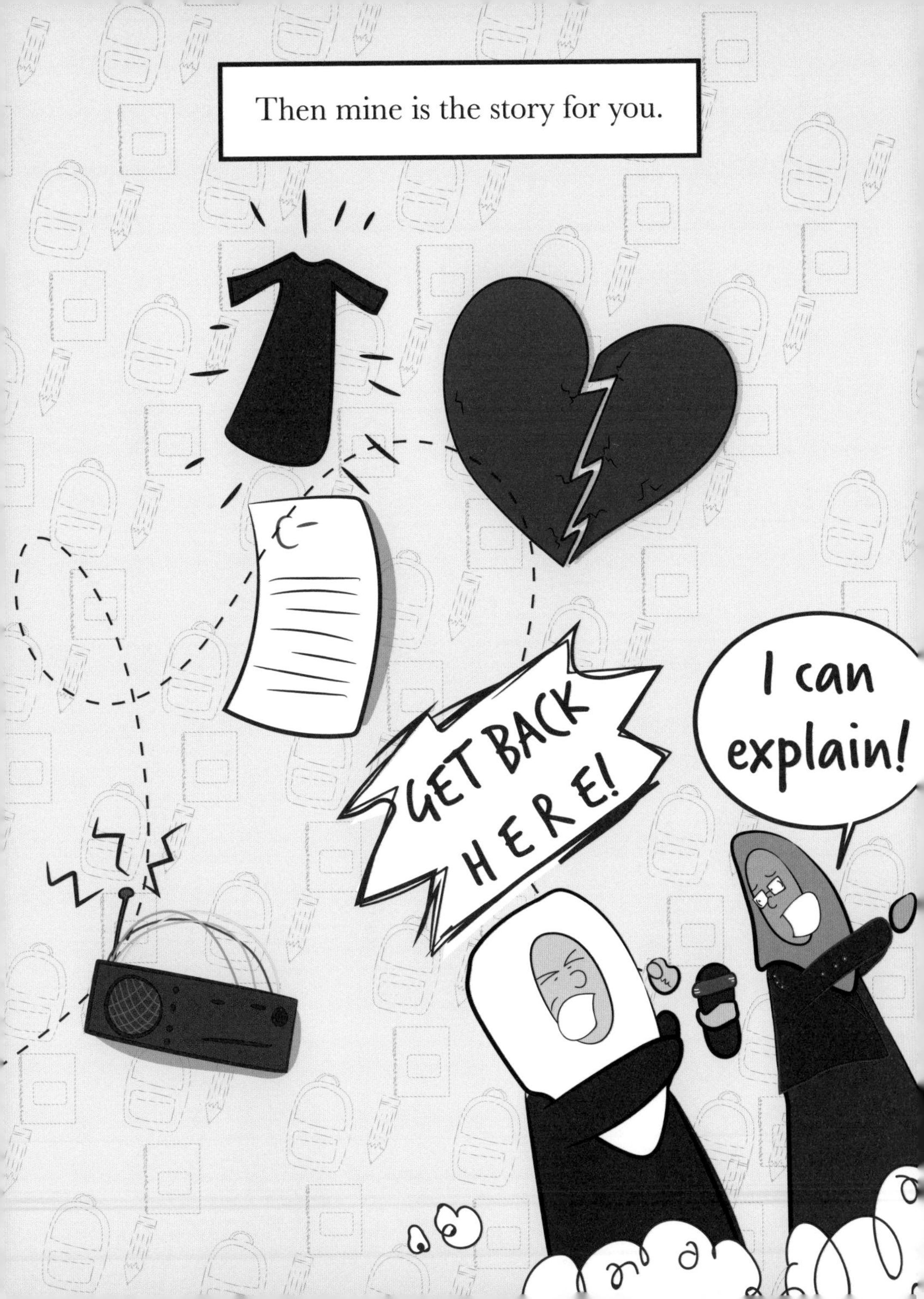
Then mine is the story for you.
GET BACK HERE!
I can explain!

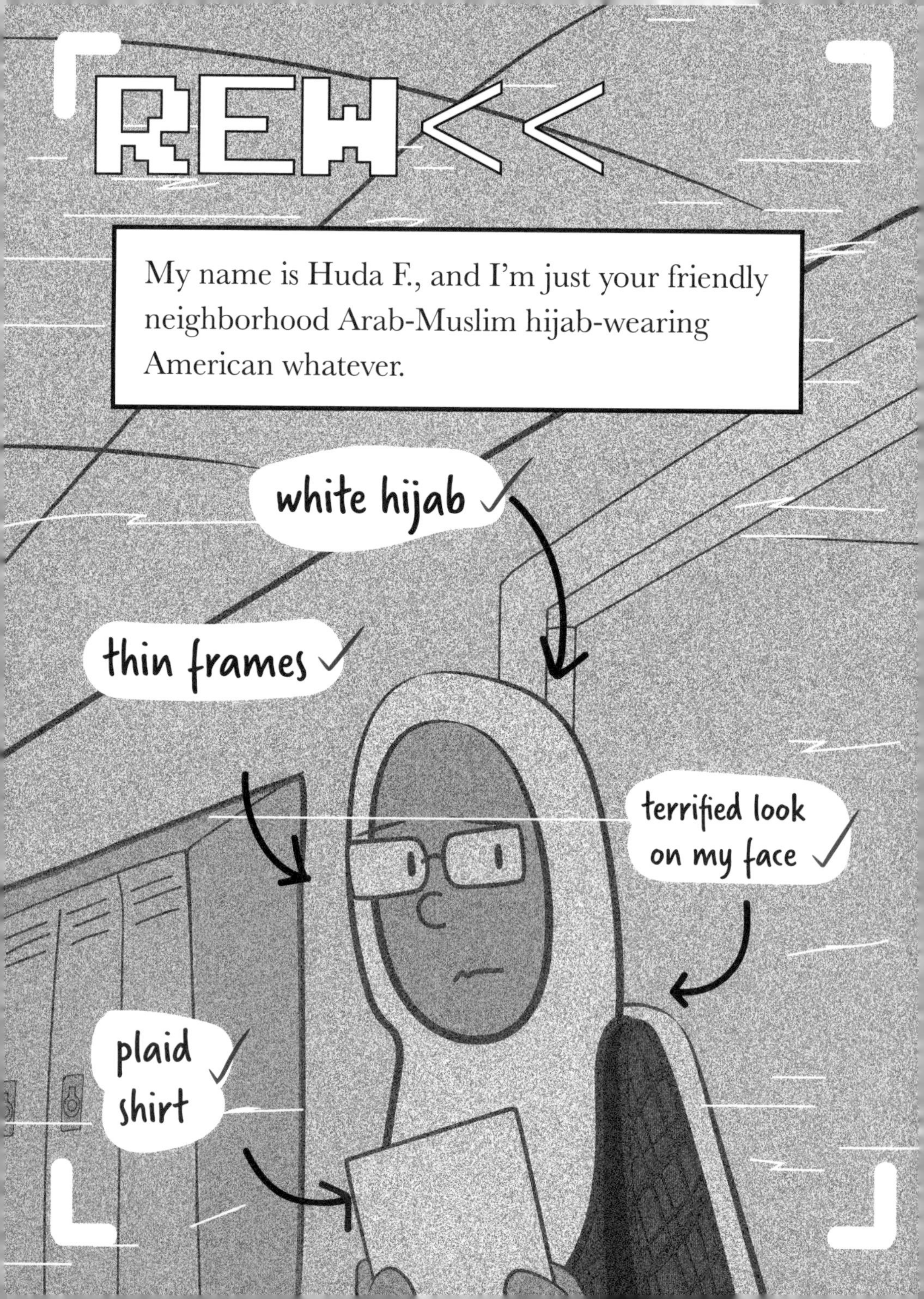
REW<<
My name is Huda F., and I'm just your friendly neighborhood Arab-Muslim hijab-wearing American whatever.
white hijab
thin frames
terrified look on my face
plaid shirt

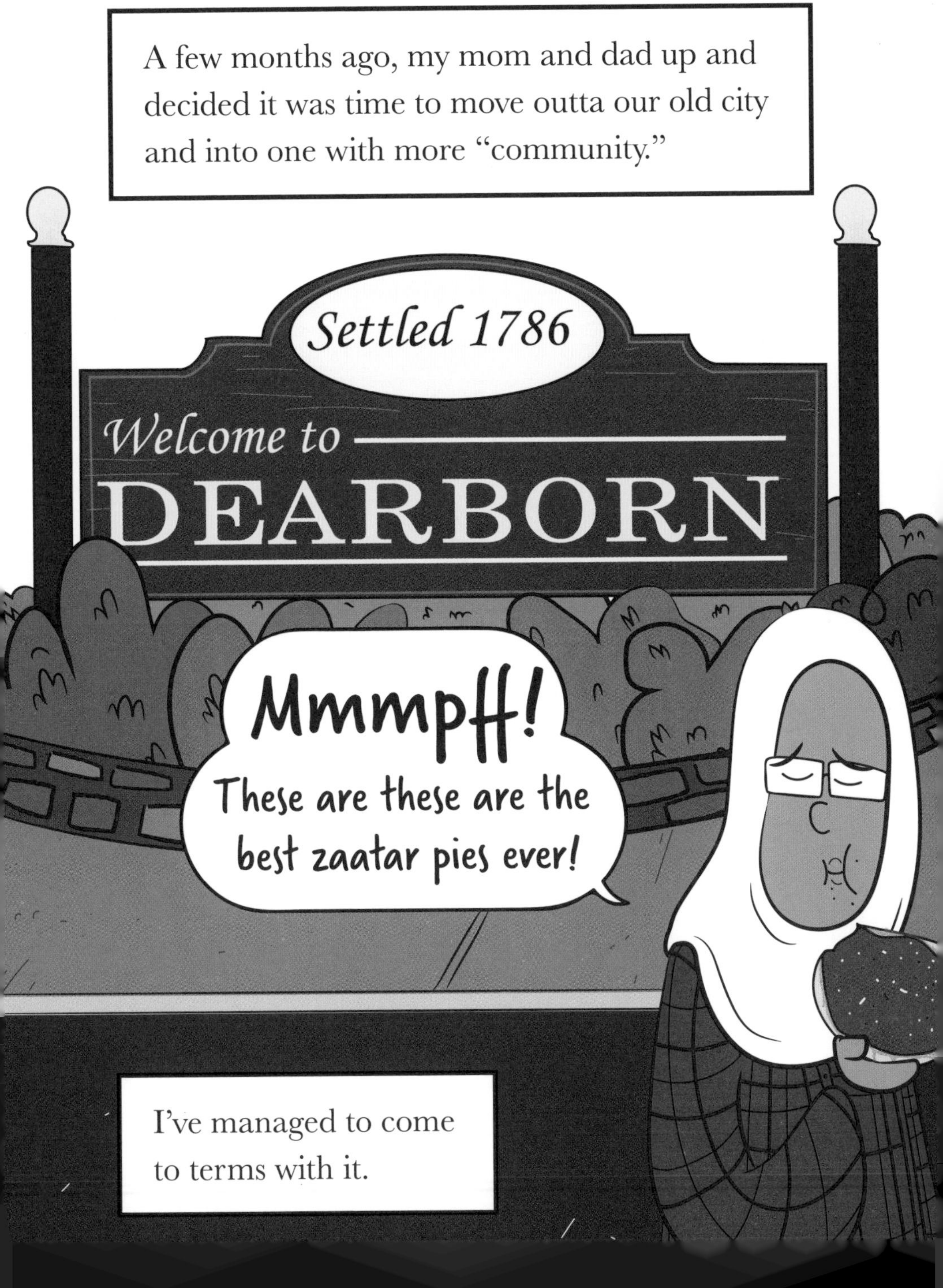
A few months ago, my mom and dad up and decided it was time to move outta our old city and into one with more "community."
Settled 1786
Welcome to DEARBORN
Mmmpff! These are these are the best zaatar pies ever!
I've managed to come to terms with it.

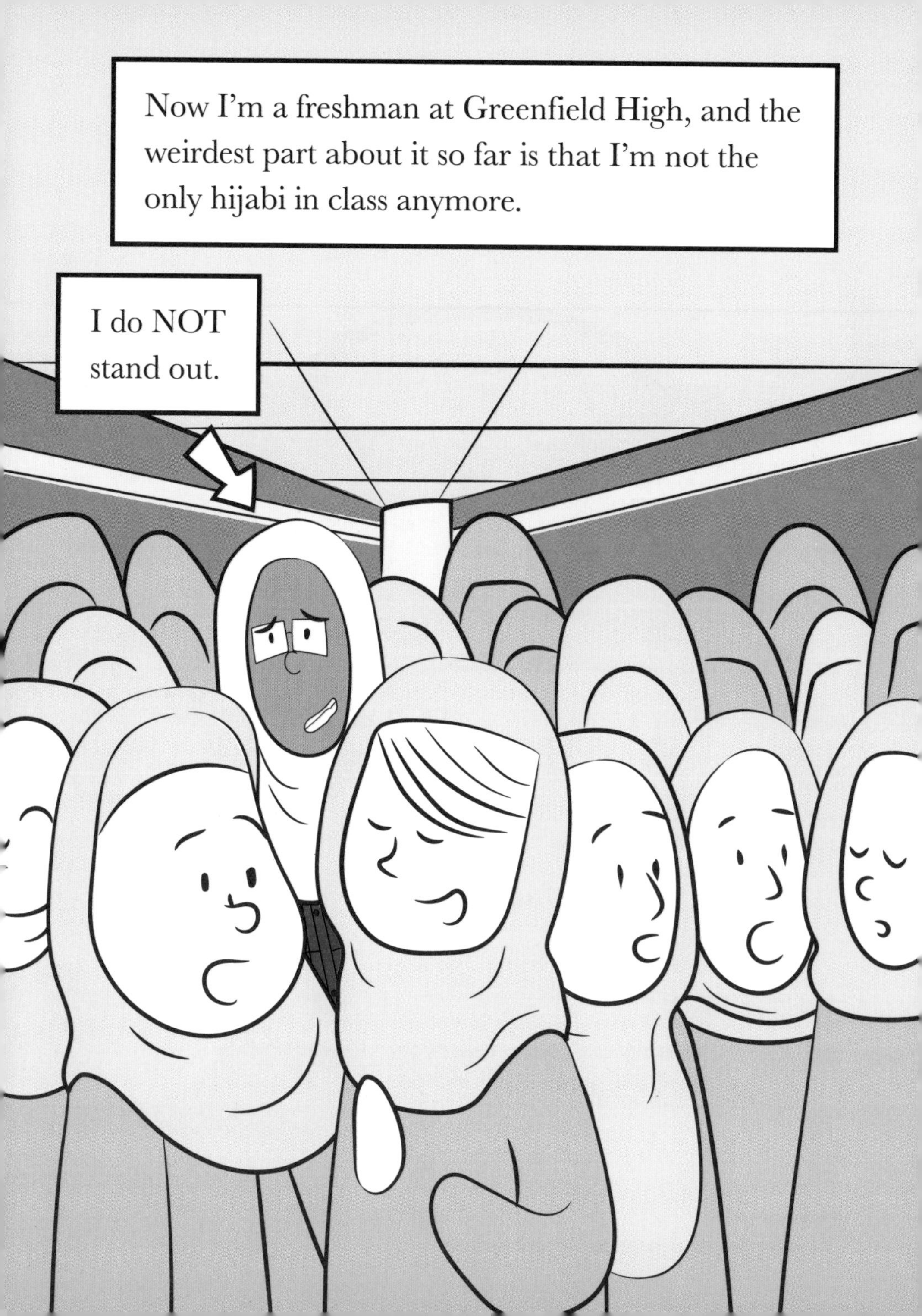
Now I'm a freshman at Greenfield High, and the weirdest part about it so far is that I'm not the only hijabi in class anymore.
I do NOT stand out.

Baba is a complicated man. Sometimes I feel like he *wants* me to struggle, but, like, only enough to learn how to take care of myself.

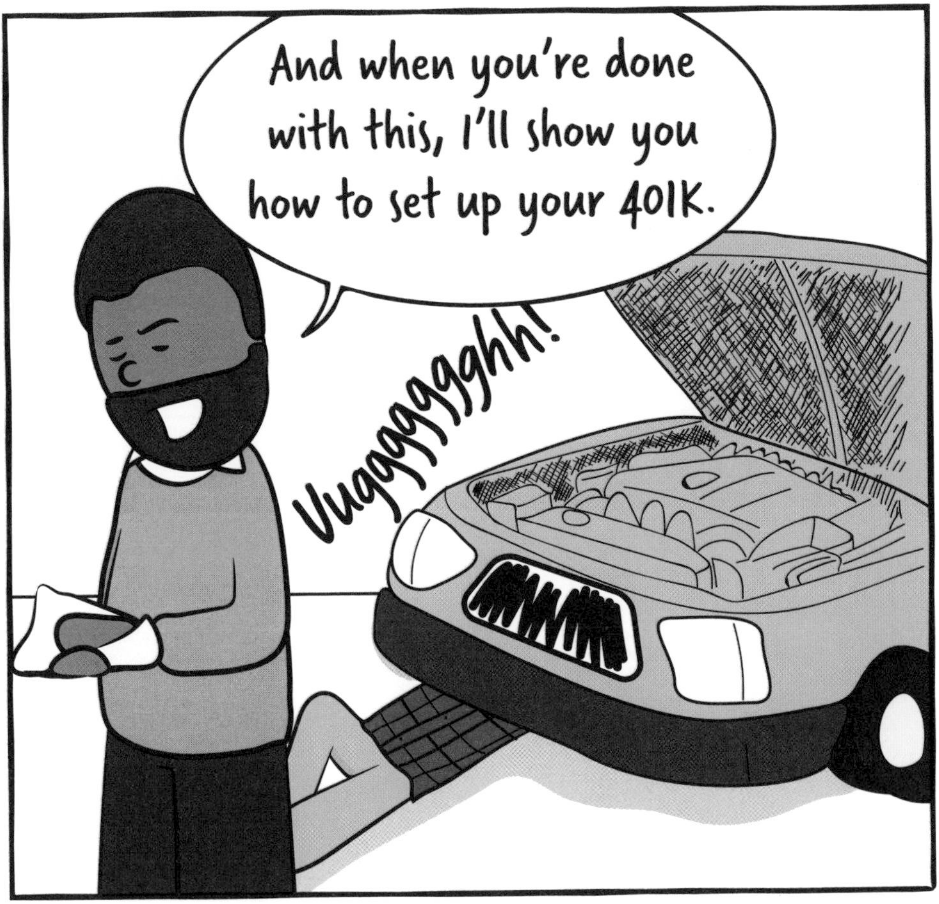
And when you're done with this, I'll show you how to set up your 401K.
Vuggggggghh!

He moved to the U.S. from Egypt when he was seventeen, went to school full-time, worked three jobs,

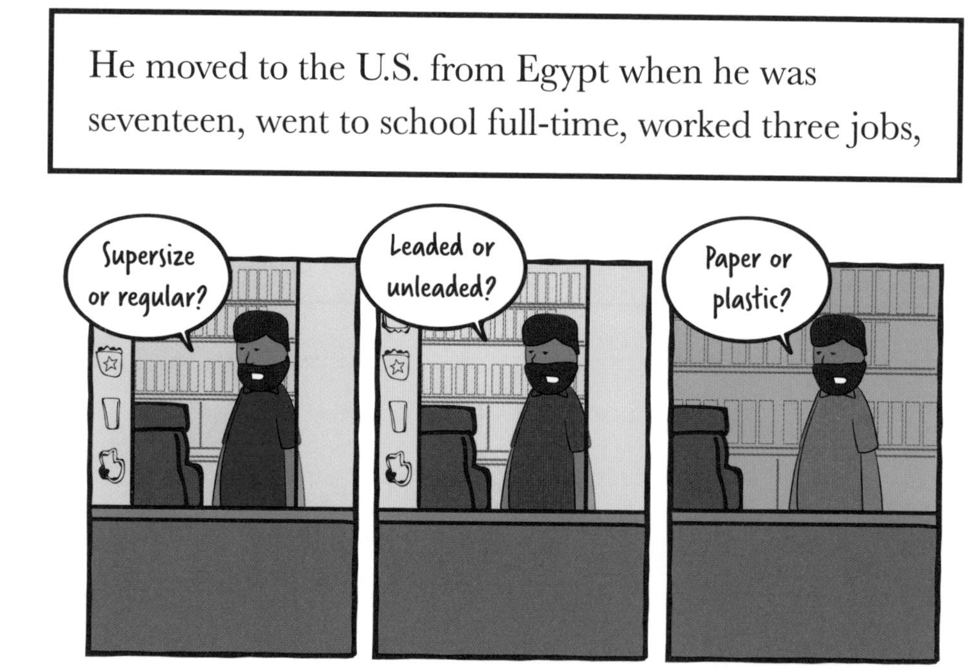
Supersize or regular?
Leaded or unleaded?
Paper or plastic?

Job #1 Job #2 Job #3

and did everything he could to survive.

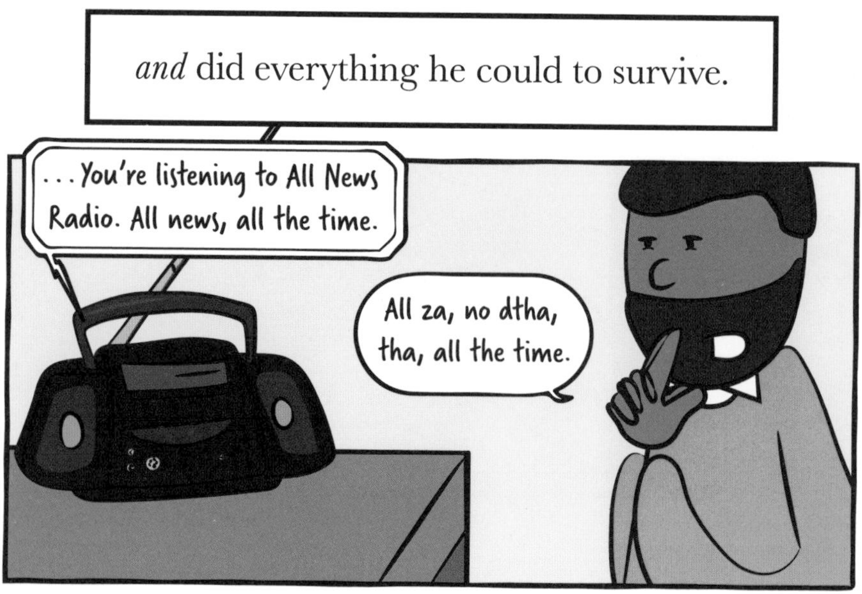
. . . You're listening to All News Radio. All news, all the time.
All za, no dtha, tha, all the time.

At twenty, he married my mom and brought her back to the States with the promise that they wouldn't stay long.

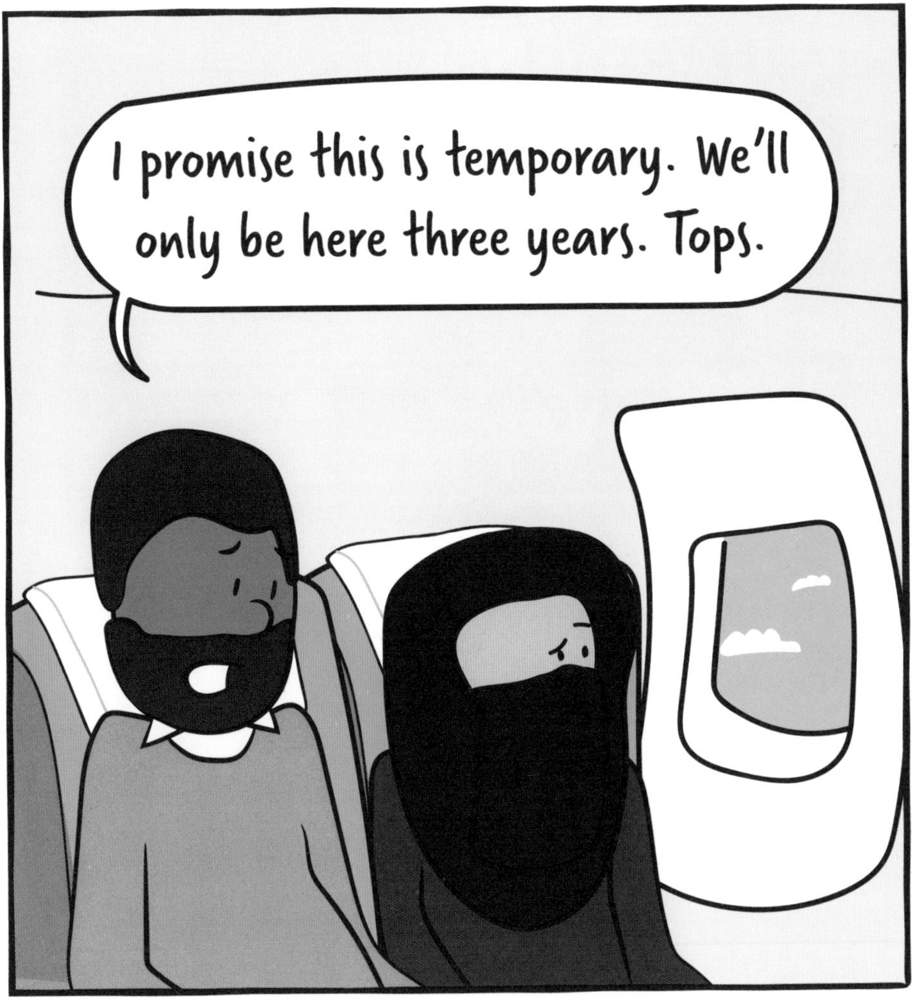
I promise this is temporary. We'll only be here three years. Tops.

She had a hard time adjusting.

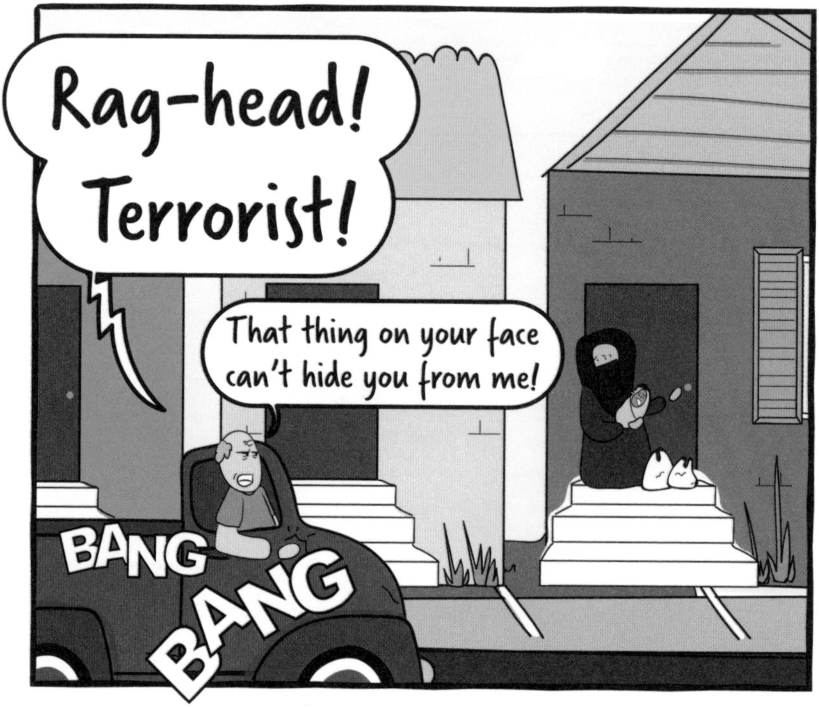
Rag-head! Terrorist!
That thing on your face can't hide you from me!
BANG
BANG

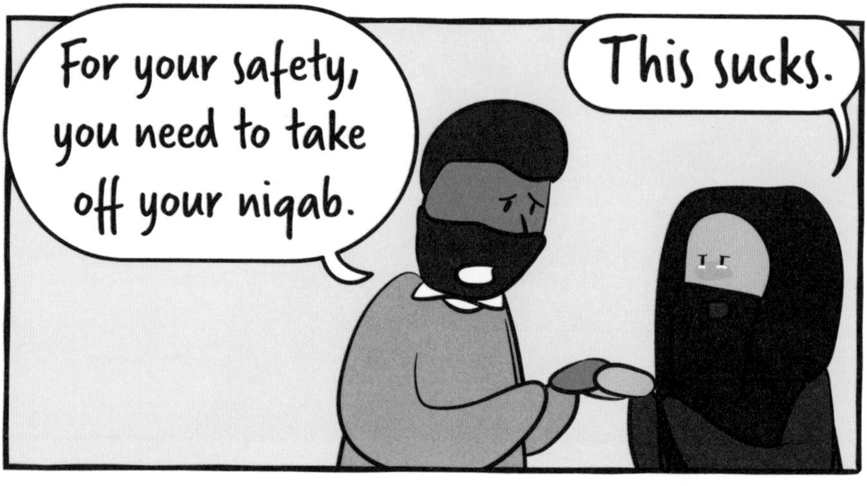
For your safety, you need to take off your niqab.
This sucks.

I don't think it's something she's ever forgotten.

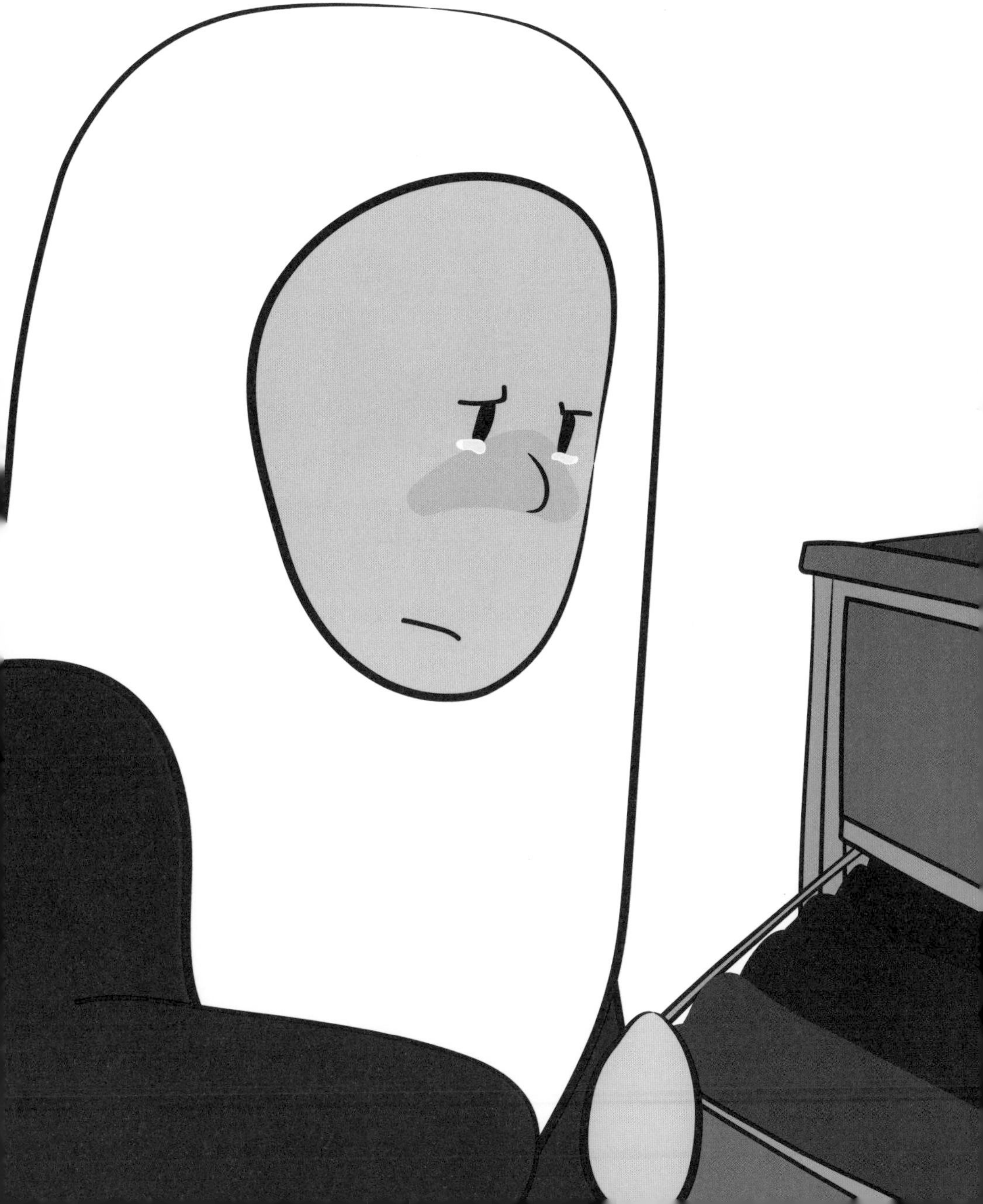

Three years kinda turned into more, and before they knew it, Mama and Baba went from a family of two to a family of seven.

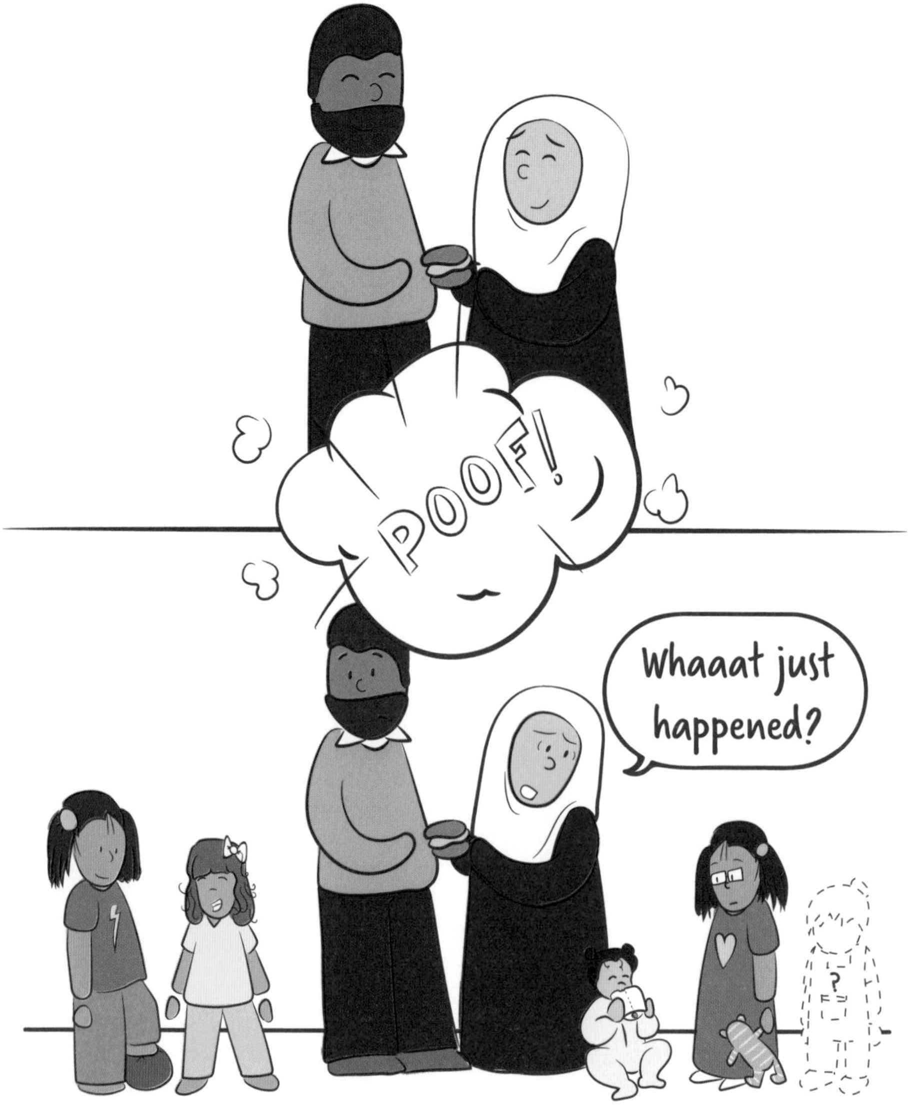
POOF!
Whaaat just happened?

Yup! They basically birthed a girl band.

Fourteen years later.

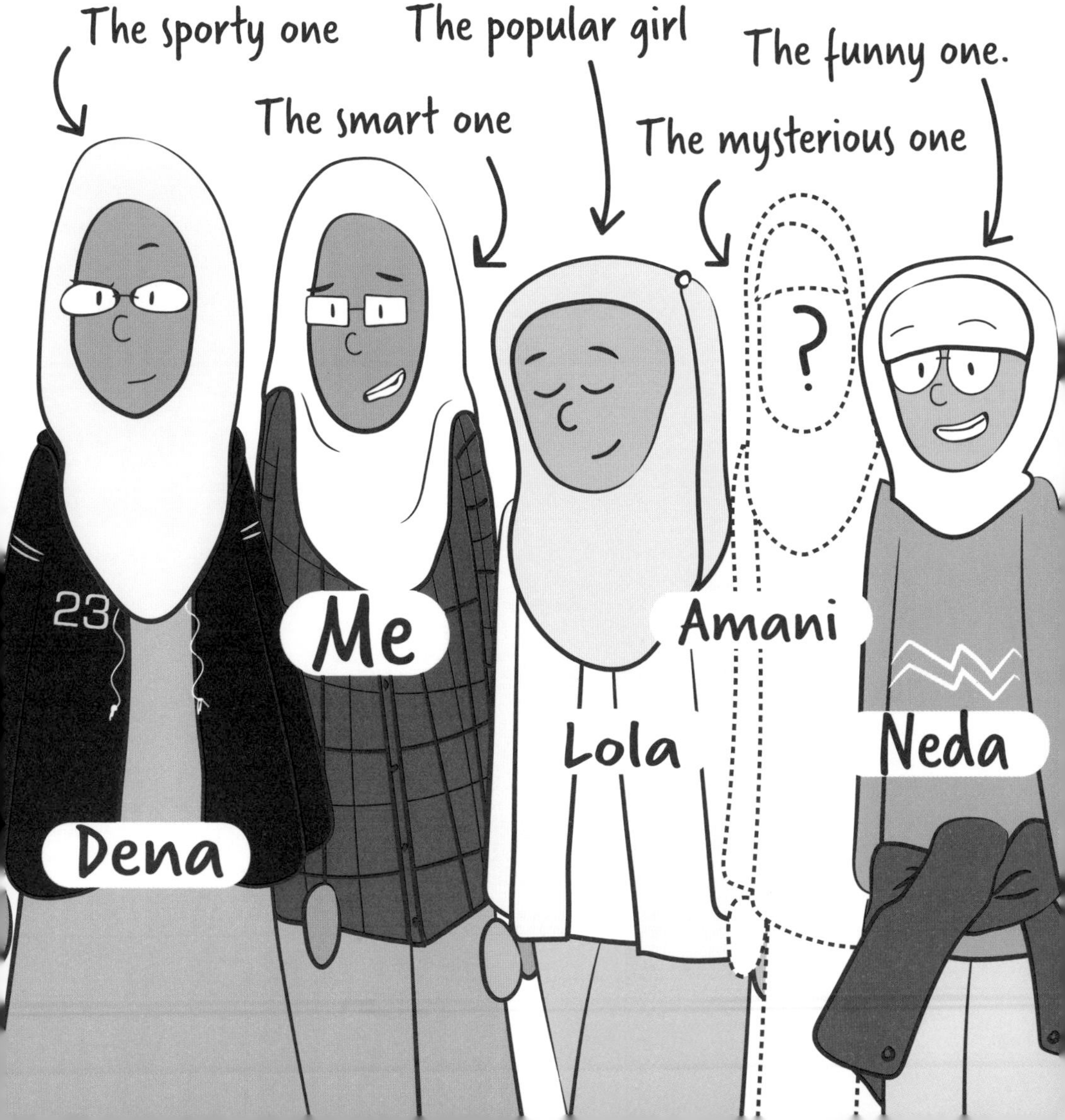
The sporty one
The popular girl
The funny one.
The smart one
The mysterious one
?
Dena
Me
Lola
Amani
Neda

Believe me when I say five girls under one roof is A LOT. It's exhausting, cramped, and don't even get me started on the bathroom to girl ratio.

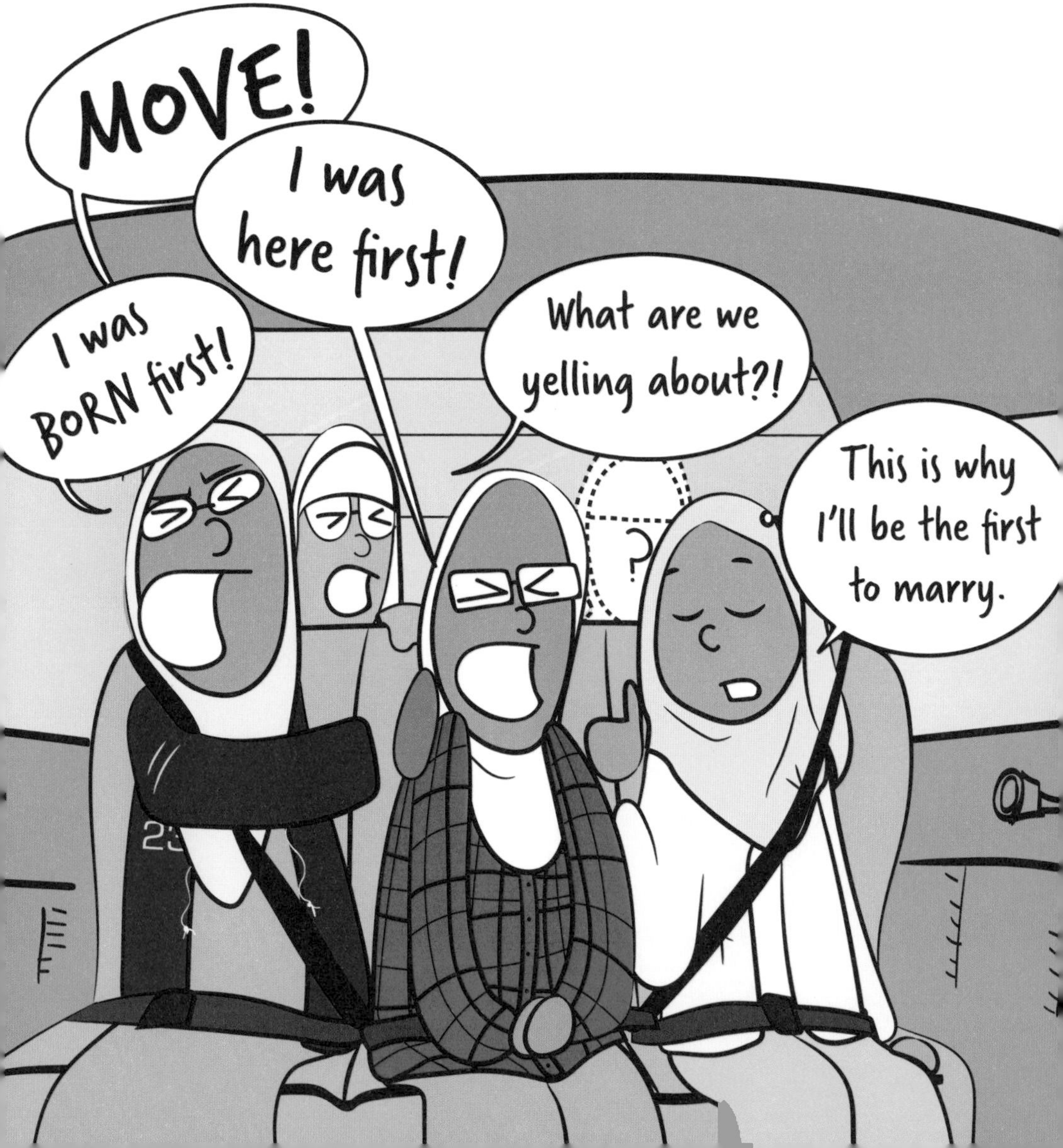
MOVE!
I was here first!
I was BORN first!
What are we yelling about?!
This is why I'll be the first to marry.

But as far as sisters go, we get along okay.

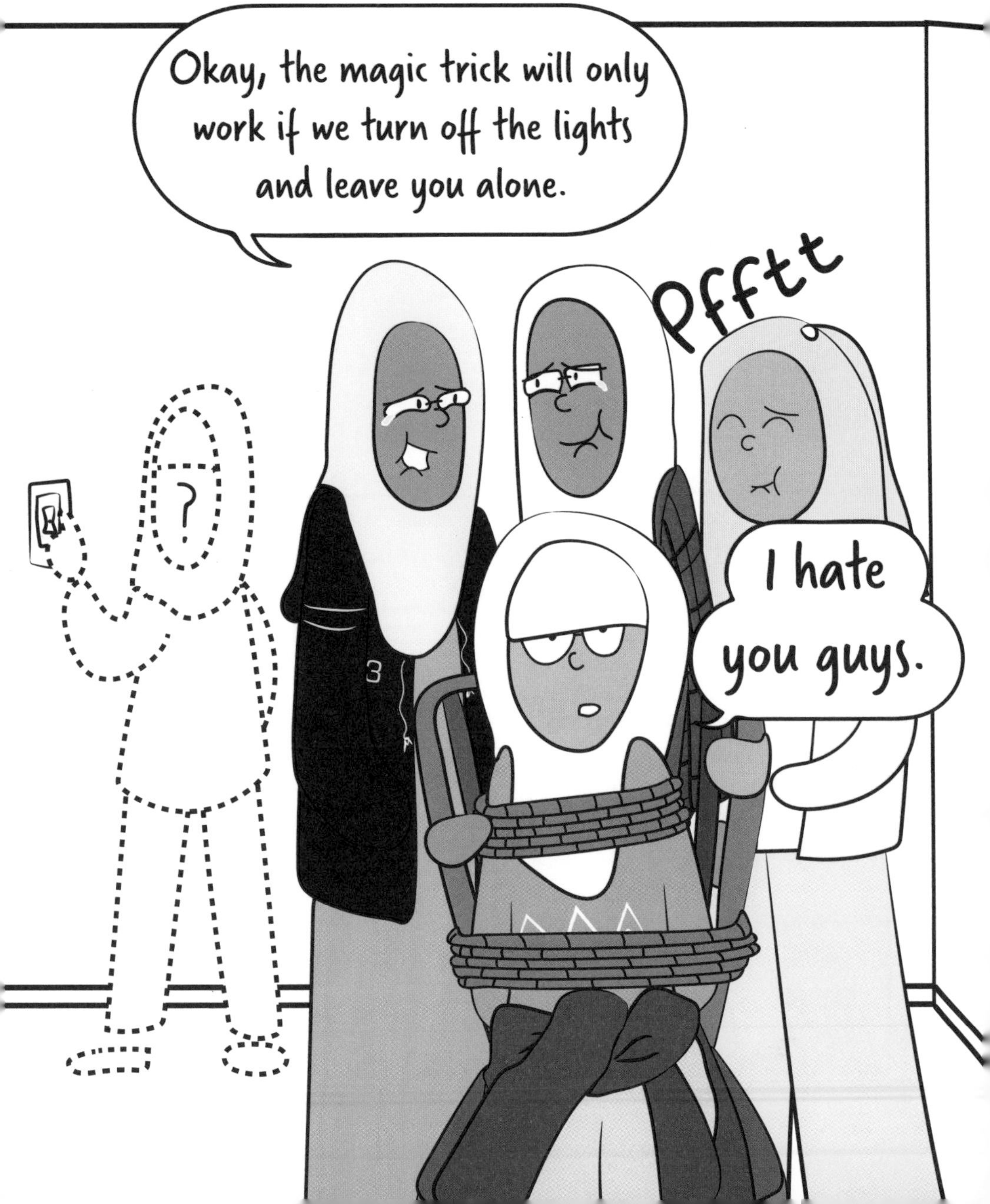
Okay, the magic trick will only work if we turn off the lights and leave you alone.
Pfftt
I hate you guys.
3

Mama makes sure of that. Whenever she thinks we need to "bond" more, she switches up who's bunking with who. This year is my turn to bunk with Neda.

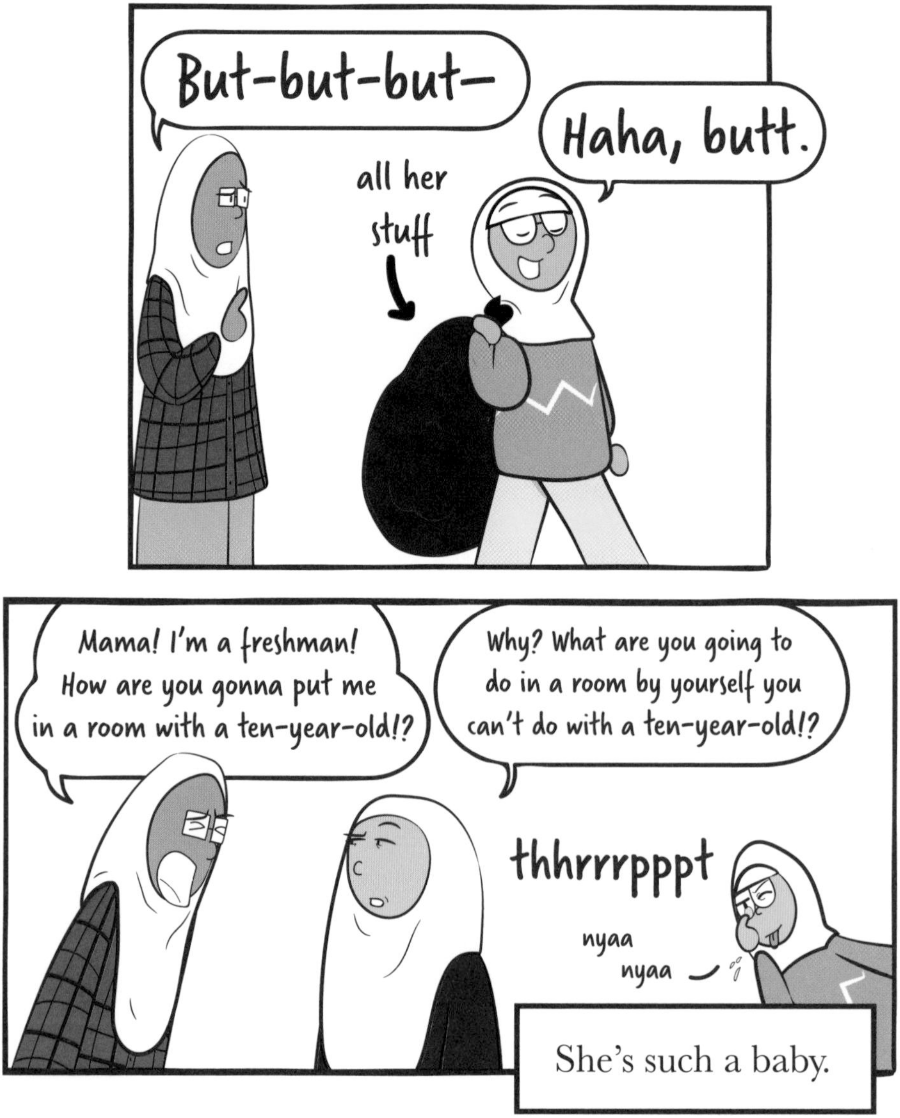
But-but-but–
Haha, butt.
all her stuff
Mama! I'm a freshman! How are you gonna put me in a room with a ten-year-old!?
Why? What are you going to do in a room by yourself you can't do with a ten-year-old!?
thhrrrpppt
nyaa nyaa
She's such a baby.

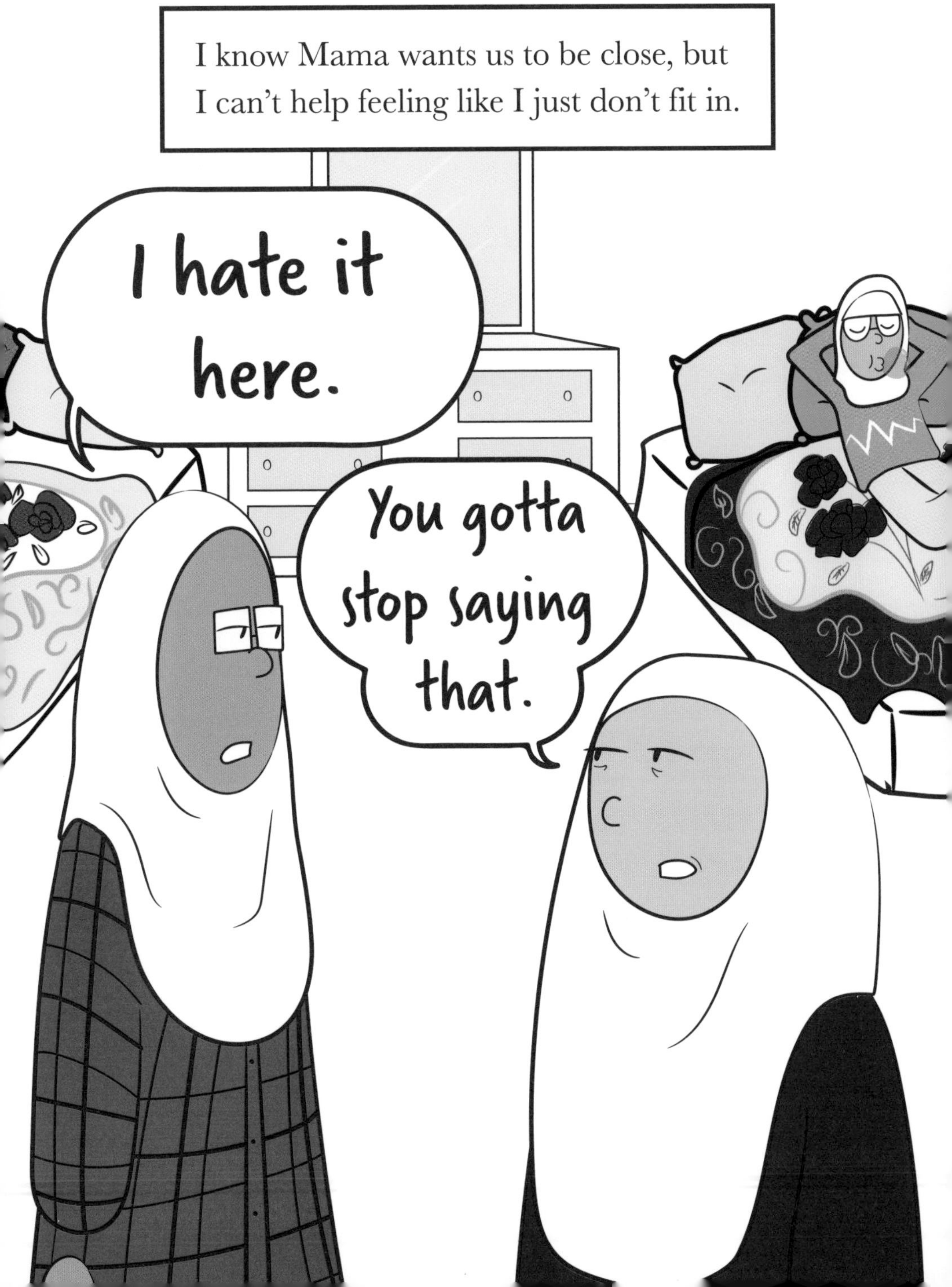

I know Mama wants us to be close, but I can't help feeling like I just don't fit in.
I hate it here.
You gotta stop saying that.

It doesn't matter, though. We're forced to do pretty much everything together. And because we were born back to back, we'll eventually be going to college together too.

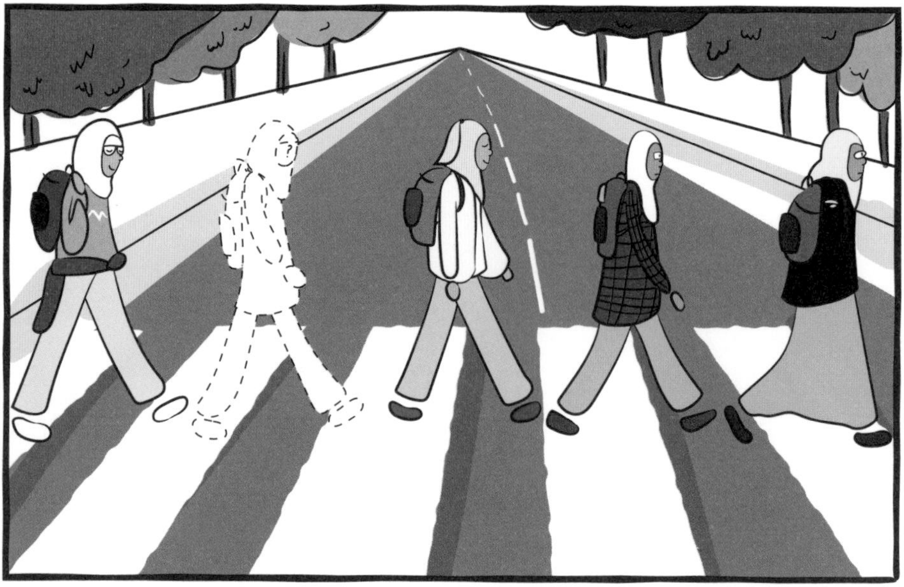

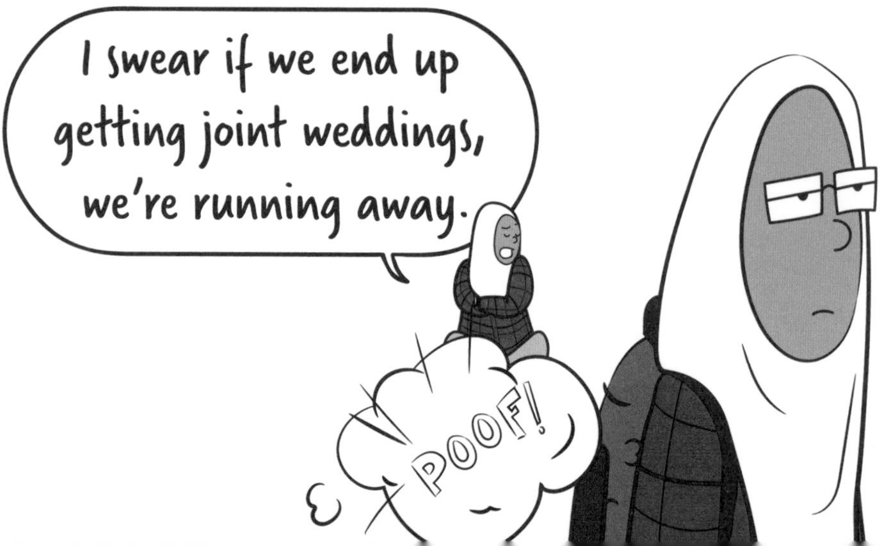
I swear if we end up getting joint weddings, we're running away.
POOF!

And going to college is definitely a must. My parents value education. I mean like *really* value it.

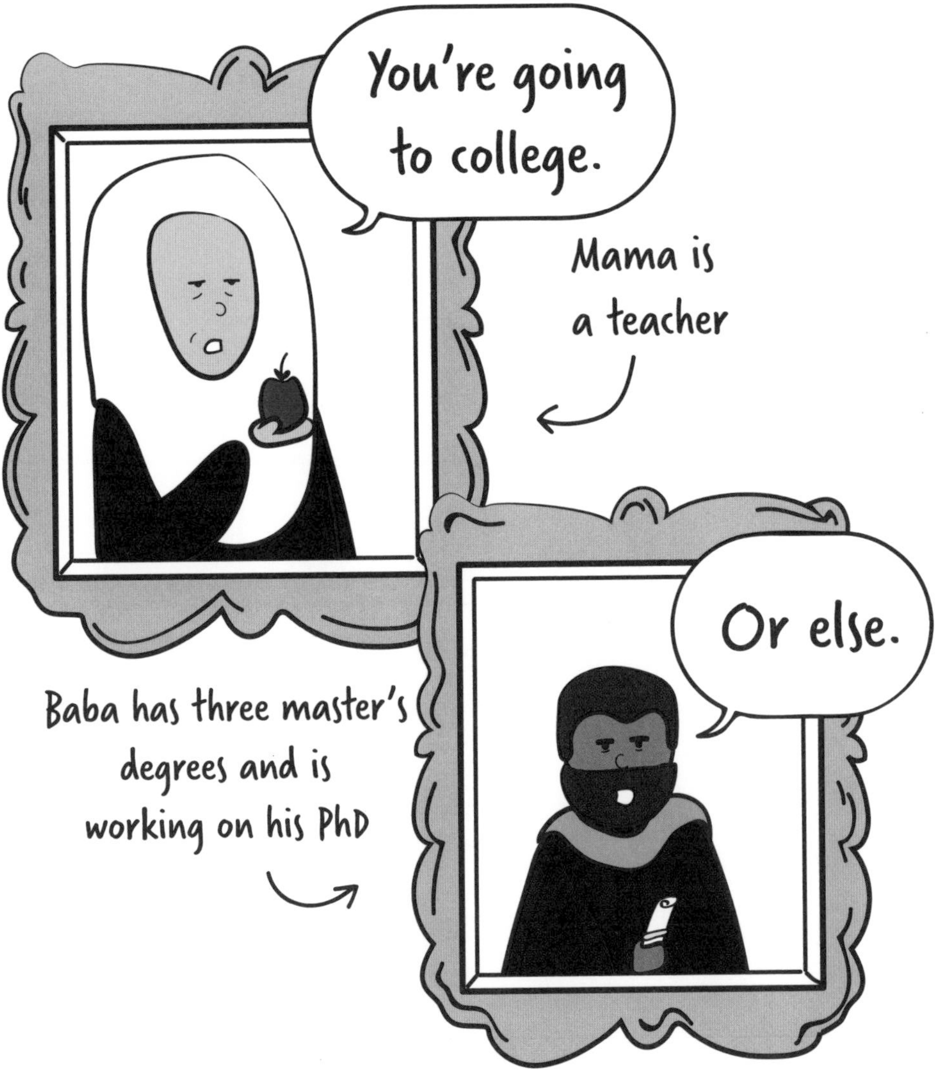
You're going to college.
Mama is a teacher
Or else.
Baba has three master's degrees and is working on his PhD

But college is expensive.

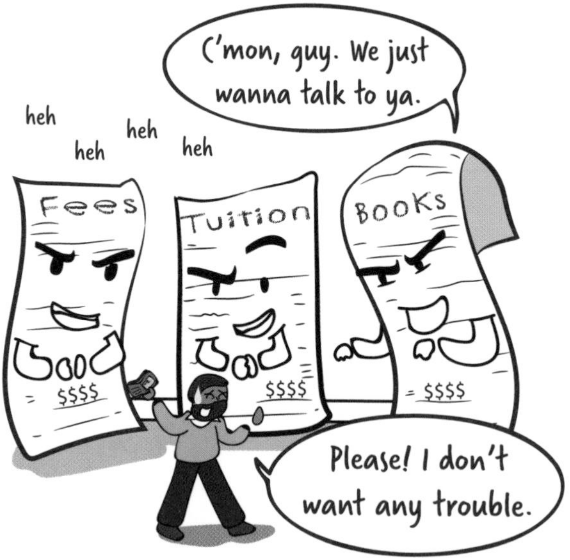
heh
heh
heh
heh
C'mon, guy. We just wanna talk to ya.
Fees
$$$$
Tuition
$$$$
BOOKS
$$$$
Please! I don't want any trouble.

And taking out loans is a big no-no for Muslims.

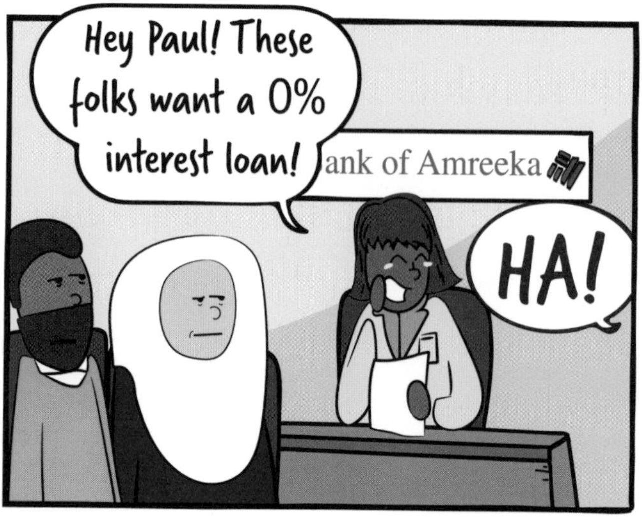
Hey Paul! These folks want a 0% interest loan!
ank of Amreeka
HA!

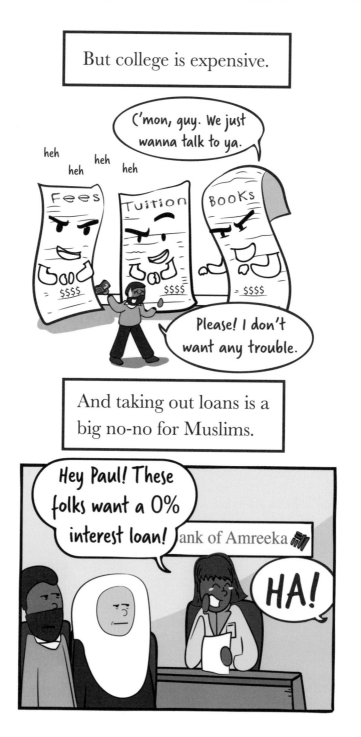

So my parents' expectations of us are pretty high up there.

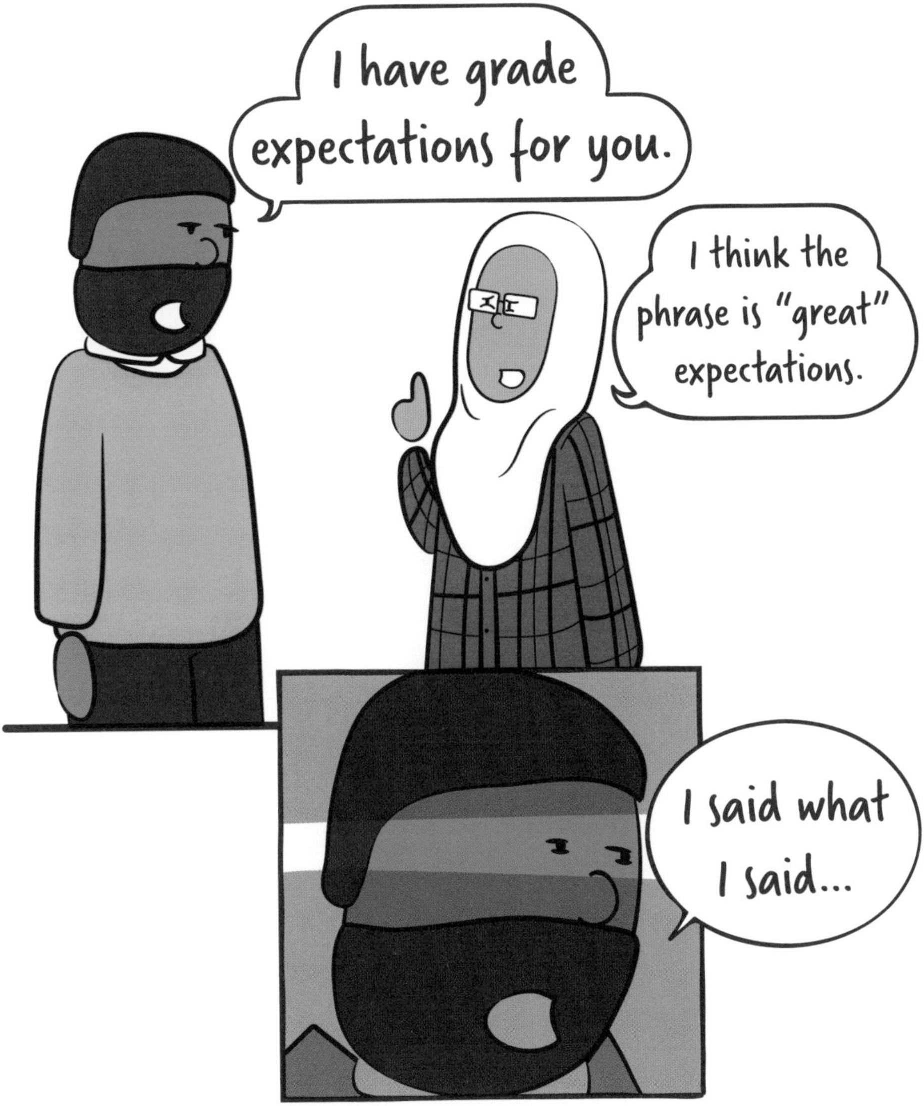
I have grade expectations for you.
I think the phrase is "great" expectations.
I said what I said...

Nothing short of great grades and full scholarships are gonna be accepted.

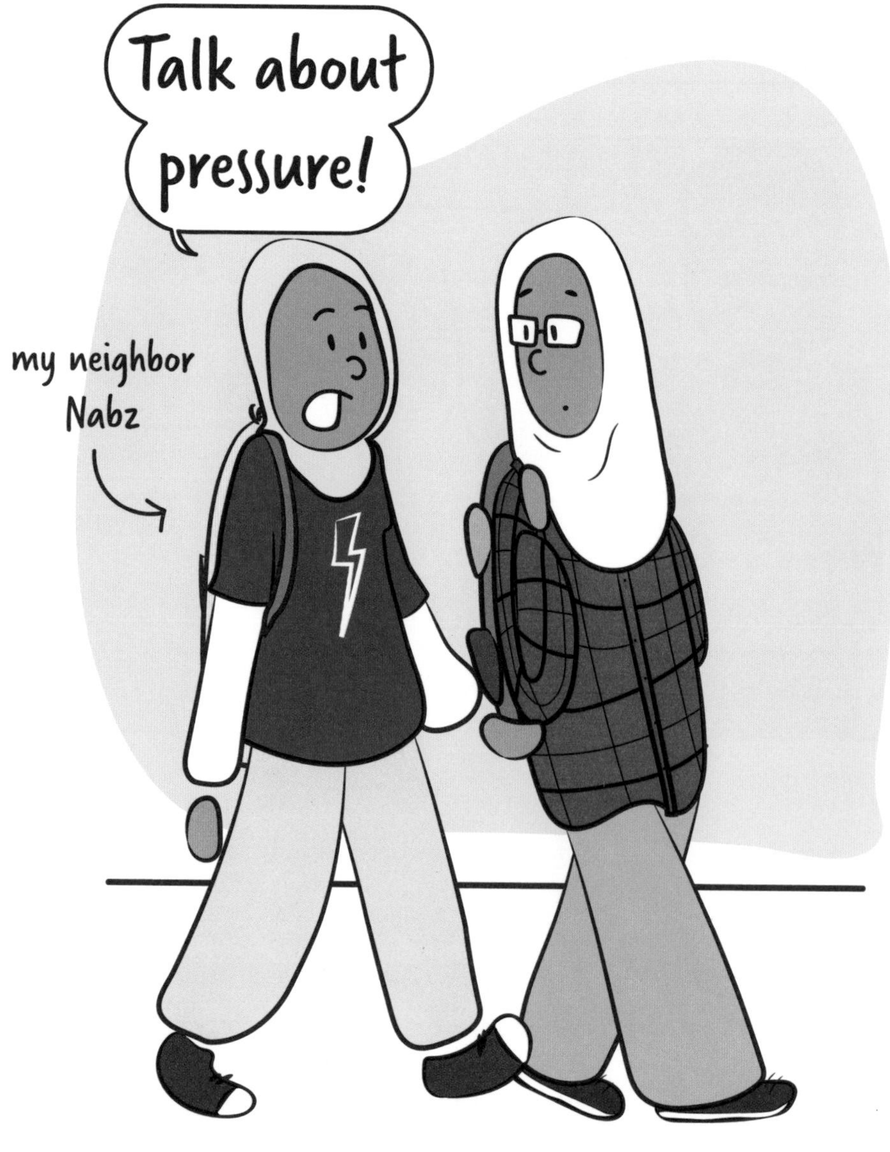
Talk about pressure!
my neighbor Nabz

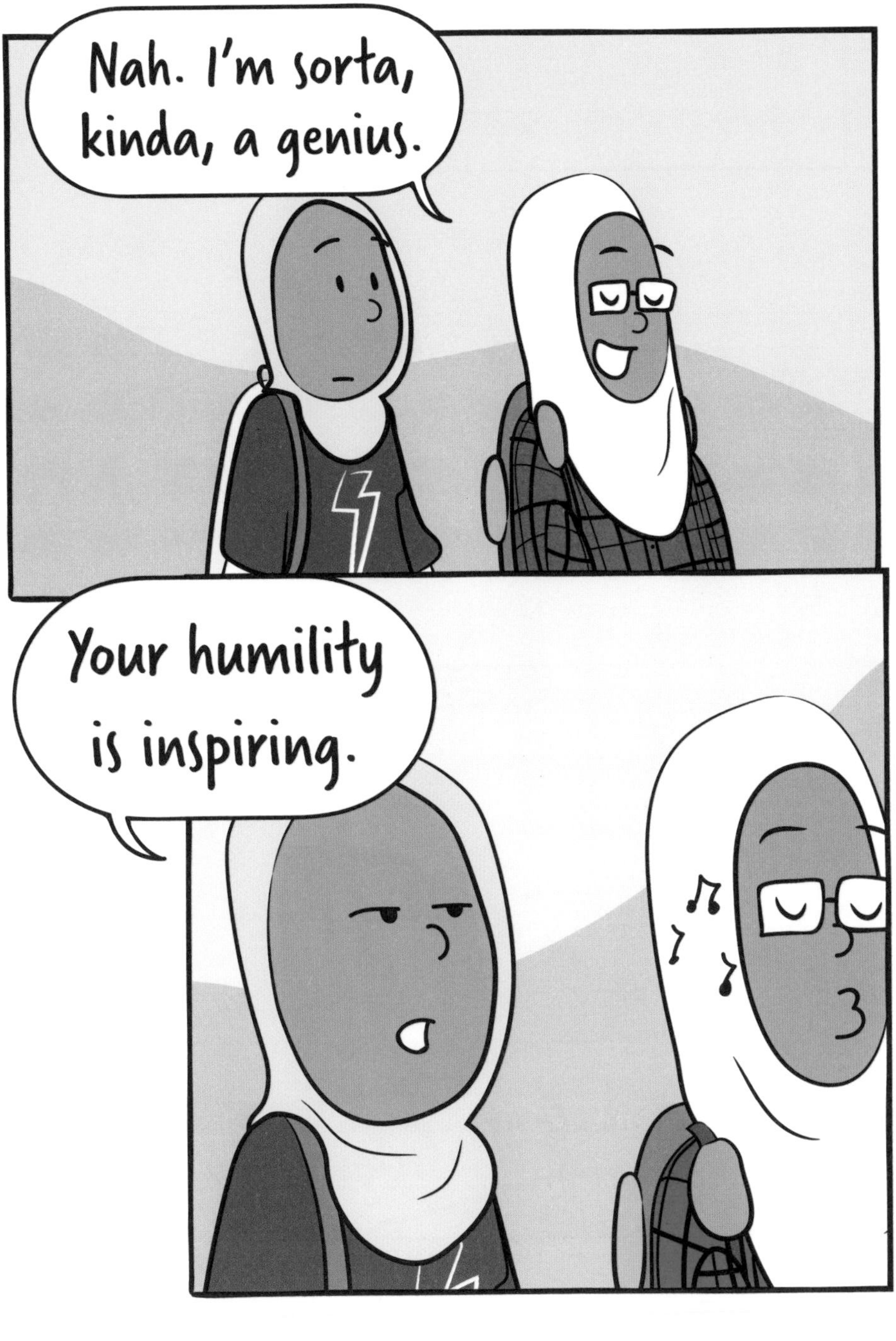
Nah. I'm sorta, kinda, a genius.
Your humility is inspiring.

But seriously, being smart is kinda my thing. I'm totally gonna coast through the next four years.

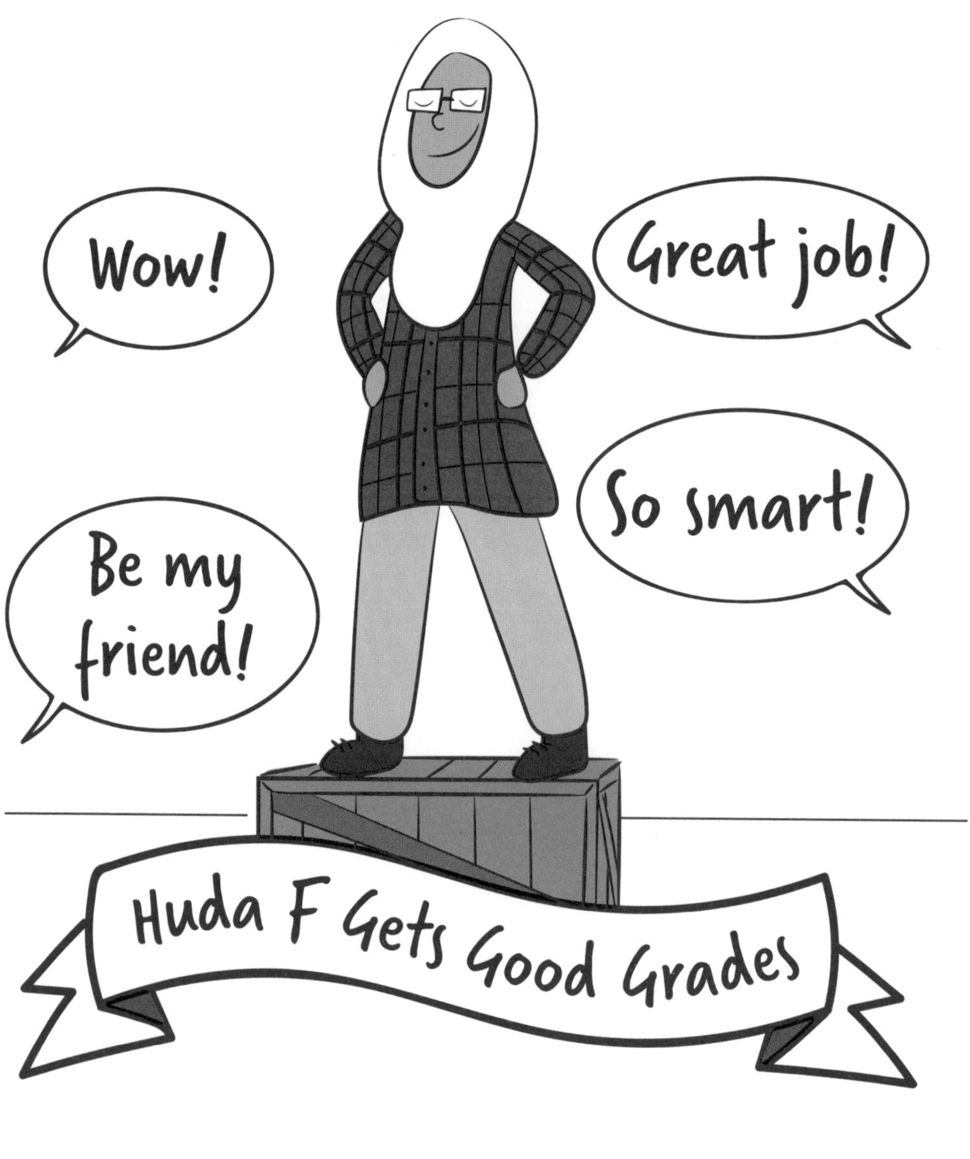
Wow!
Great job!
So smart!
Be my friend!
Huda F Gets Good Grades

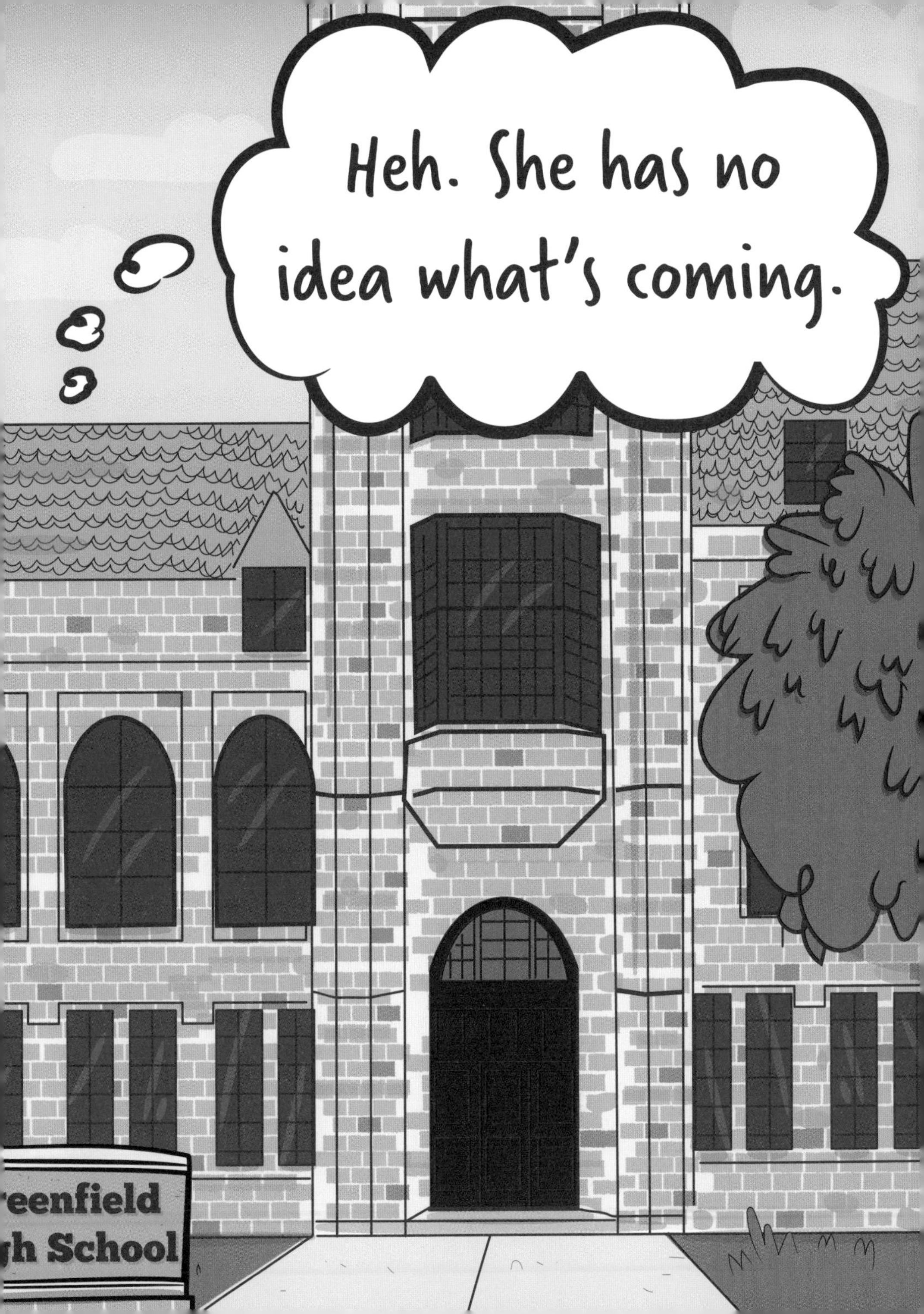
Heh. She has no idea what's coming.
eenfield
gh School

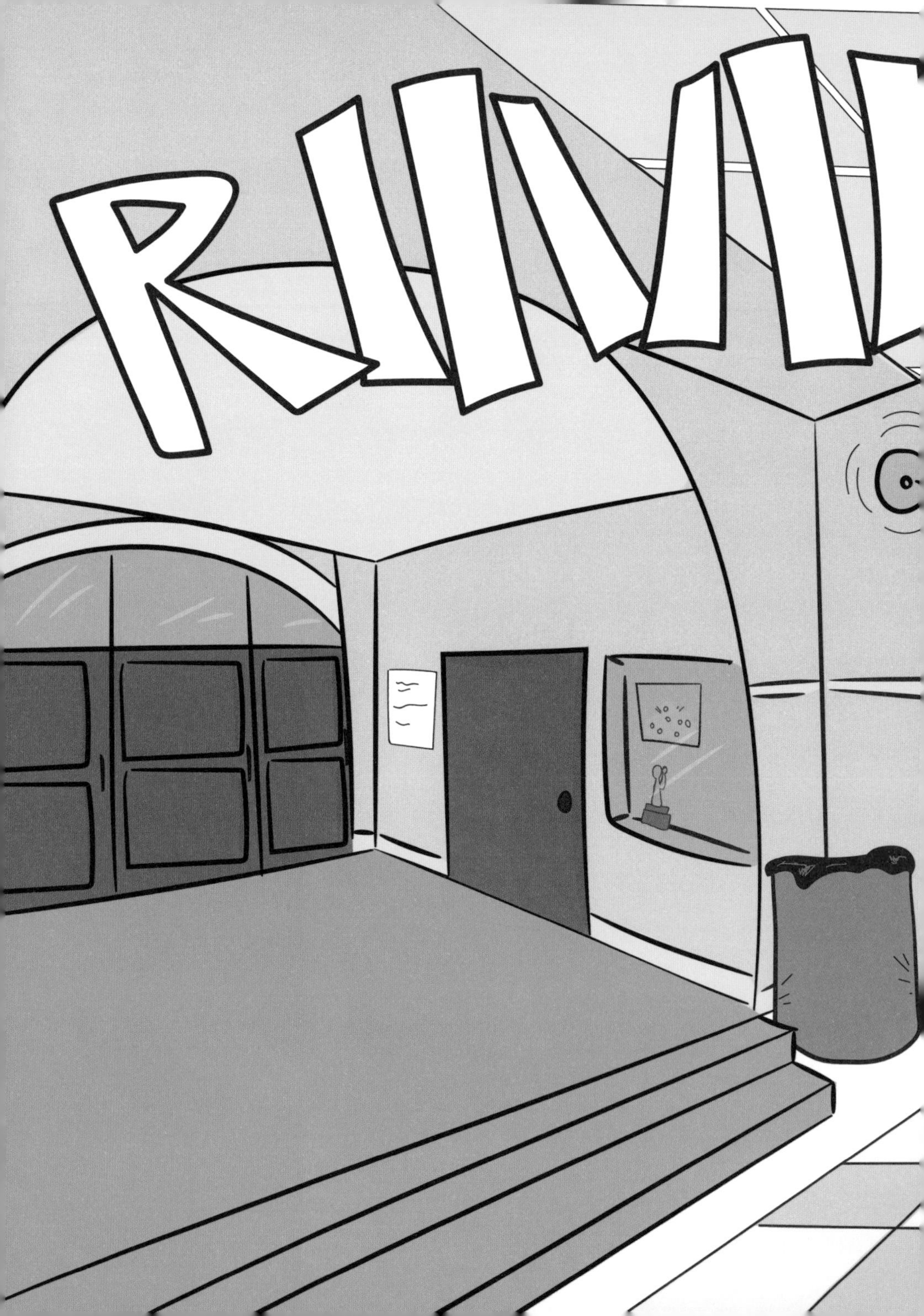

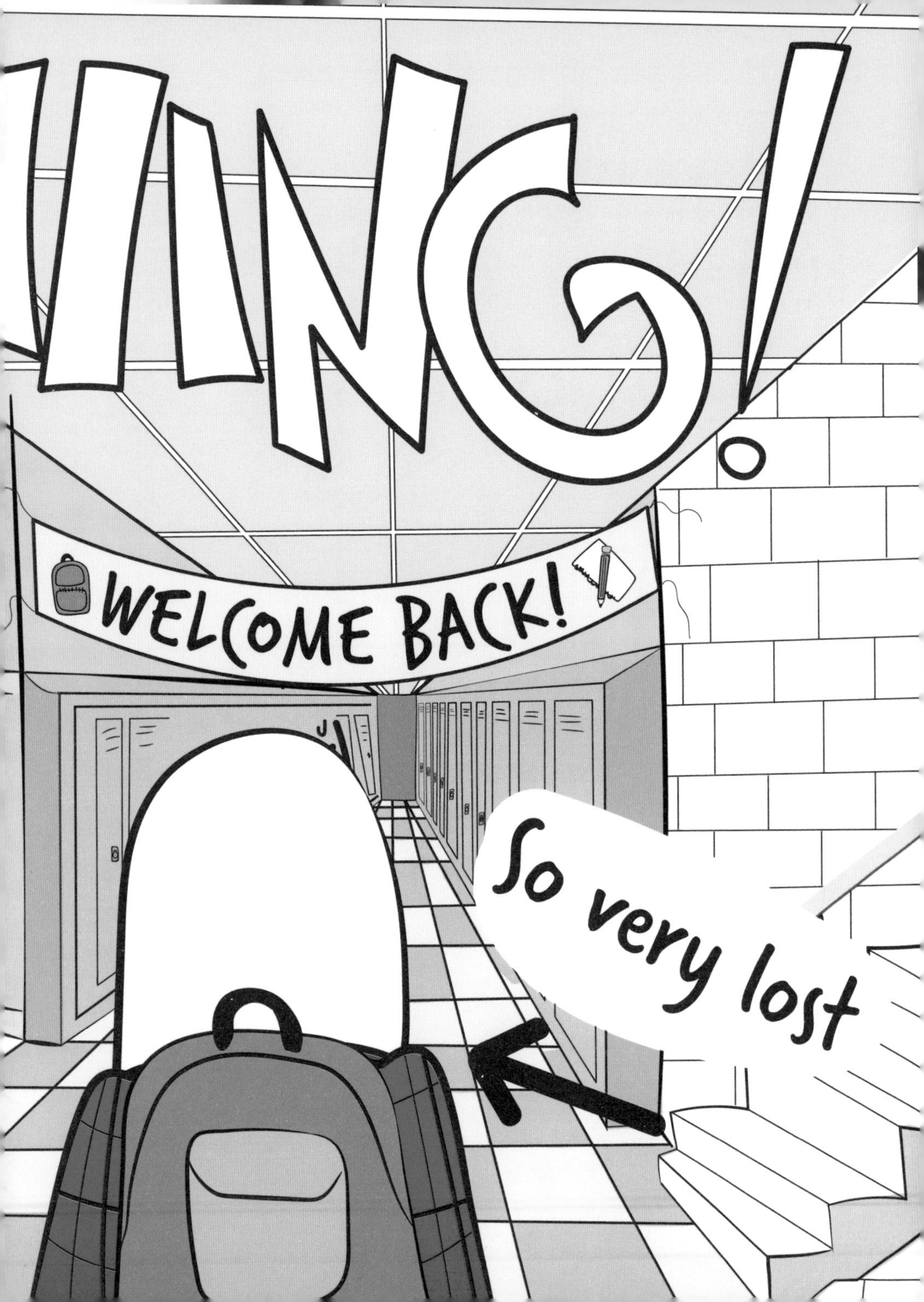

ING!
WELCOME BACK!
So very lost

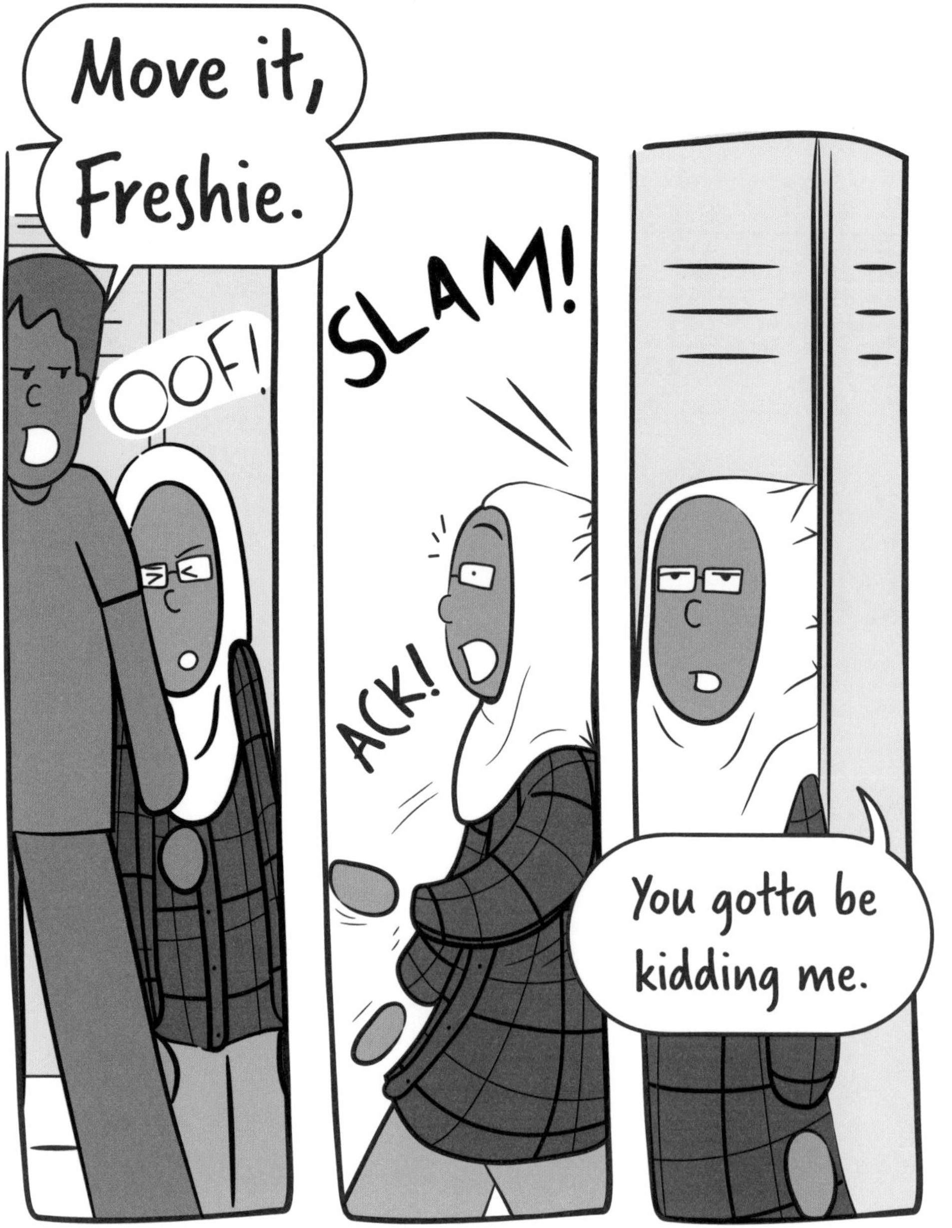
Move it, Freshie.
OOF!
SLAM!
ACK!
You gotta be kidding me.

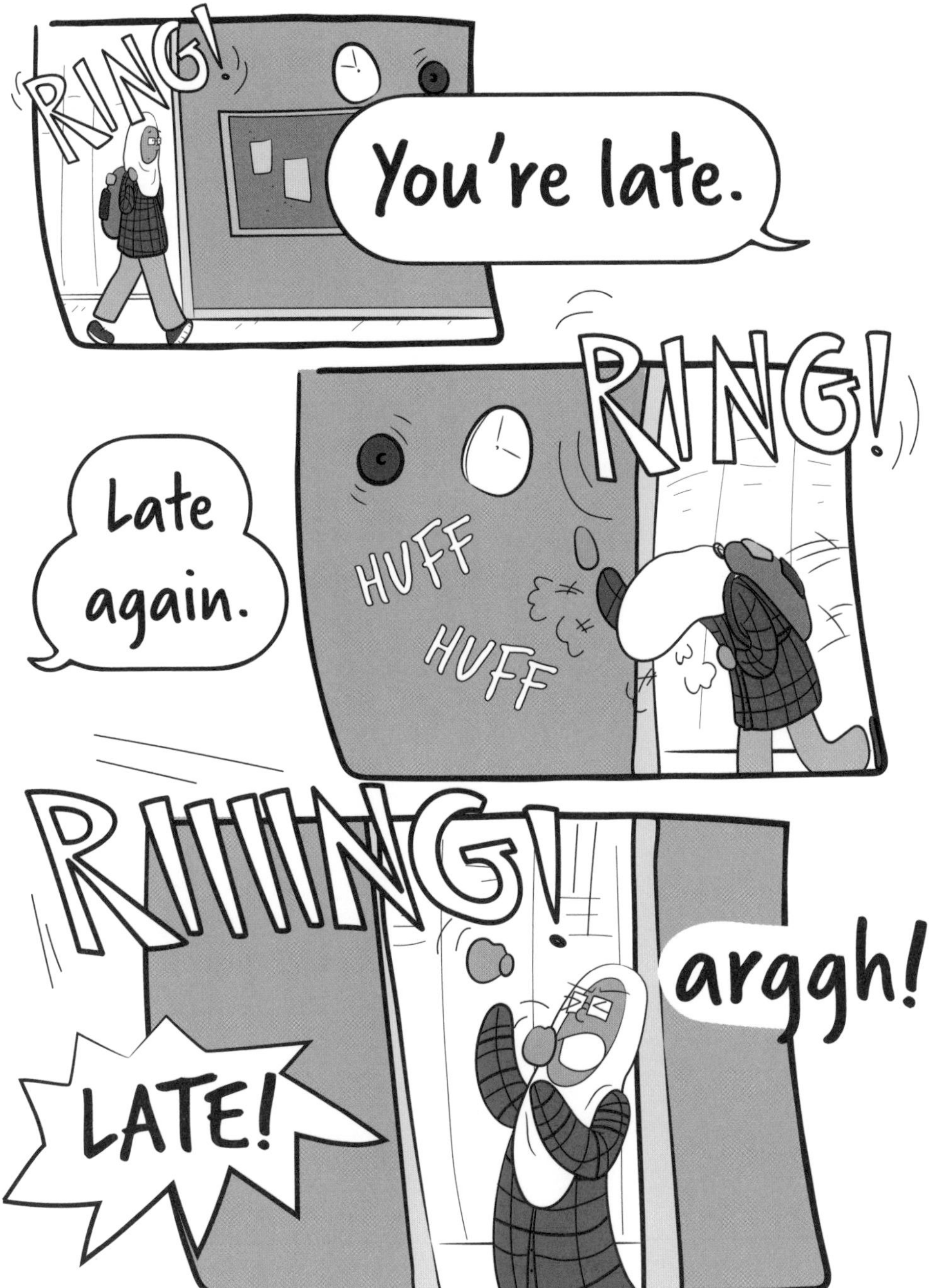
RING!
You're late.
RING!
Late again.
HUFF
HUFF
RIIIING!
arggh!
LATE!

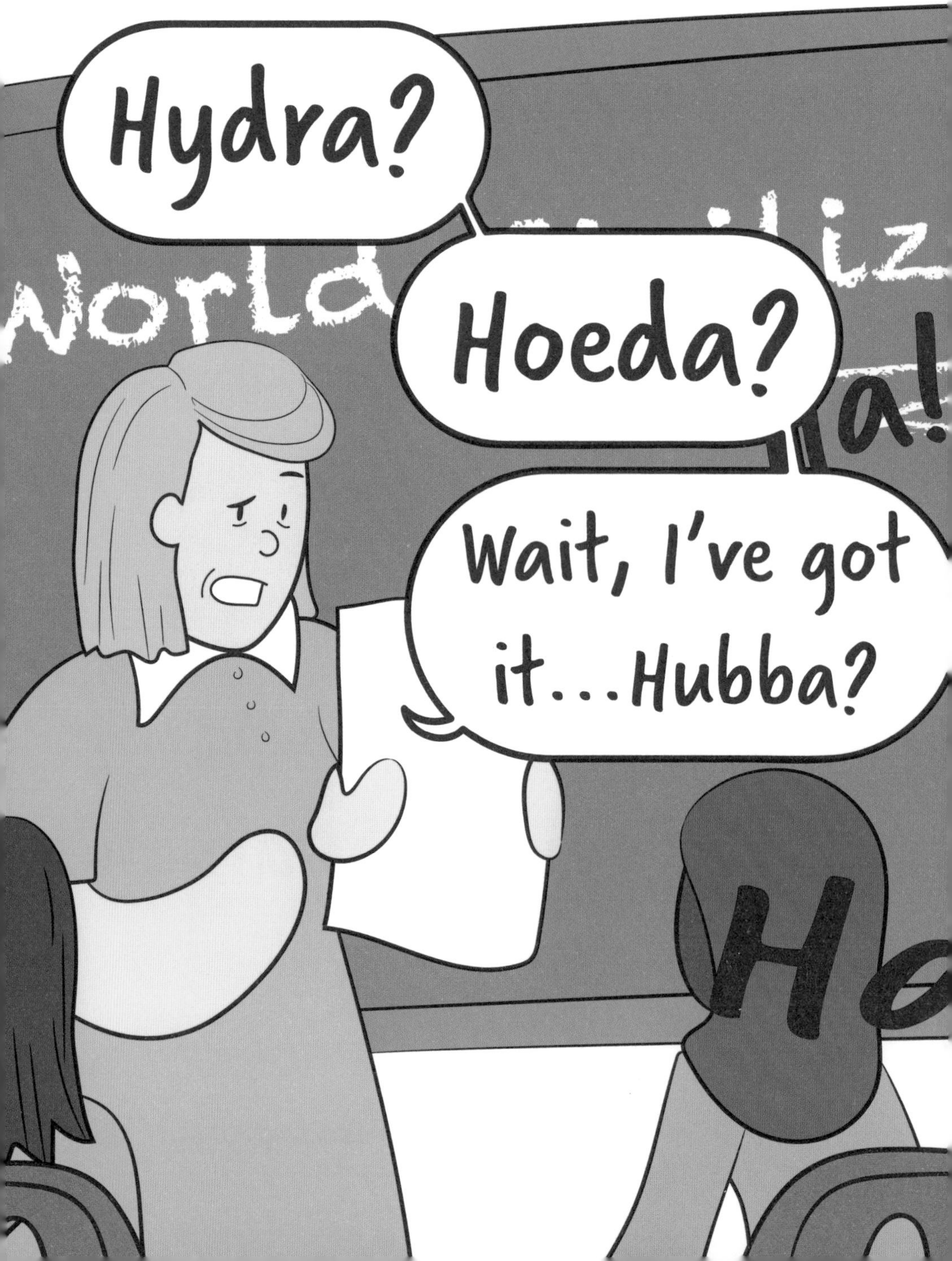
Hydra?
Hoeda?
Wait, I've got it...Hubba?

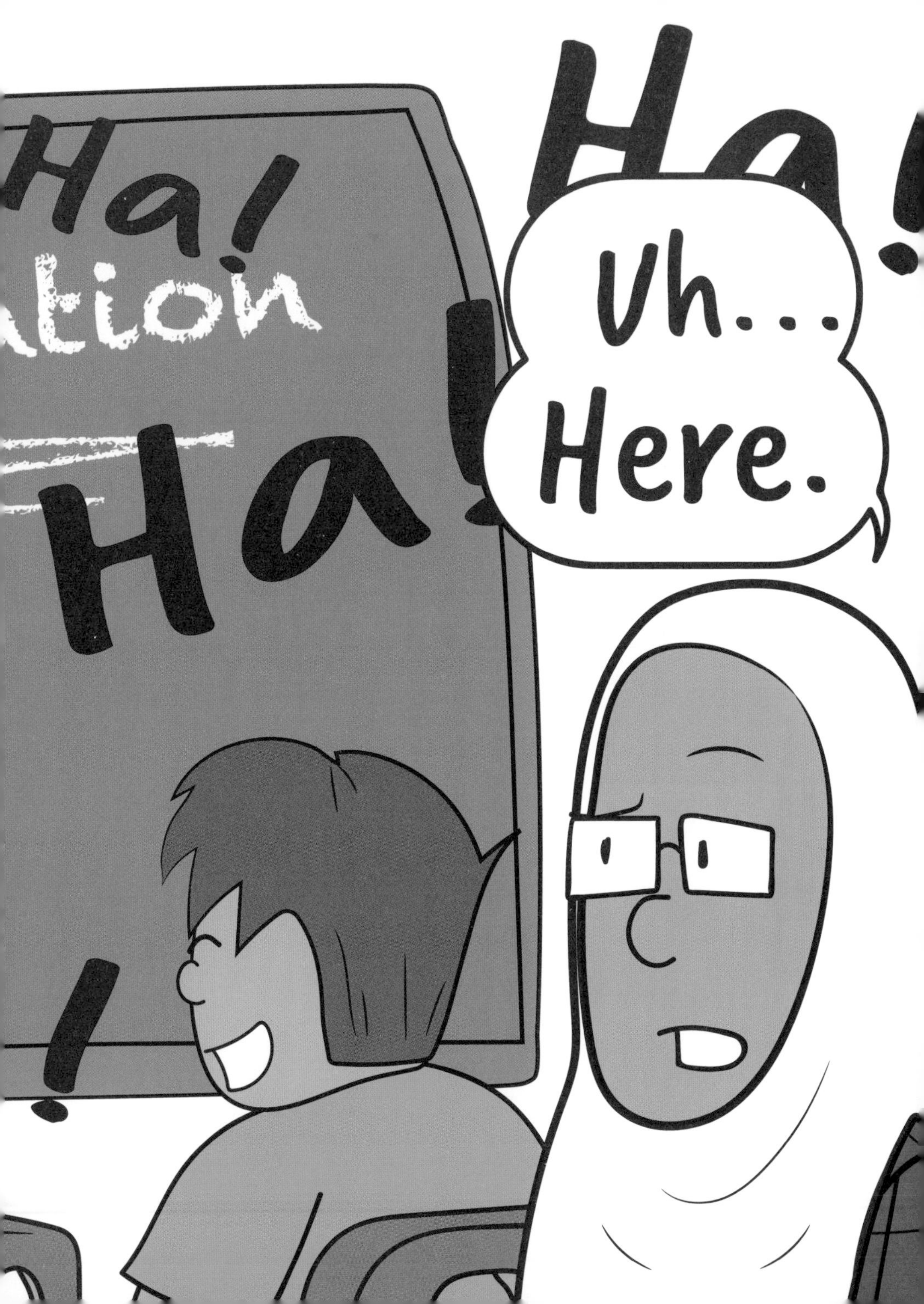
Ha!
ation
Ha!
Ha!
Ha!
Uh... Here.

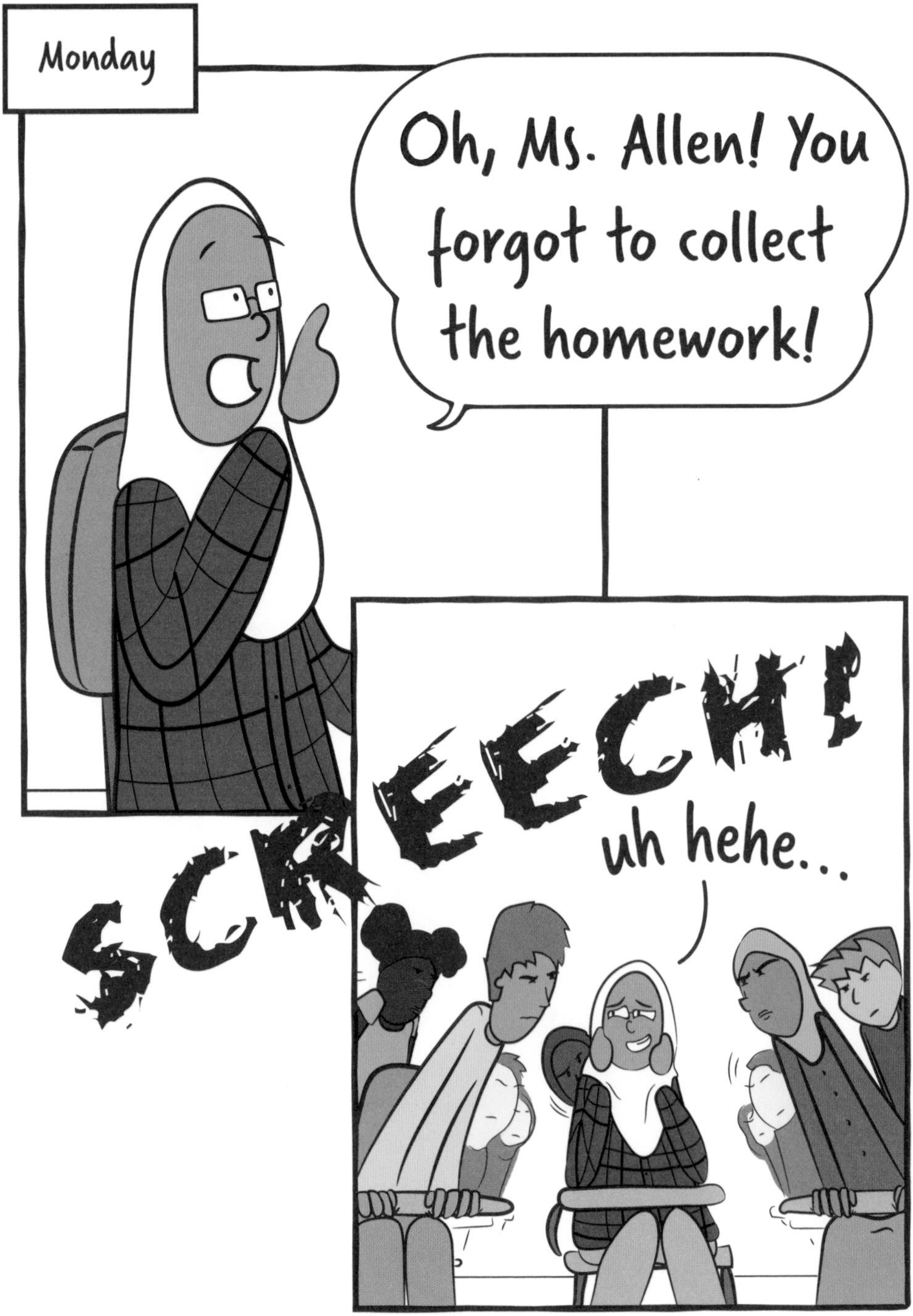
Monday
Oh, Ms. Allen! You forgot to collect the homework!
SCREEECH!
uh hehe...

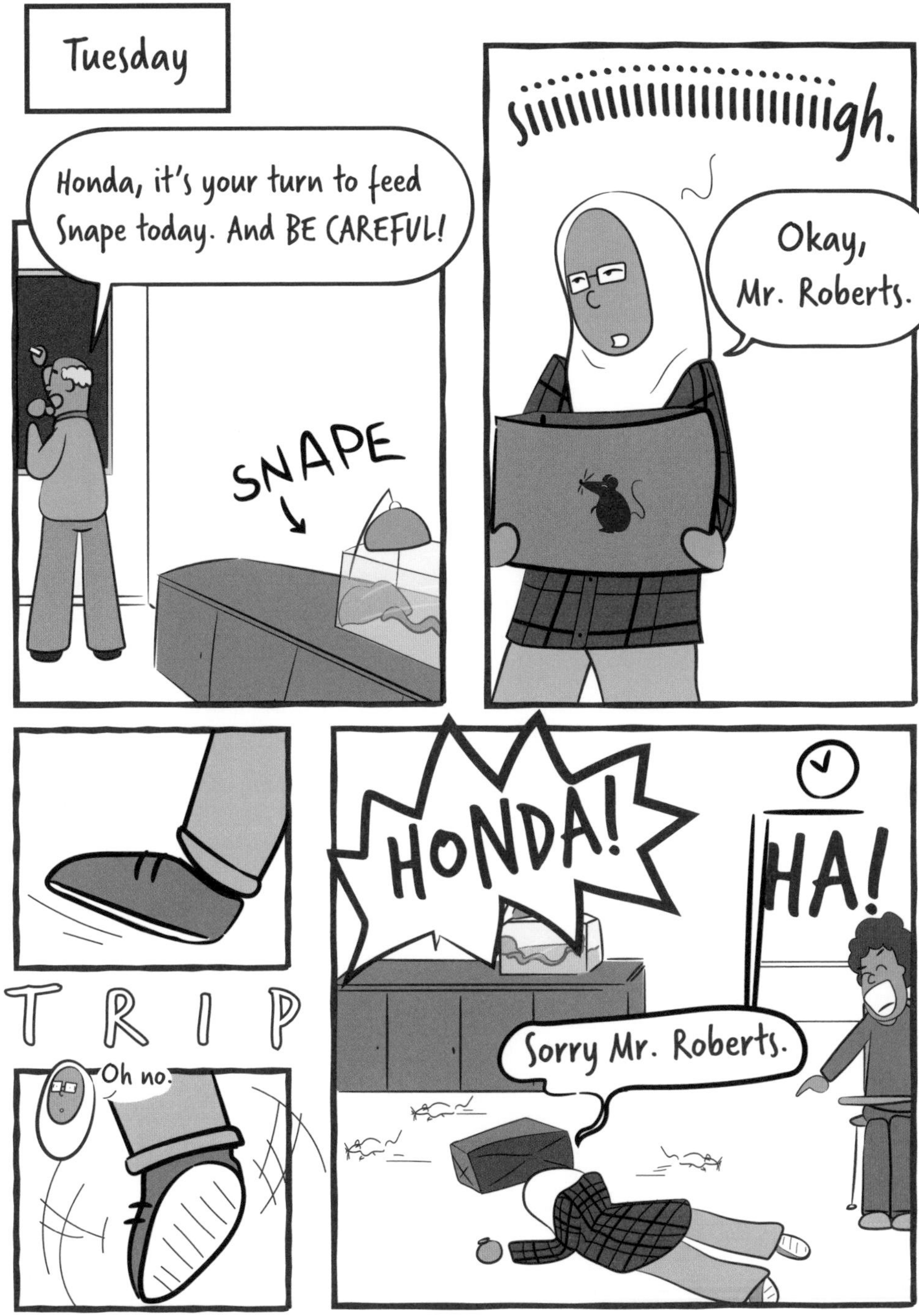
Tuesday
Honda, it's your turn to feed Snape today. And BE CAREFUL!
SNAPE
siiiiiiiiiiiiiiiiiiiiiigh.
Okay, Mr. Roberts.
TRIP
Oh no.
HONDA!
HA!
Sorry Mr. Roberts.

Wednesday

Okay, so school might not be going that great, but at least it can't get much worse, right?

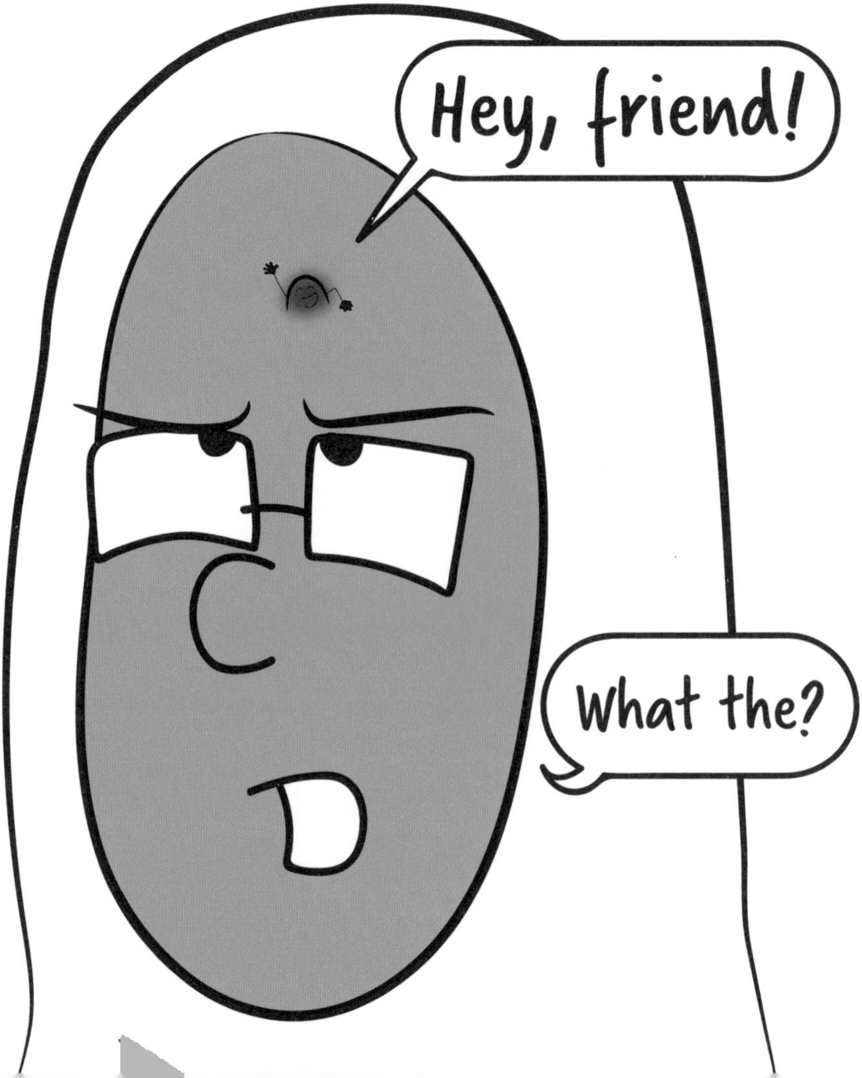
Hey, friend!
What the?

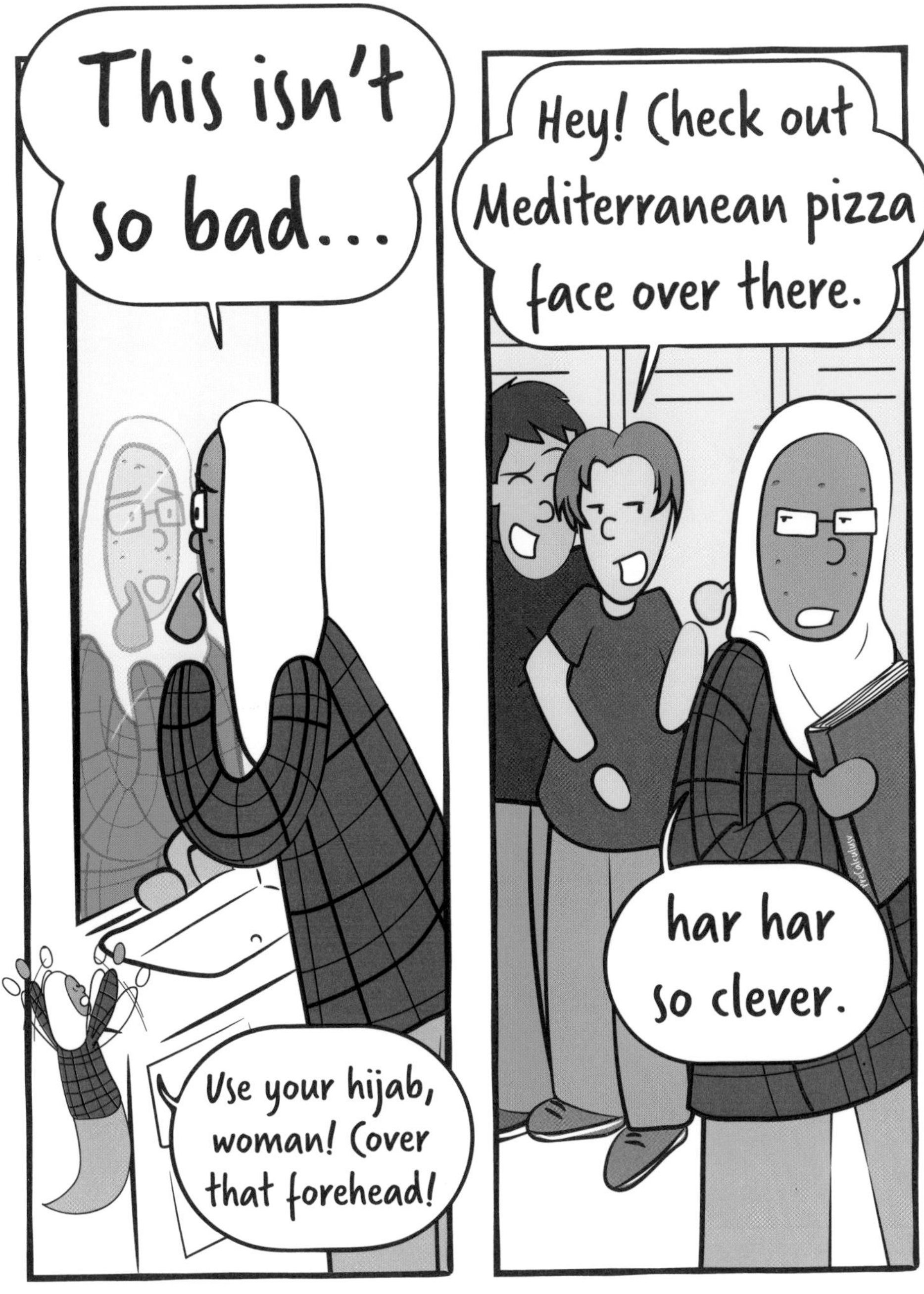
This isn't so bad...
Use your hijab, woman! Cover that forehead!
Hey! Check out Mediterranean pizza face over there.
har har so clever.

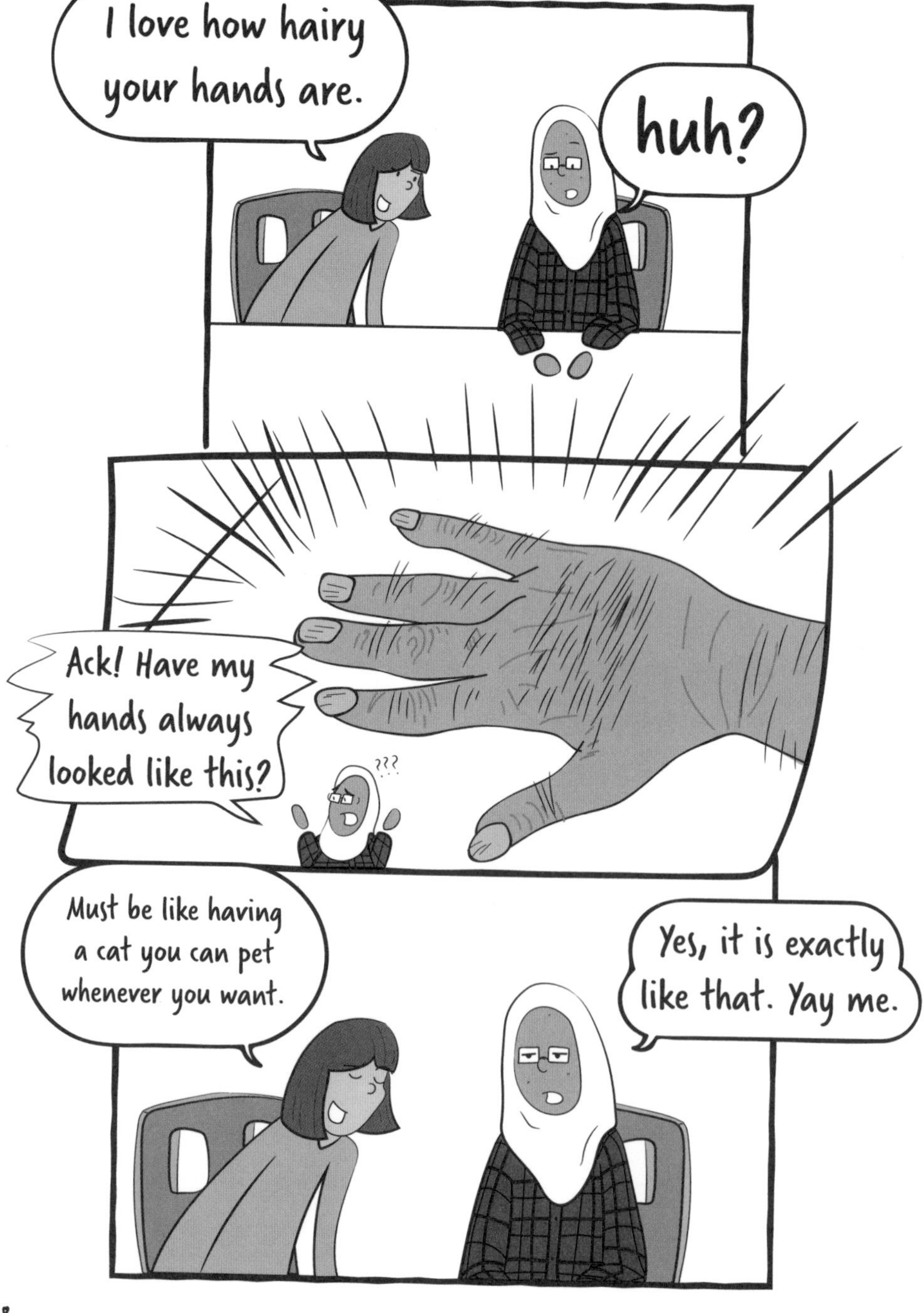
I love how hairy your hands are.
huh?
Ack! Have my hands always looked like this?
???
Must be like having a cat you can pet whenever you want.
Yes, it is exactly like that. Yay me.

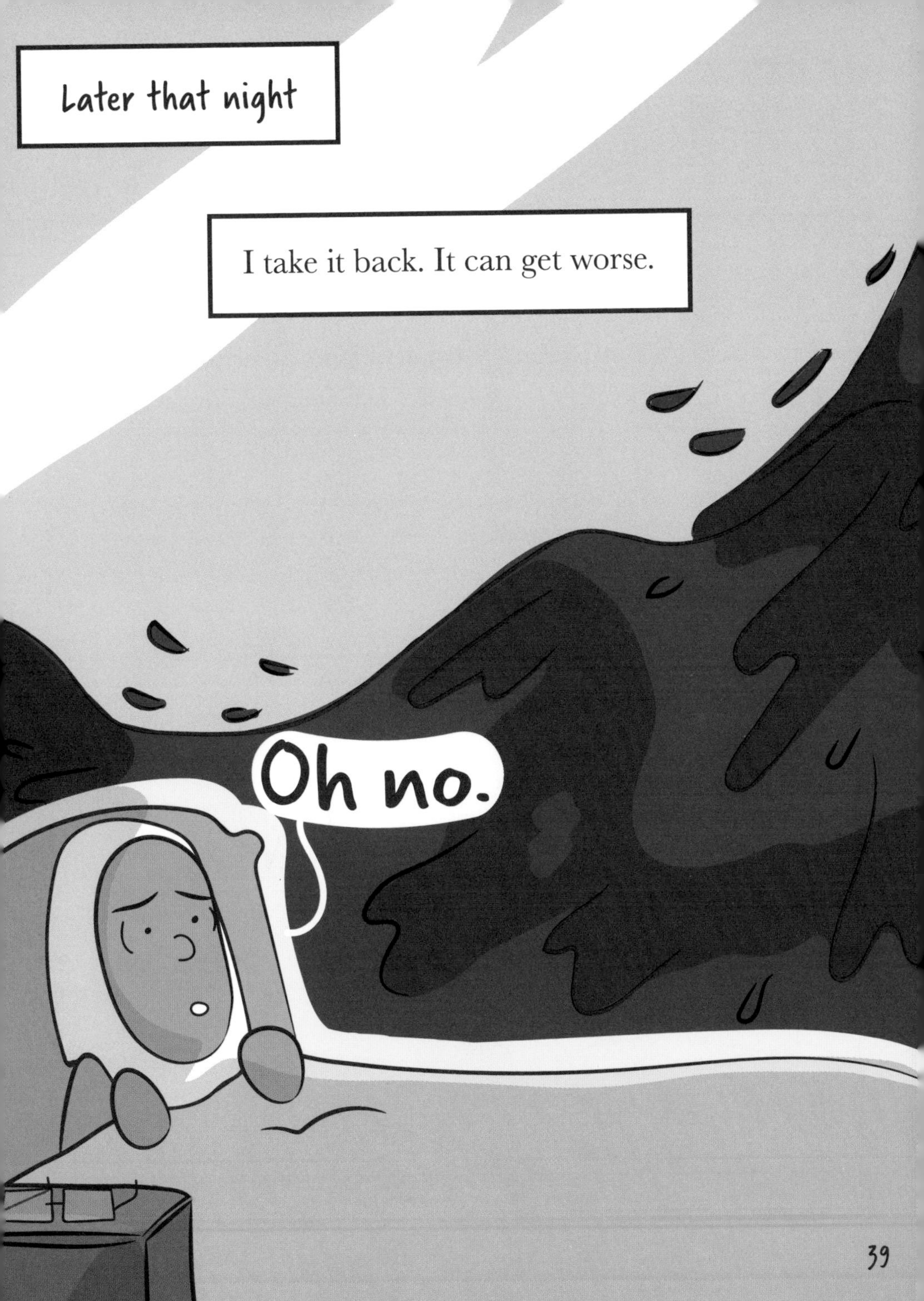
Later that night
I take it back. It can get worse.
Oh no.

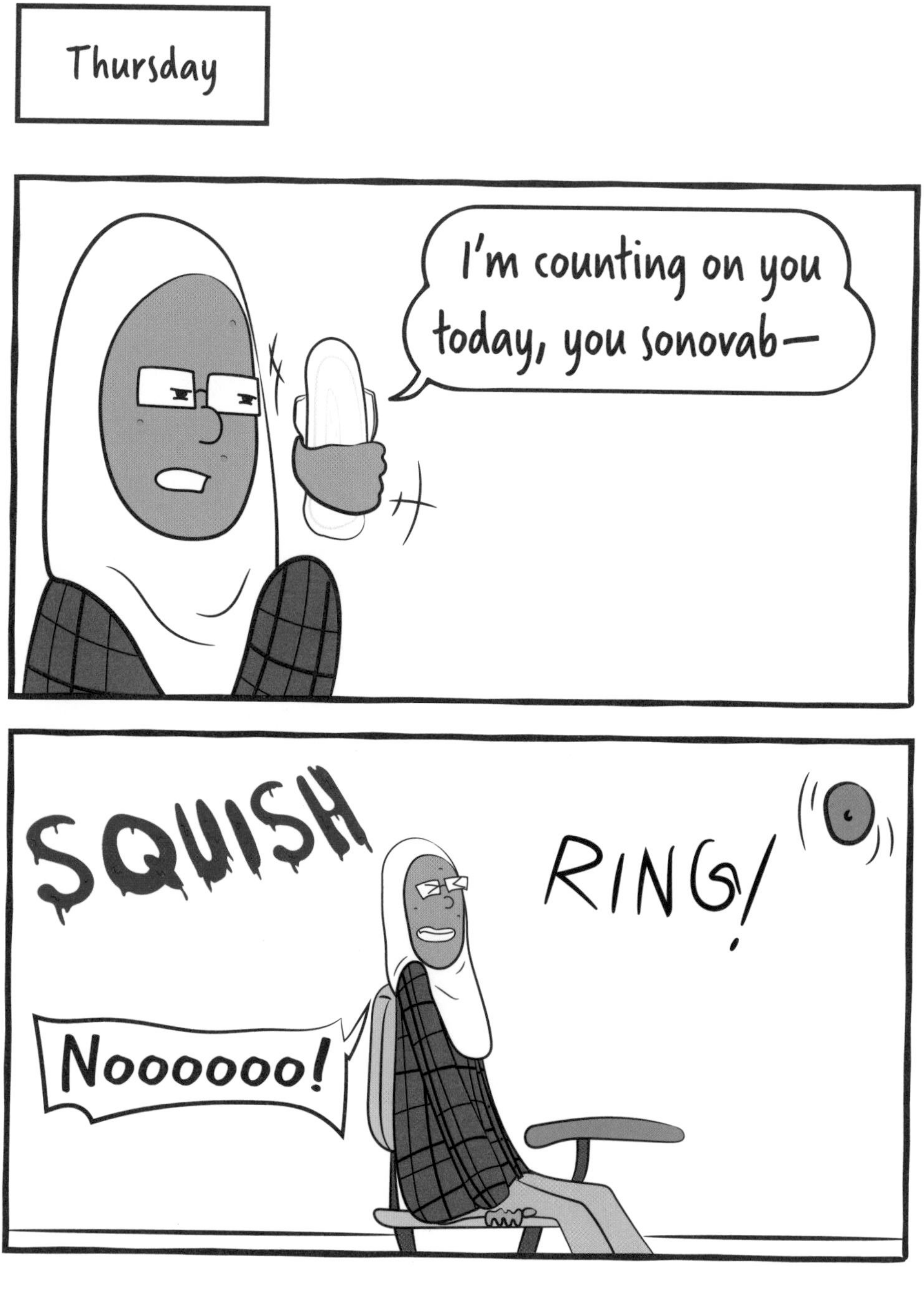

Thursday
I'm counting on you today, you sonovab—
SQUISH
RING!
Nooooooo!

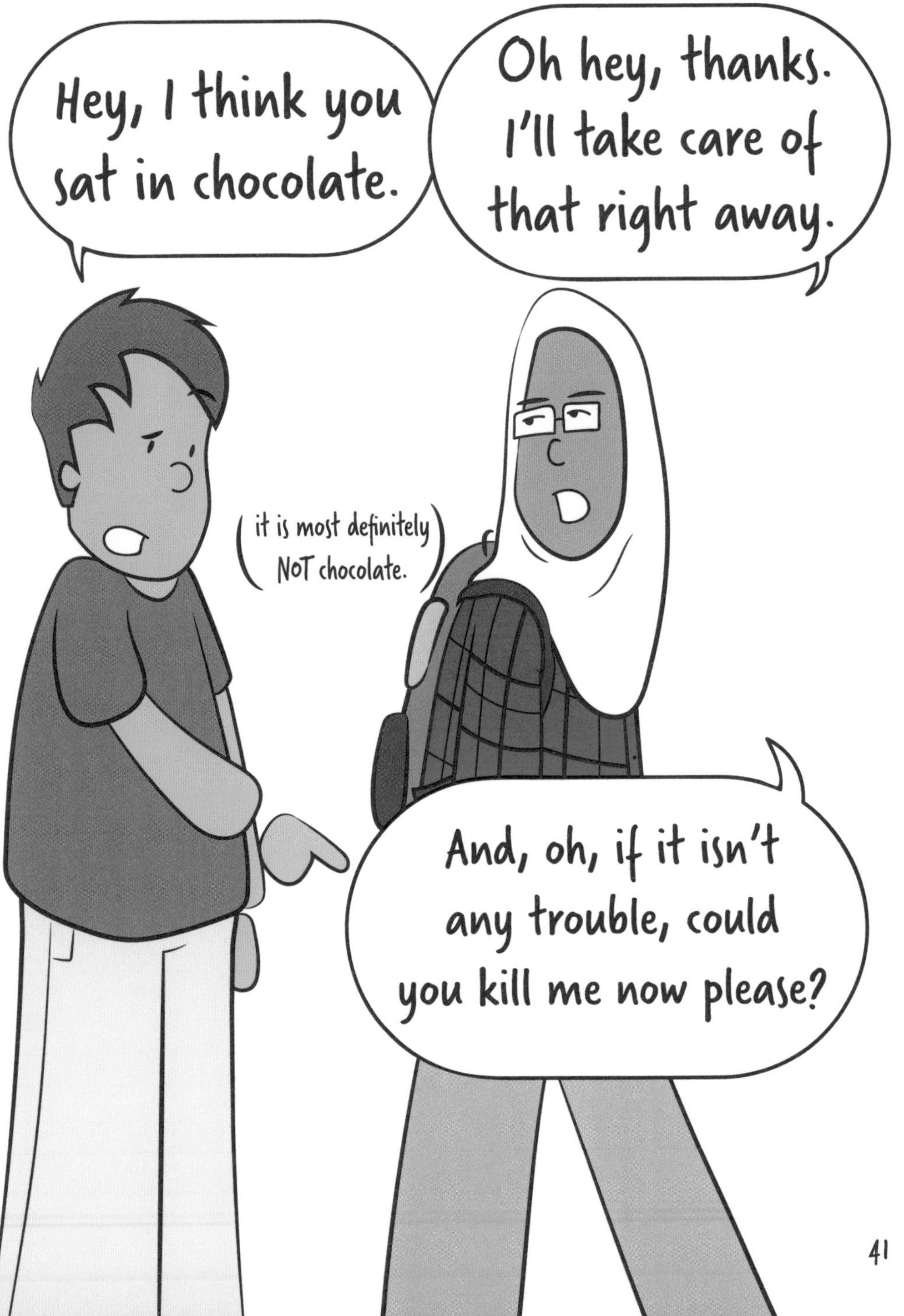
Hey, I think you sat in chocolate.
Oh hey, thanks. I'll take care of that right away.
(it is most definitely NOT chocolate.)
And, oh, if it isn't any trouble, could you kill me now please?

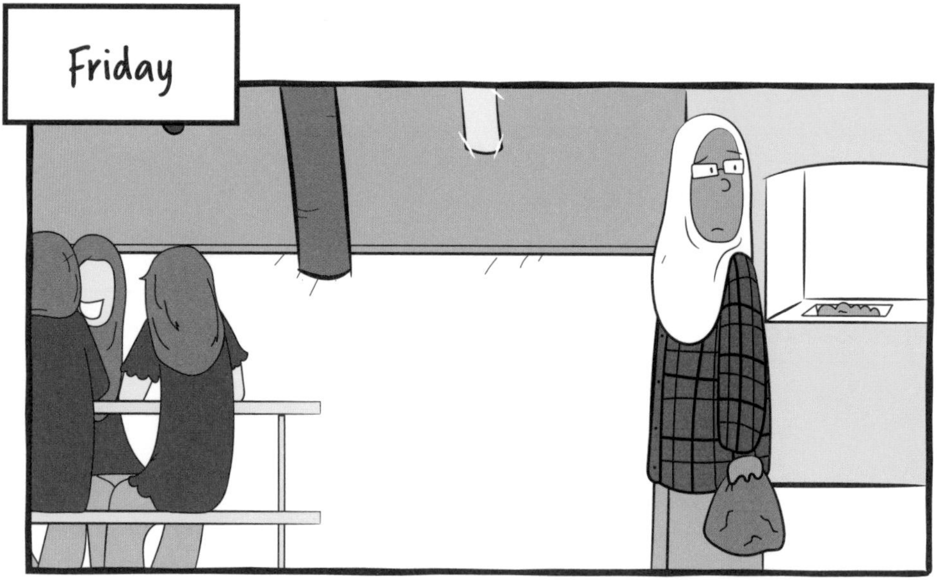
Friday

If only I had a group of friends to suffer high school with.

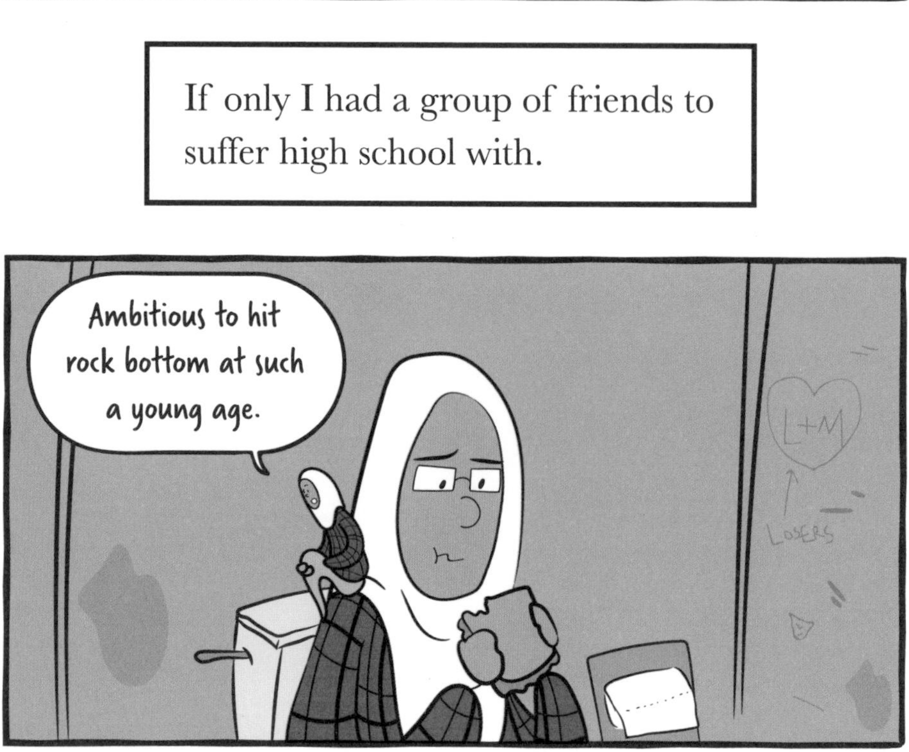
Ambitious to hit rock bottom at such a young age.
L+M
LOSERS

I guess I should be used to this. I didn't have friends in middle school either. I mean, I had people who hung out with me.

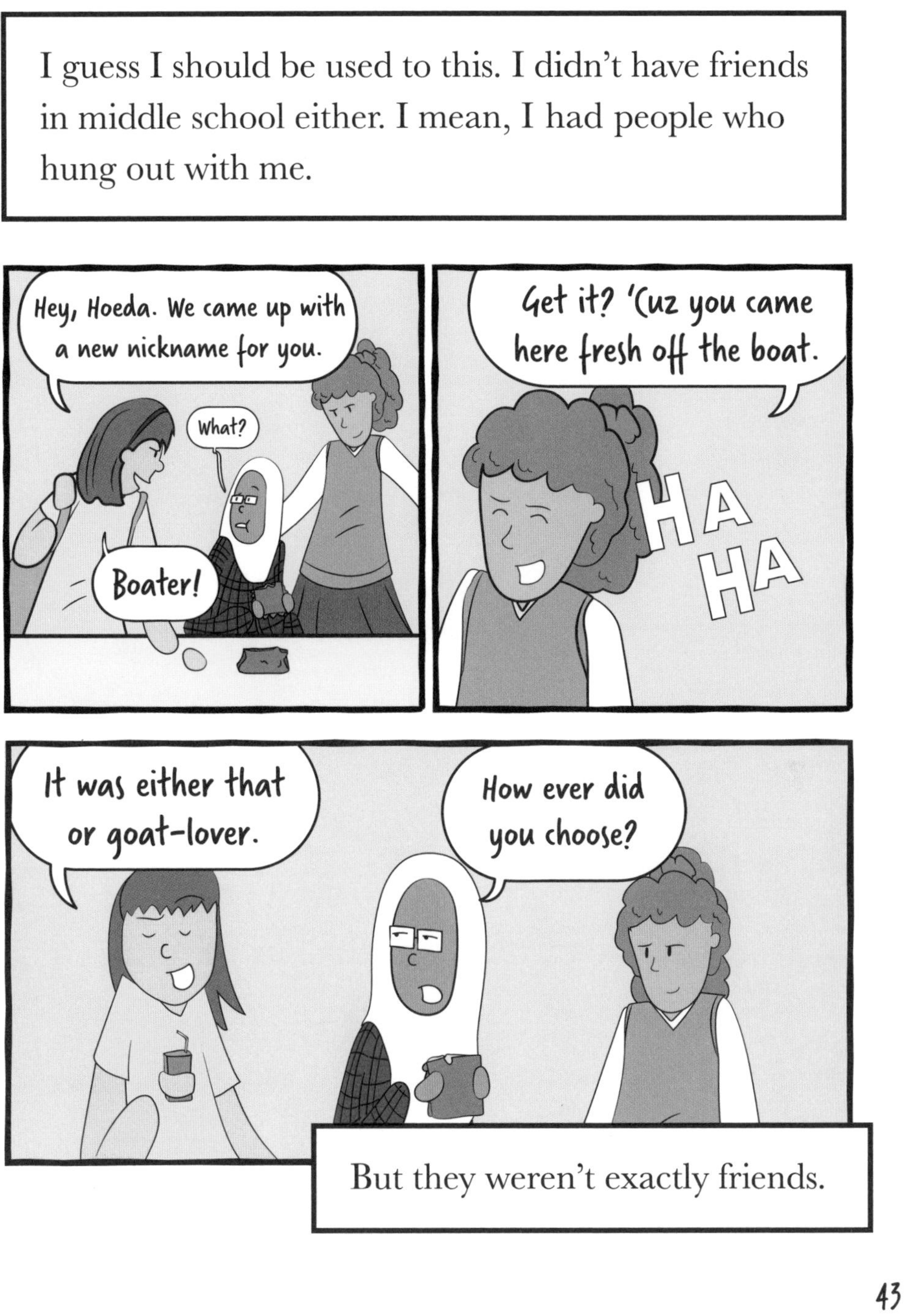
Hey, Hoeda. We came up with a new nickname for you.
What?
Boater!
Get it? 'Cuz you came here fresh off the boat.
HA HA
It was either that or goat-lover.
How ever did you choose?

But they weren't exactly friends.

Yeah, I definitely don't miss those guys. But I'm in high school now! I can rebrand. New city! New school! New me! Right?

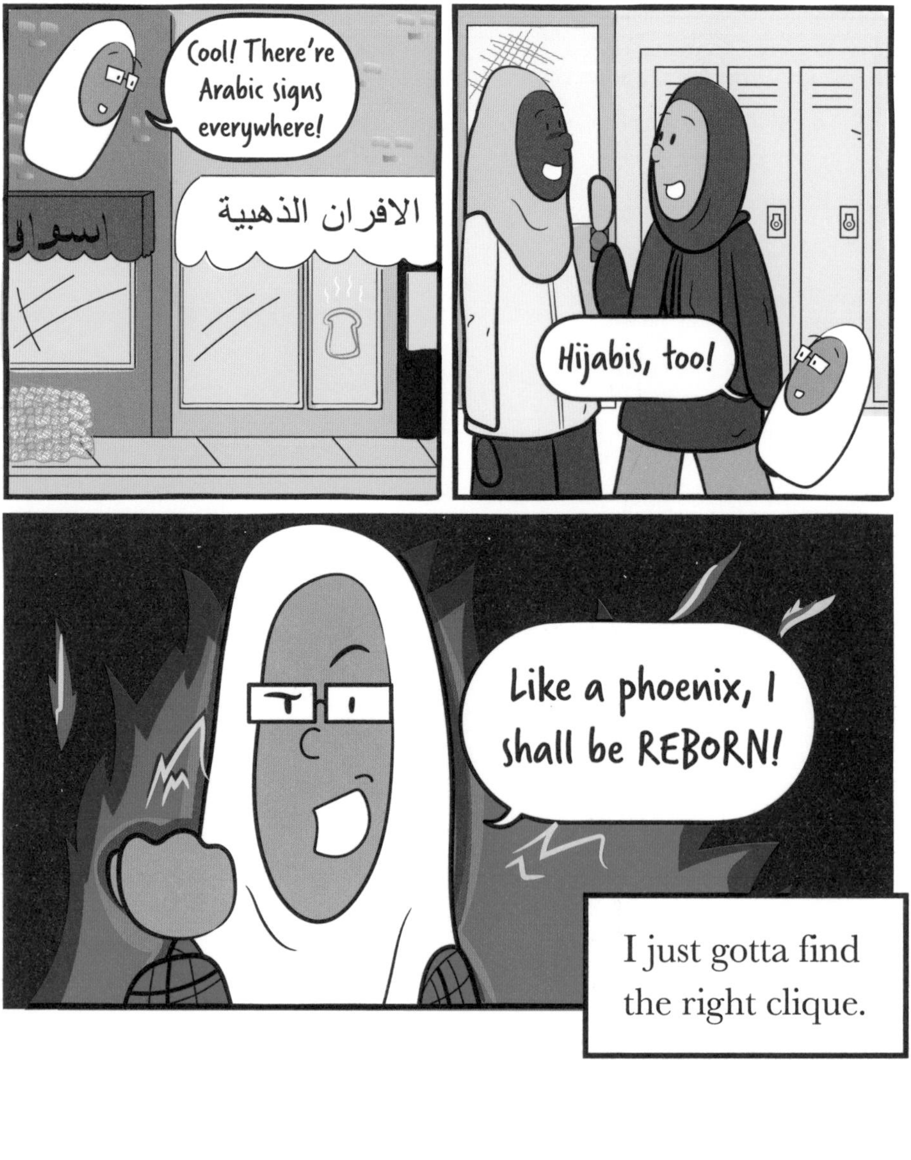
Cool! There're Arabic signs everywhere!
الافران الذهبية
Hijabis, too!
Like a phoenix, I shall be REBORN!
I just gotta find the right clique.

That should be easy in Dearborn, right?
I'll just hang out with the other hijabis.

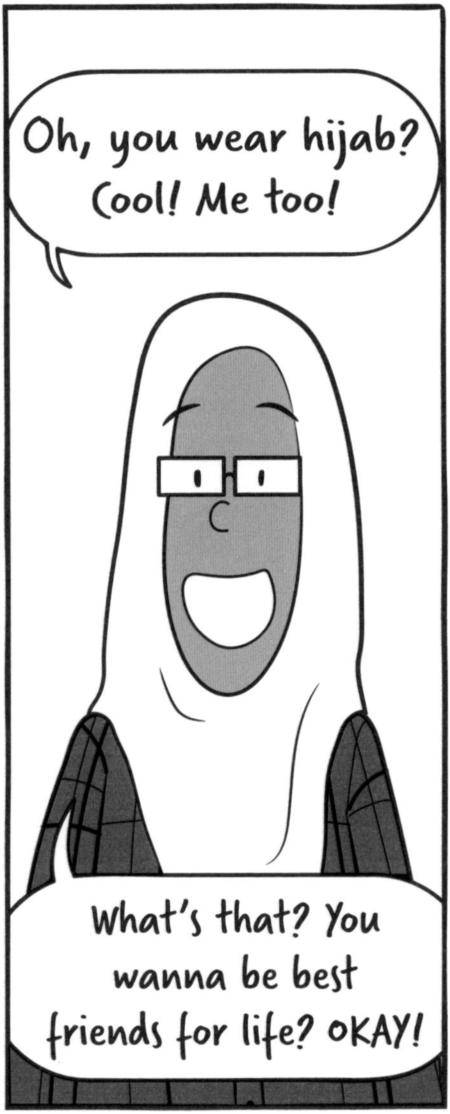
Oh, you wear hijab? Cool! Me too!
What's that? You wanna be best friends for life? OKAY!

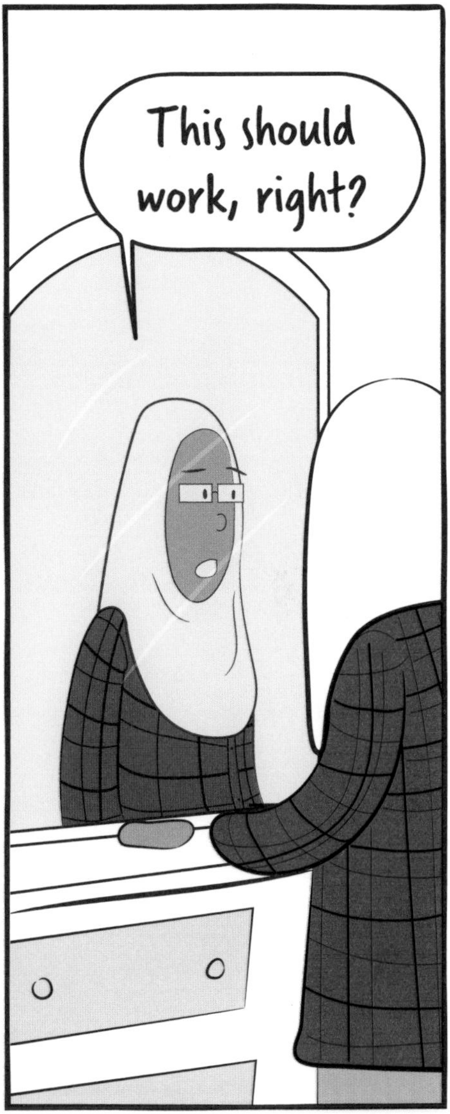
This should work, right?

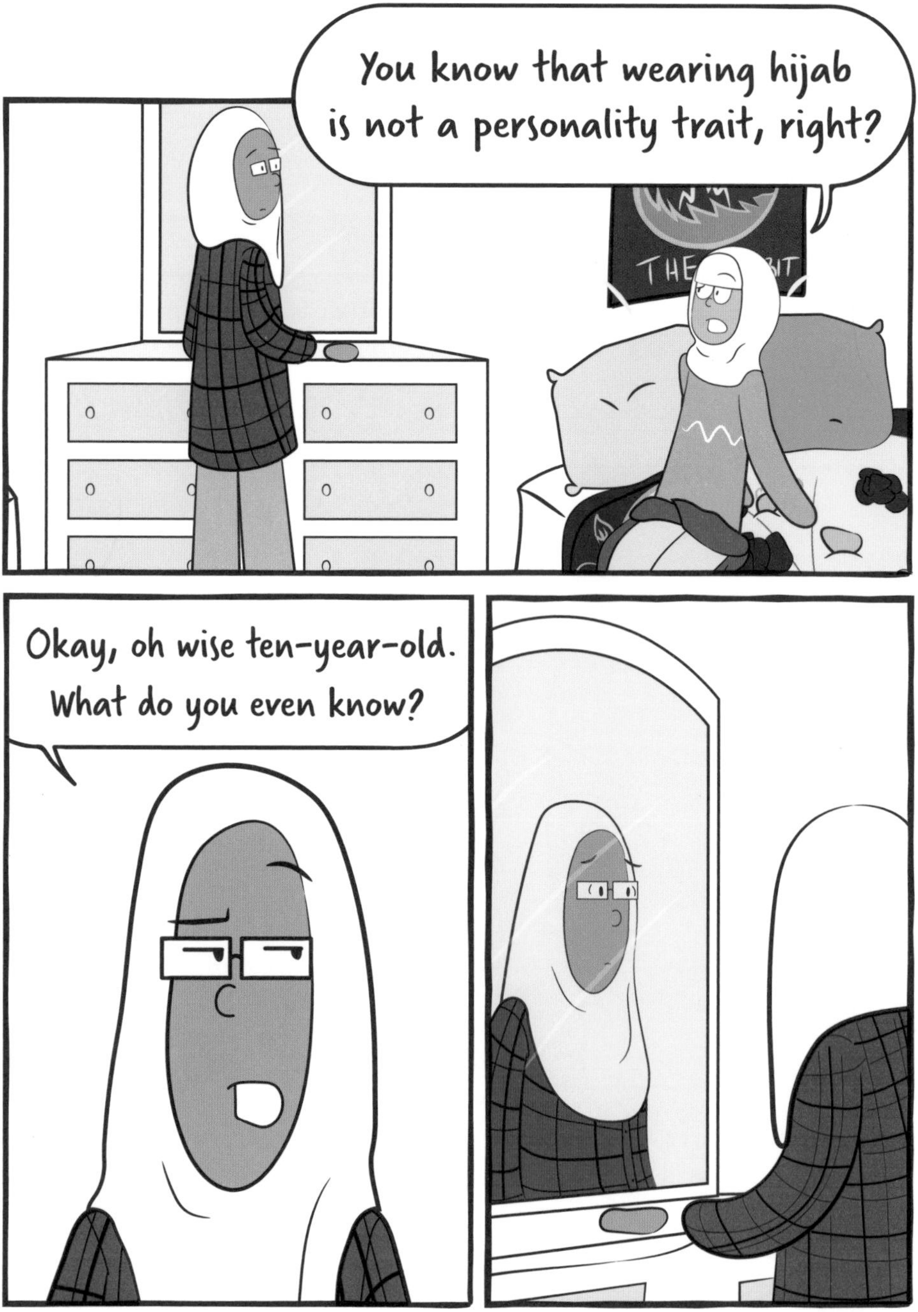
You know that wearing hijab is not a personality trait, right?
Okay, oh wise ten-year-old. What do you even know?

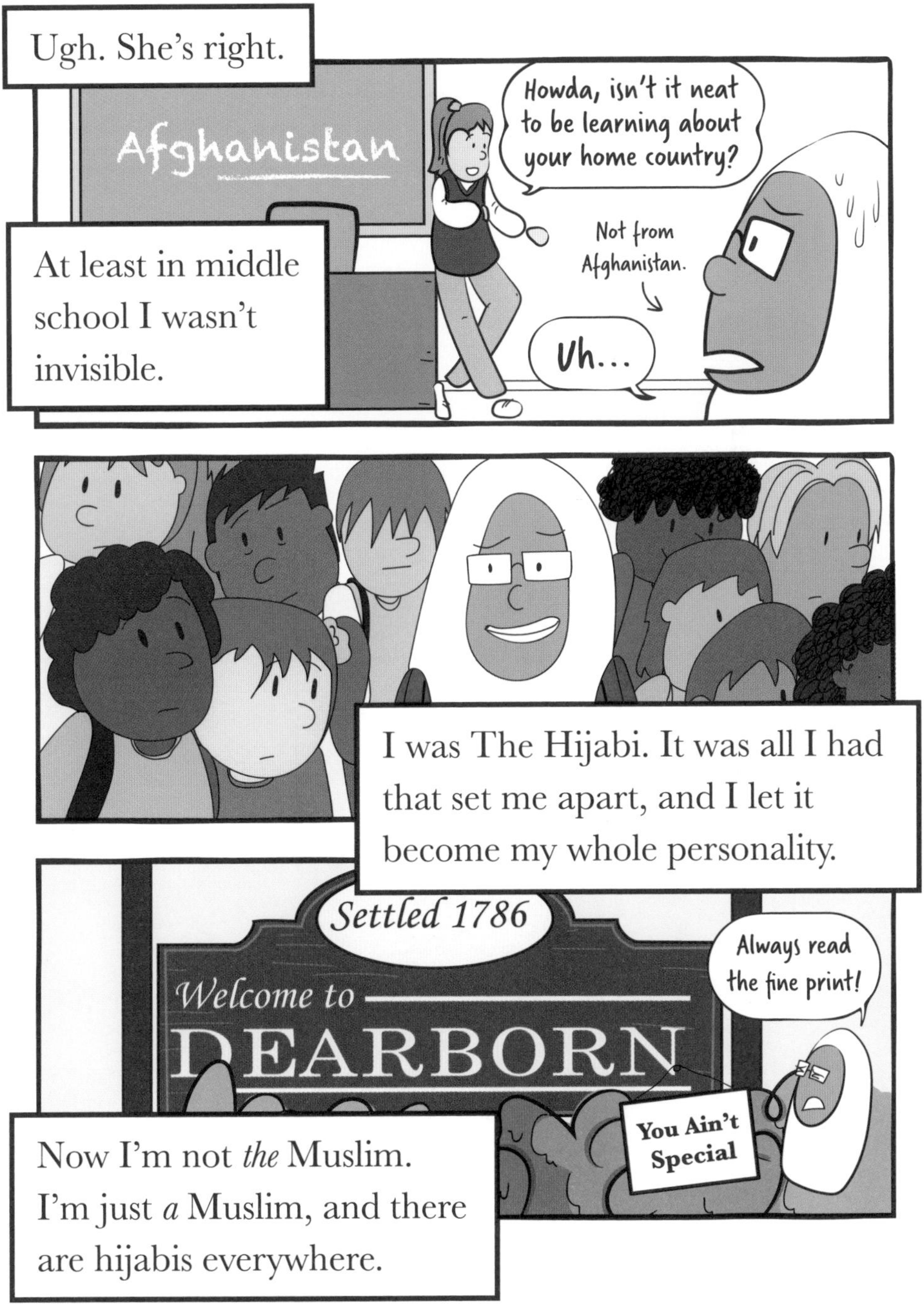
Ugh. She's right.
Afghanistan
Howda, isn't it neat to be learning about your home country?
Not from Afghanistan.
Uh...
At least in middle school I wasn't invisible.
I was The Hijabi. It was all I had that set me apart, and I let it become my whole personality.
Settled 1786
Welcome to
DEARBORN
Always read the fine print!
You Ain't Special
Now I'm not *the* Muslim. I'm just *a* Muslim, and there are hijabis everywhere.

There are hijabi athletes.

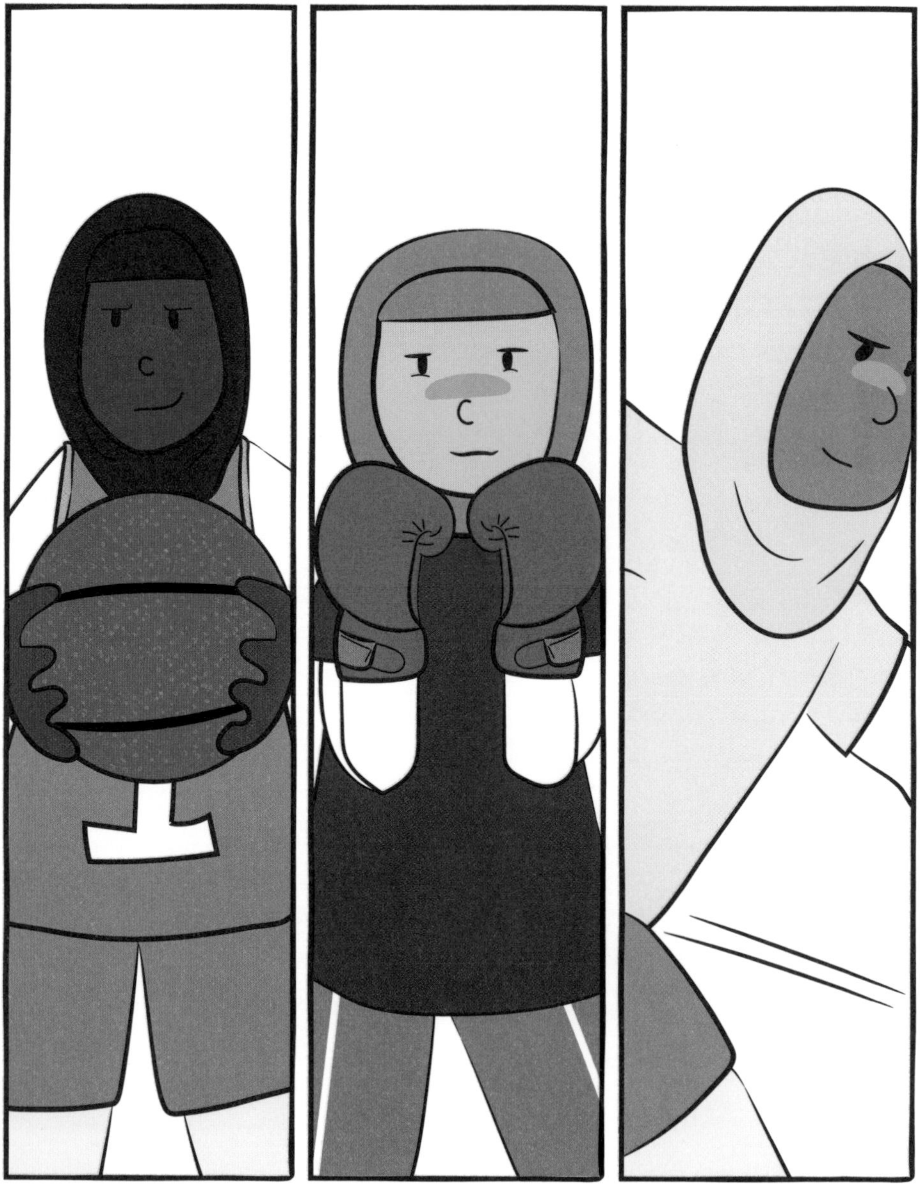

Hijabi gamers.

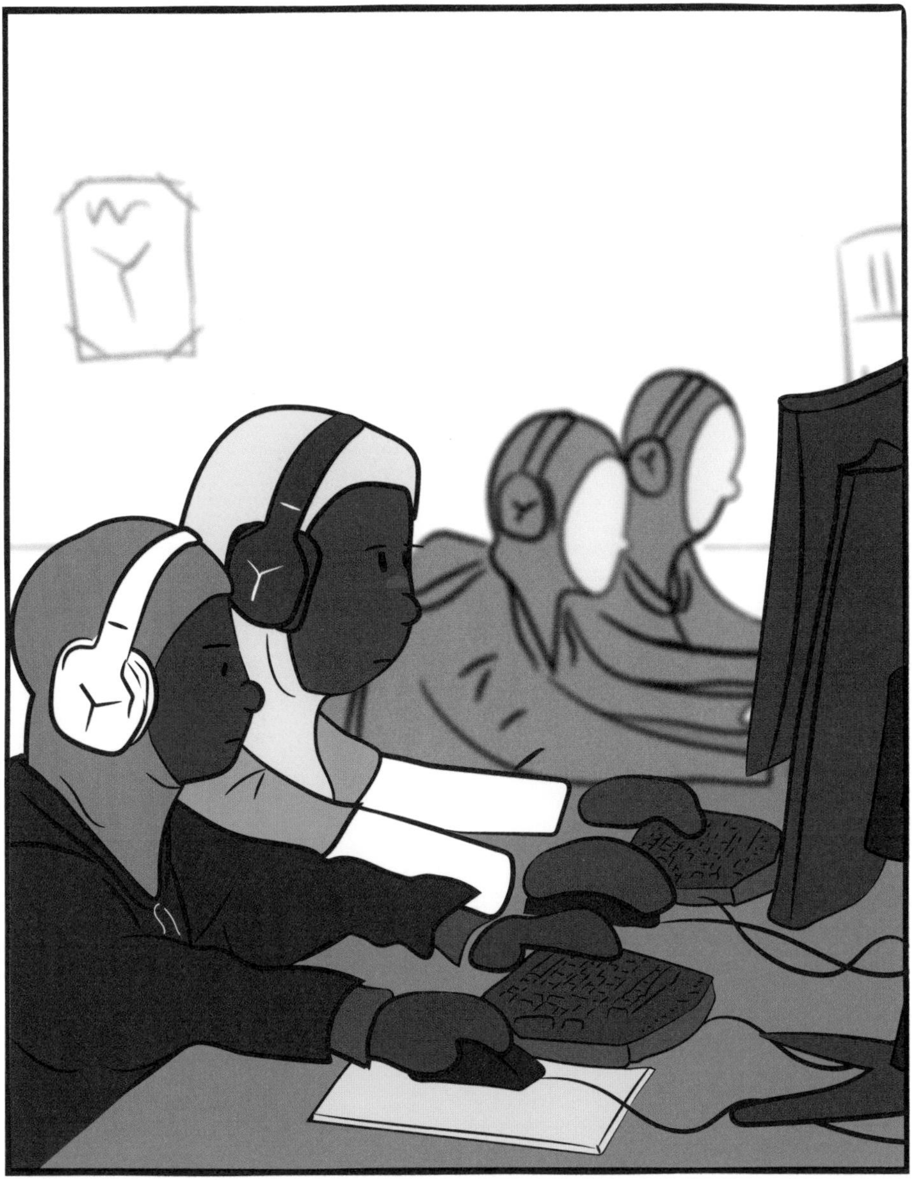

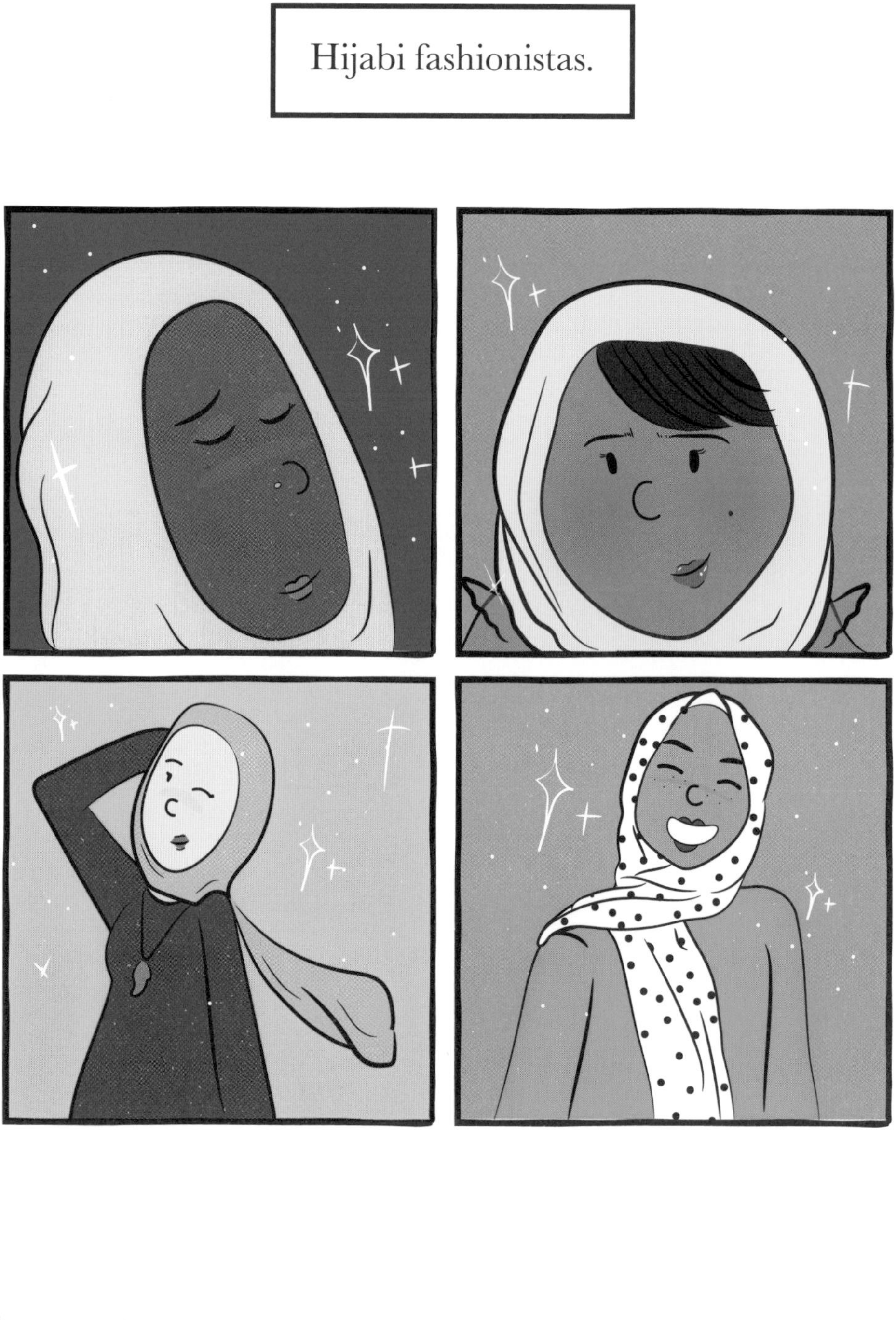
Hijabi fashionistas.

And then there's me.

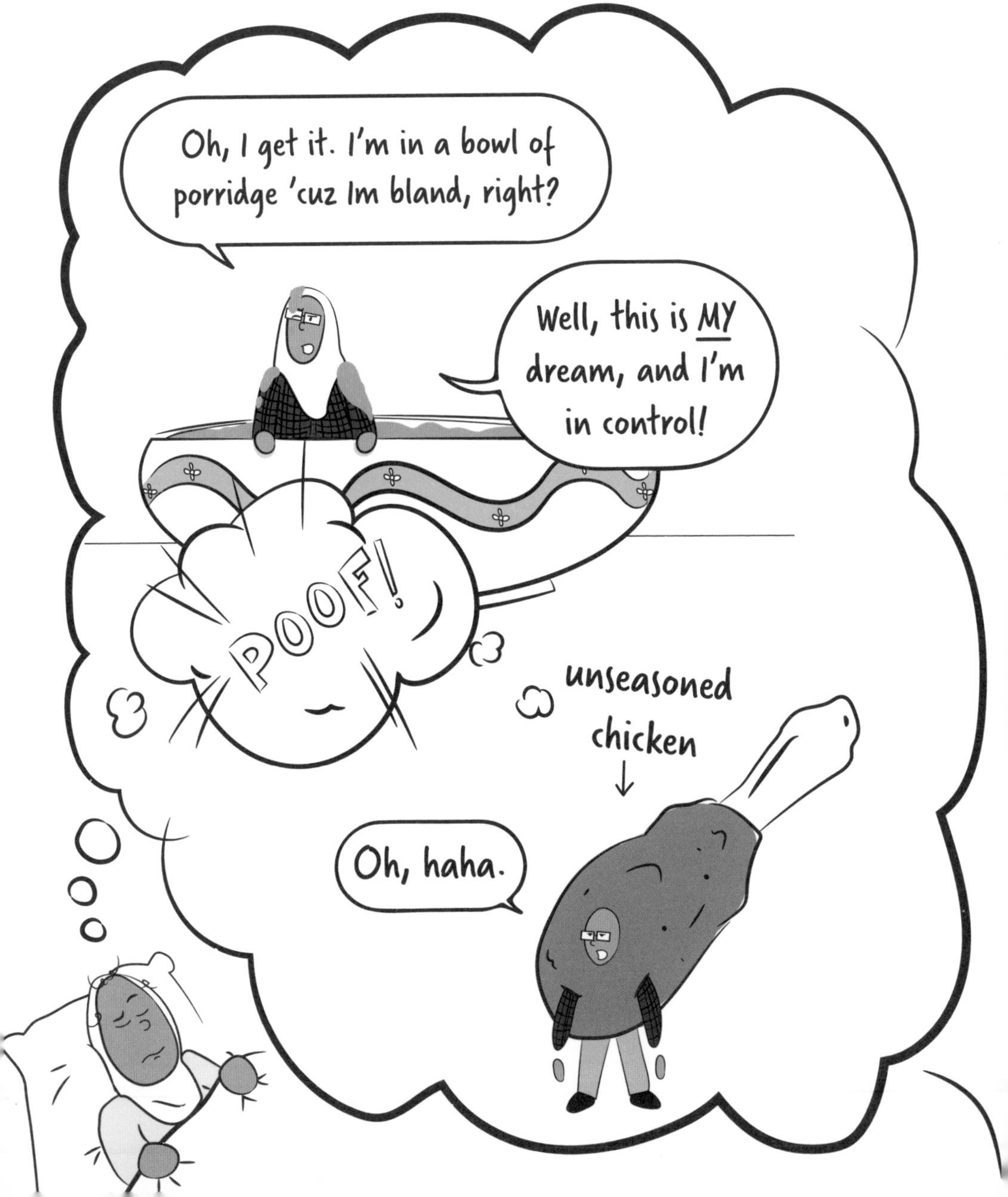
Oh, I get it. I'm in a bowl of porridge 'cuz Im bland, right?
Well, this is MY dream, and I'm in control!
POOF!
unseasoned chicken
Oh, haha.

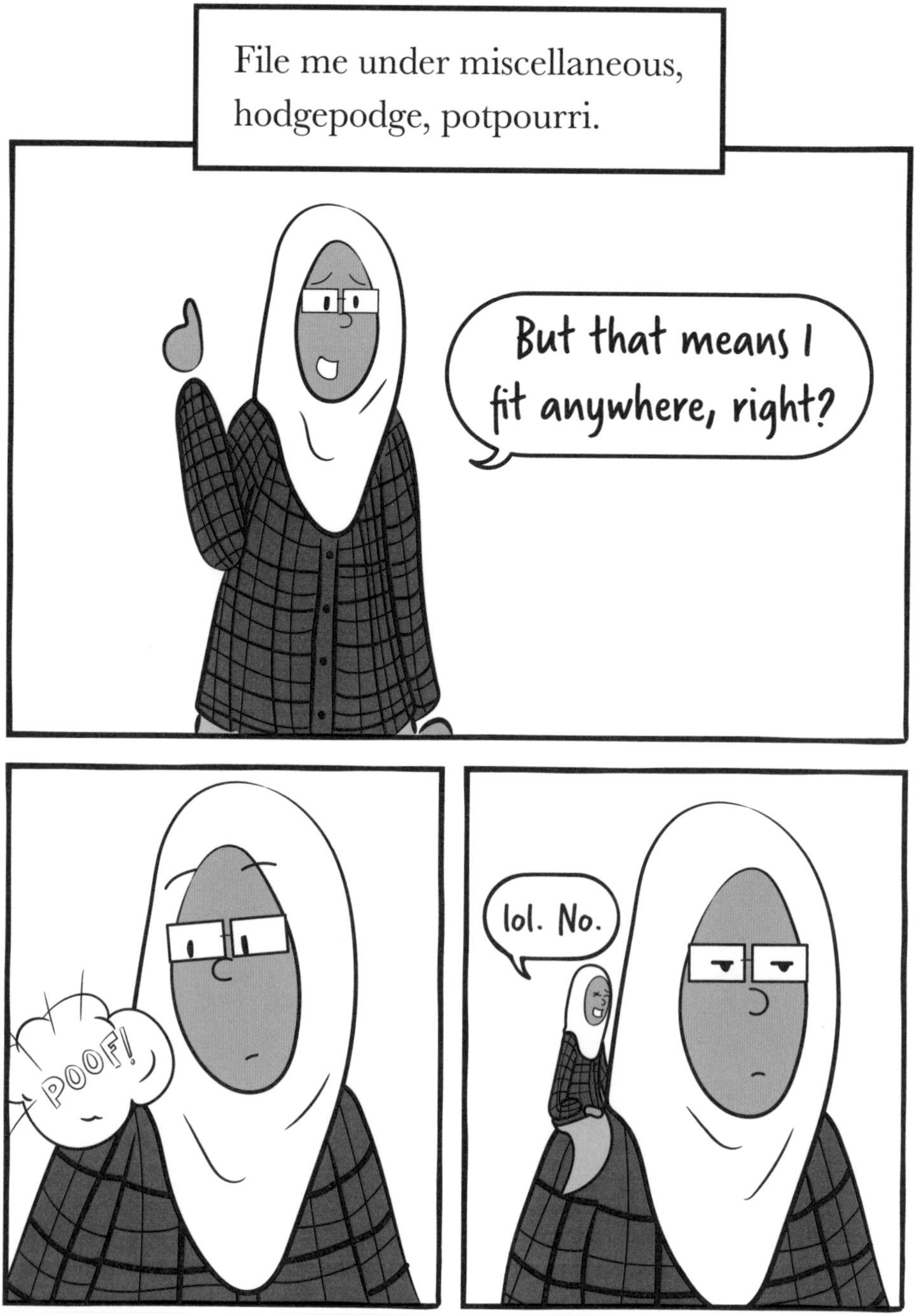
File me under miscellaneous, hodgepodge, potpourri.
But that means I fit anywhere, right?
POOF!
lol. No.

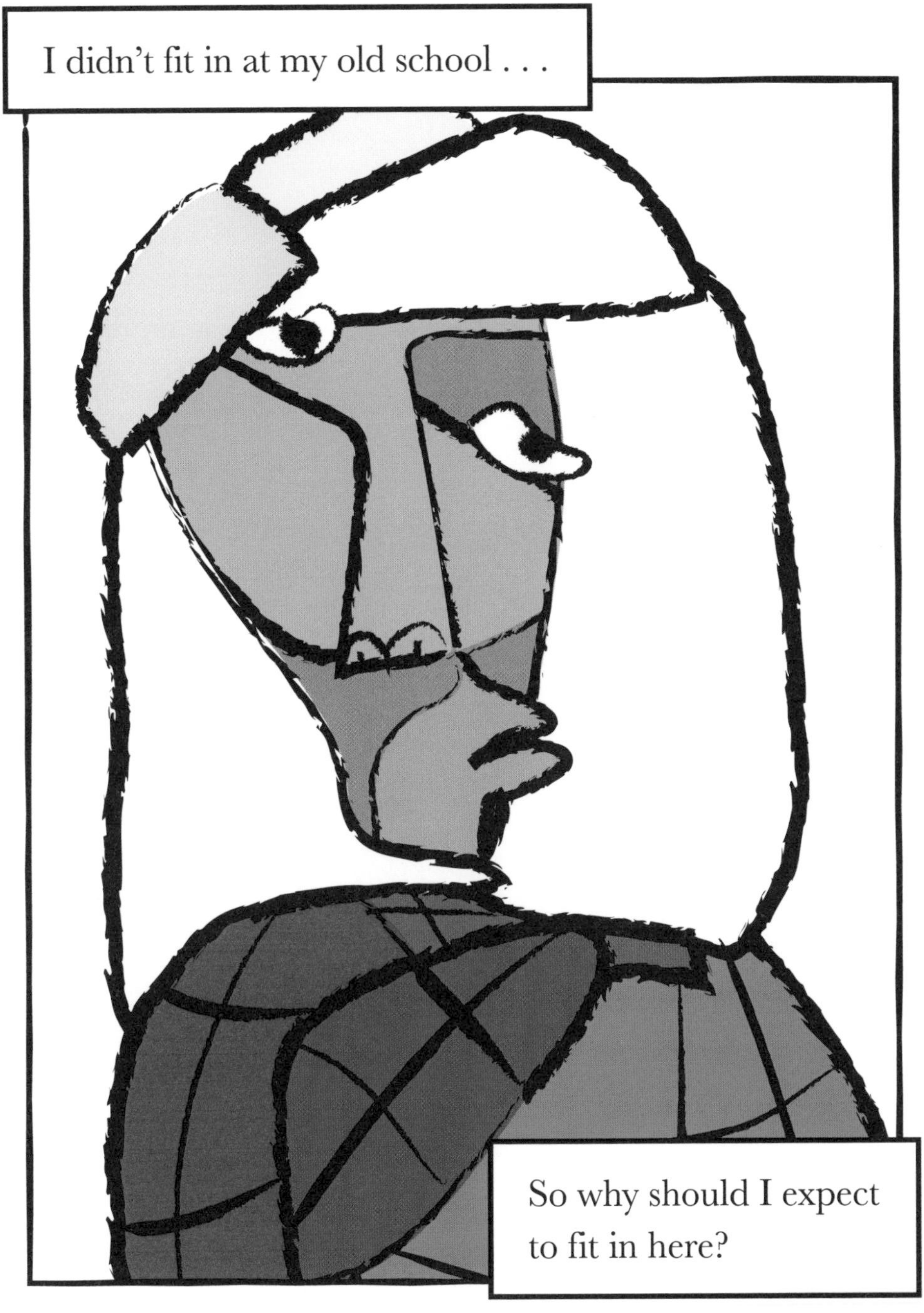
I didn't fit in at my old school . . .
So why should I expect to fit in here?

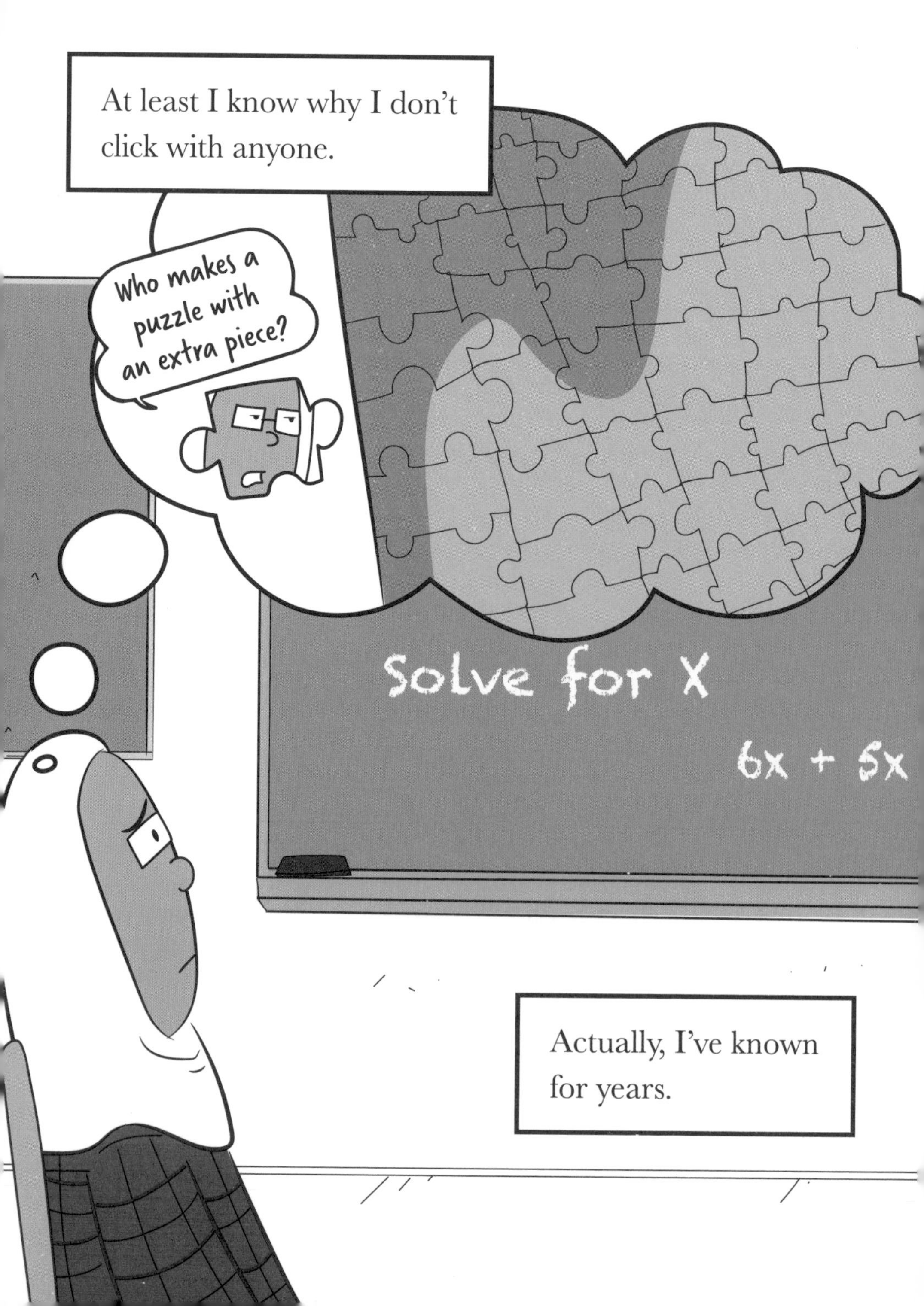
At least I know why I don't click with anyone.
Who makes a puzzle with an extra piece?
Solve for X
6x + 5x
Actually, I've known for years.

I am a pod person.

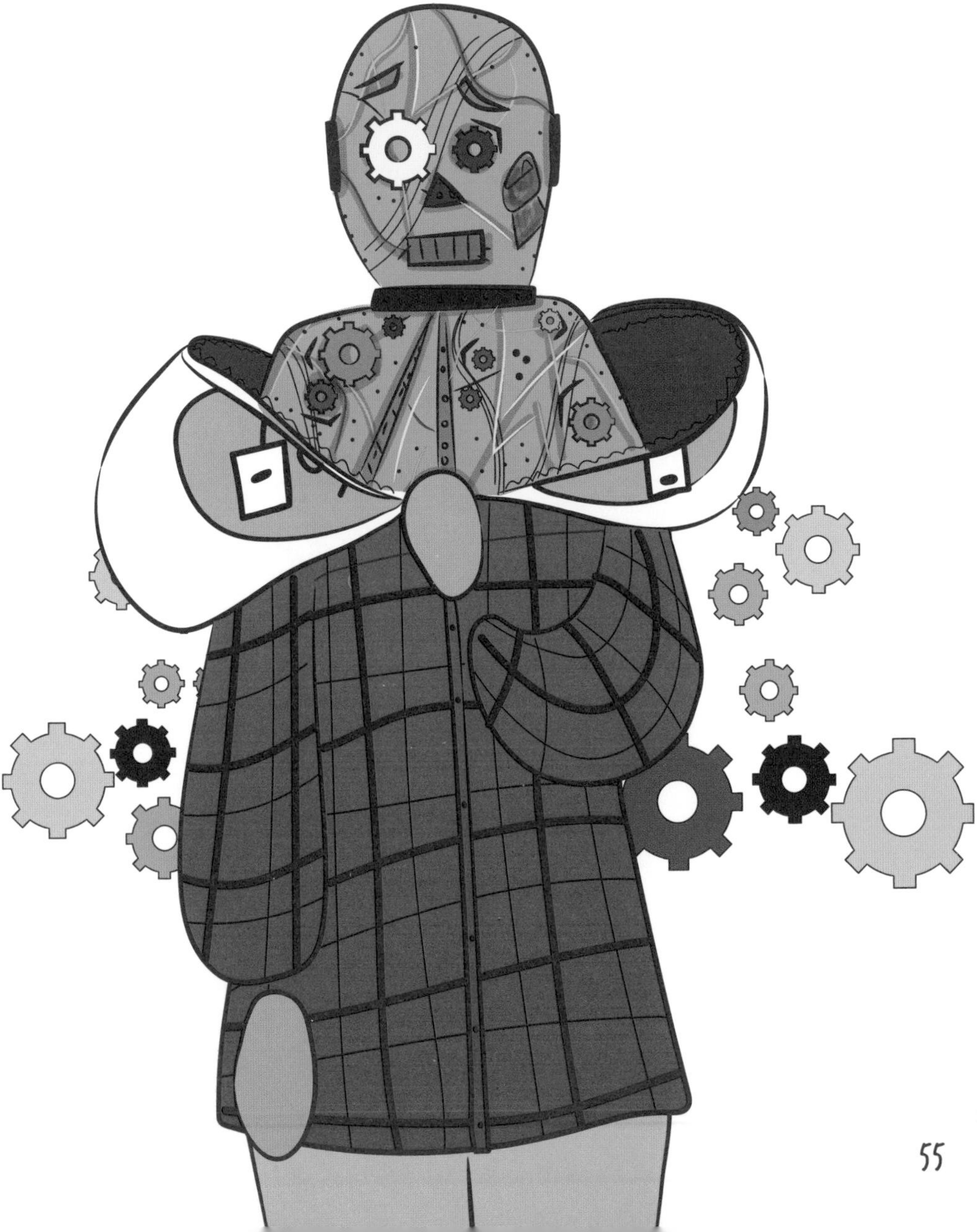

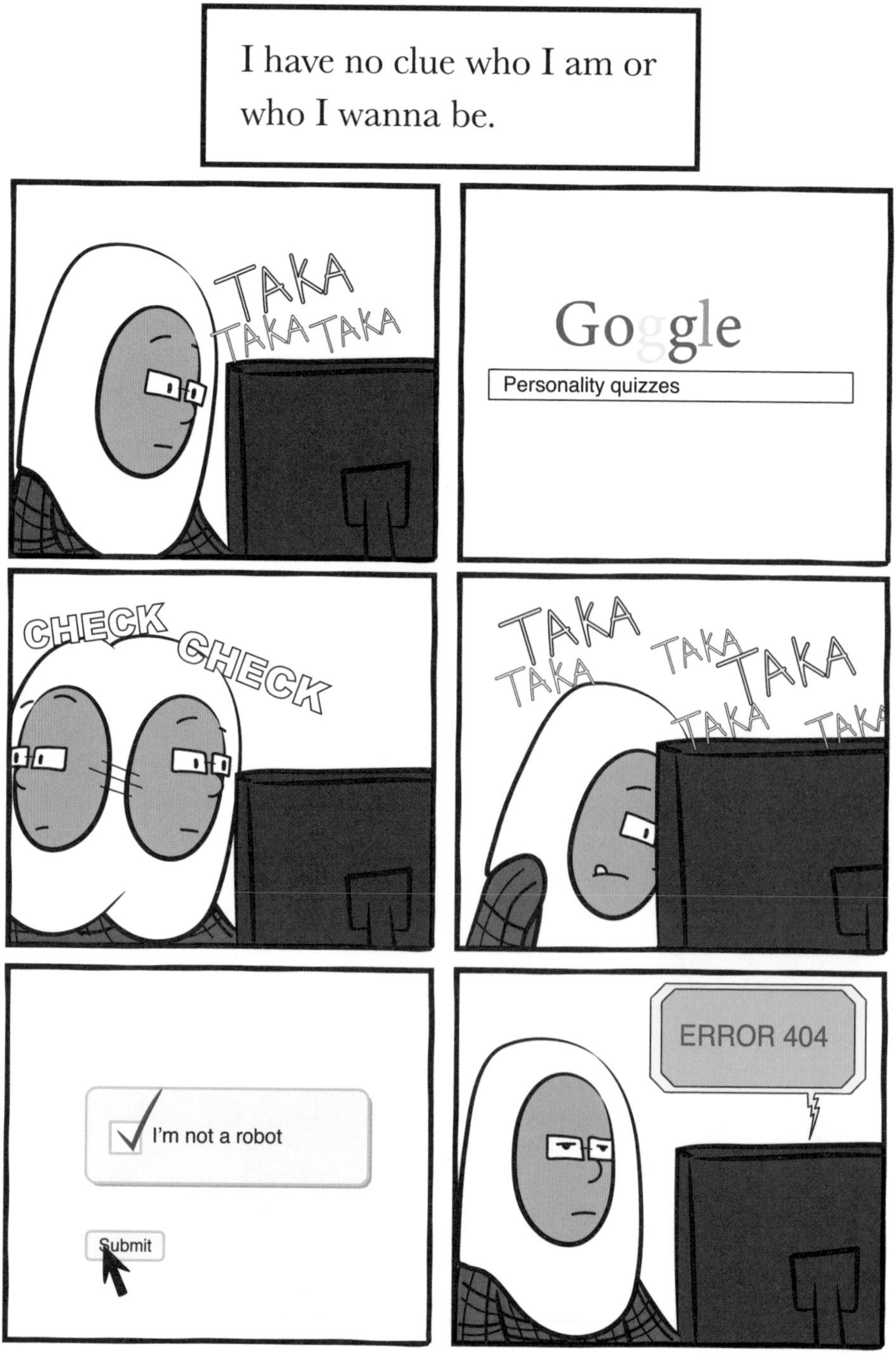
I have no clue who I am or who I wanna be.
TAKA
TAKA TAKA
Goggle
Personality quizzes
CHECK
CHECK
TAKA
TAKA
TAKA
TAKA
TAKA
I'm not a robot
Submit
ERROR 404

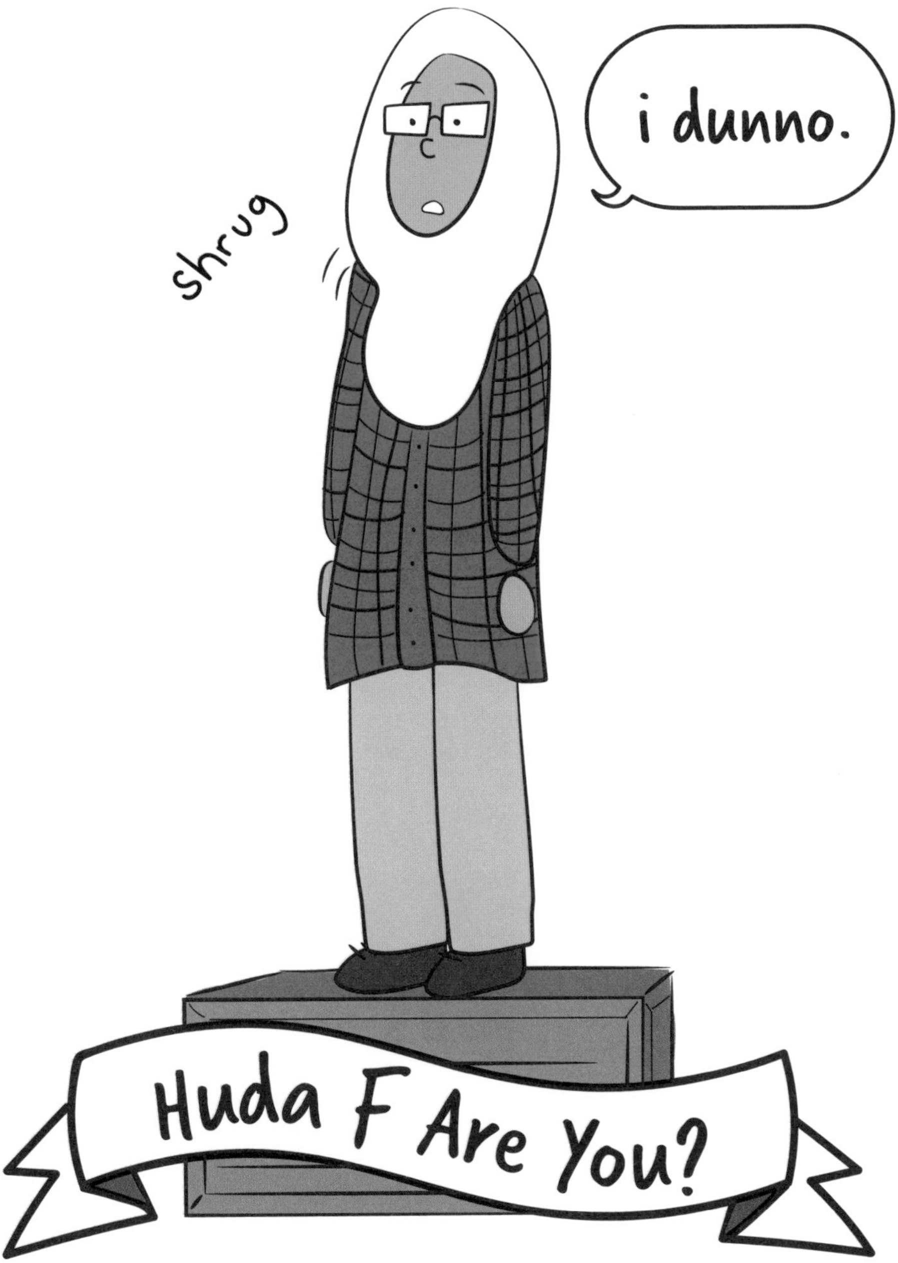
shrug
i dunno.
Huda F Are You?

If someone asked me what I wanted to do with my life, I'd say:

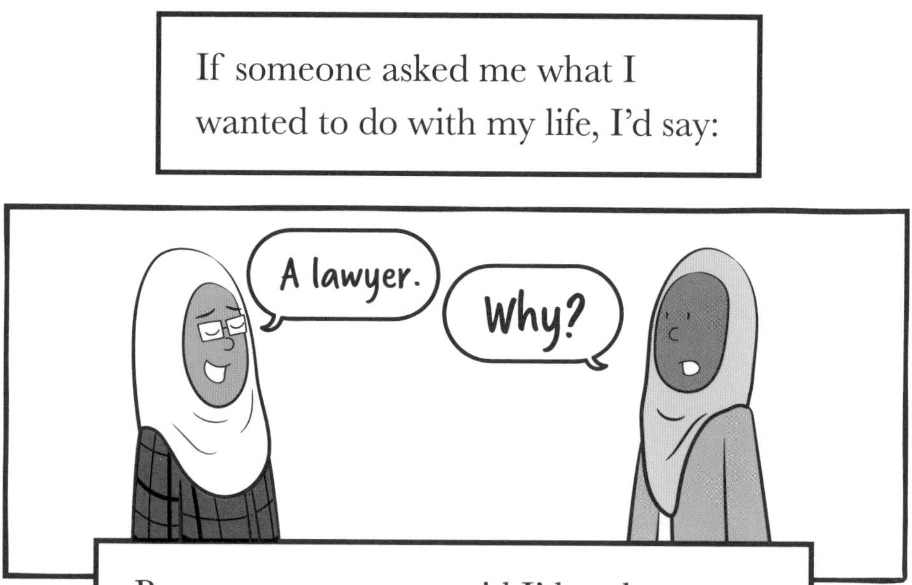
A lawyer.
Why?

Because my parents said I'd make a great lawyer? I DON'T KNOW.

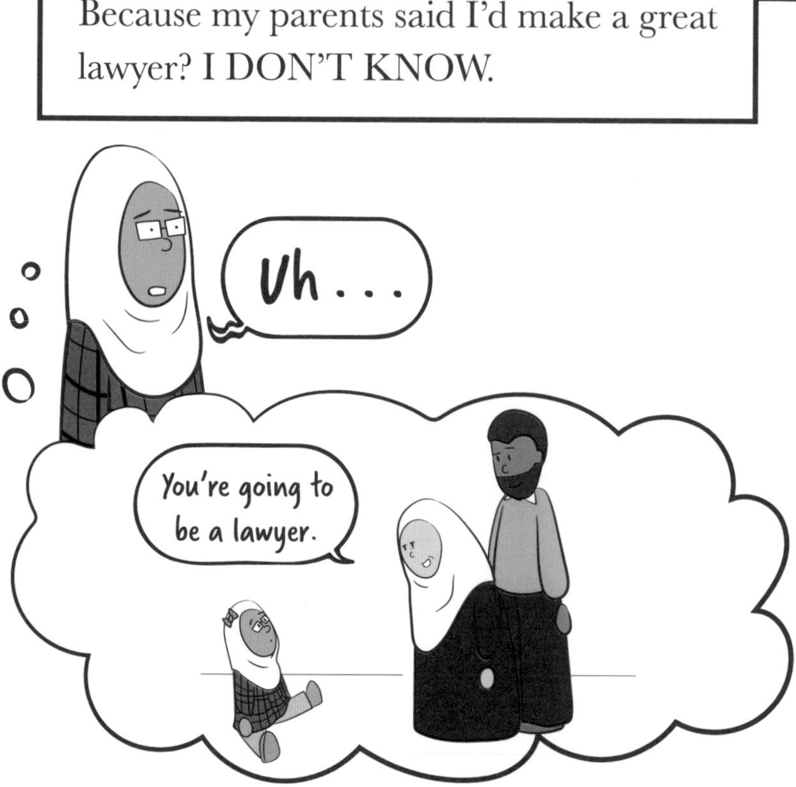
Uh . . .
You're going to be a lawyer.

I don't have any likes or dislikes. I fake interest in whatever other people are talking about.

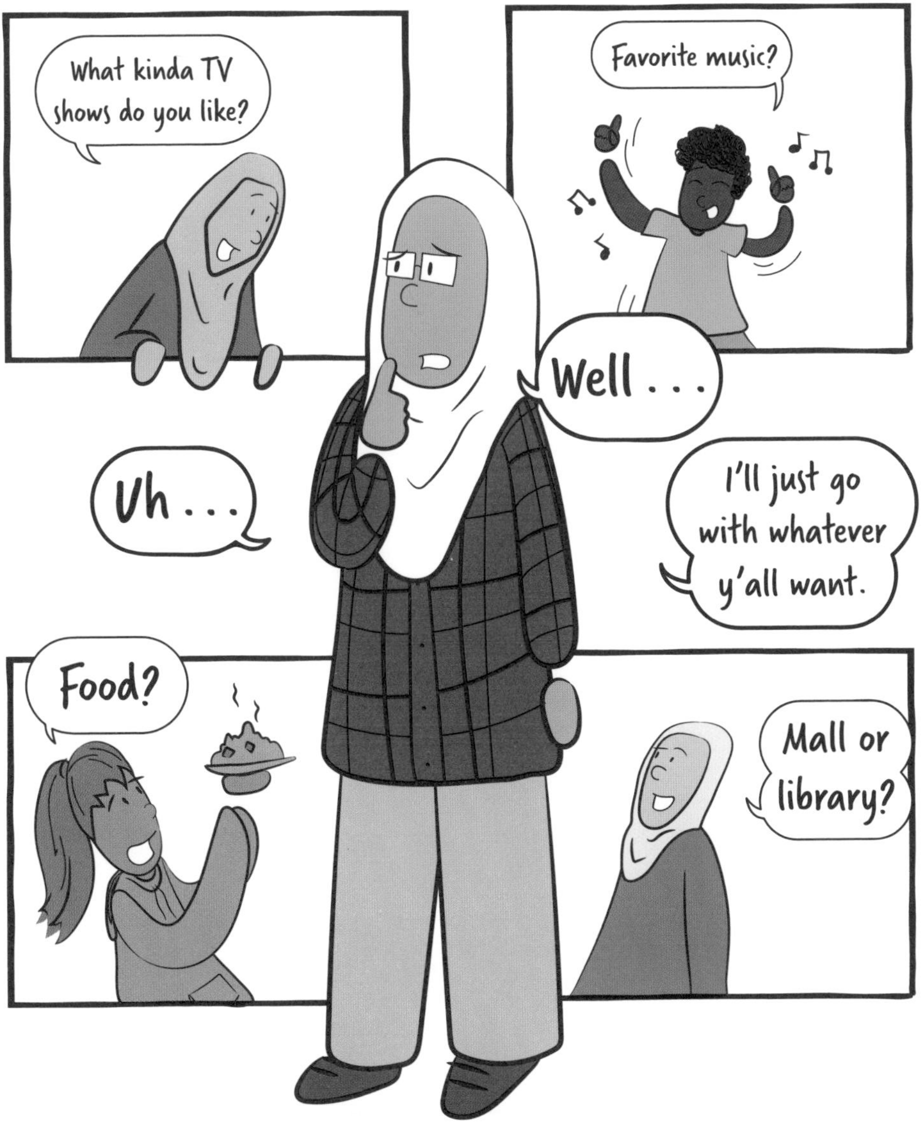

What kinda TV shows do you like?
Favorite music?
Well . . .
Uh . . .
I'll just go with whatever y'all want.
Food?
Mall or library?

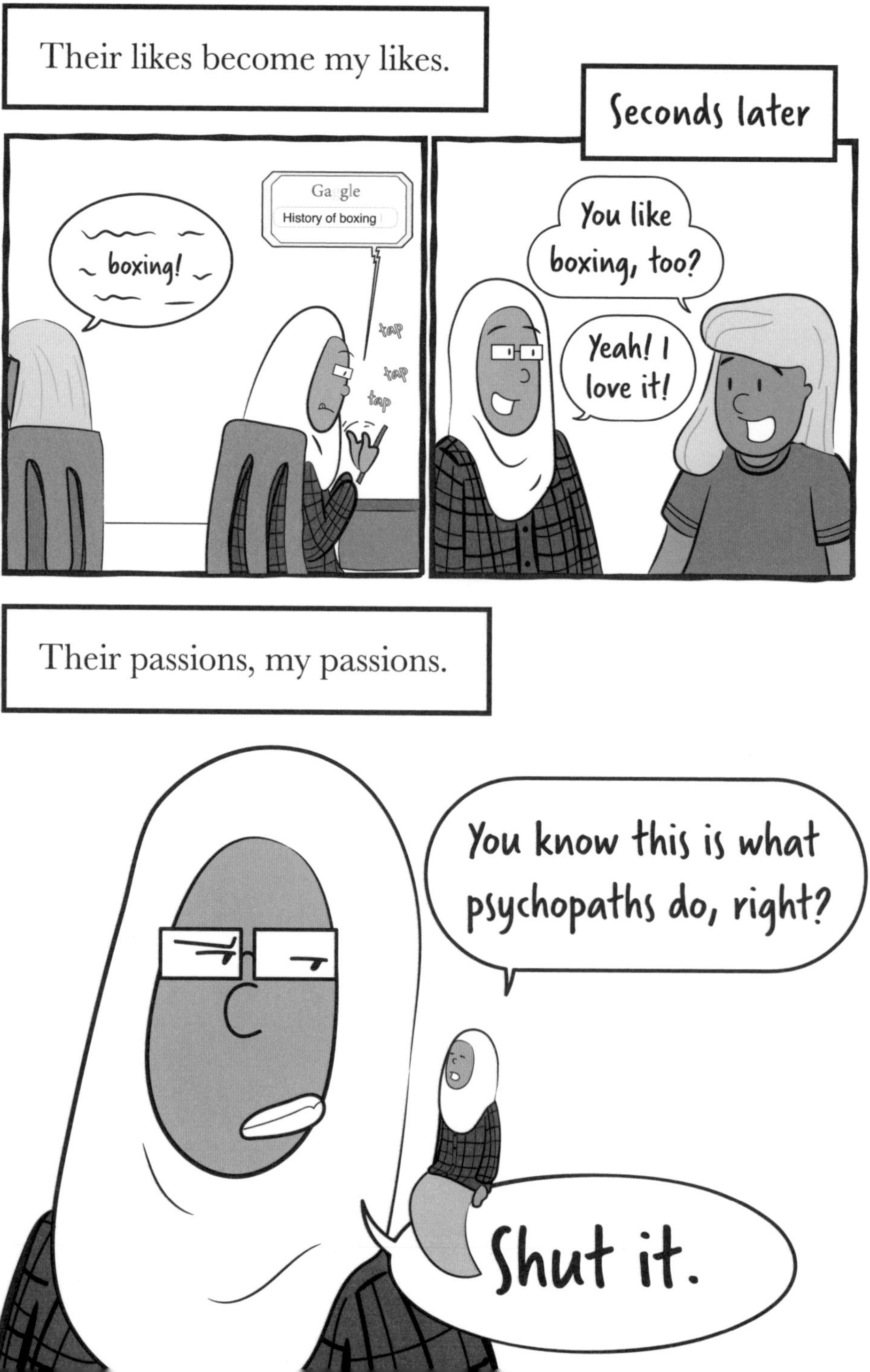
Their likes become my likes.
boxing!
History of boxing
tap
tap
tap
Seconds later
You like boxing, too?
Yeah! I love it!
Their passions, my passions.
You know this is what psychopaths do, right?
Shut it.

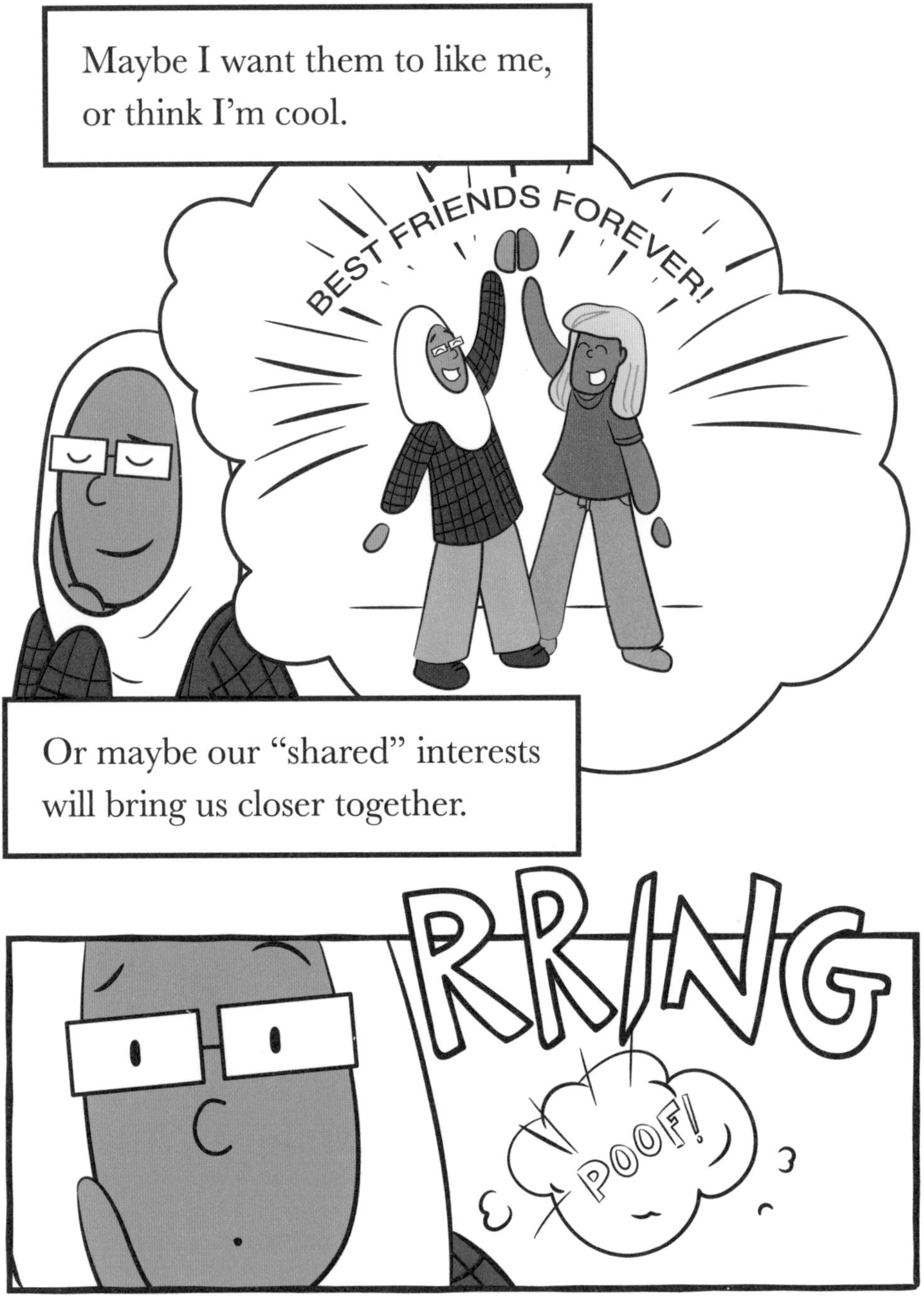
Maybe I want them to like me, or think I'm cool.
BEST FRIENDS FOREVER!
Or maybe our "shared" interests will bring us closer together.
RRING
POOF!

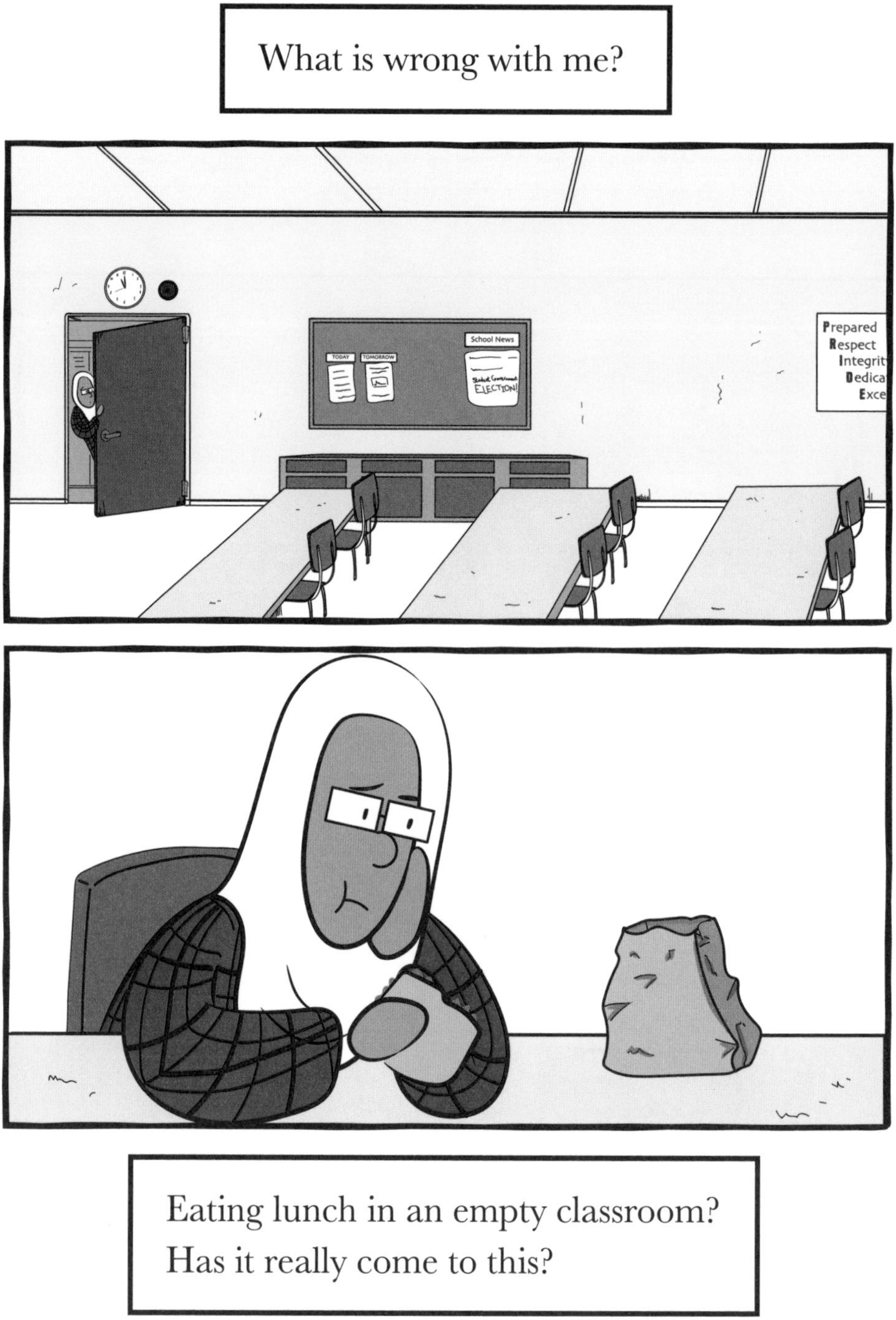
What is wrong with me?
School News
TODAY
TOMORROW
ELECTION!
Prepared
Respect
Eating lunch in an empty classroom?
Has it really come to this?

The only thing I seem to be good at is doing homework and taking tests.

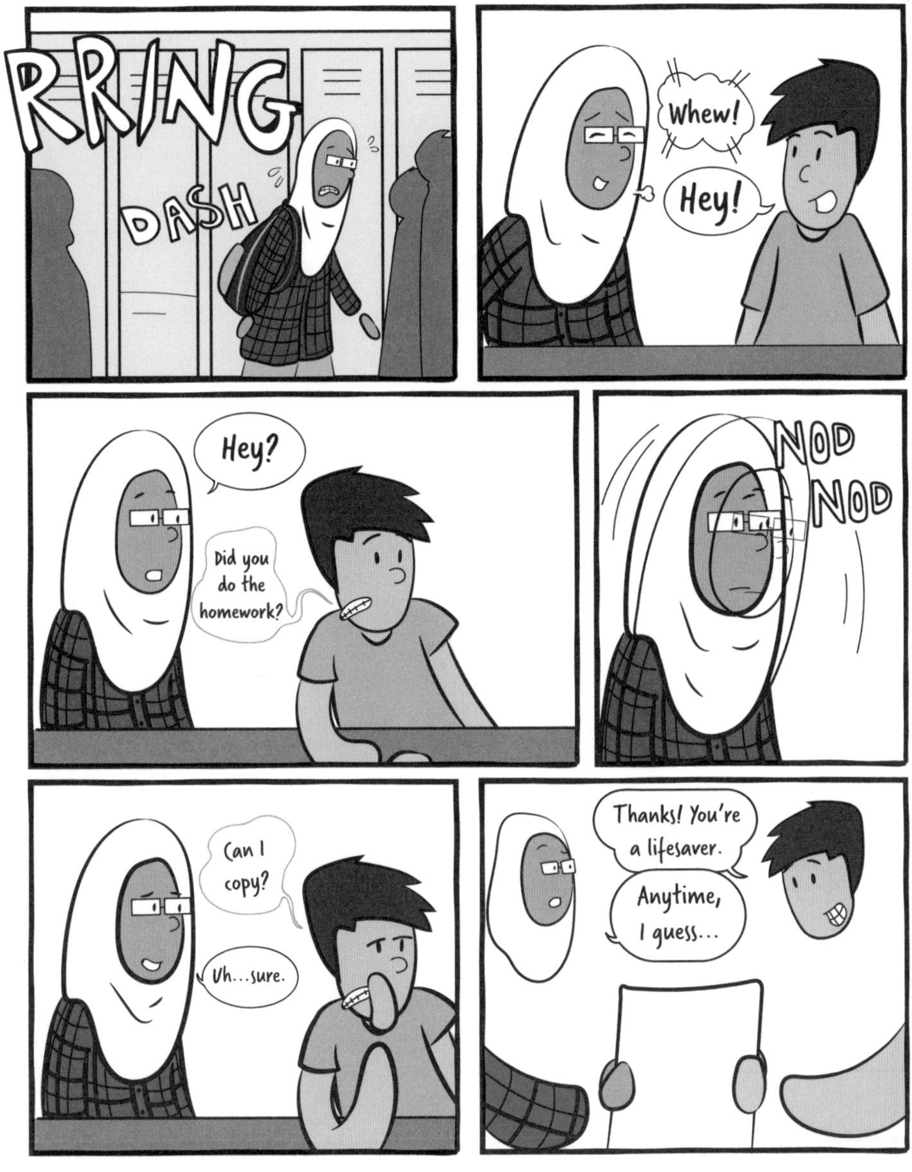
RRING
DASH
Whew!
Hey!
Hey?
Did you do the homework?
NOD NOD
Can I copy?
Uh...sure.
Thanks! You're a lifesaver.
Anytime, I guess...

And I can't base a whole personality on being smart.

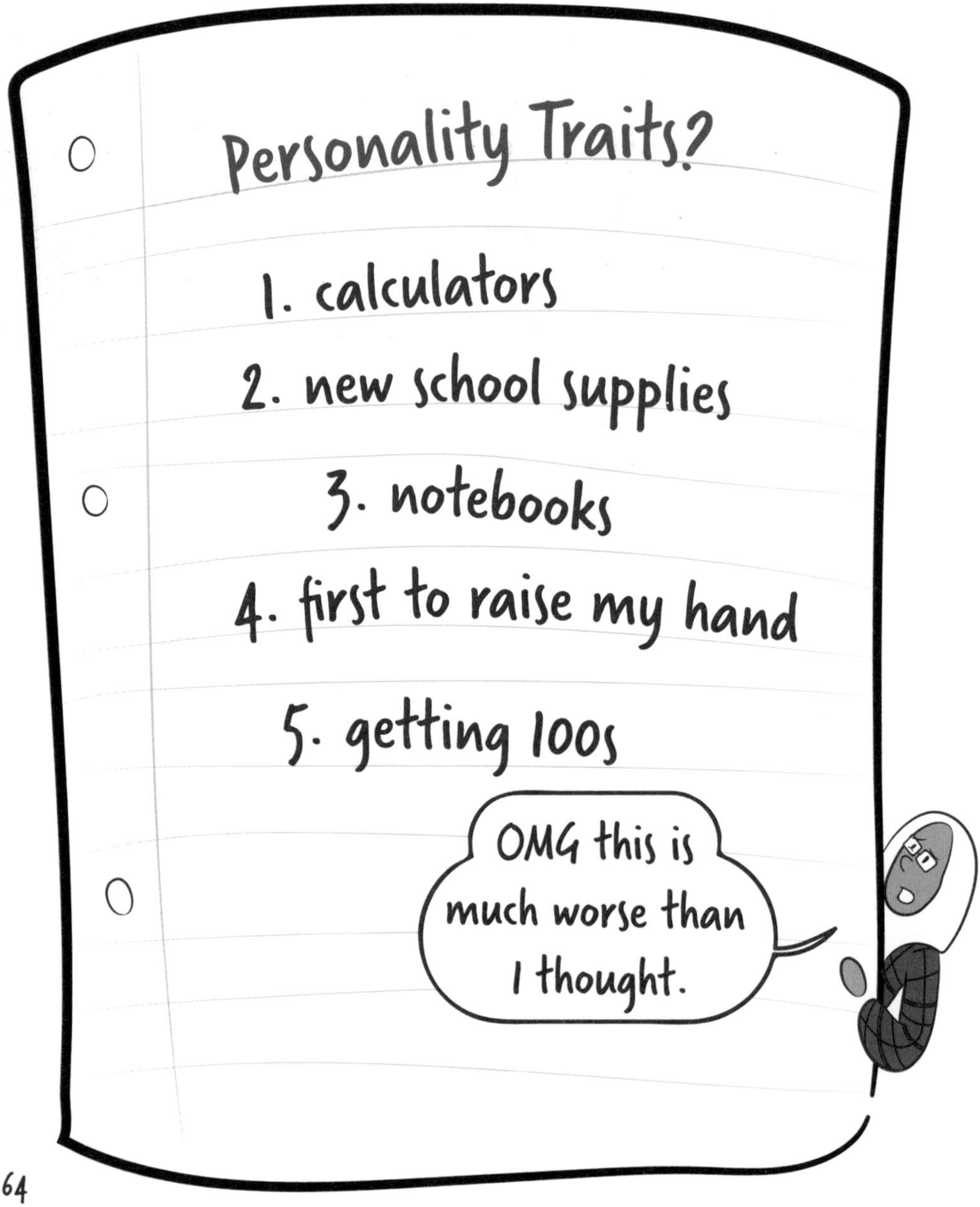
Personality Traits?
1. calculators
2. new school supplies
3. notebooks
4. first to raise my hand
5. getting 100s
OMG this is much worse than I thought.

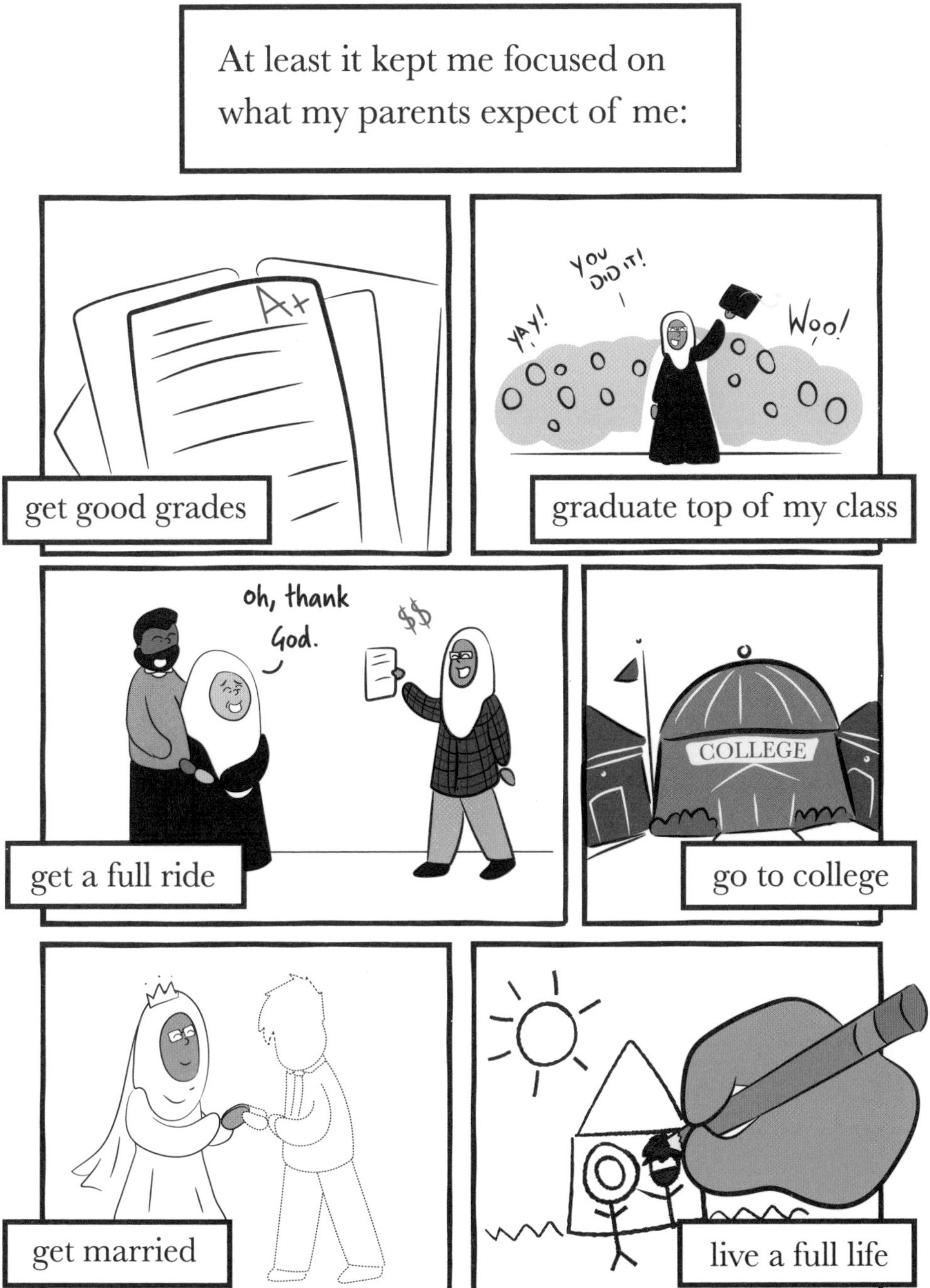
At least it kept me focused on what my parents expect of me:
A+
get good grades
YOU DID IT!
YAY!
WOO!
graduate top of my class
oh, thank God.
$$
get a full ride
COLLEGE
go to college
get married
live a full life

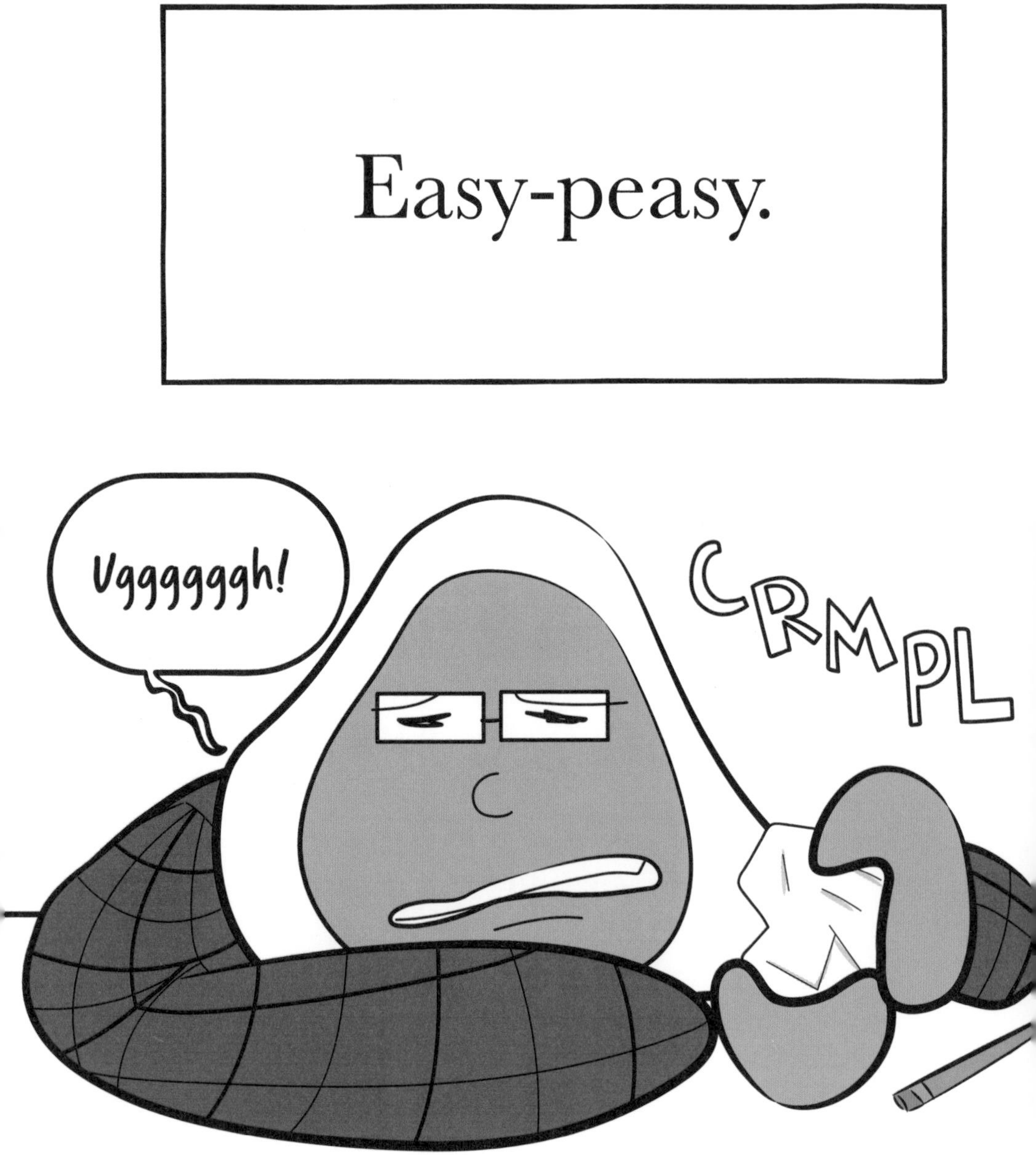
Easy-peasy.
Ugggggggh!
CRMPL

Except of course it's never easy-peasy.

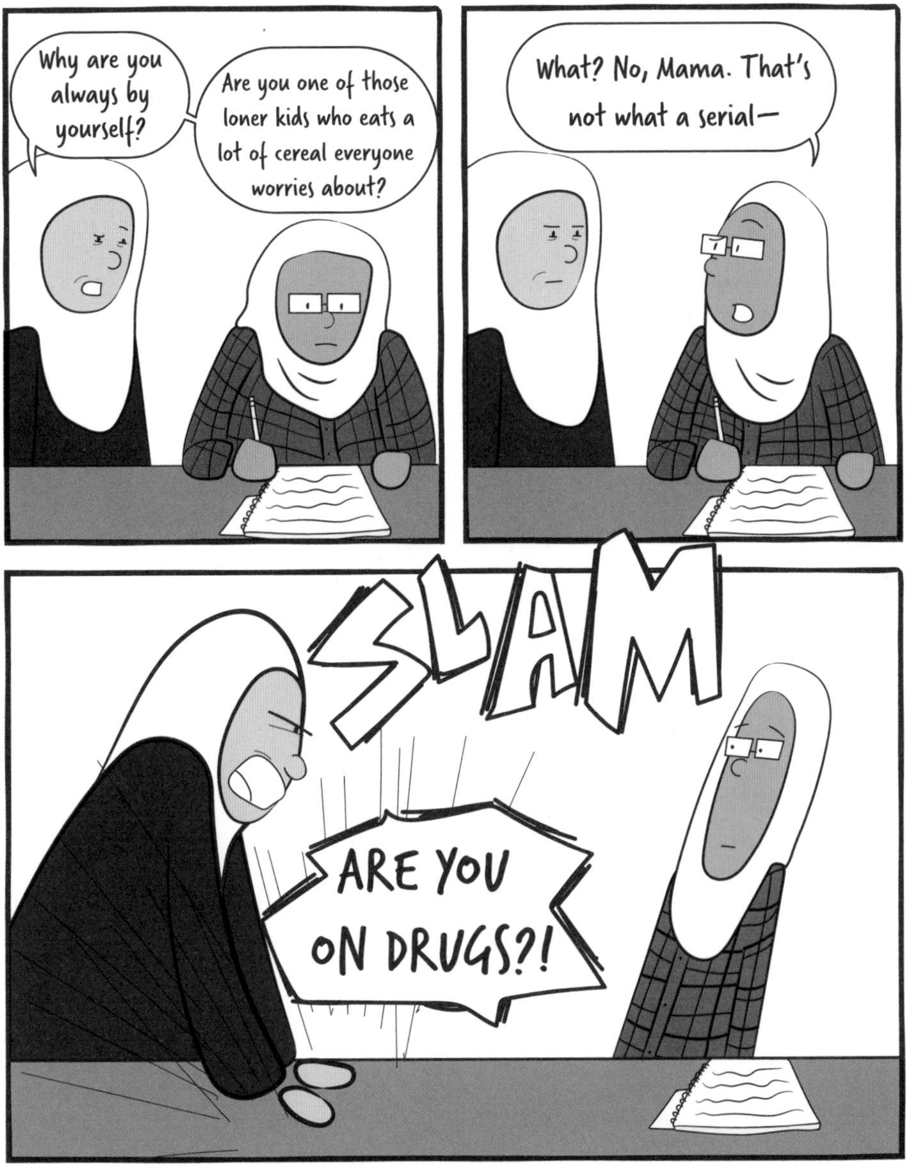
Why are you always by yourself?
Are you one of those loner kids who eats a lot of cereal everyone worries about?
What? No, Mama. That's not what a serial—
SLAM
ARE YOU ON DRUGS?!

So yes, I feel like a fraud, and yes, I'm terrified of spending too much time with anyone lest they figure out.

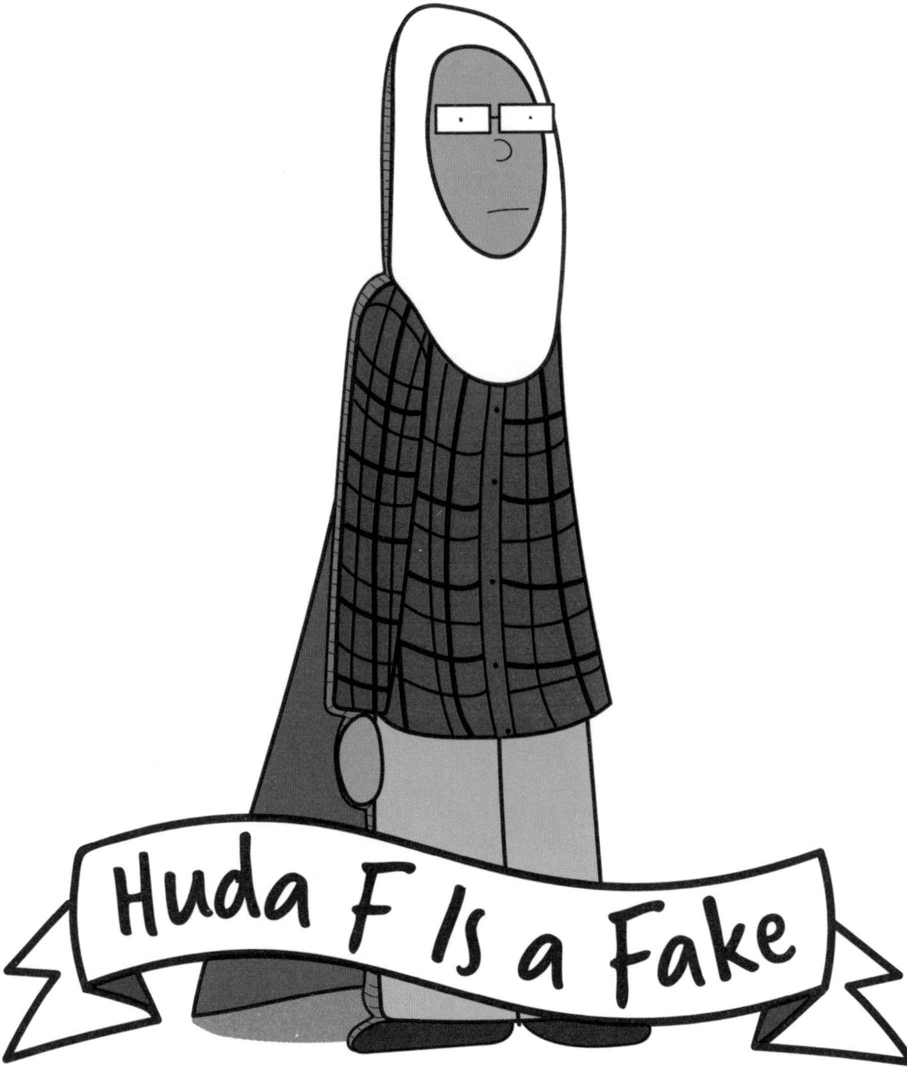
Huda F Is a Fake

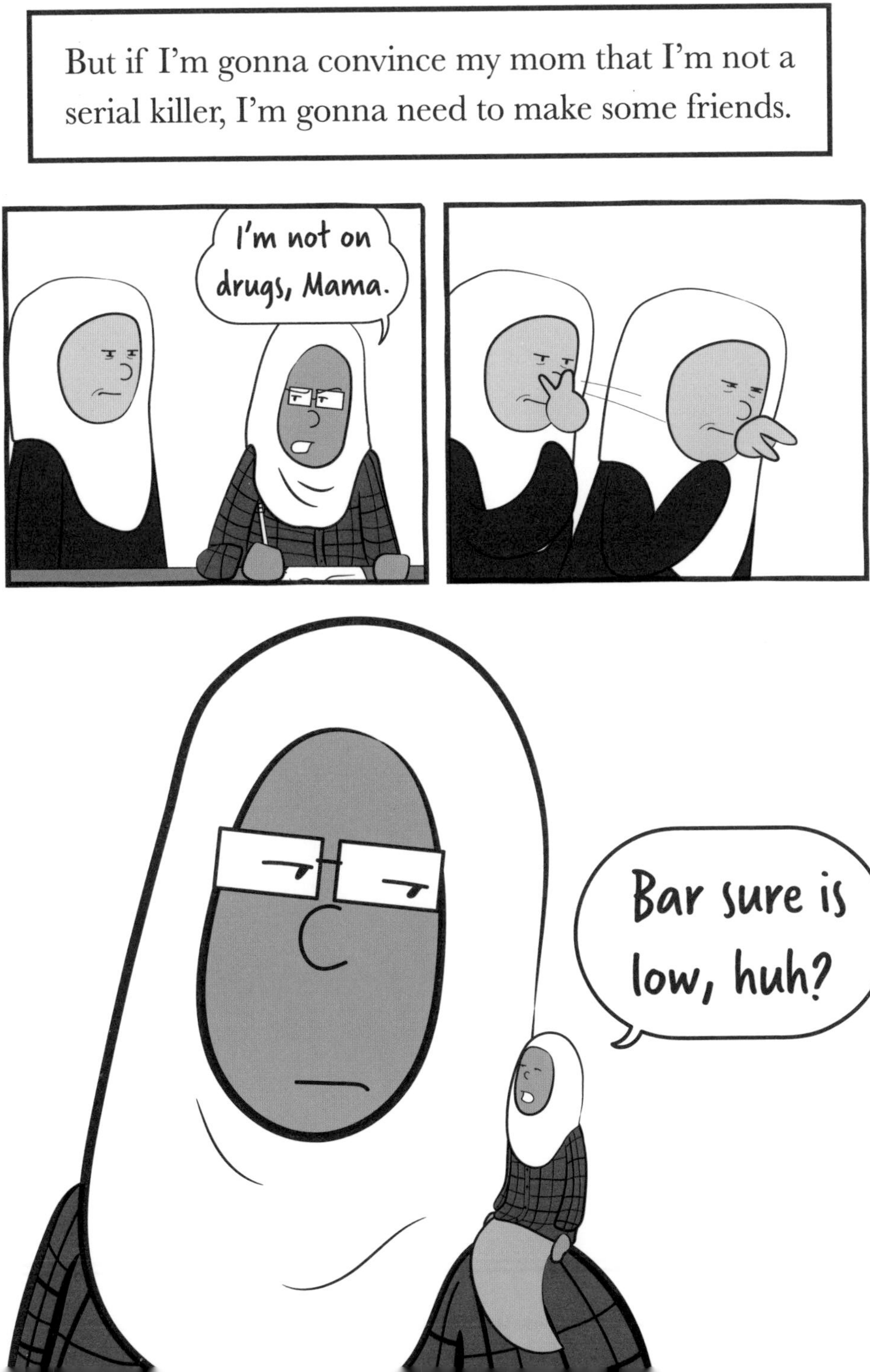
But if I'm gonna convince my mom that I'm not a serial killer, I'm gonna need to make some friends.
I'm not on drugs, Mama.
Bar sure is low, huh?

And I think I can forget about being an athlete.

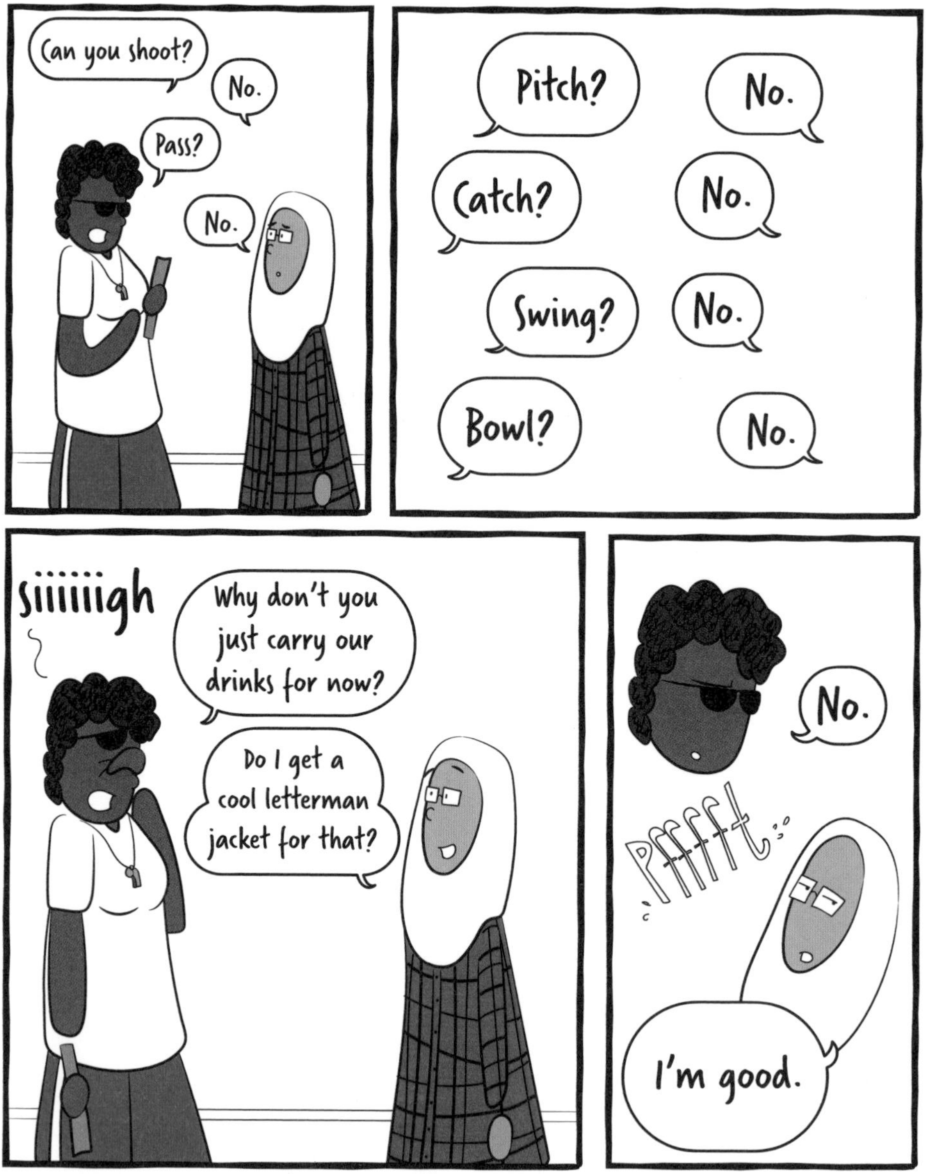

Can you shoot?
No.
Pass?
No.
Pitch?
No.
Catch?
No.
Swing?
No.
Bowl?
No.
siiiiiigh
Why don't you just carry our drinks for now?
Do I get a cool letterman jacket for that?
No.
Pfffft
I'm good.

That's okay. I'll just try my hand at being a hijabi gamer.

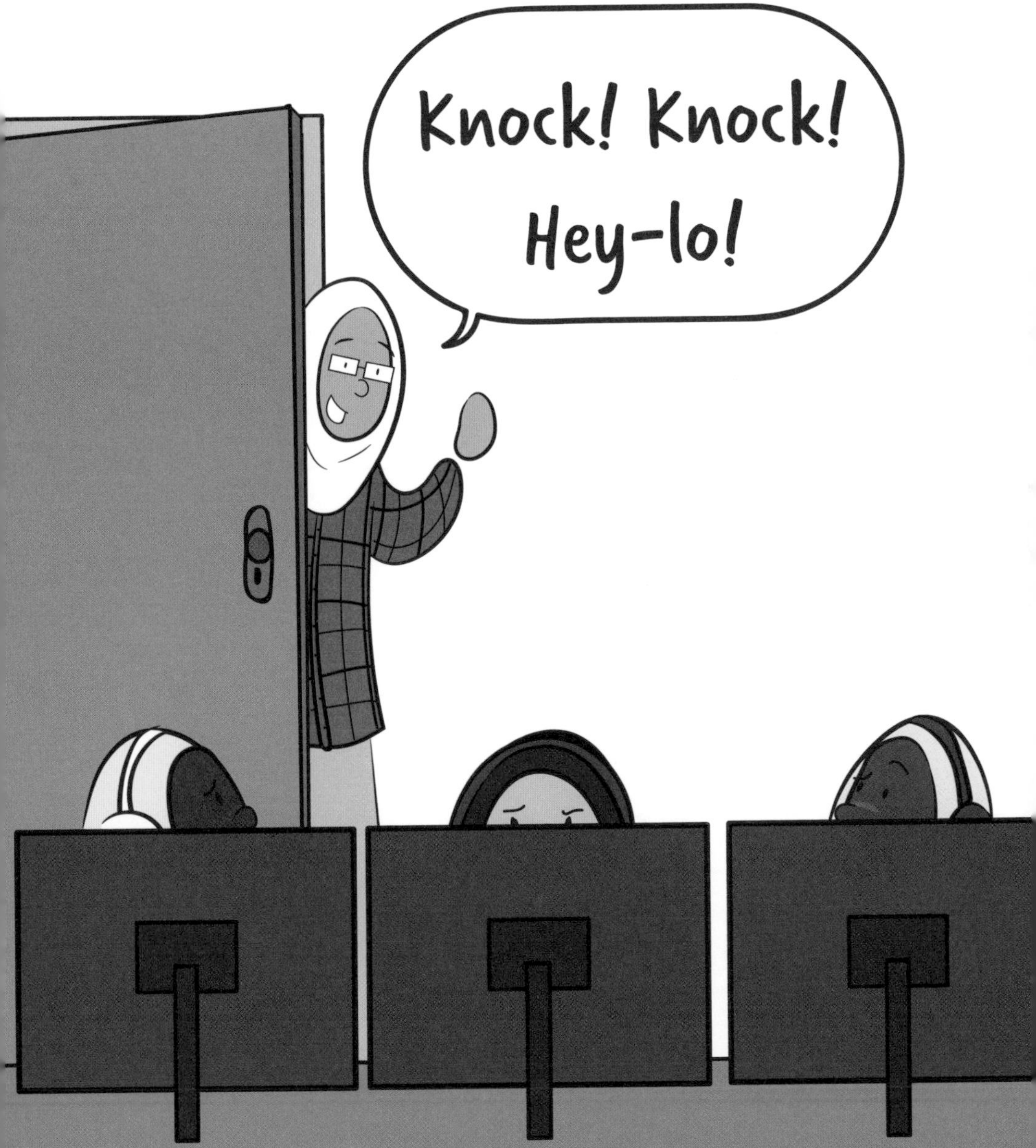

Knock! Knock! Hey-lo!

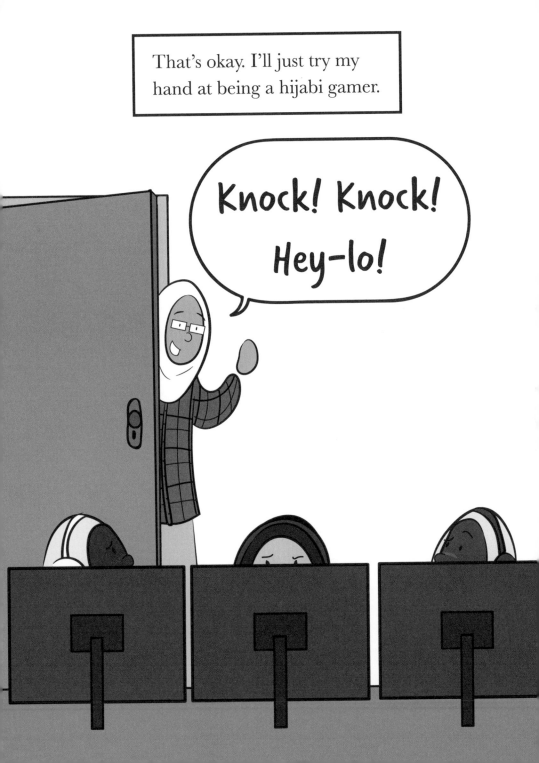

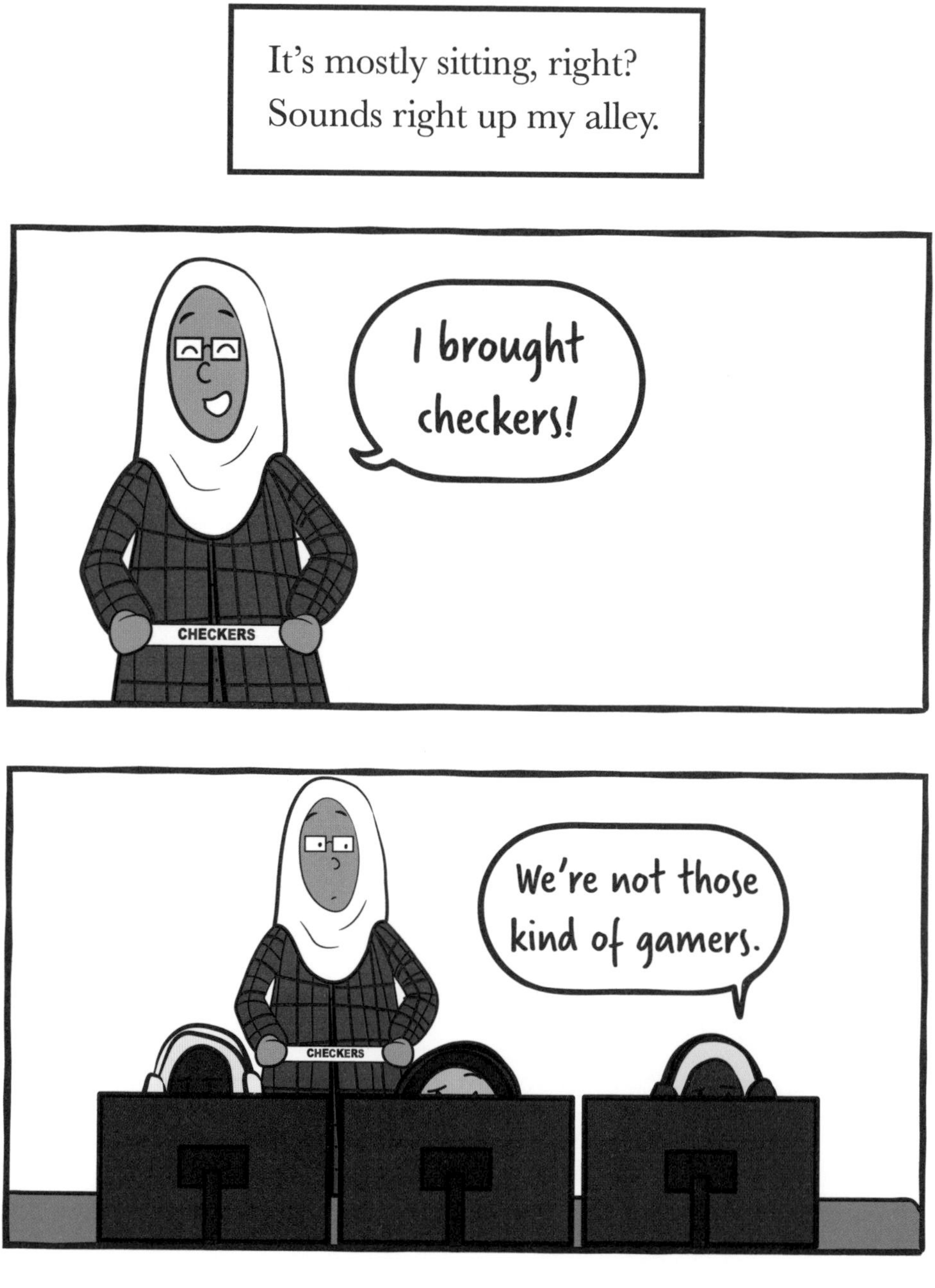
It's mostly sitting, right?
Sounds right up my alley.
I brought checkers!
CHECKERS
We're not those kind of gamers.
CHECKERS

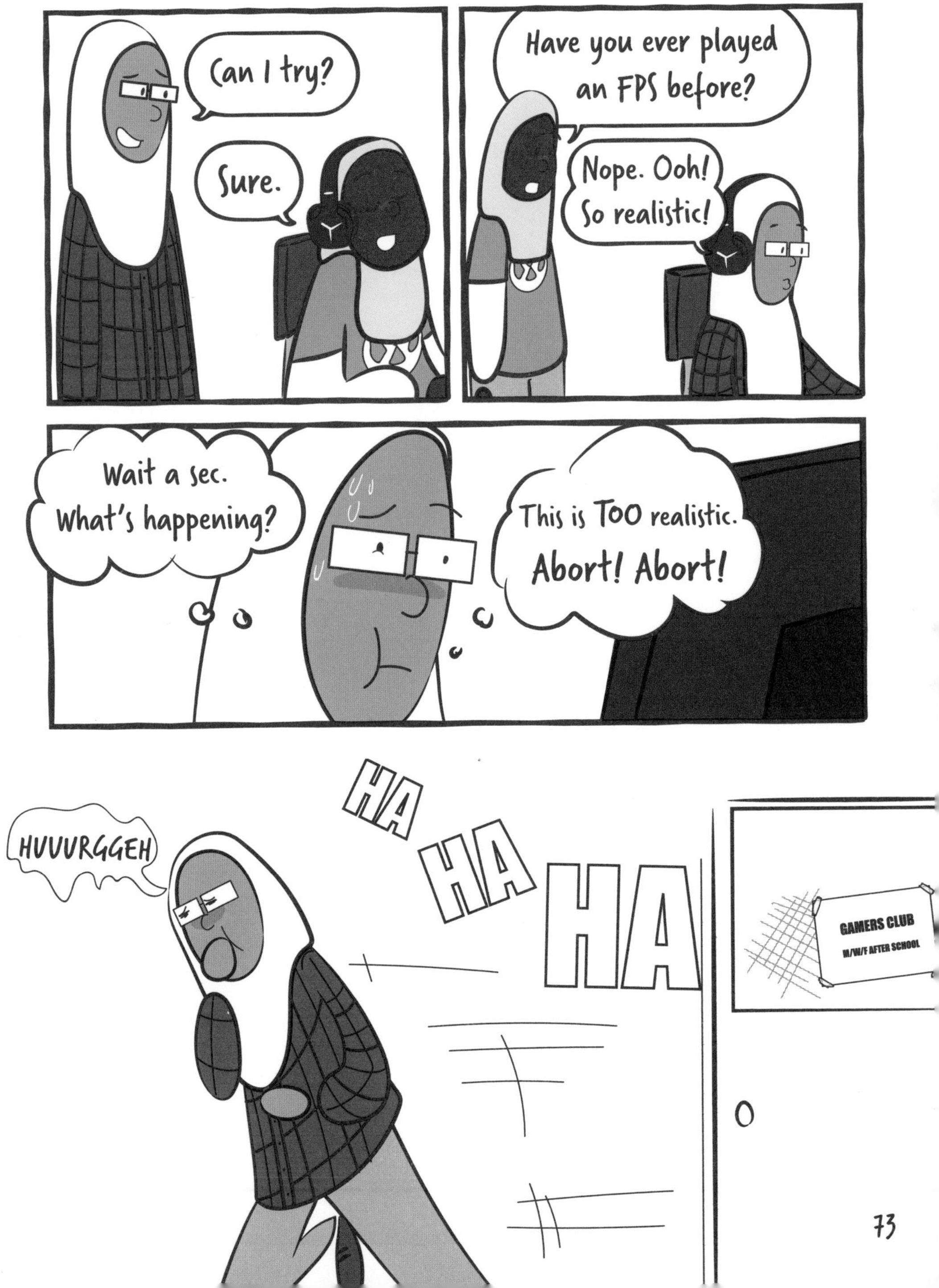
Can I try?
Sure.
Have you ever played an FPS before?
Nope. Ooh! So realistic!
Wait a sec. What's happening?
This is TOO realistic. Abort! Abort!
HUUURGGEH
HA
HA
HA
GAMERS CLUB
M/W/F AFTER SCHOOL

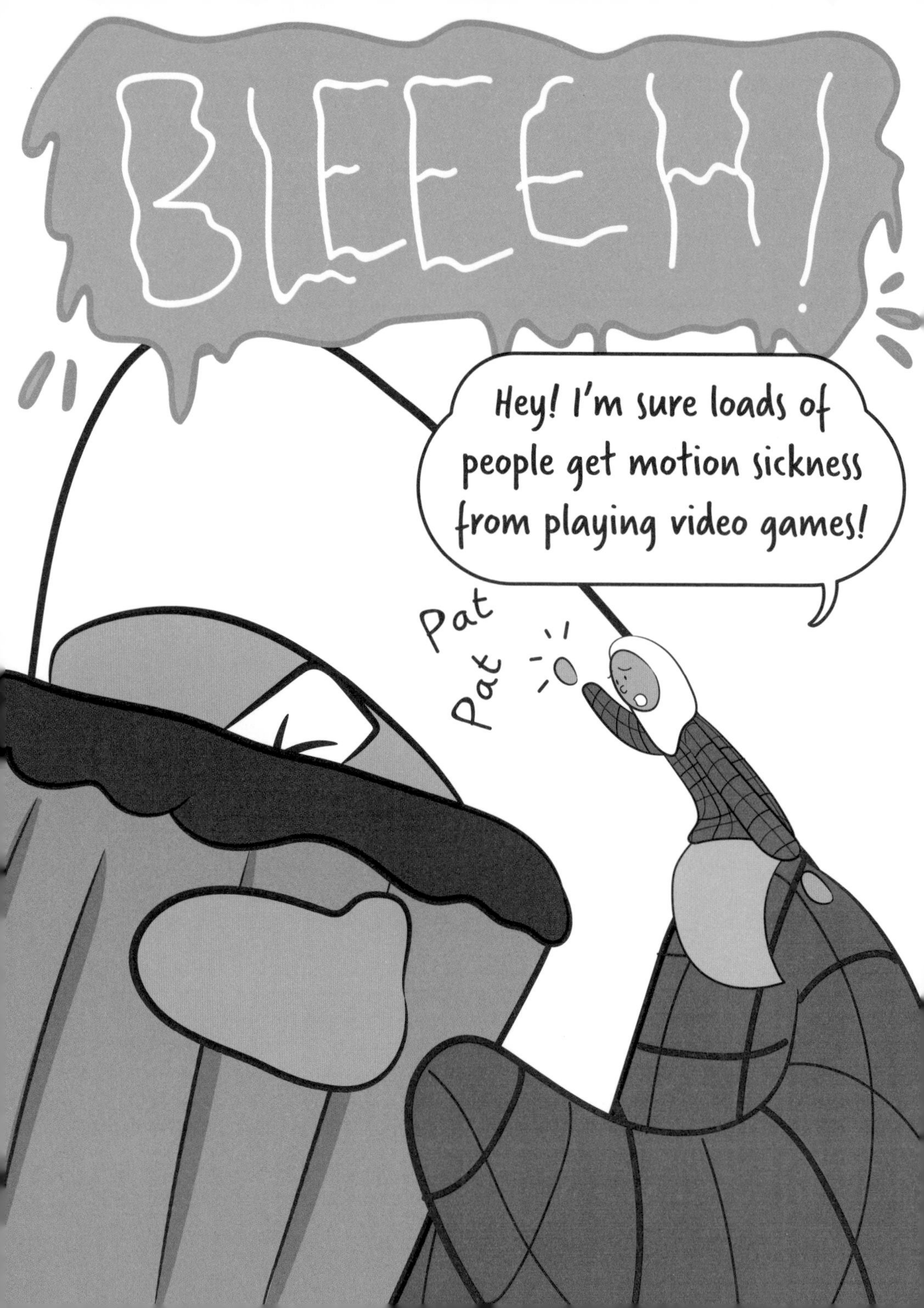
BLEEEH!
Hey! I'm sure loads of people get motion sickness from playing video games!
Pat Pat

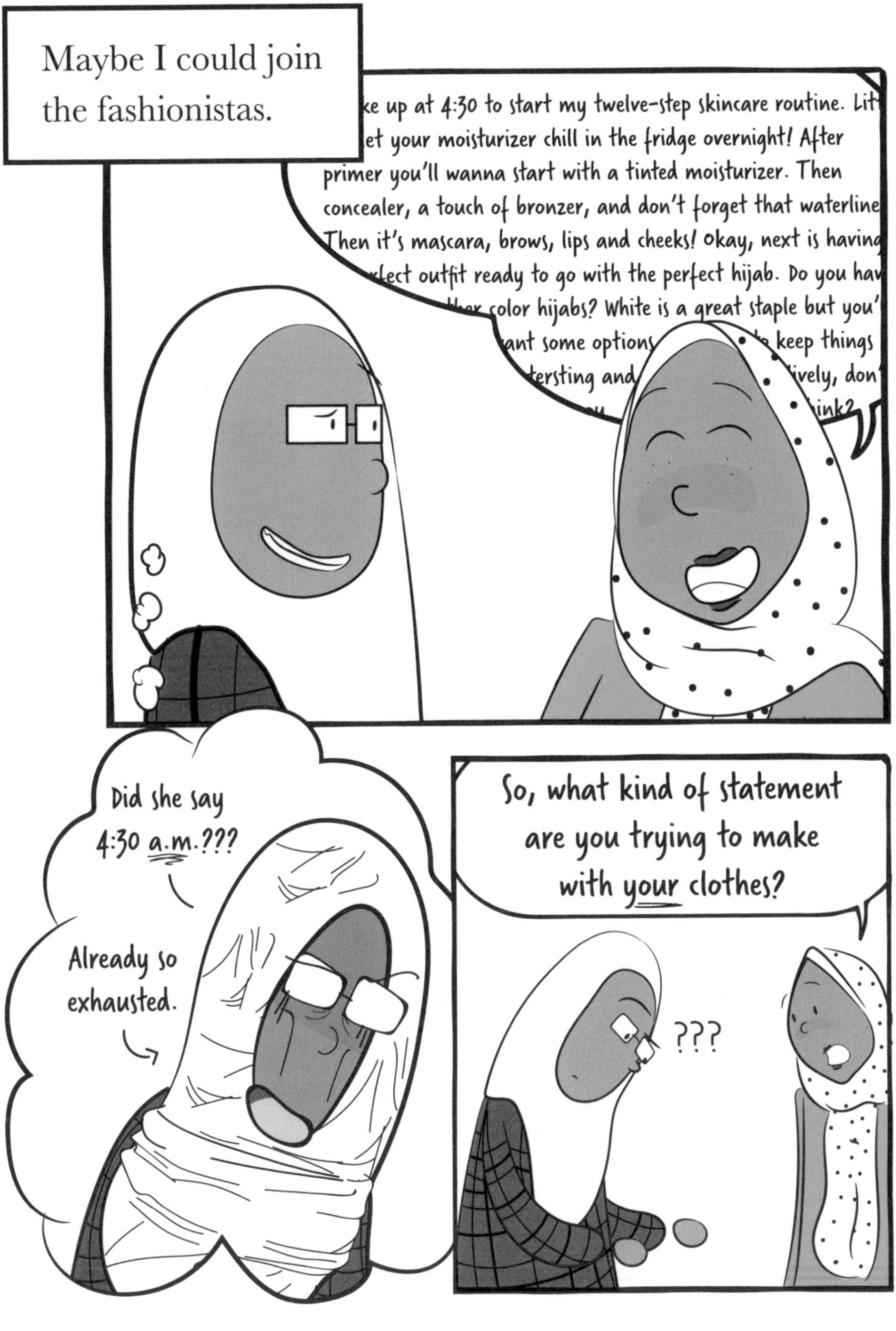
Maybe I could join the fashionistas.
ke up at 4:30 to start my twelve-step skincare routine.
et your moisturizer chill in the fridge overnight! After primer you'll wanna start with a tinted moisturizer. Then concealer, a touch of bronzer, and don't forget that waterline
Then it's mascara, brows, lips and cheeks! Okay, next is having
ect outfit ready to go with the perfect hijab. Do you hav
color hijabs? White is a great staple but you'
ant some options
keep things
tersting and
ively, don'
Did she say 4:30 a.m.???
Already so exhausted.
So, what kind of statement are you trying to make with your clothes?
???

Statement? I own precisely five of the same color plaid shirt, one for each day of the week. They are comfy and convenient: my only two criteria for an outfit.

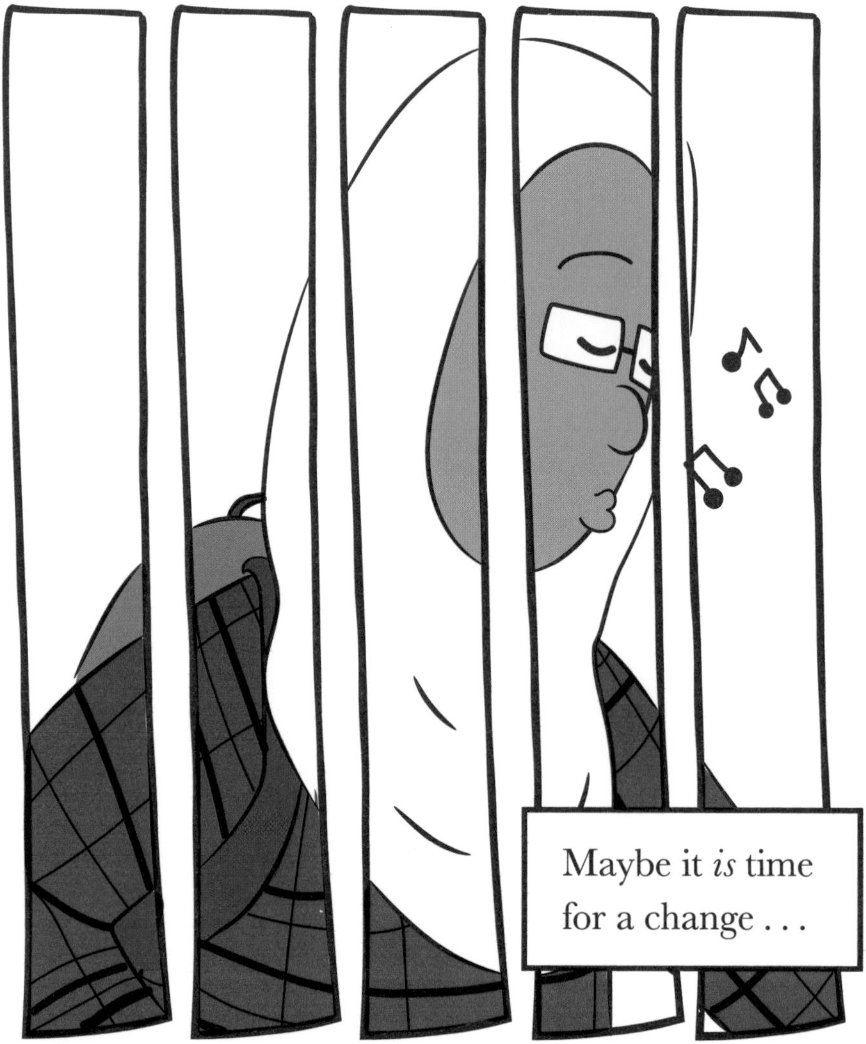
Maybe it *is* time for a change . . .

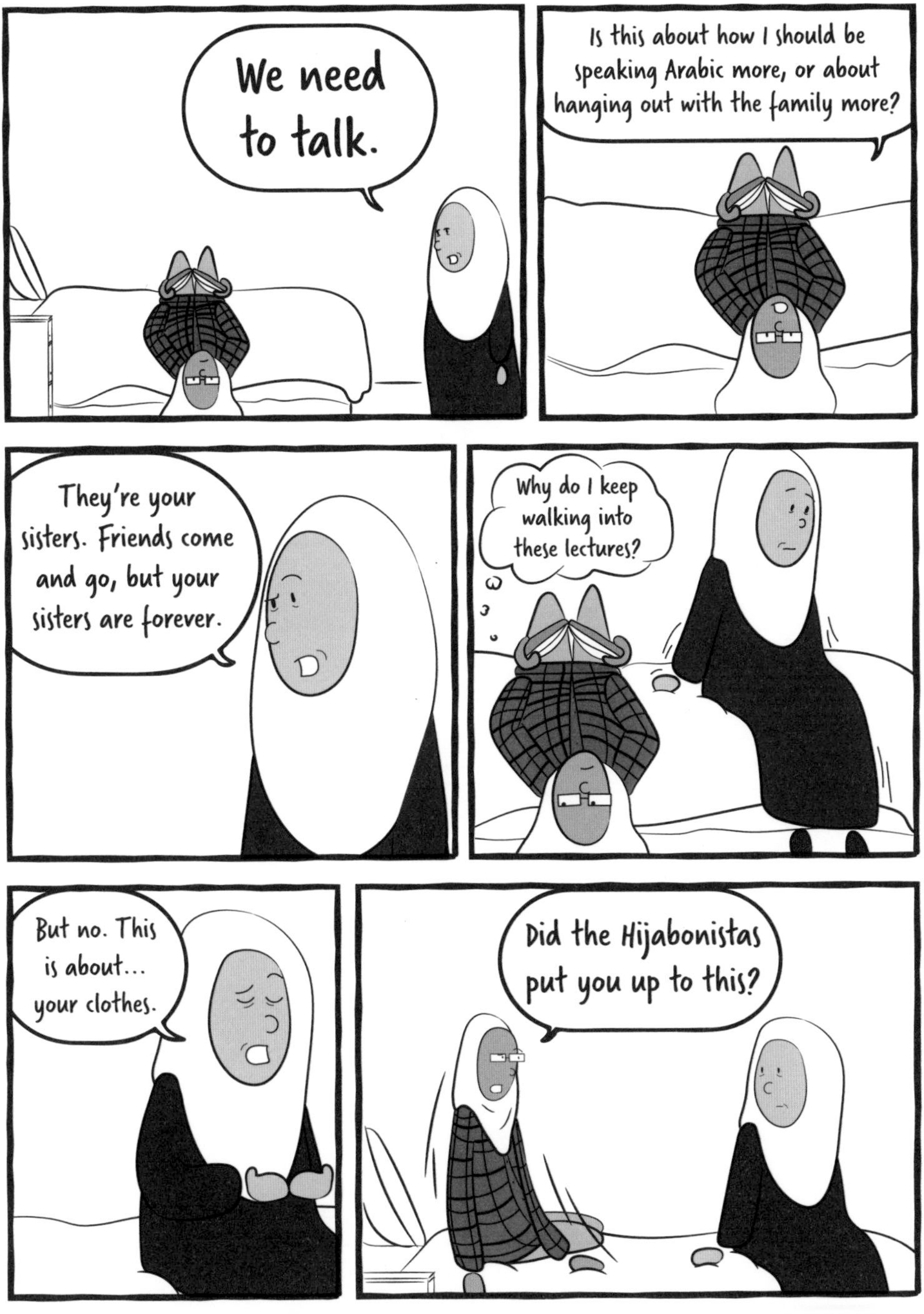
We need to talk.
Is this about how I should be speaking Arabic more, or about hanging out with the family more?
They're your sisters. Friends come and go, but your sisters are forever.
Why do I keep walking into these lectures?
But no. This is about... your clothes.
Did the Hijabonistas put you up to this?

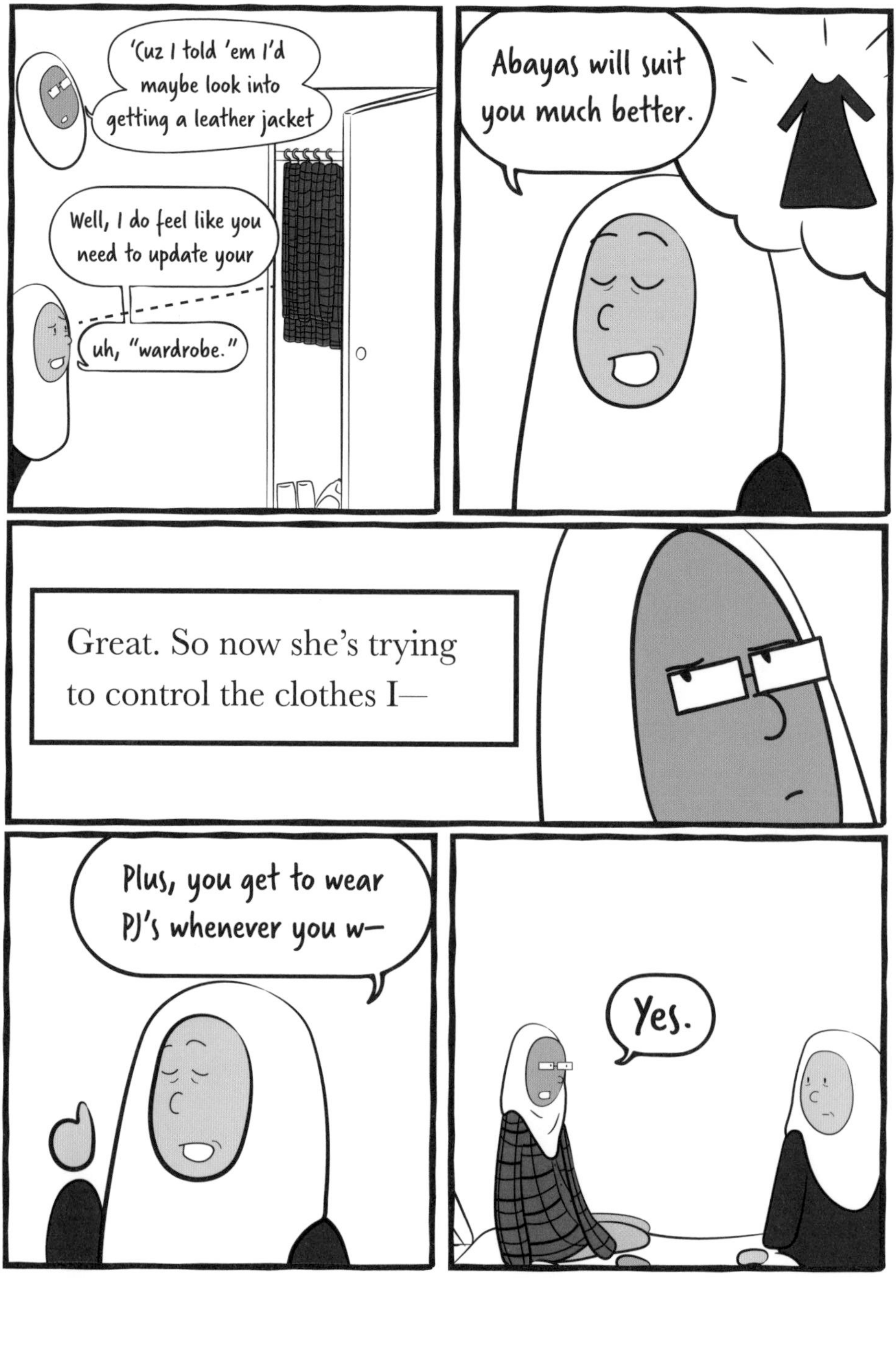
'Cuz I told 'em I'd maybe look into getting a leather jacket
Well, I do feel like you need to update your
uh, "wardrobe."
Abayas will suit you much better.
Great. So now she's trying to control the clothes I—
Plus, you get to wear PJ's whenever you w–
Yes.

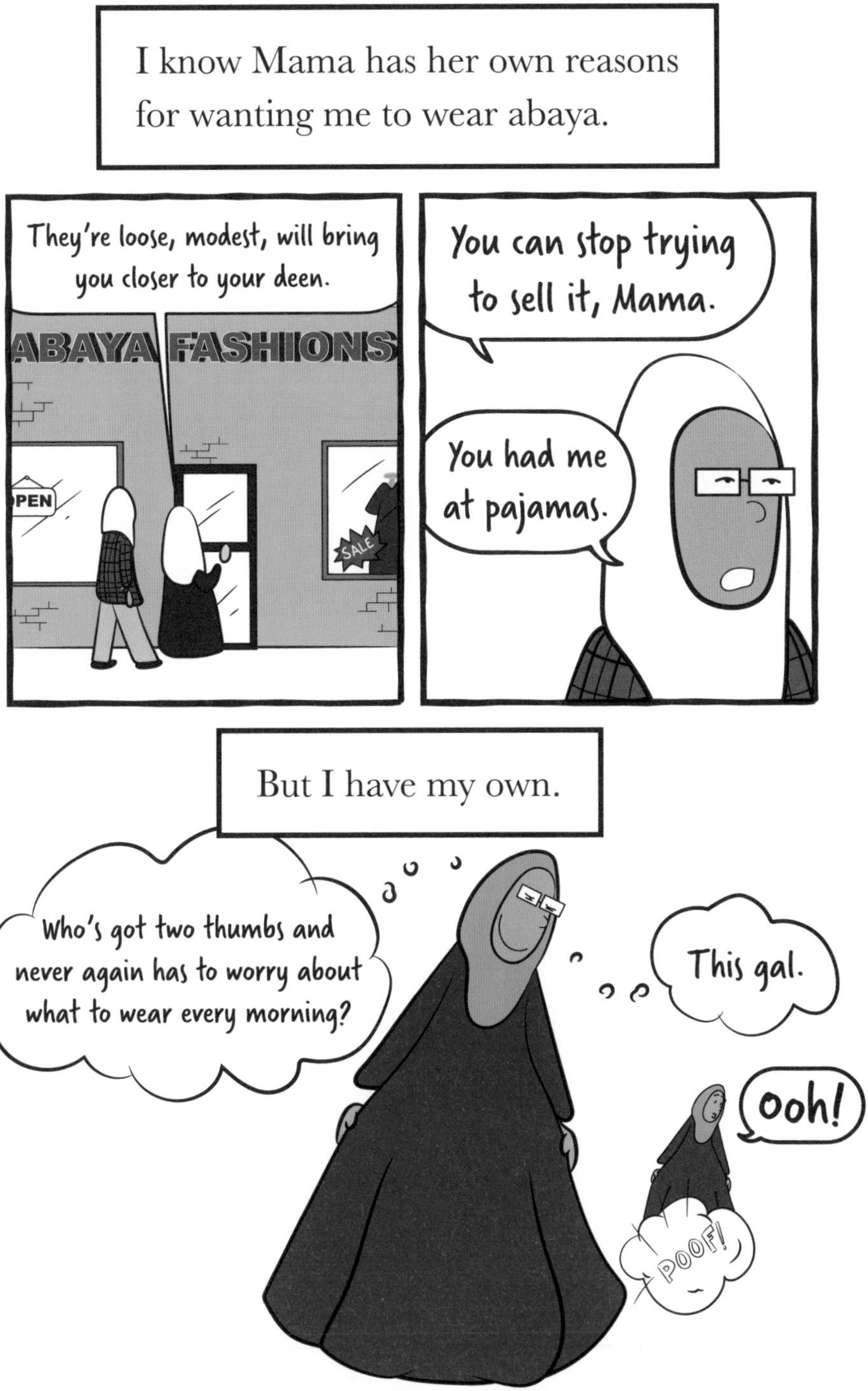
I know Mama has her own reasons for wanting me to wear abaya.
They're loose, modest, will bring you closer to your deen.
ABAYA FASHIONS
OPEN
SALE
You can stop trying to sell it, Mama.
You had me at pajamas.
But I have my own.
Who's got two thumbs and never again has to worry about what to wear every morning?
This gal.
Ooh!
POOF!

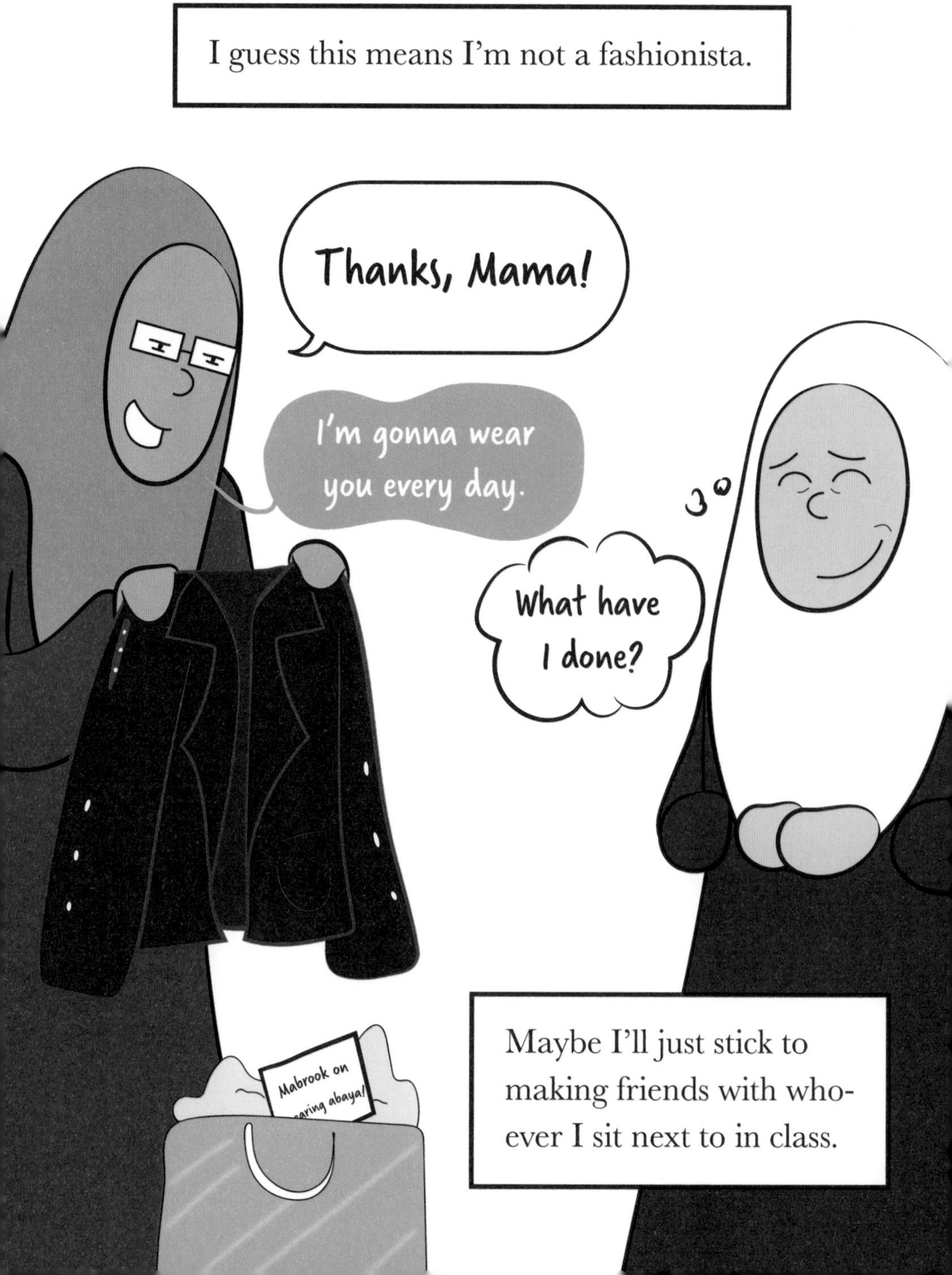
I guess this means I'm not a fashionista.
Thanks, Mama!
I'm gonna wear you every day.
What have I done?
Mabrook on
Maybe I'll just stick to making friends with who-ever I sit next to in class.

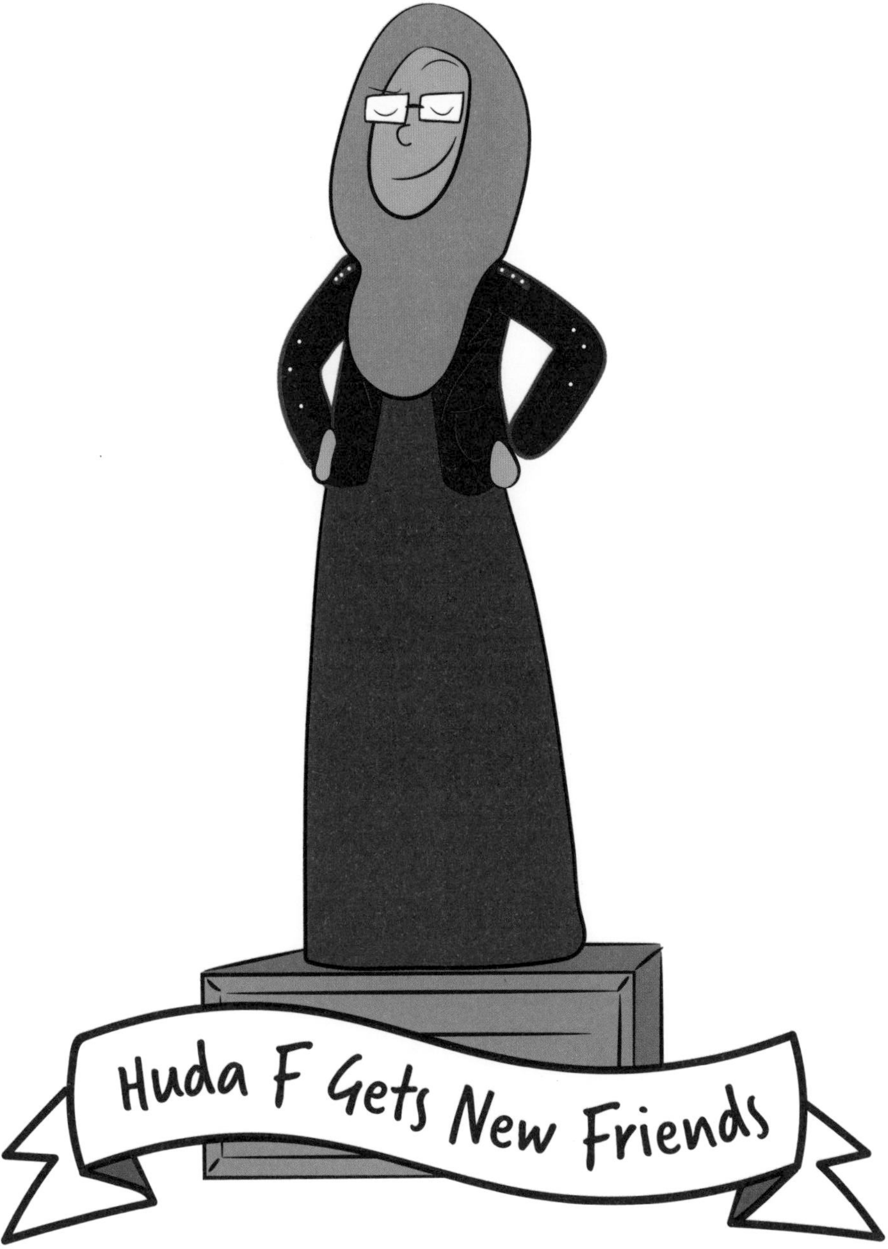
Huda F Gets New Friends

Hailey's pretty nice. She supplies me with a steady flow of romance novels from her vast personal cache, and she's got tons of scandalous —albeit hard to believe—stories of her own.

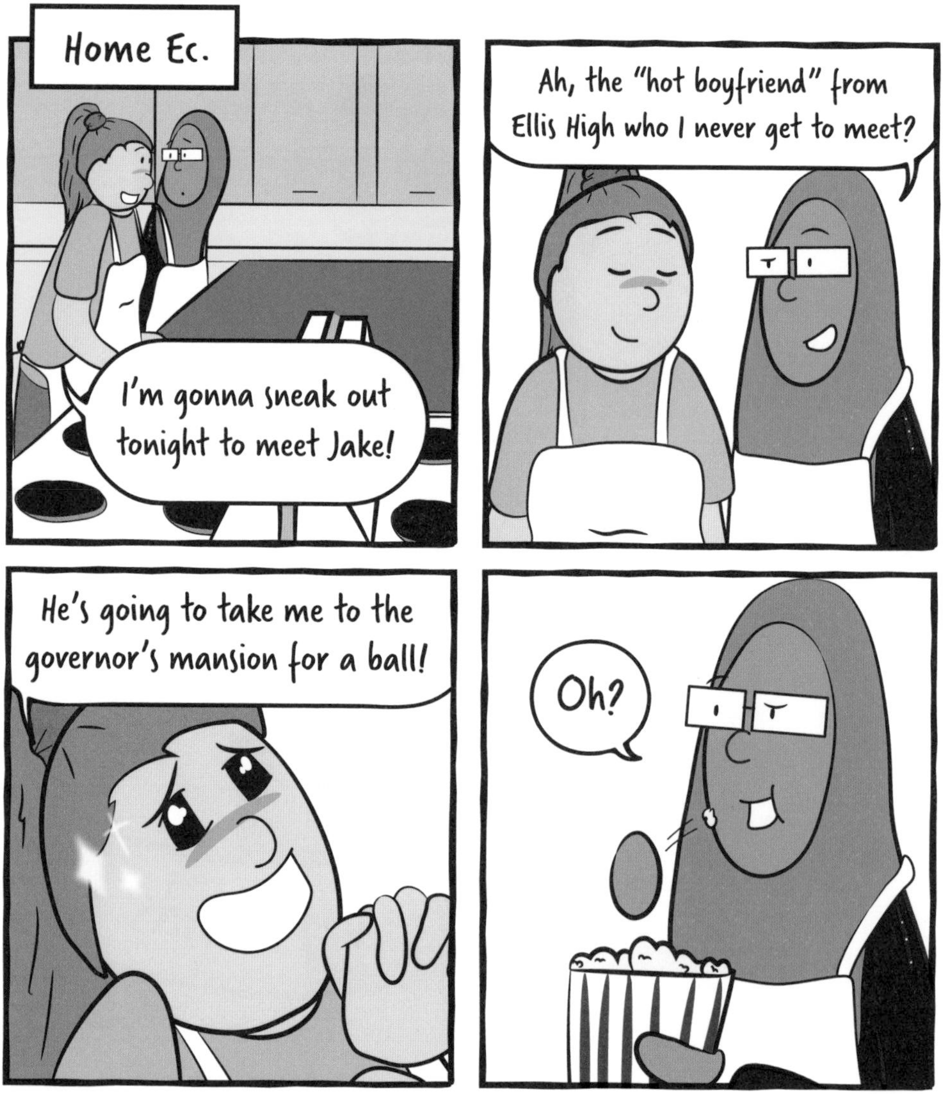

Home Ec.
I'm gonna sneak out tonight to meet Jake!
Ah, the "hot boyfriend" from Ellis High who I never get to meet?
He's going to take me to the governor's mansion for a ball!
Oh?

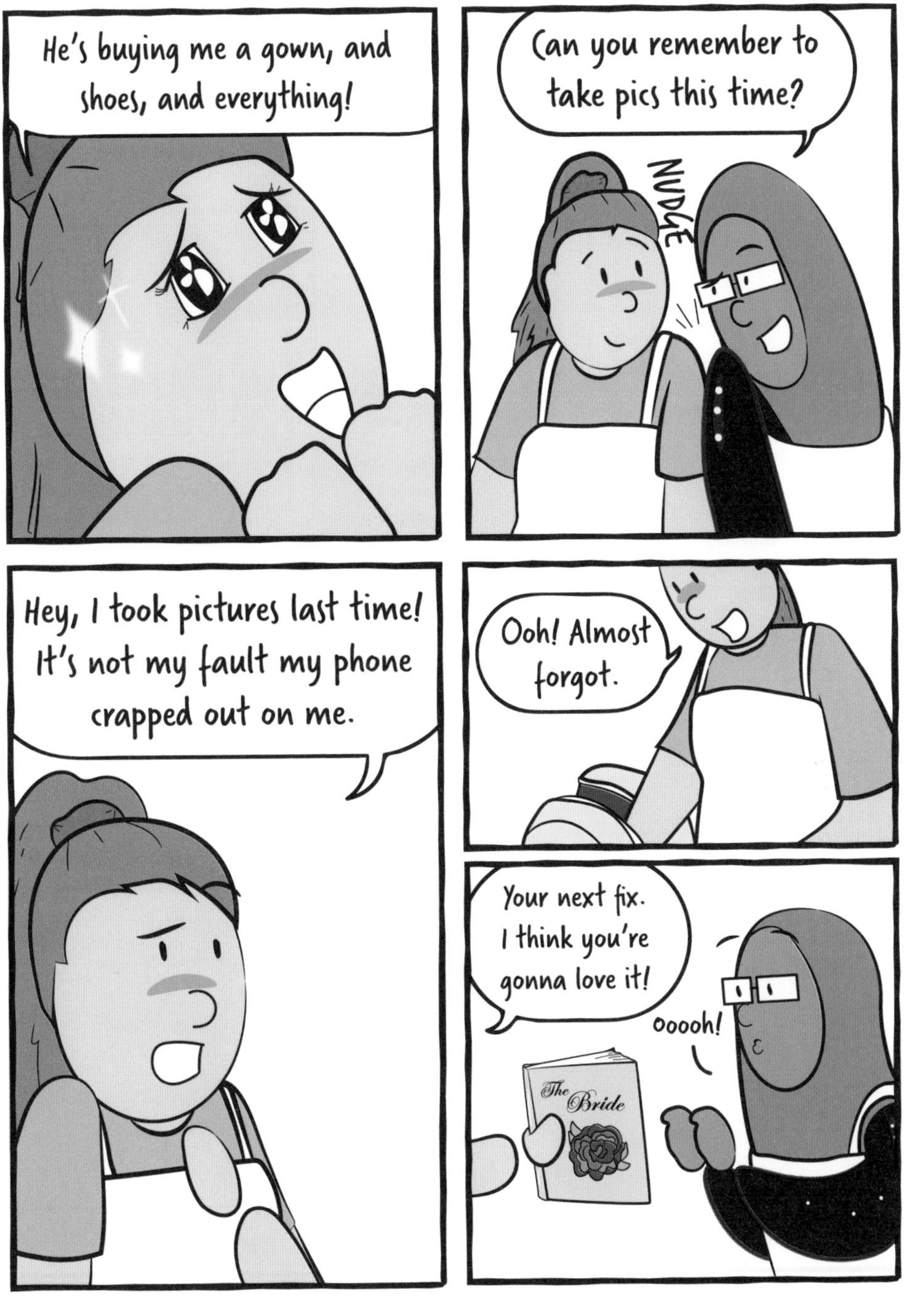
He's buying me a gown, and shoes, and everything!
Can you remember to take pics this time?
NUDGE
Hey, I took pictures last time! It's not my fault my phone crapped out on me.
Ooh! Almost forgot.
Your next fix. I think you're gonna love it!
ooooh!
The Bride

Aliya and I have pre-calc together.
She's really big on female empowerment.

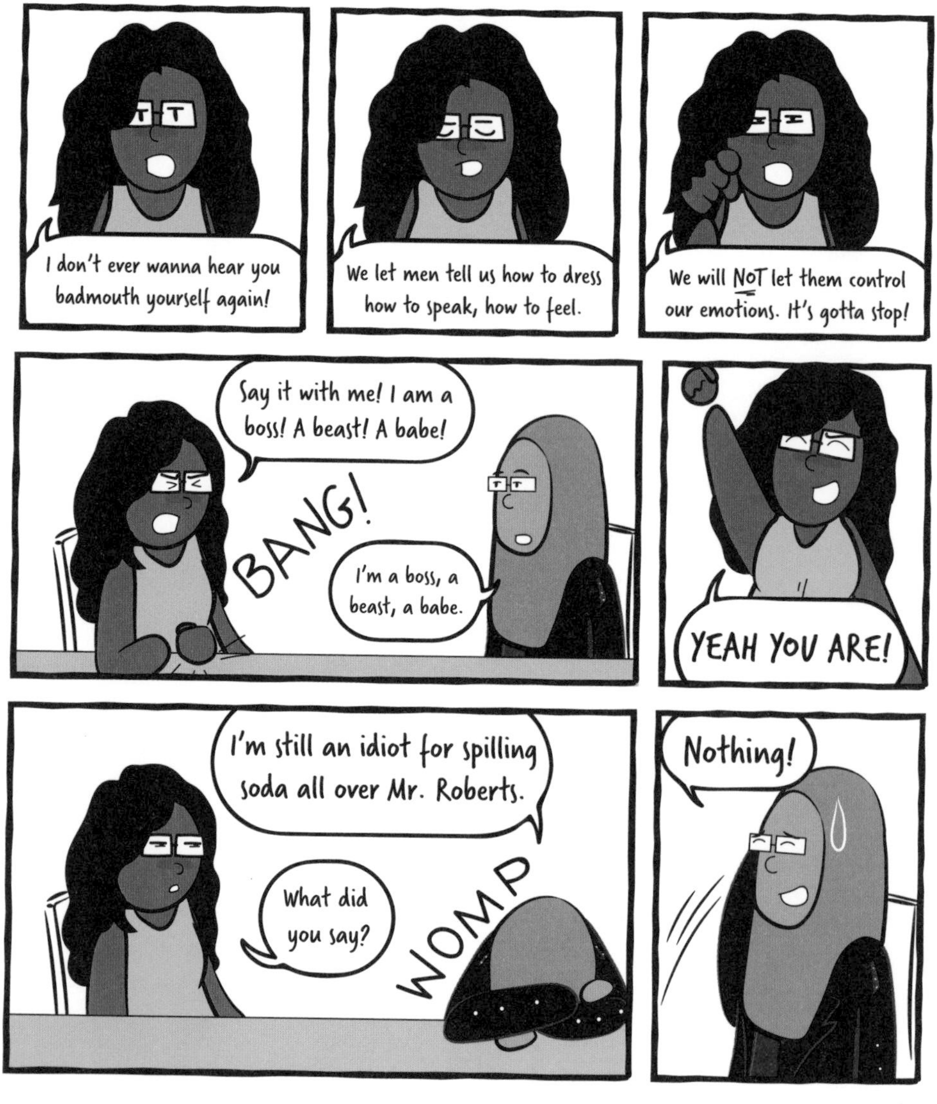
I don't ever wanna hear you badmouth yourself again!
We let men tell us how to dress how to speak, how to feel.
We will NOT let them control our emotions. It's gotta stop!
Say it with me! I am a boss! A beast! A babe!
BANG!
I'm a boss, a beast, a babe.
YEAH YOU ARE!
I'm still an idiot for spilling soda all over Mr. Roberts.
What did you say?
WOMP
Nothing!

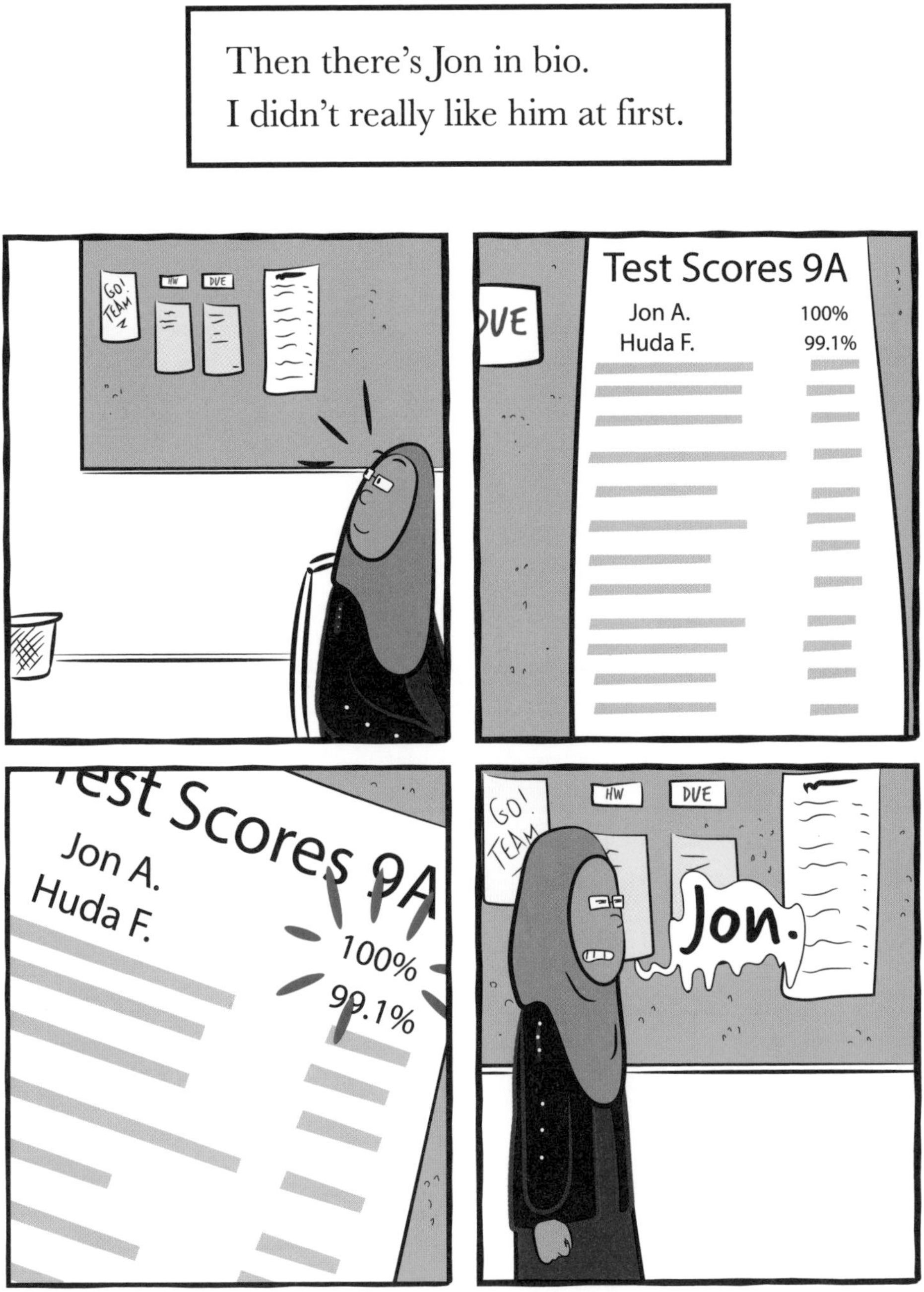
Then there's Jon in bio.
I didn't really like him at first.
GO! TEAM
HW
DUE
Test Scores 9A
Jon A. 100%
Huda F. 99.1%
Jon.

But he turned out to be pretty cool. AND he got me hooked on a lot of great stuff.

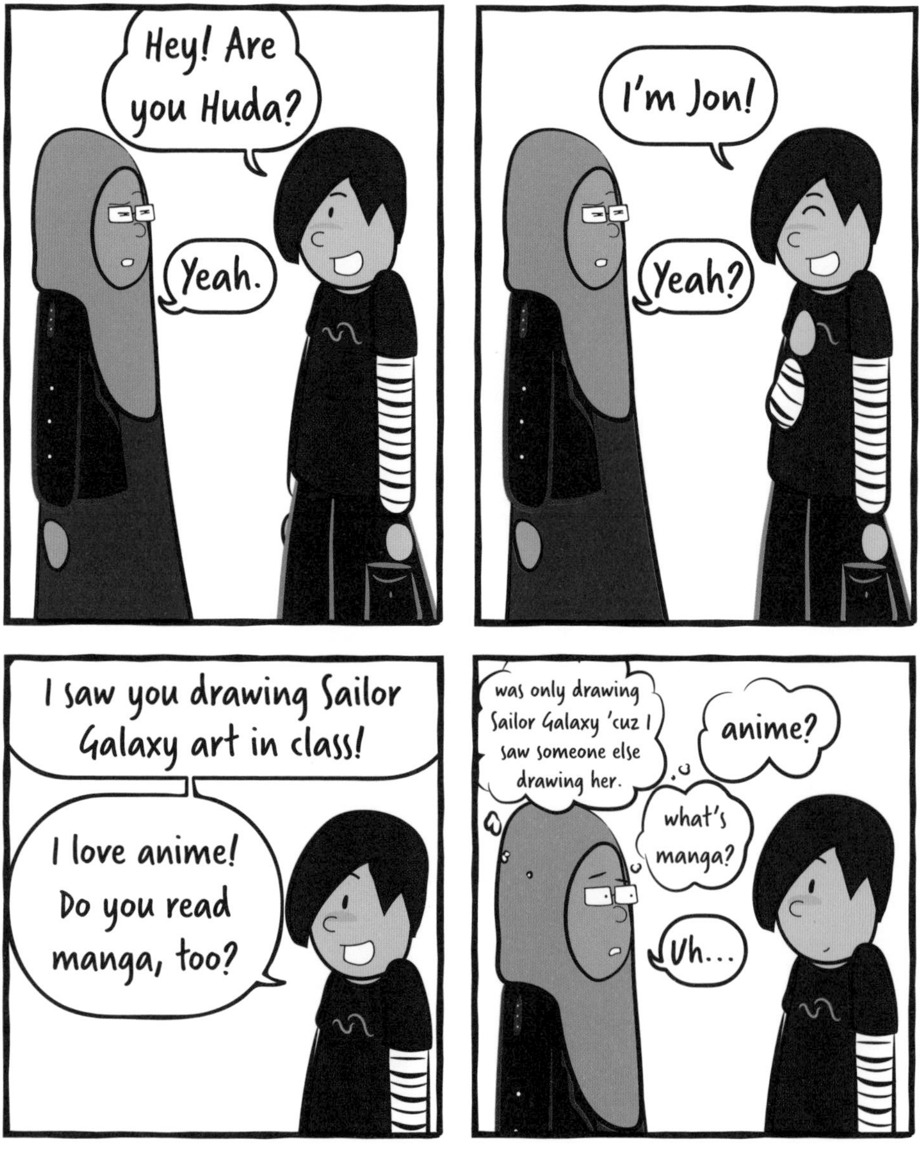
Hey! Are you Huda?
Yeah.
I'm Jon!
Yeah?
I saw you drawing Sailor Galaxy art in class!
I love anime! Do you read manga, too?
was only drawing Sailor Galaxy 'cuz I saw someone else drawing her.
anime?
what's manga?
Uh...

Including Jolt soda.

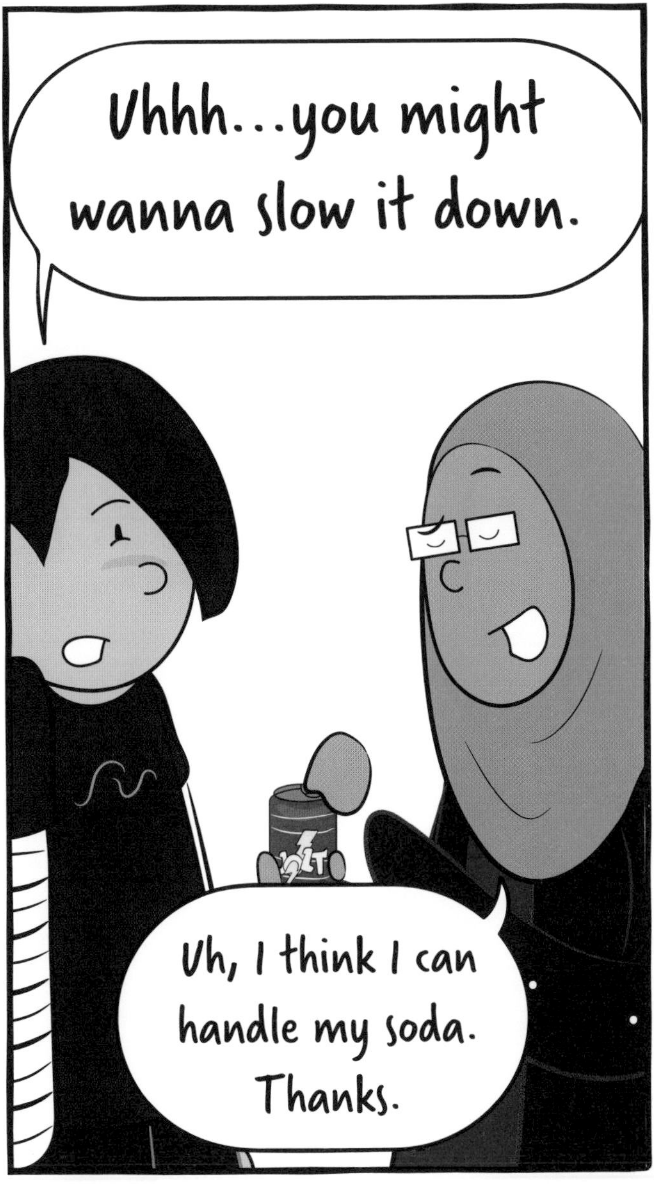

Uhhh...you might wanna slow it down.
Uh, I think I can handle my soda. Thanks.

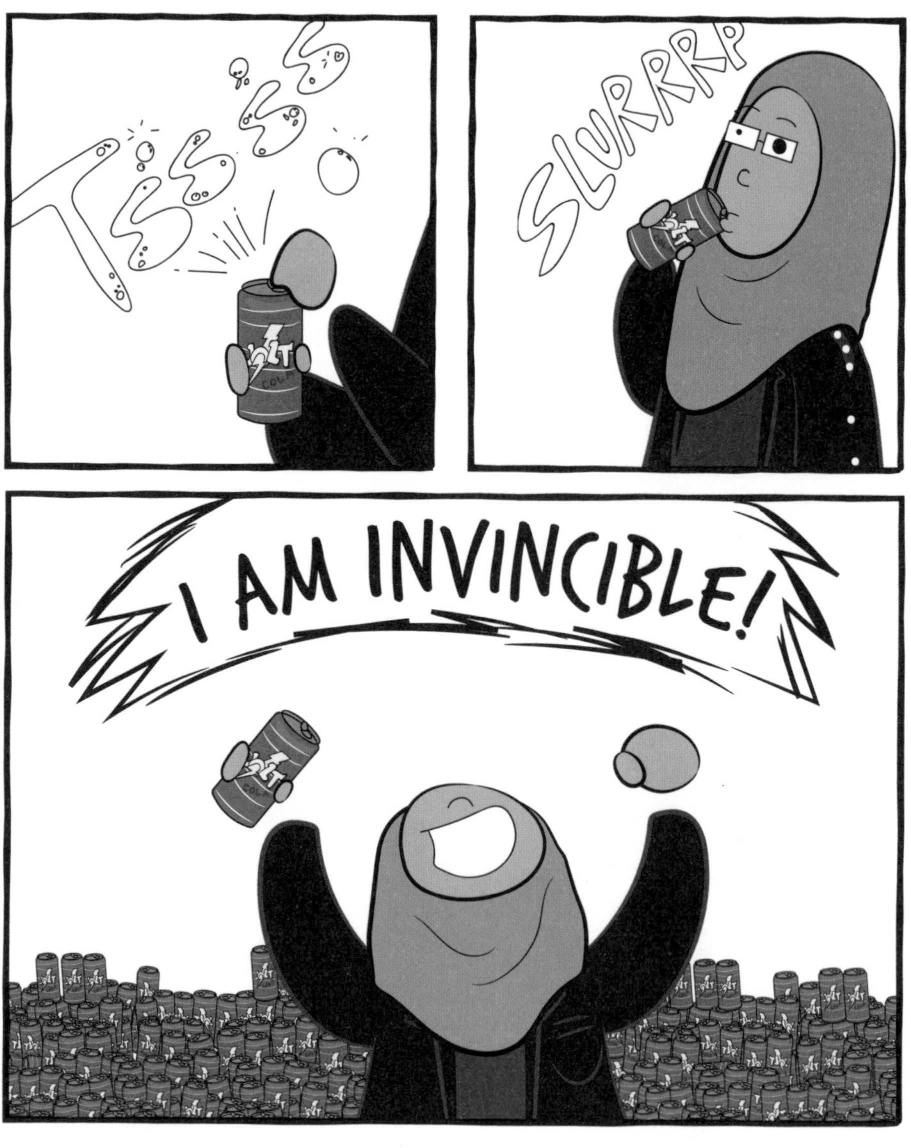
TSSSSS
SLURRRP
I AM INVINCIBLE!

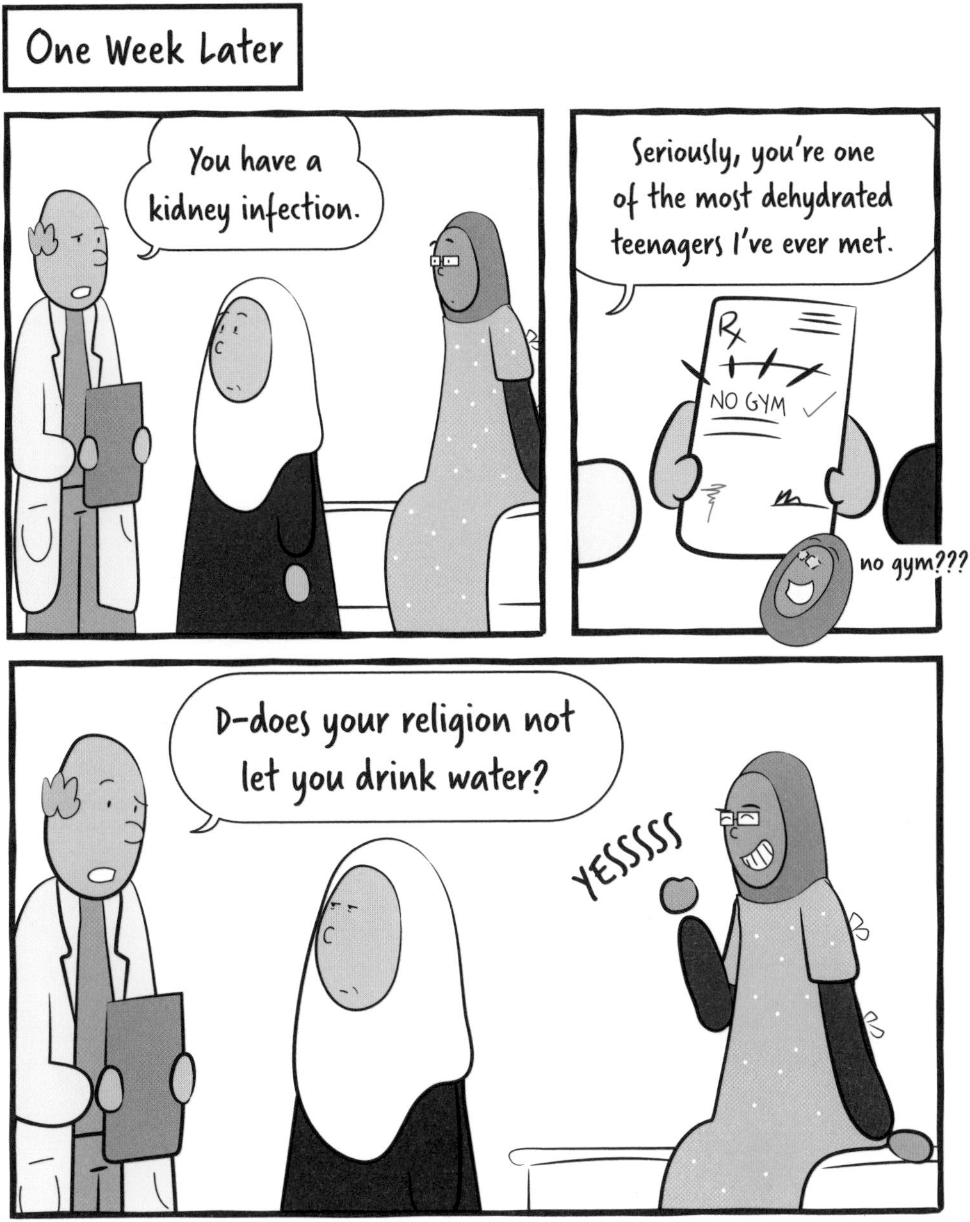
One Week Later
You have a kidney infection.
Seriously, you're one of the most dehydrated teenagers I've ever met.
NO GYM
no gym???
D-does your religion not let you drink water?
YESSSSS

Then there's Nabz. We're the only two freshmen who tested into AP Lang. We also happen to be next-door neighbors. She loves cosplay, Star Trek, and mail-in rebates.

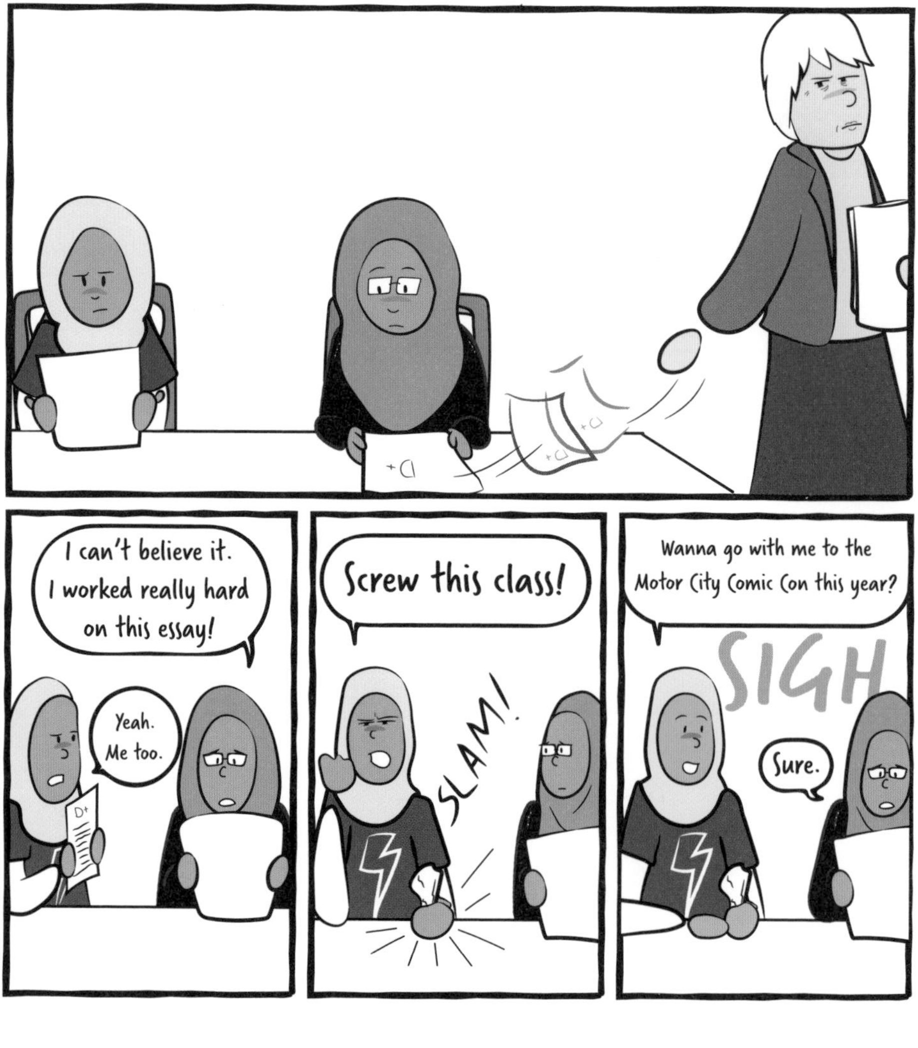
I can't believe it. I worked really hard on this essay!
Yeah. Me too.
D+
Screw this class!
SLAM!
Wanna go with me to the Motor City Comic Con this year?
SIGH
Sure.

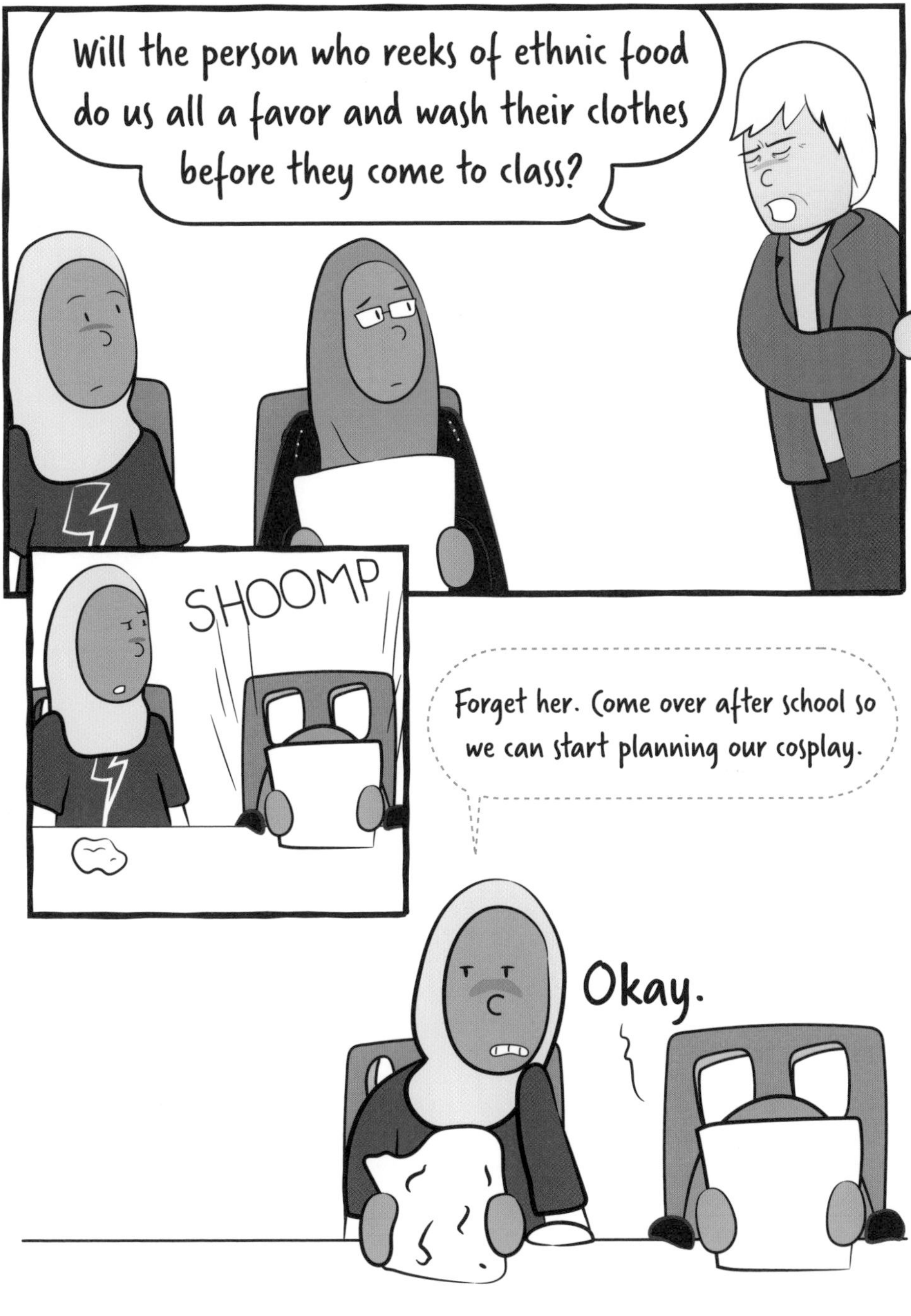
Will the person who reeks of ethnic food do us all a favor and wash their clothes before they come to class?
SHOOMP
Forget her. Come over after school so we can start planning our cosplay.
Okay.

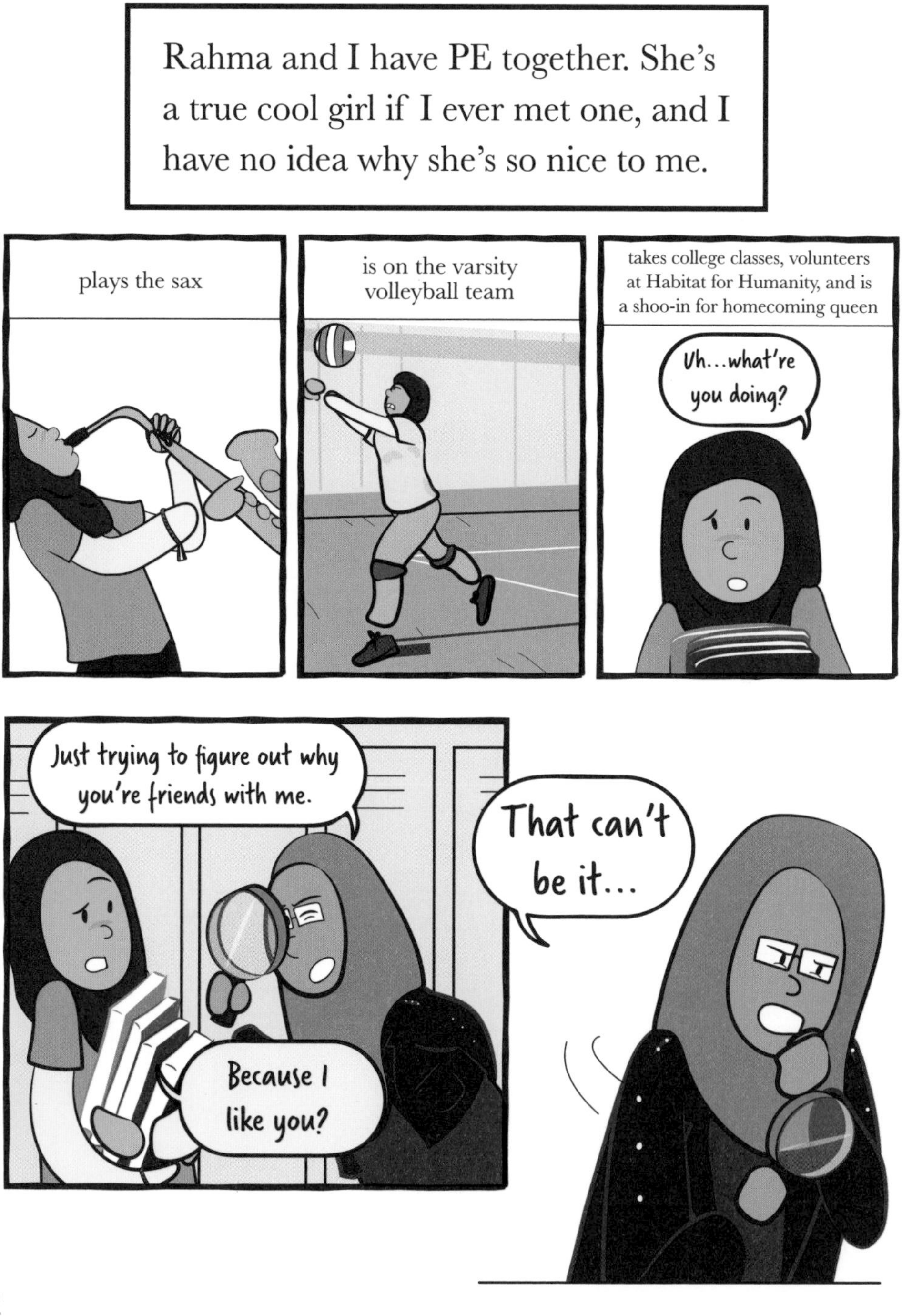
Rahma and I have PE together. She's a true cool girl if I ever met one, and I have no idea why she's so nice to me.
plays the sax
is on the varsity volleyball team
takes college classes, volunteers at Habitat for Humanity, and is a shoo-in for homecoming queen
Uh...what're you doing?
Just trying to figure out why you're friends with me.
Because I like you?
That can't be it...

Joe and I are usually paired up for group projects. Mainly 'cuz we're the last two left without partners. He skips class a lot and is super mellow. Perfect friend material, if you ask me.

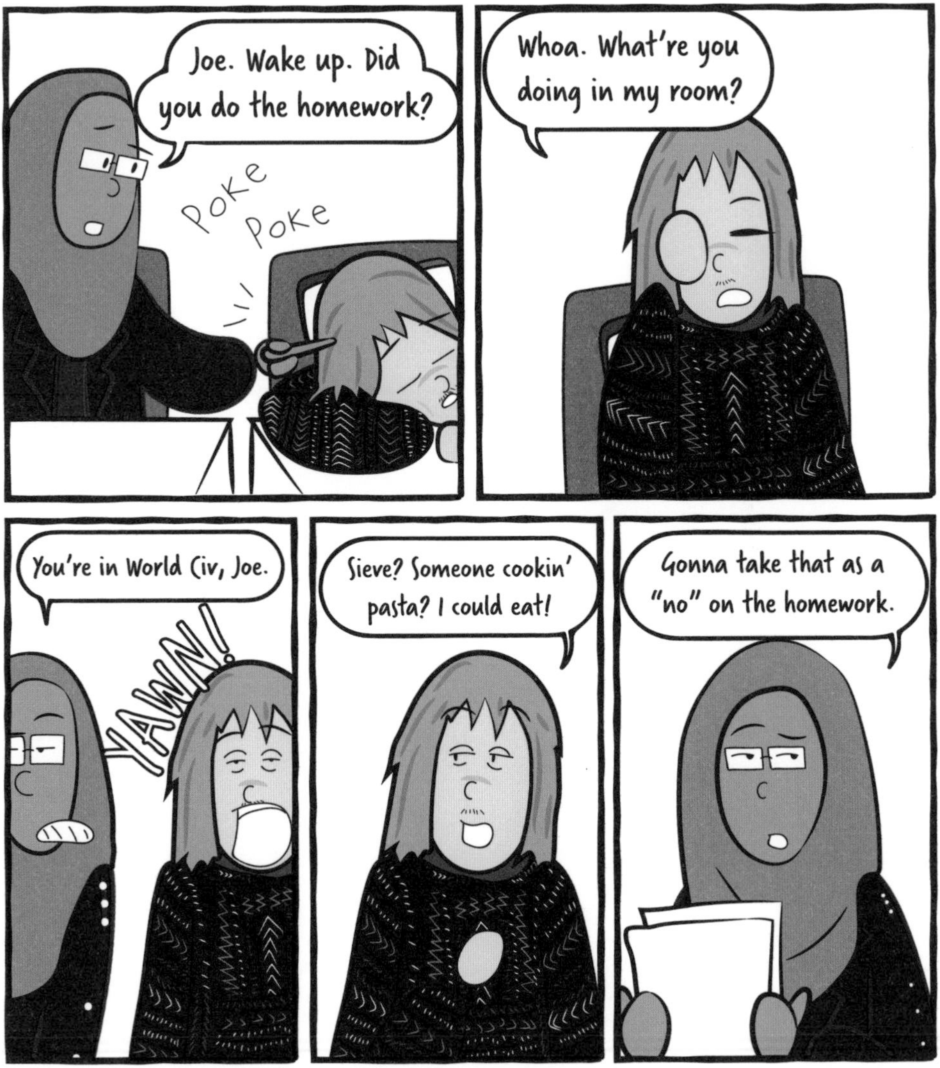
Joe. Wake up. Did you do the homework?
POKE POKE
Whoa. What're you doing in my room?
You're in World Civ, Joe.
YAWN!
Sieve? Someone cookin' pasta? I could eat!
Gonna take that as a "no" on the homework.

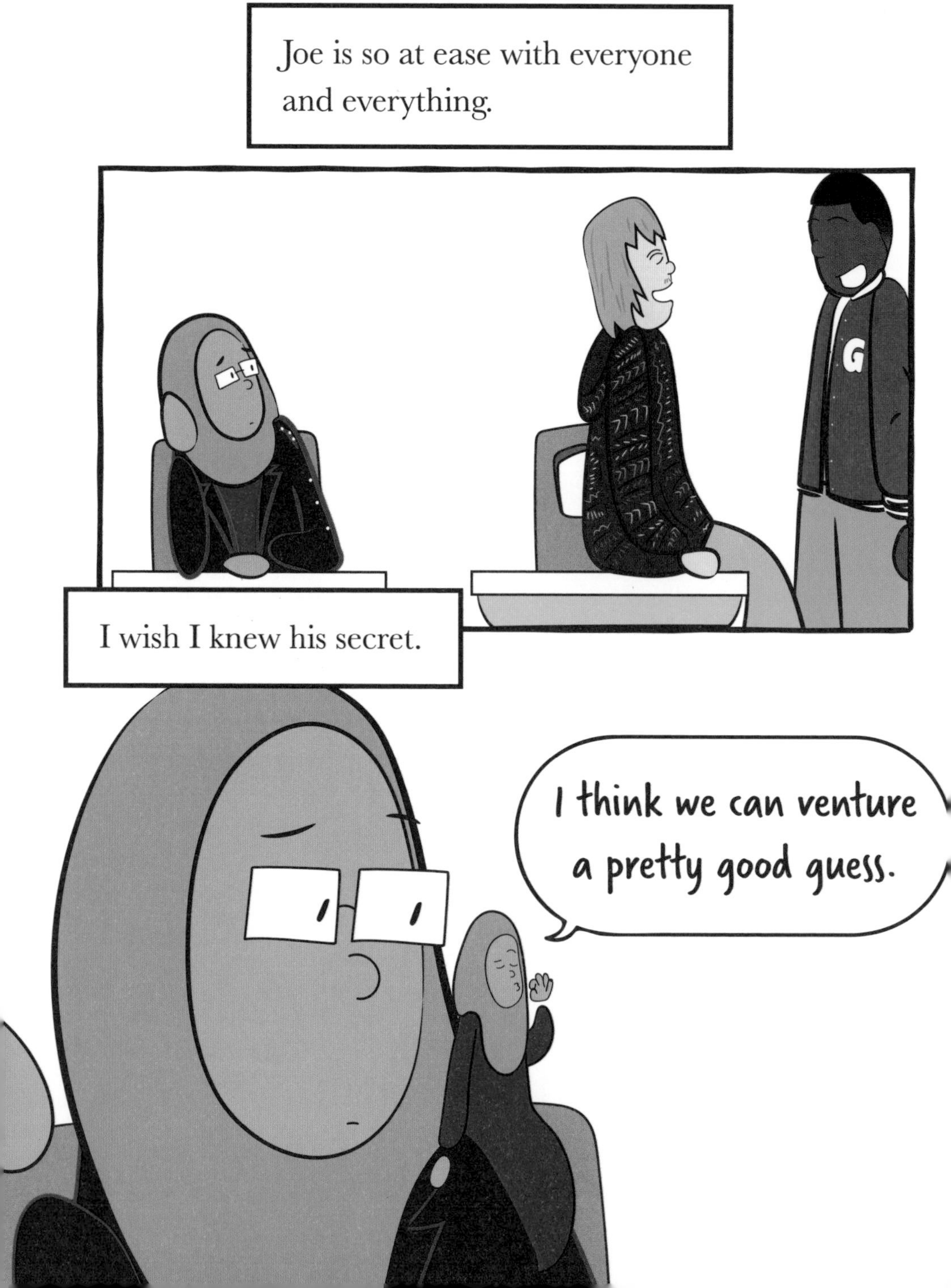
Joe is so at ease with everyone and everything.
I wish I knew his secret.
I think we can venture a pretty good guess.

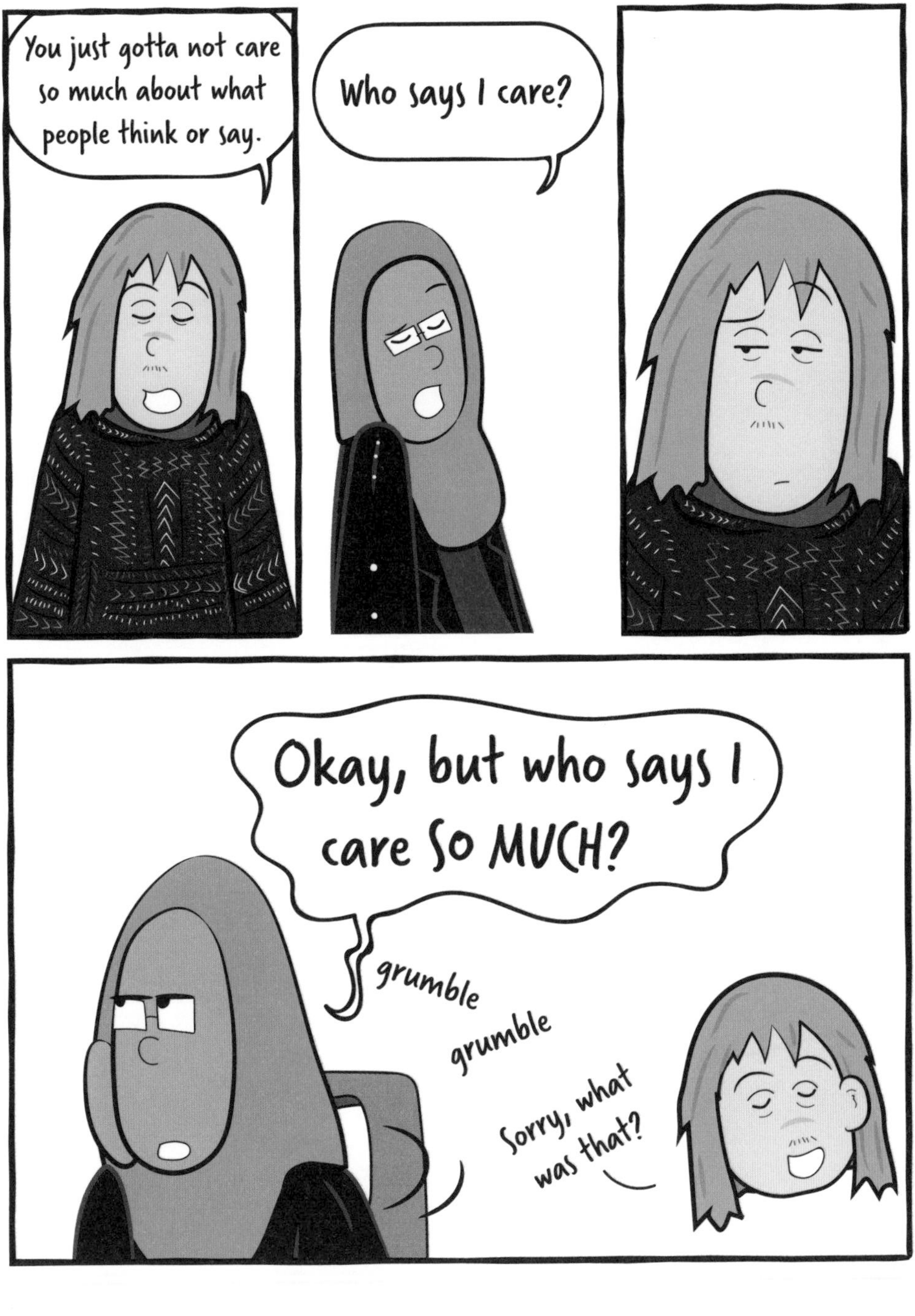
You just gotta not care so much about what people think or say.
Who says I care?
Okay, but who says I care SO MUCH?
grumble
grumble
Sorry, what was that?

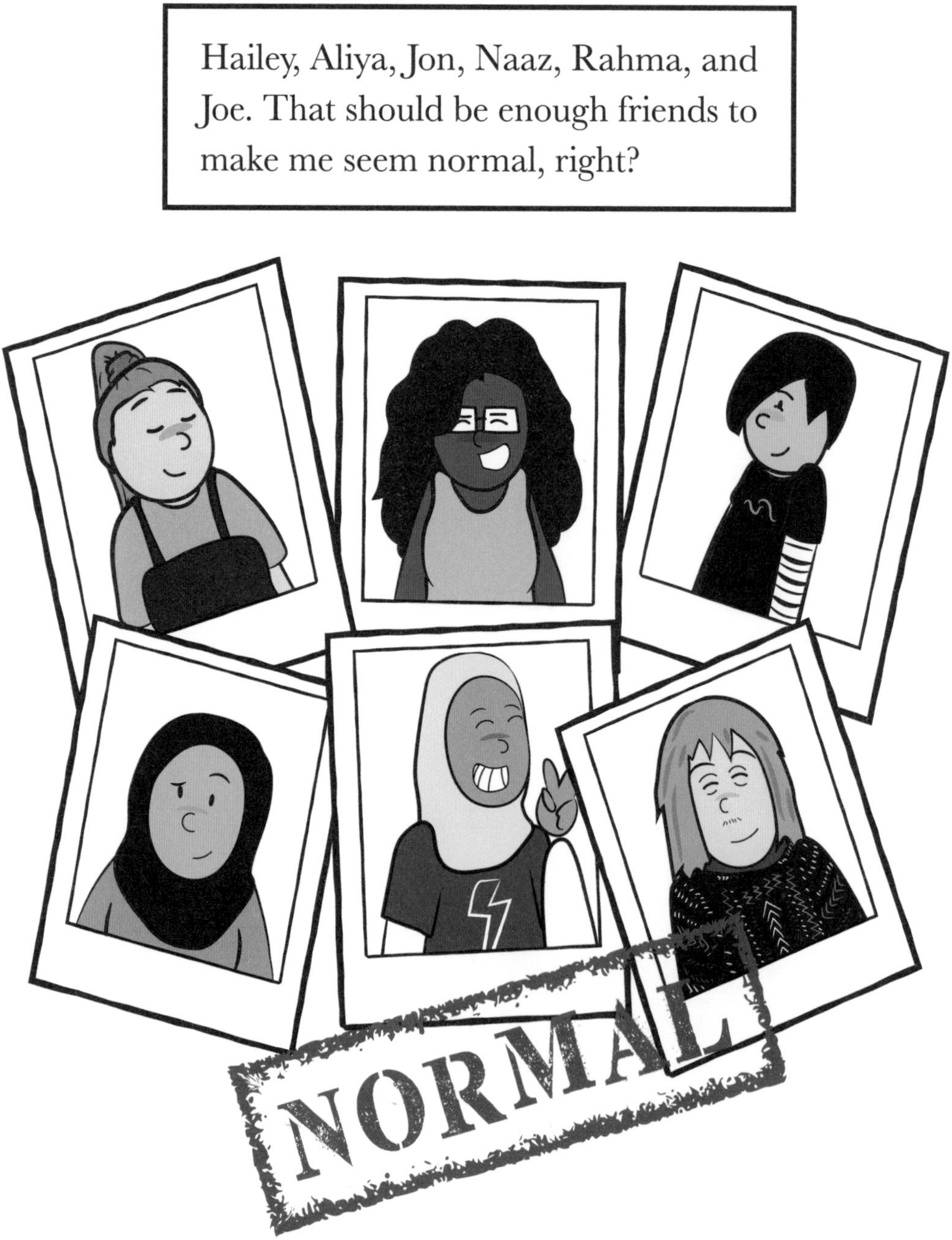

Hailey, Aliya, Jon, Naaz, Rahma, and Joe. That should be enough friends to make me seem normal, right?
NORMAL

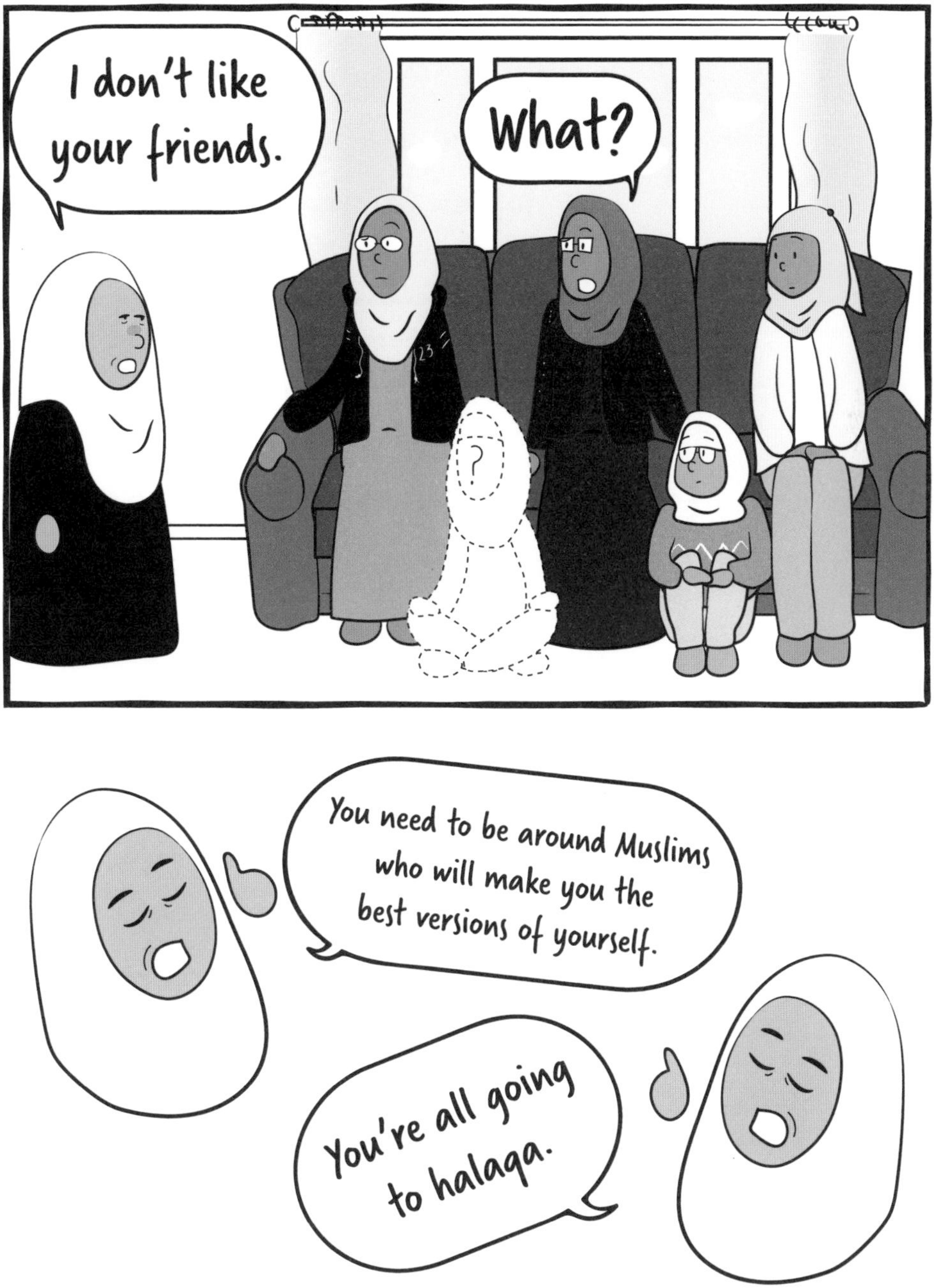
I don't like your friends.
What?
You need to be around Muslims who will make you the best versions of yourself.
You're all going to halaqa.

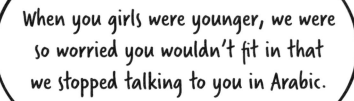

When you girls were younger, we were so worried you wouldn't fit in that we stopped talking to you in Arabic.

We put you in schools where it seemed like every religion and culture was celebrated except yours.

Is THIS why we moved to Dearborn?

But it was more than that.

Something happened when Dena started high school last year, but no one would say what. That was when the hour after dinner was suddenly designated "family time." And if we wanted to speak, it had to be in Arabic. But our Arabic was subpar, so family time was long, awkward, and mostly silent.

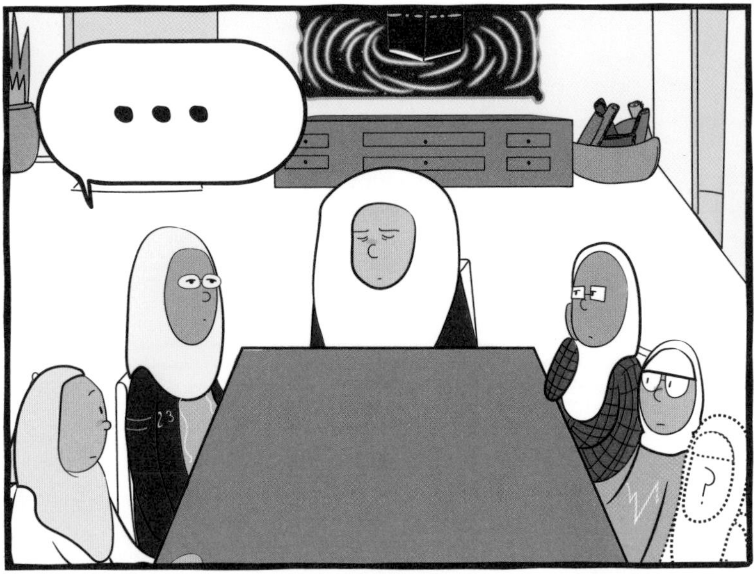
...

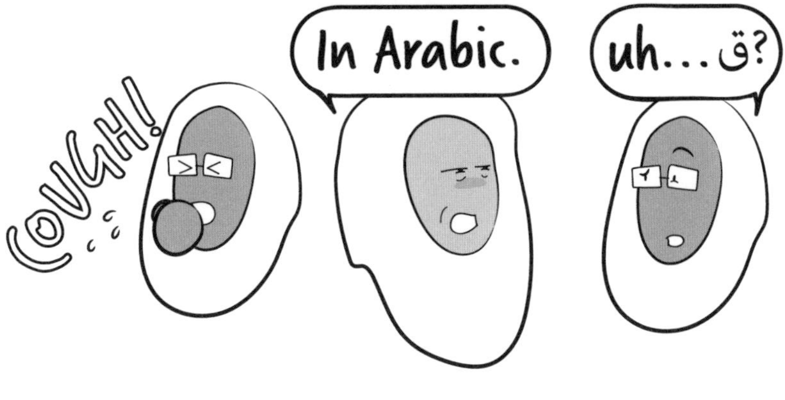
COUGH!
In Arabic.
uh...ق?

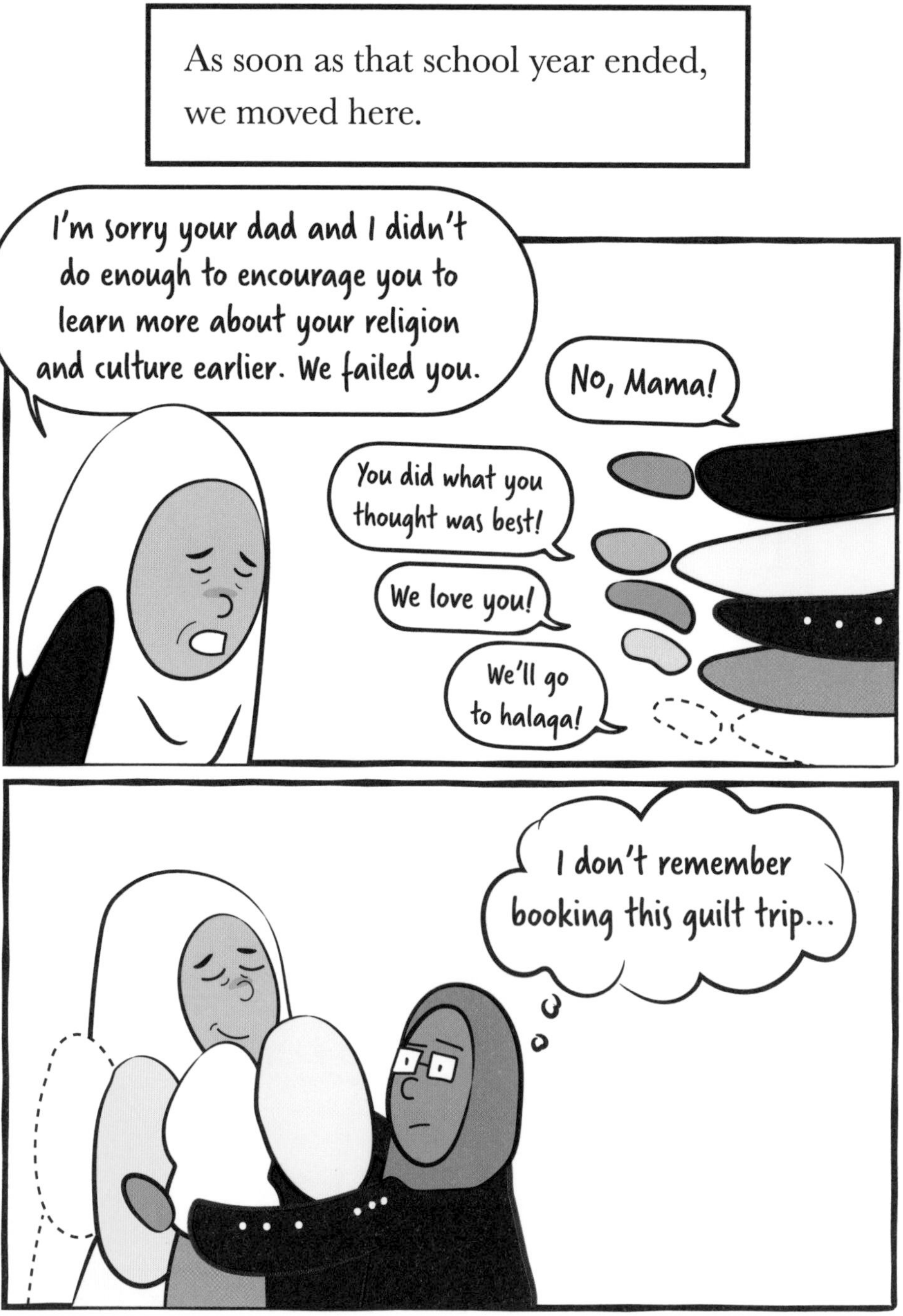
As soon as that school year ended, we moved here.
I'm sorry your dad and I didn't do enough to encourage you to learn more about your religion and culture earlier. We failed you.
No, Mama!
You did what you thought was best!
We love you!
We'll go to halaqa!
I don't remember booking this guilt trip...

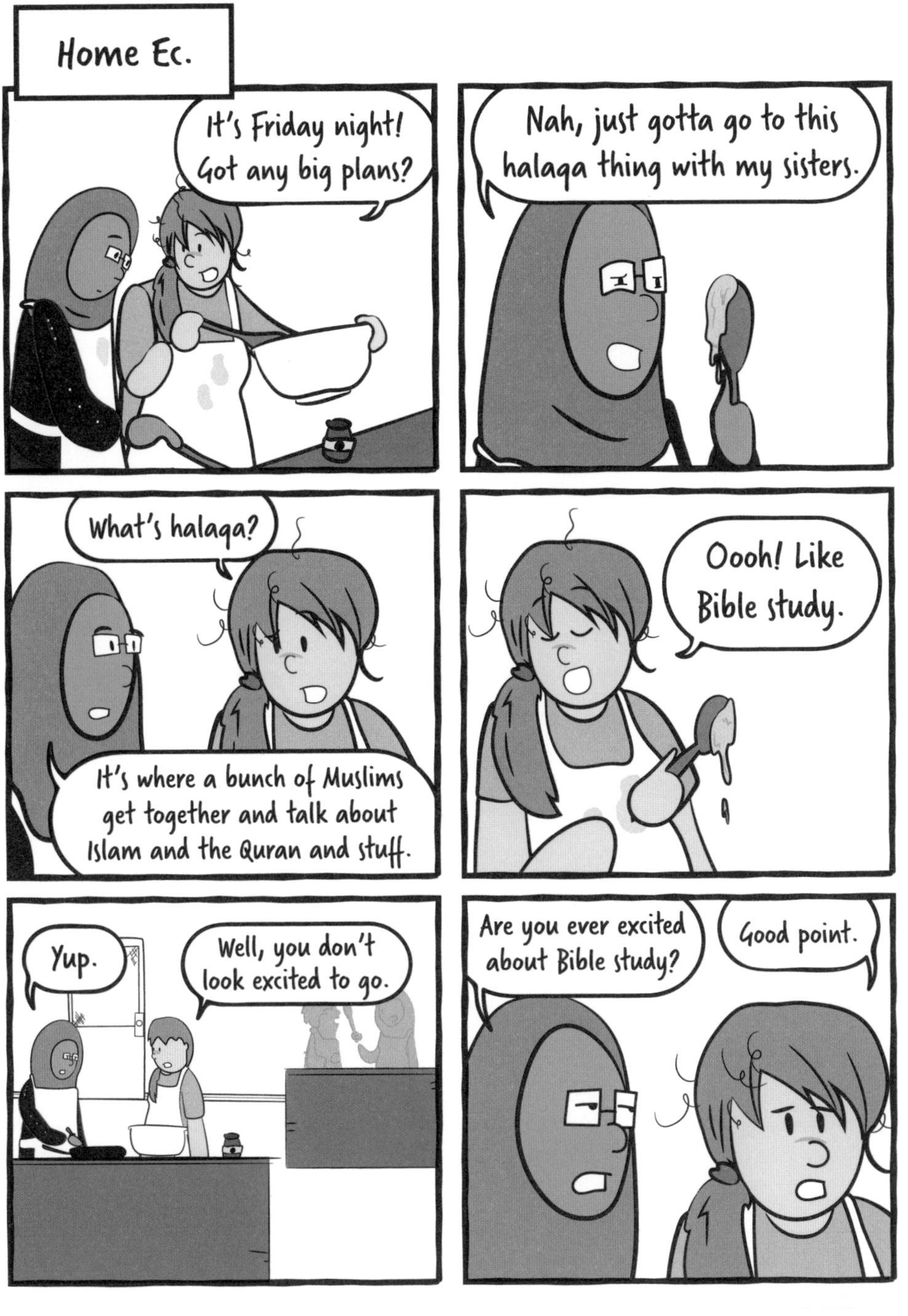

Home Ec.
It's Friday night! Got any big plans?
Nah, just gotta go to this halaqa thing with my sisters.
What's halaqa?
It's where a bunch of Muslims get together and talk about Islam and the Quran and stuff.
Oooh! Like Bible study.
Yup.
Well, you don't look excited to go.
Are you ever excited about Bible study?
Good point.

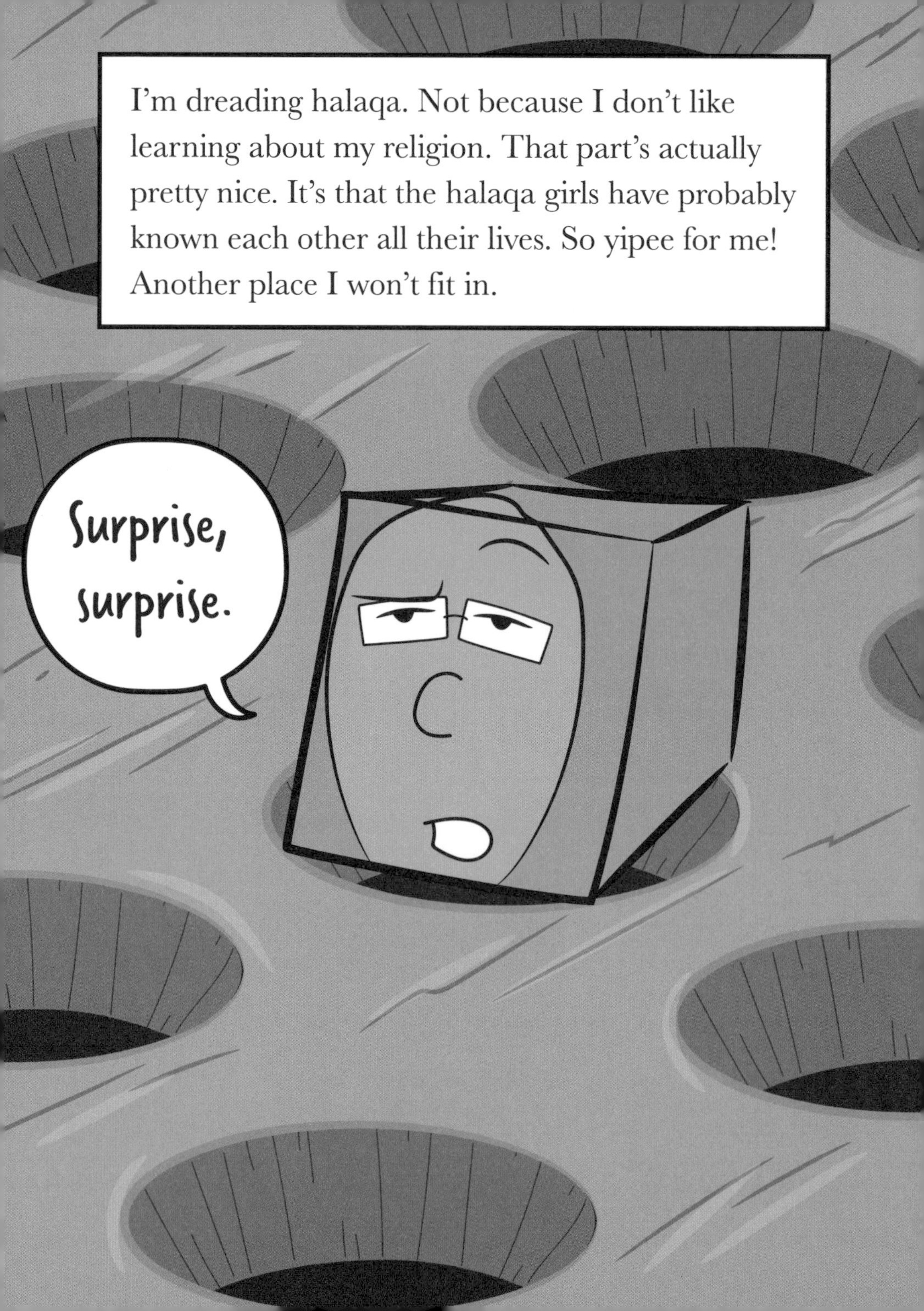
I'm dreading halaqa. Not because I don't like learning about my religion. That part's actually pretty nice. It's that the halaqa girls have probably known each other all their lives. So yipee for me! Another place I won't fit in.
Surprise, surprise.

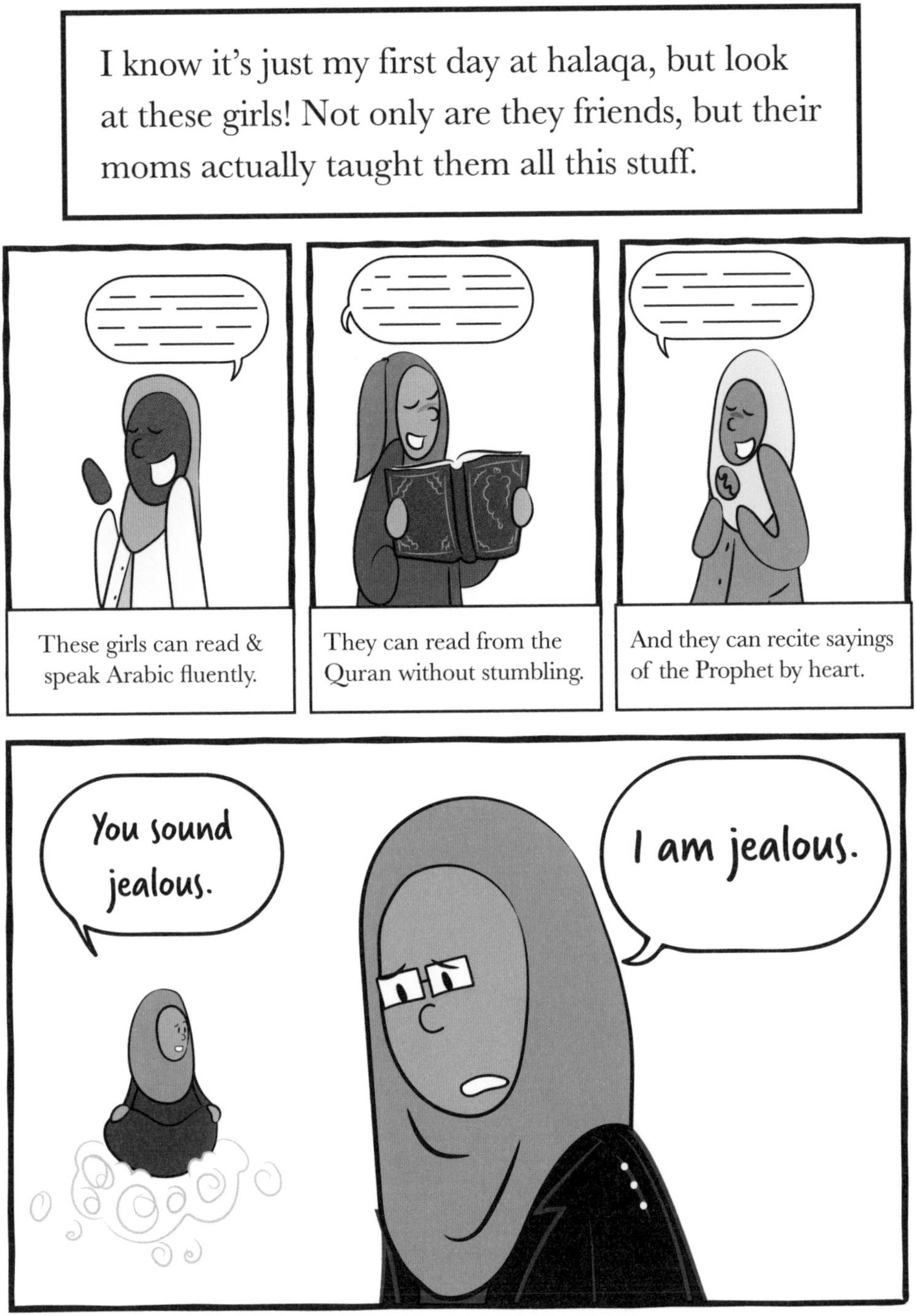
I know it's just my first day at halaqa, but look at these girls! Not only are they friends, but their moms actually taught them all this stuff.
These girls can read & speak Arabic fluently.
They can read from the Quran without stumbling.
And they can recite sayings of the Prophet by heart.
You sound jealous.
I am jealous.

At least Sister Amal, the halaqa leader, seems pretty cool.

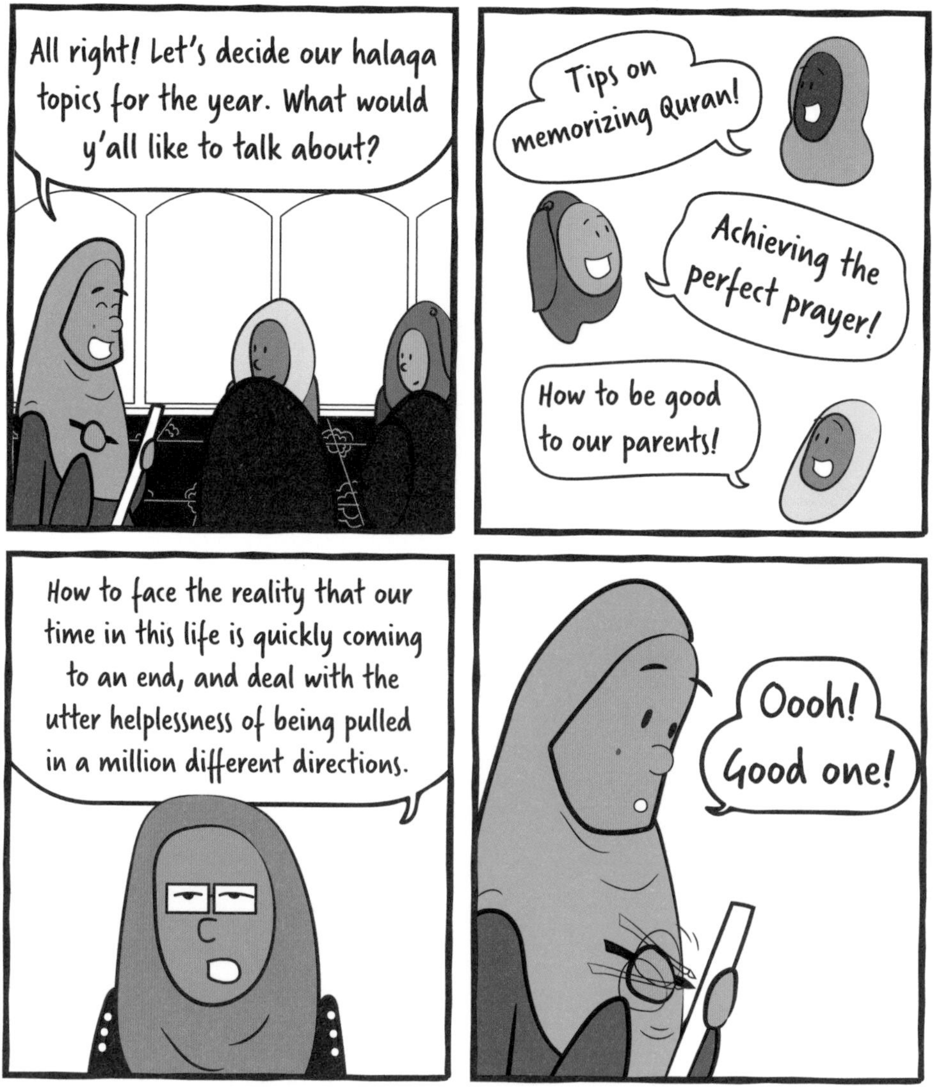
All right! Let's decide our halaqa topics for the year. What would y'all like to talk about?
Tips on memorizing Quran!
Achieving the perfect prayer!
How to be good to our parents!
How to face the reality that our time in this life is quickly coming to an end, and deal with the utter helplessness of being pulled in a million different directions.
Oooh! Good one!

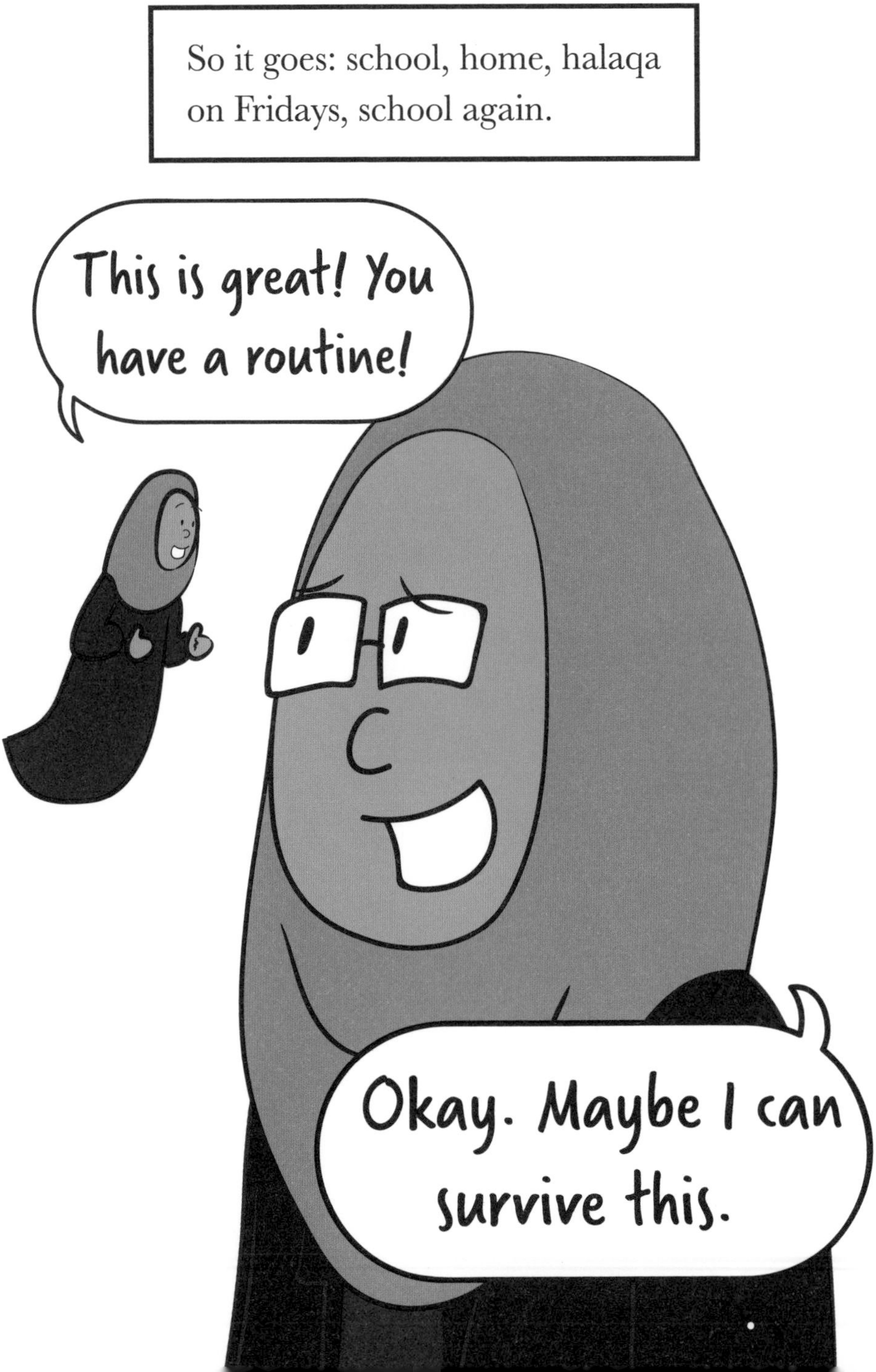
So it goes: school, home, halaqa on Fridays, school again.
This is great! You have a routine!
Okay. Maybe I can survive this.

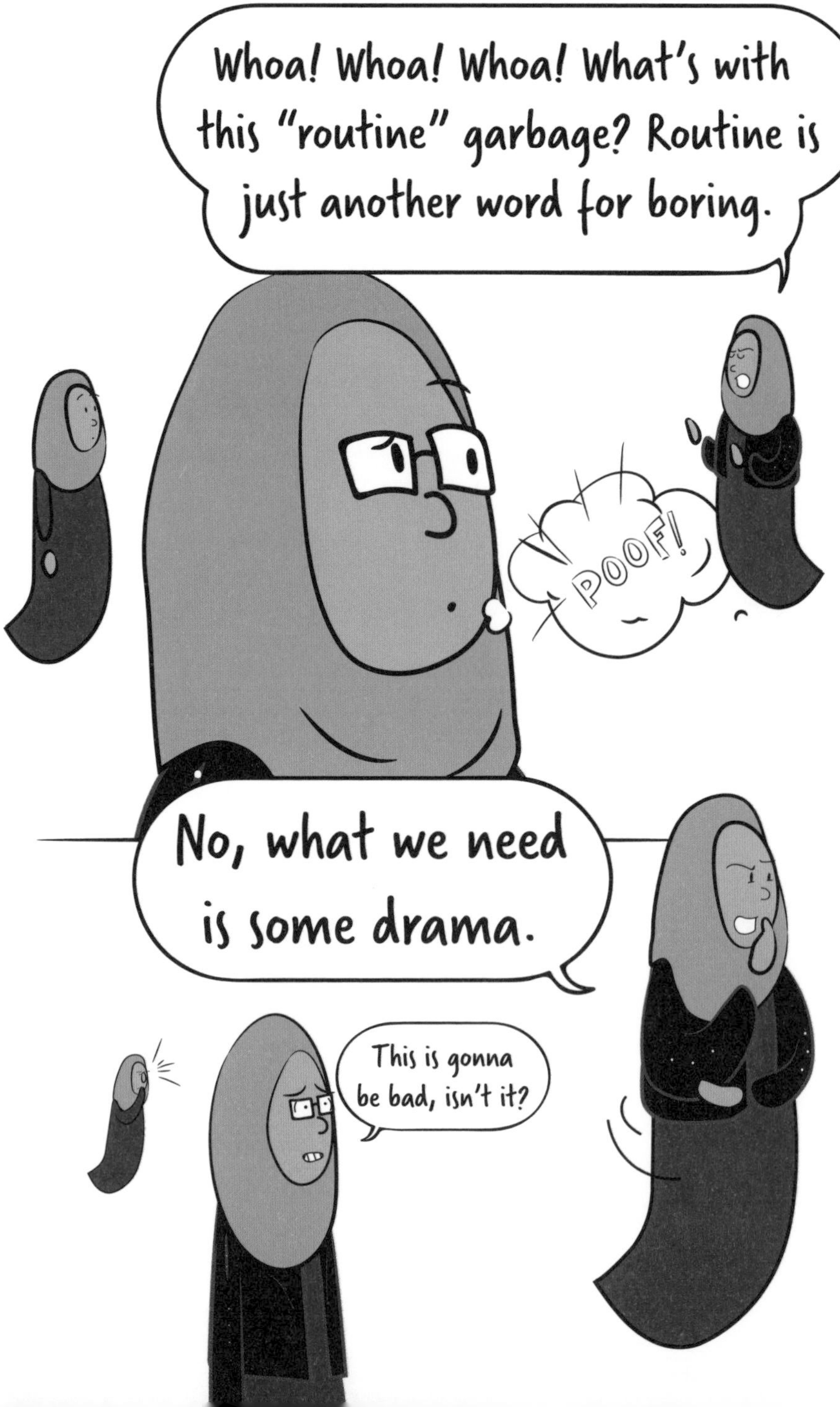
Whoa! Whoa! Whoa! What's with this "routine" garbage? Routine is just another word for boring.
POOF!
No, what we need is some drama.
This is gonna be bad, isn't it?

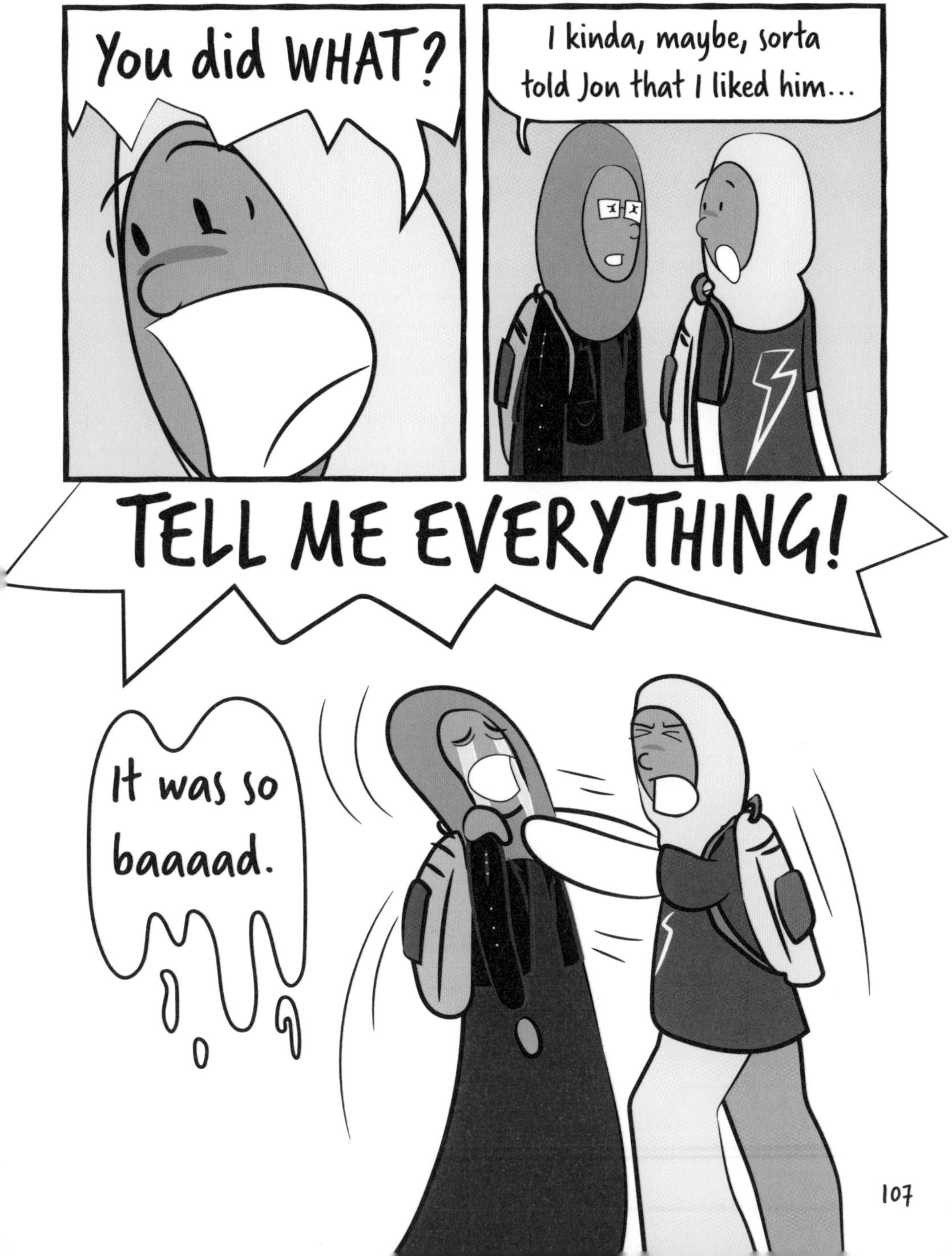

You did WHAT?
I kinda, maybe, sorta told Jon that I liked him...
TELL ME EVERYTHING!
It was so baaaad.

Earlier

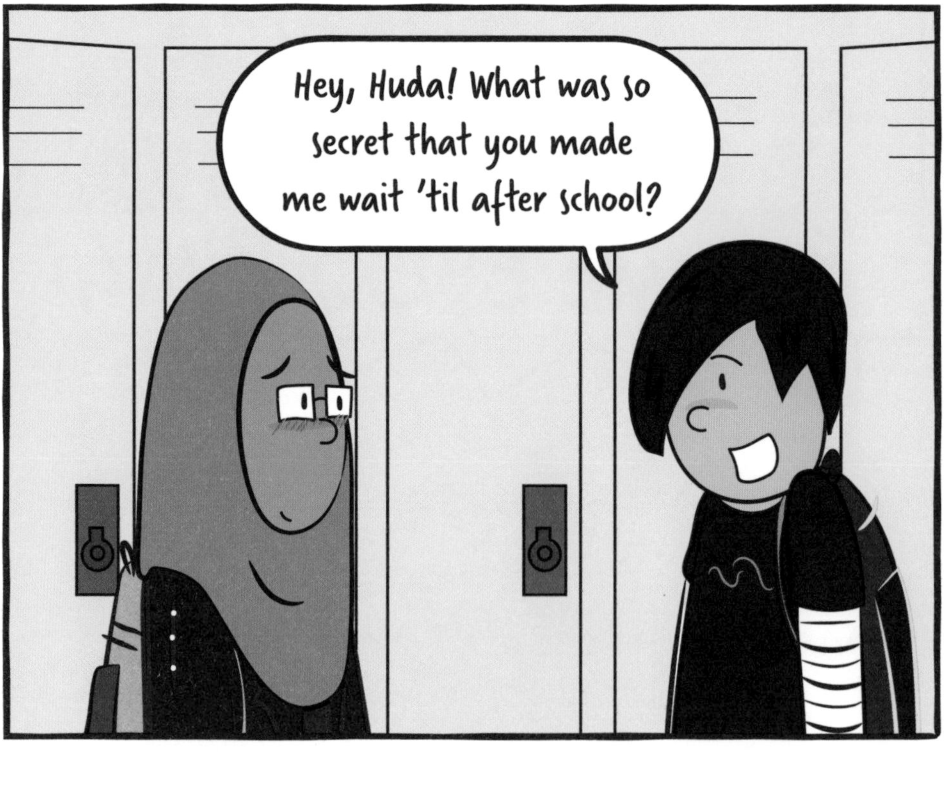
Hey, Huda! What was so secret that you made me wait 'til after school?

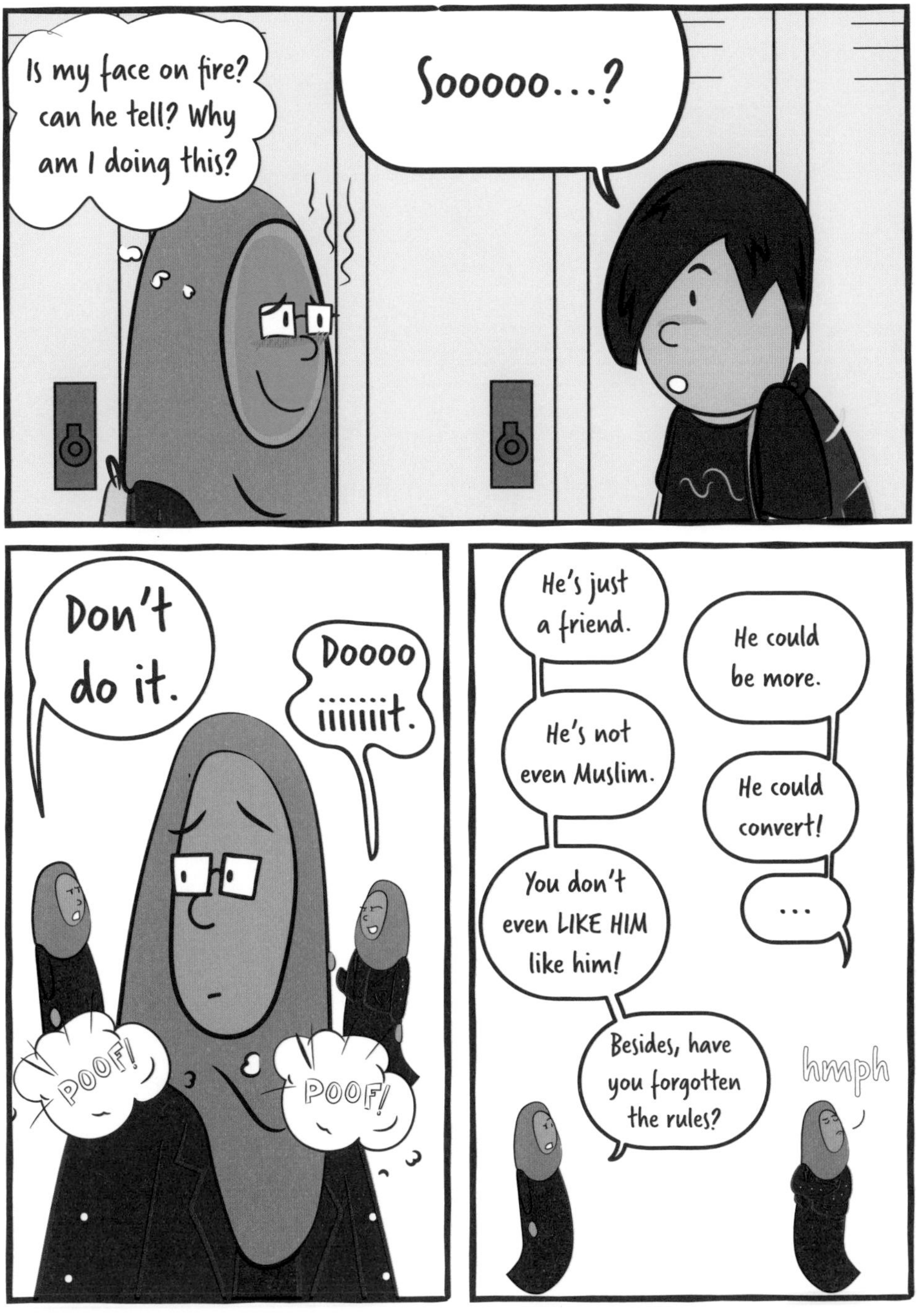
Is my face on fire? can he tell? Why am I doing this?
Sooooo...?
Don't do it.
Doooo iiiiiiiit.
POOF!
POOF!
He's just a friend.
He could be more.
He's not even Muslim.
He could convert!
You don't even LIKE HIM like him!
...
Besides, have you forgotten the rules?
hmph

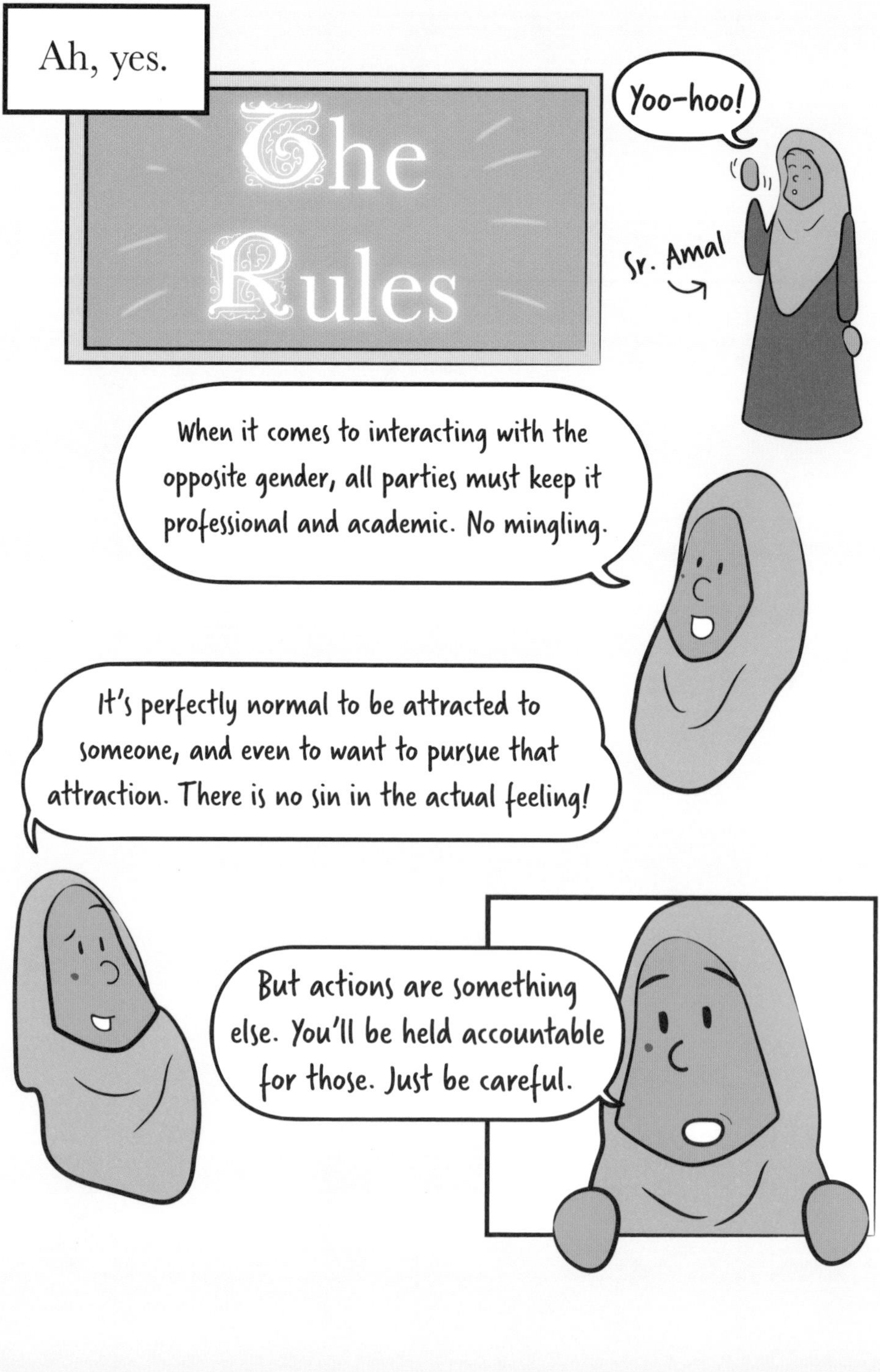
Ah, yes.
The Rules
Yoo-hoo!
Sr. Amal
When it comes to interacting with the opposite gender, all parties must keep it professional and academic. No mingling.
It's perfectly normal to be attracted to someone, and even to want to pursue that attraction. There is no sin in the actual feeling!
But actions are something else. You'll be held accountable for those. Just be careful.

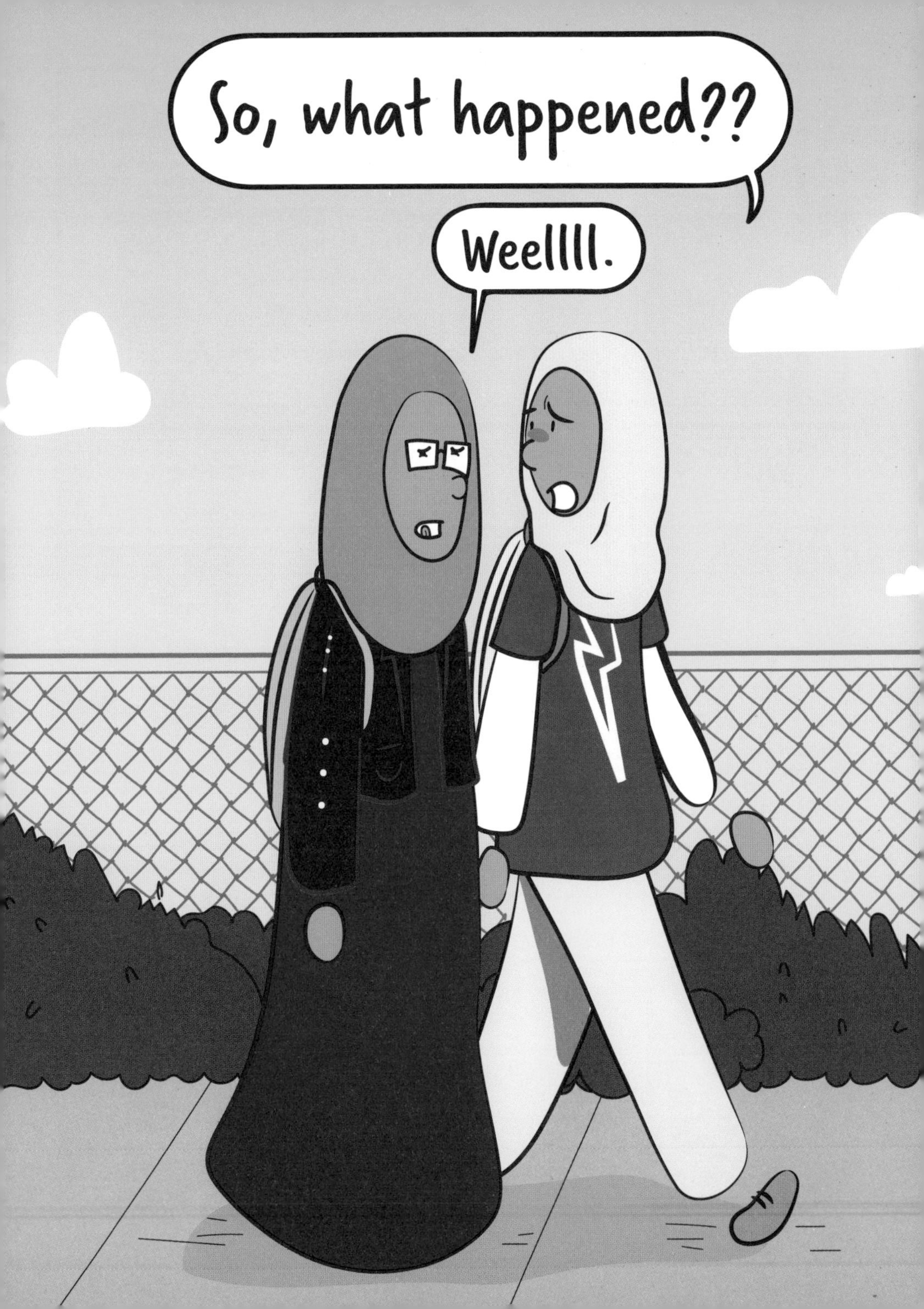
So, what happened??
Weellll.

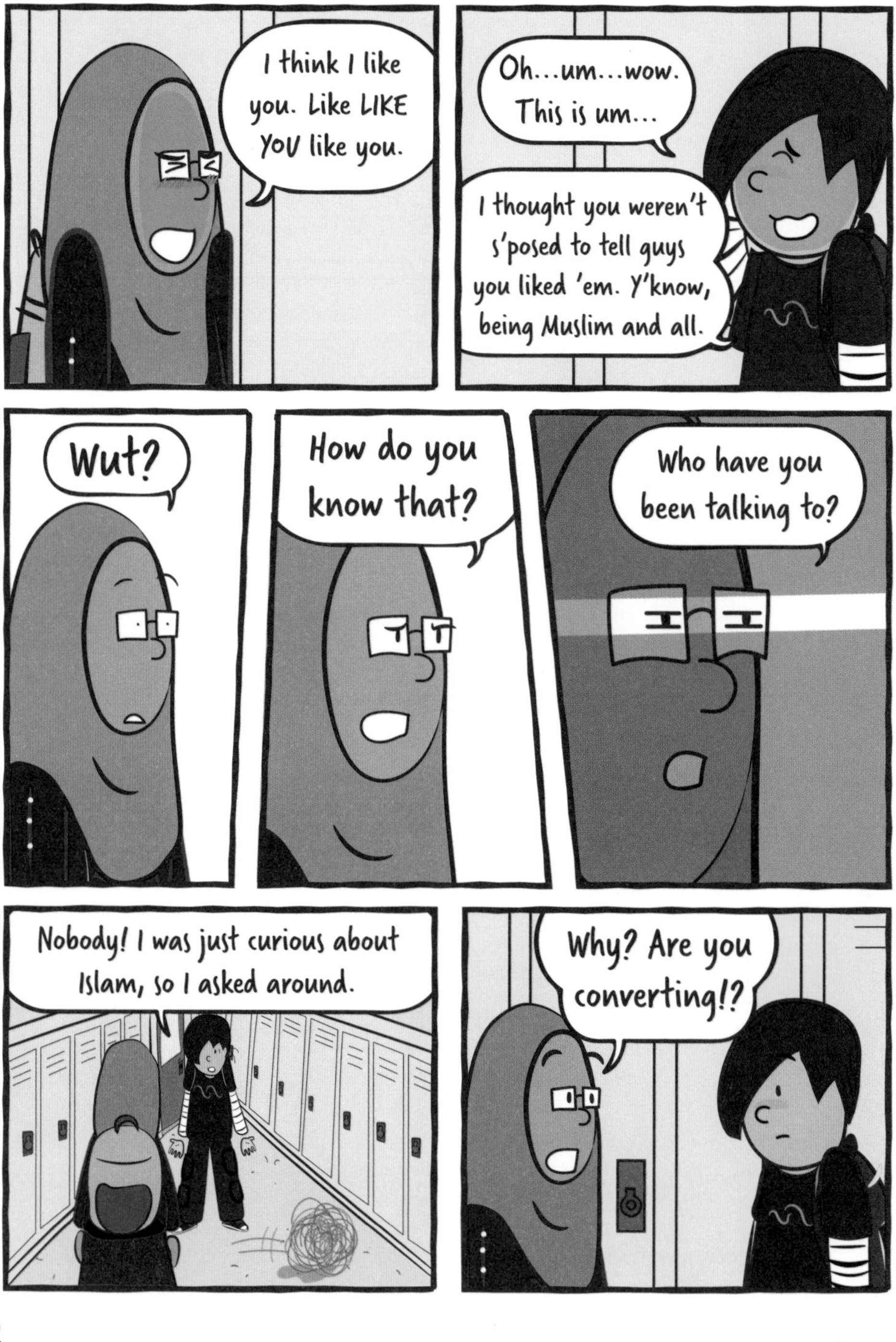
I think I like you. Like LIKE YOU like you.
Oh...um...wow. This is um...
I thought you weren't s'posed to tell guys you liked 'em. Y'know, being Muslim and all.
Wut?
How do you know that?
Who have you been talking to?
Nobody! I was just curious about Islam, so I asked around.
Why? Are you converting!?

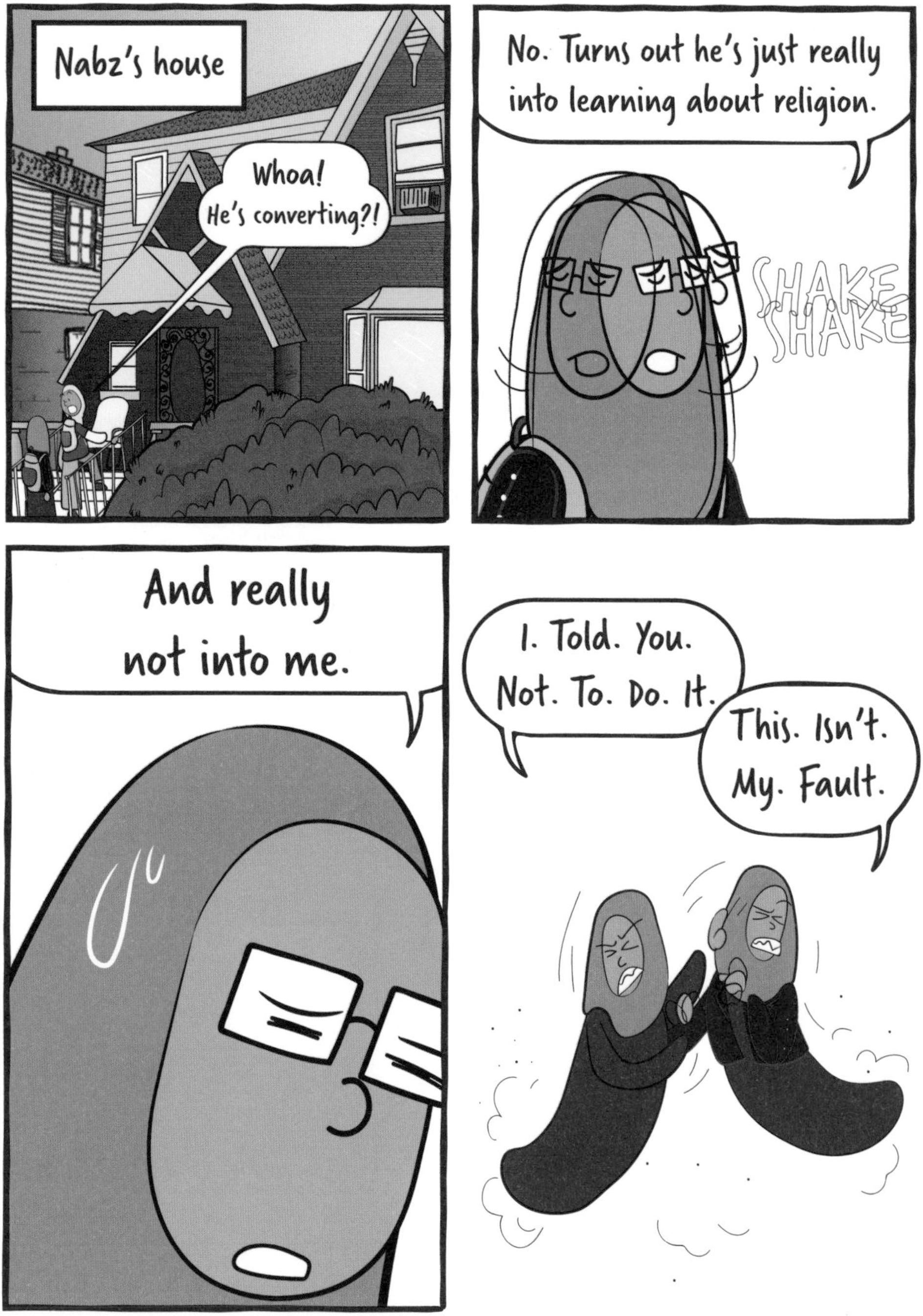
Nabz's house
Whoa! He's converting?!
No. Turns out he's just really into learning about religion.
SHAKE SHAKE
And really not into me.
I. Told. You. Not. To. Do. It.
This. Isn't. My. Fault.

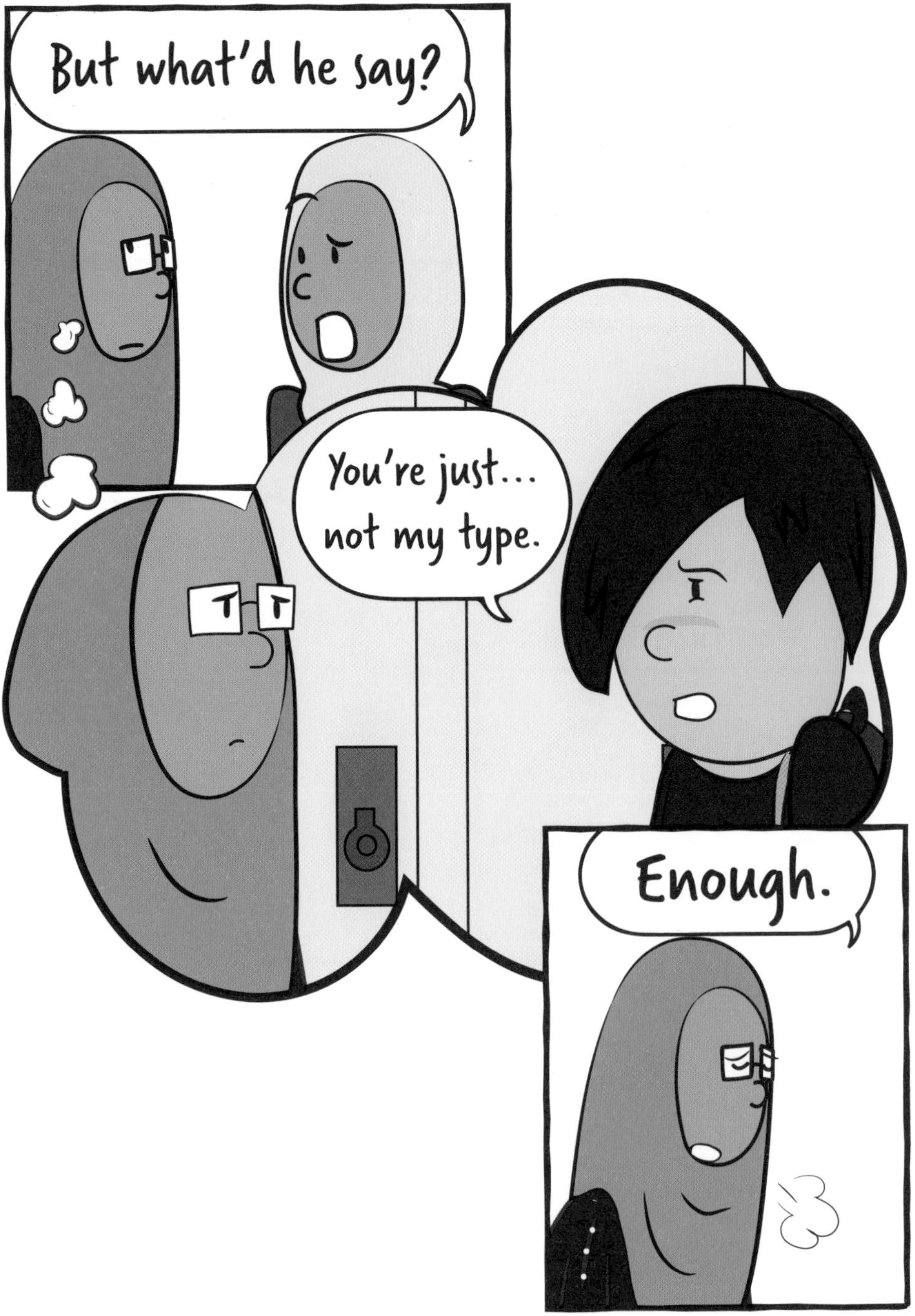

But what'd he say?
You're just... not my type.
Enough.

Huda F Is a Loser

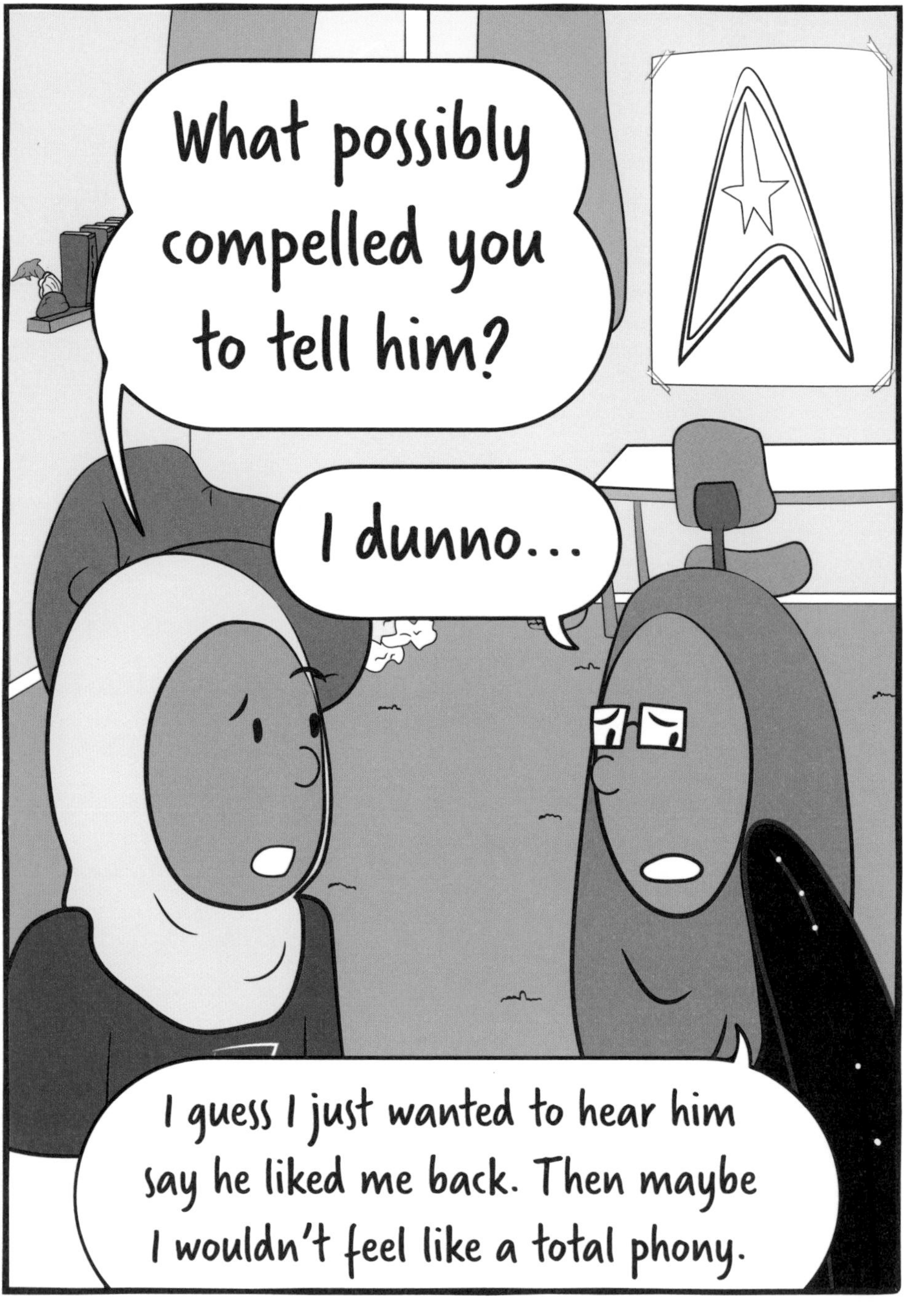
What possibly compelled you to tell him?
I dunno...
I guess I just wanted to hear him say he liked me back. Then maybe I wouldn't feel like a total phony.

Oop. Did I just say that out loud?

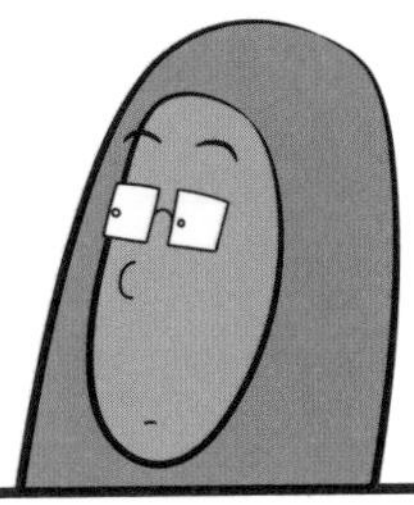

It feels weird confiding in Nabz. Up until this point, I've kept all my friends at a distance, terrified they'd find out I was a fake . . . But, God, it's getting exhausting. And if I didn't tell Nabz about my epic Huda F-up with Jon, I was going to explode.

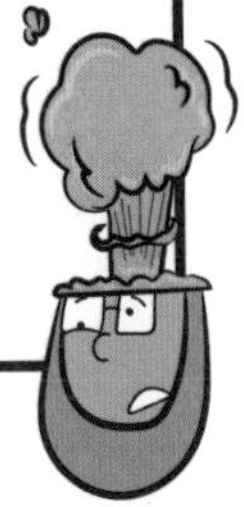

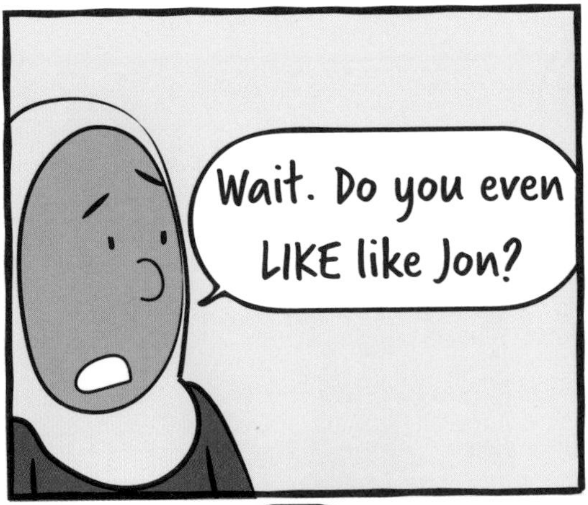
Wait. Do you even LIKE like Jon?

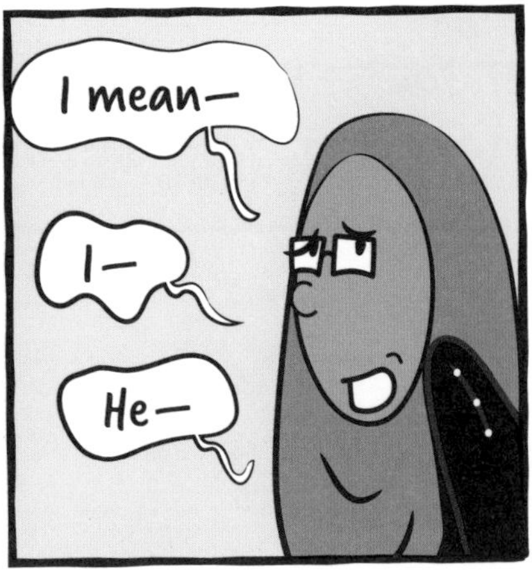
I mean—
I—
He—

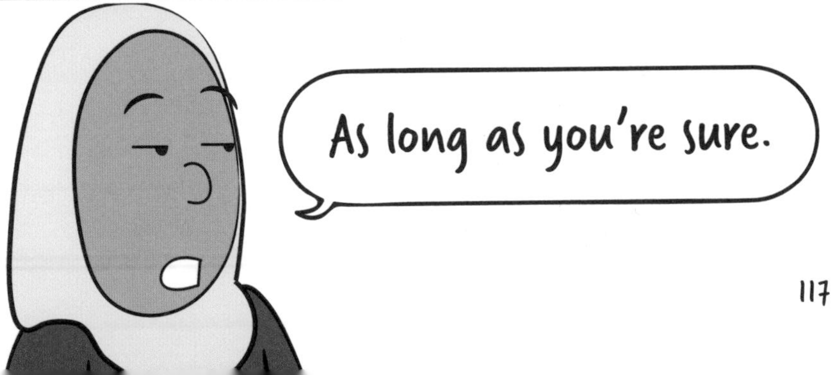
As long as you're sure.

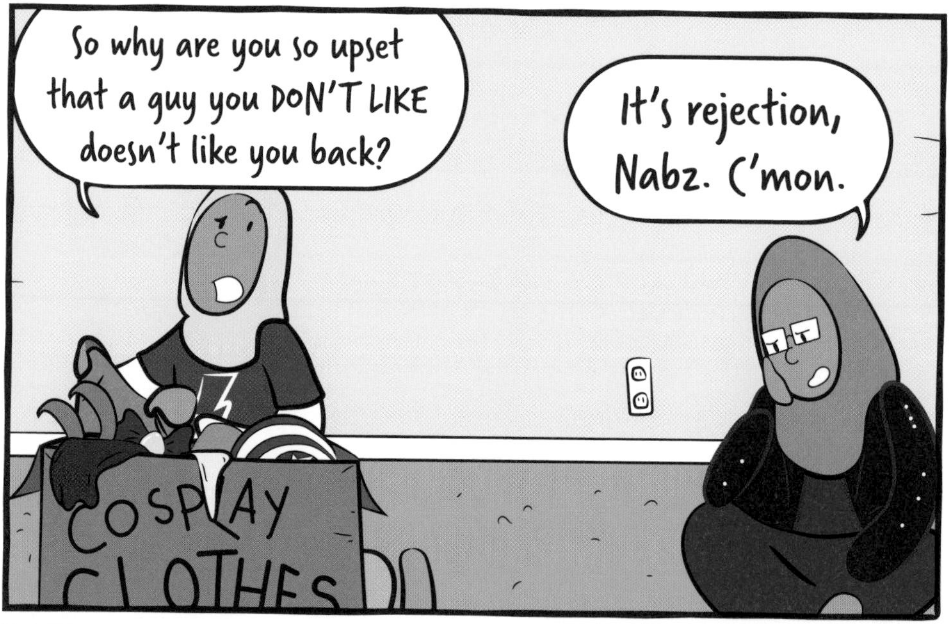
So why are you so upset that a guy you DON'T LIKE doesn't like you back?
It's rejection, Nabz. C'mon.
COSPLAY CLOTHES

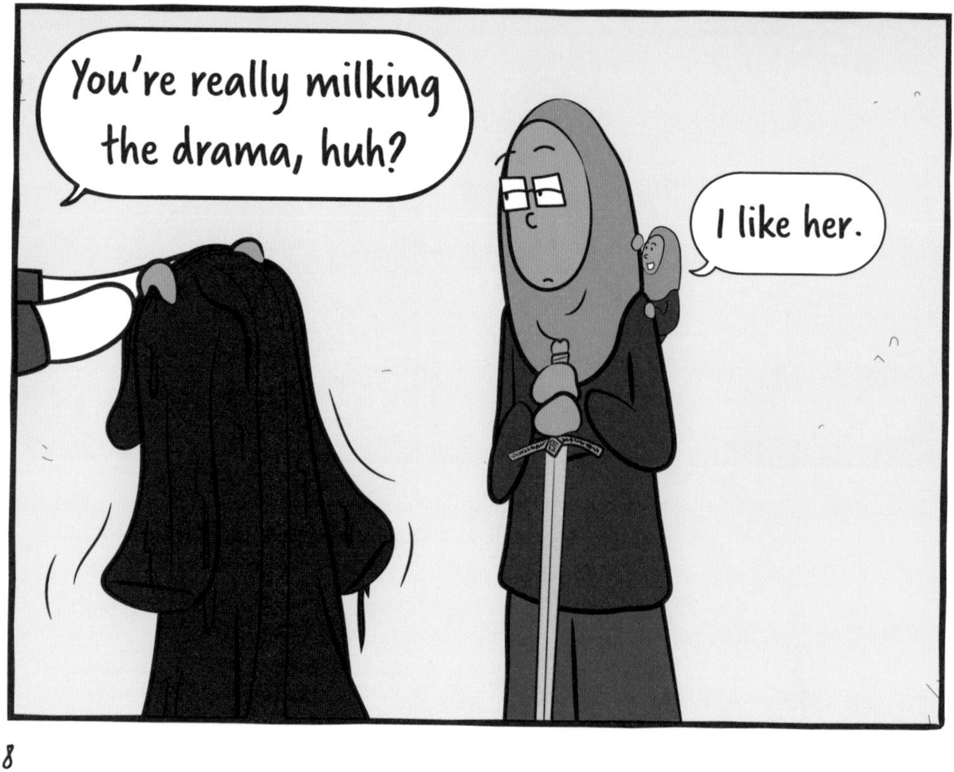
You're really milking the drama, huh?
I like her.

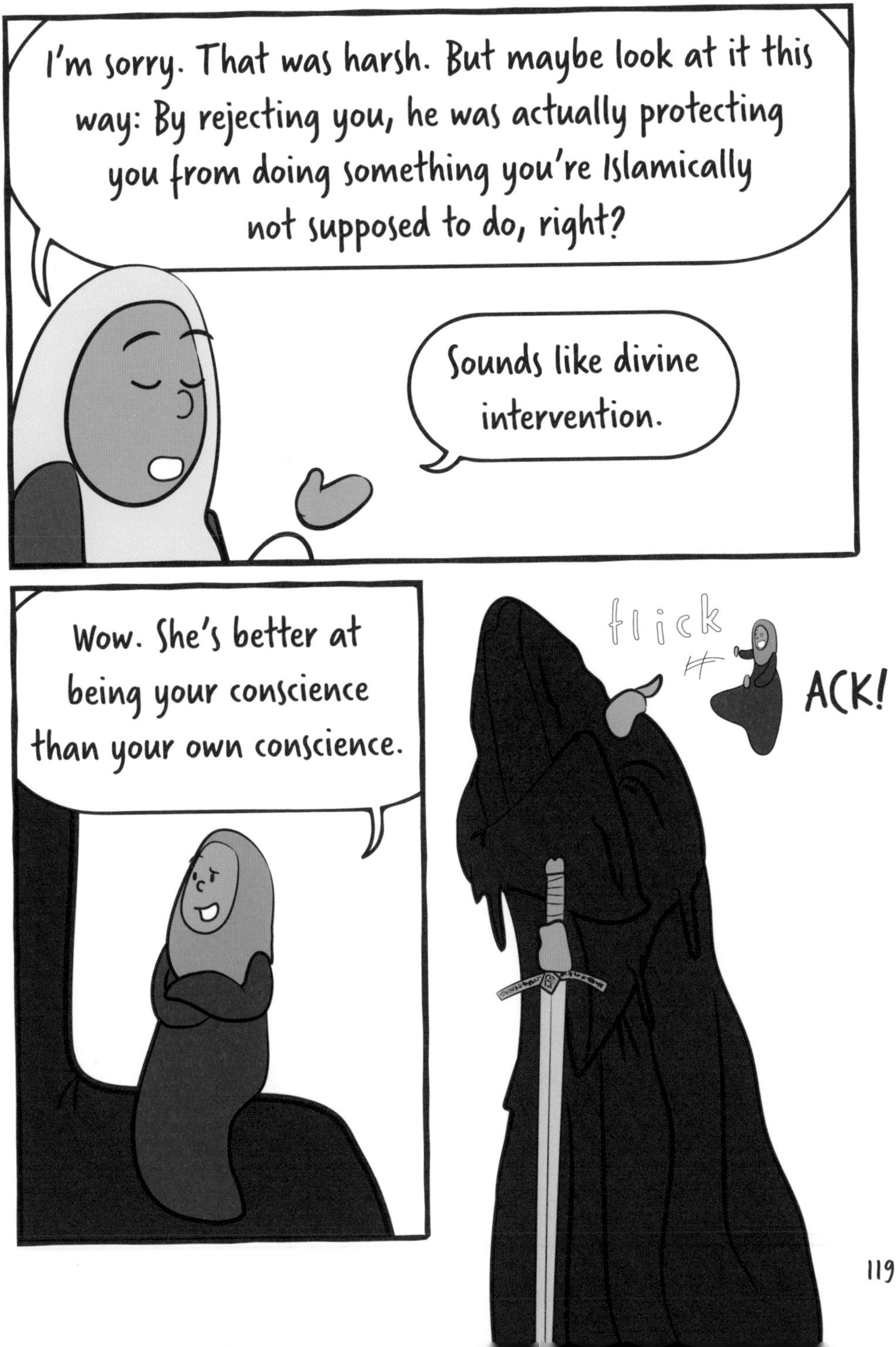
I'm sorry. That was harsh. But maybe look at it this way: By rejecting you, he was actually protecting you from doing something you're Islamically not supposed to do, right?
Sounds like divine intervention.
Wow. She's better at being your conscience than your own conscience.
flick
ACK!

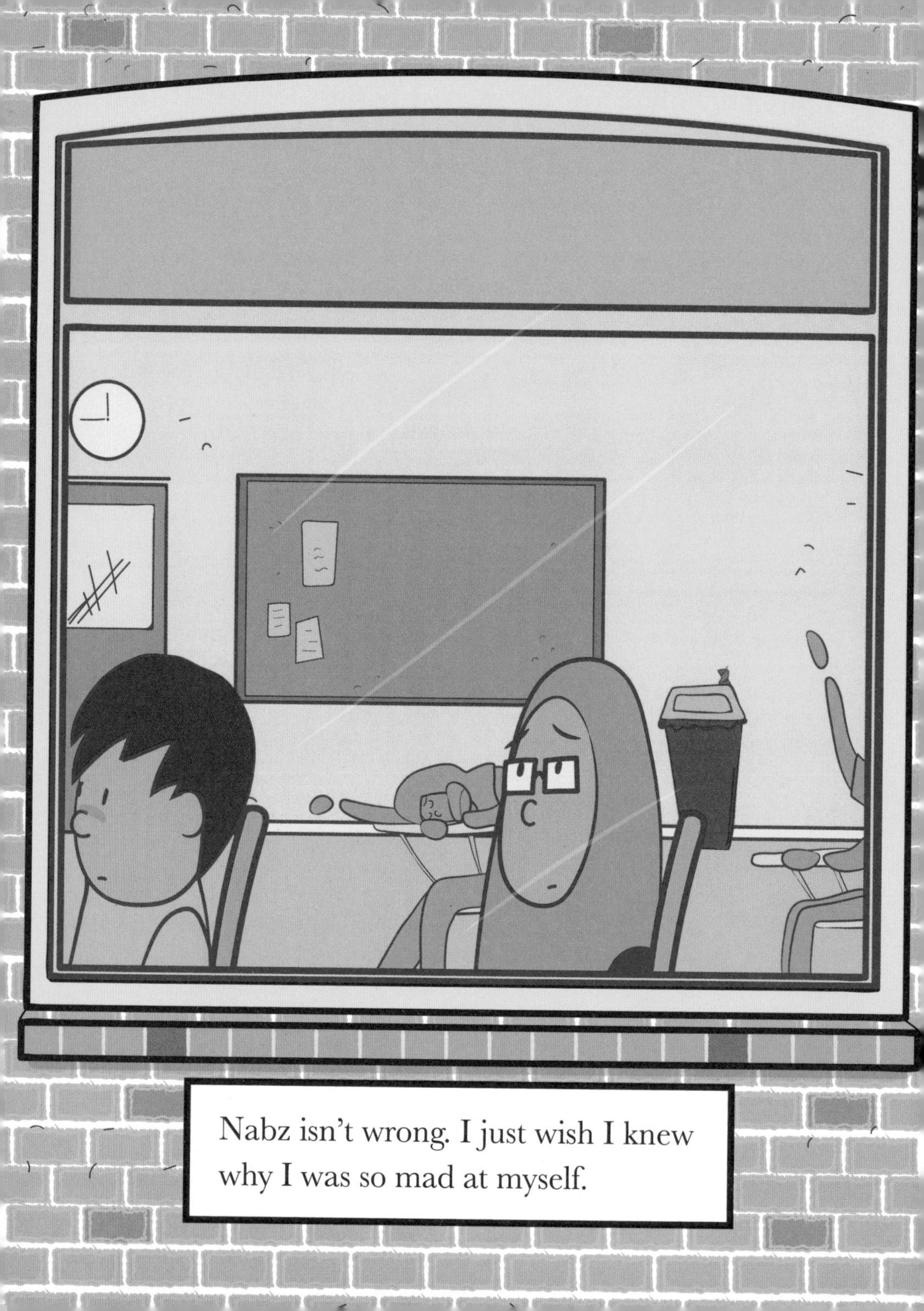
Nabz isn't wrong. I just wish I knew why I was so mad at myself.

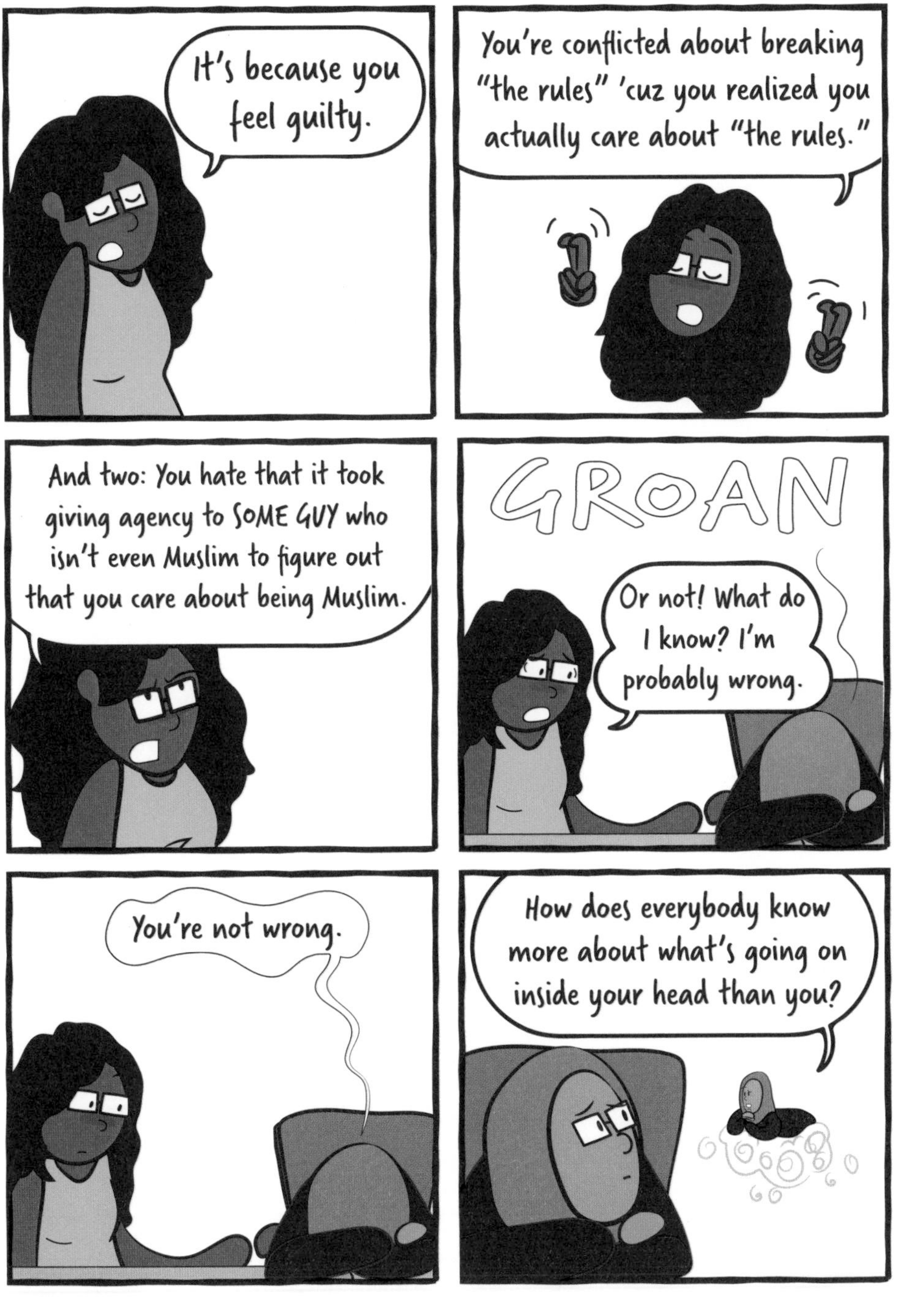
It's because you feel guilty.
You're conflicted about breaking "the rules" 'cuz you realized you actually care about "the rules."
And two: You hate that it took giving agency to SOME GUY who isn't even Muslim to figure out that you care about being Muslim.
GROAN
Or not! What do I know? I'm probably wrong.
You're not wrong.
How does everybody know more about what's going on inside your head than you?

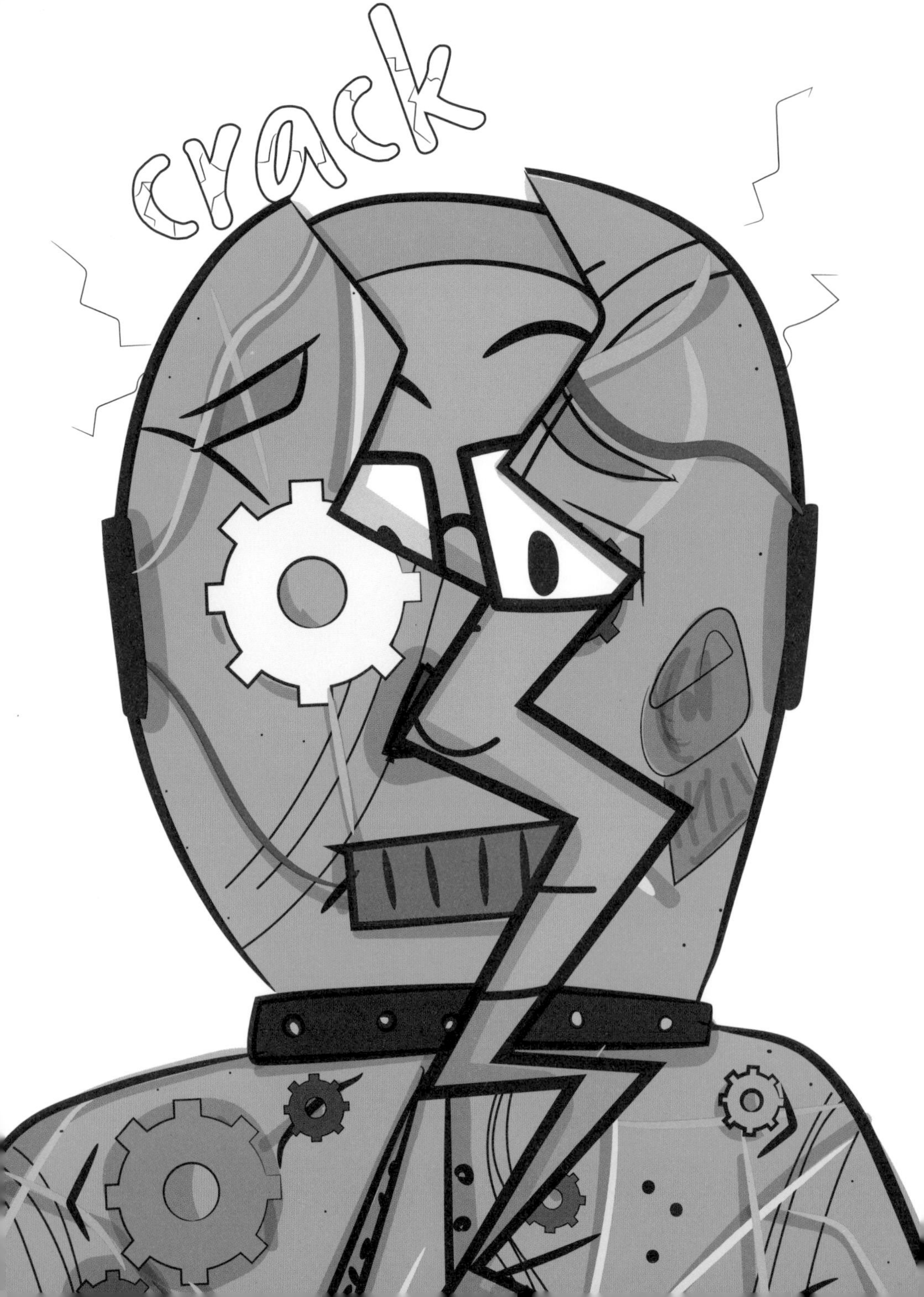
crack

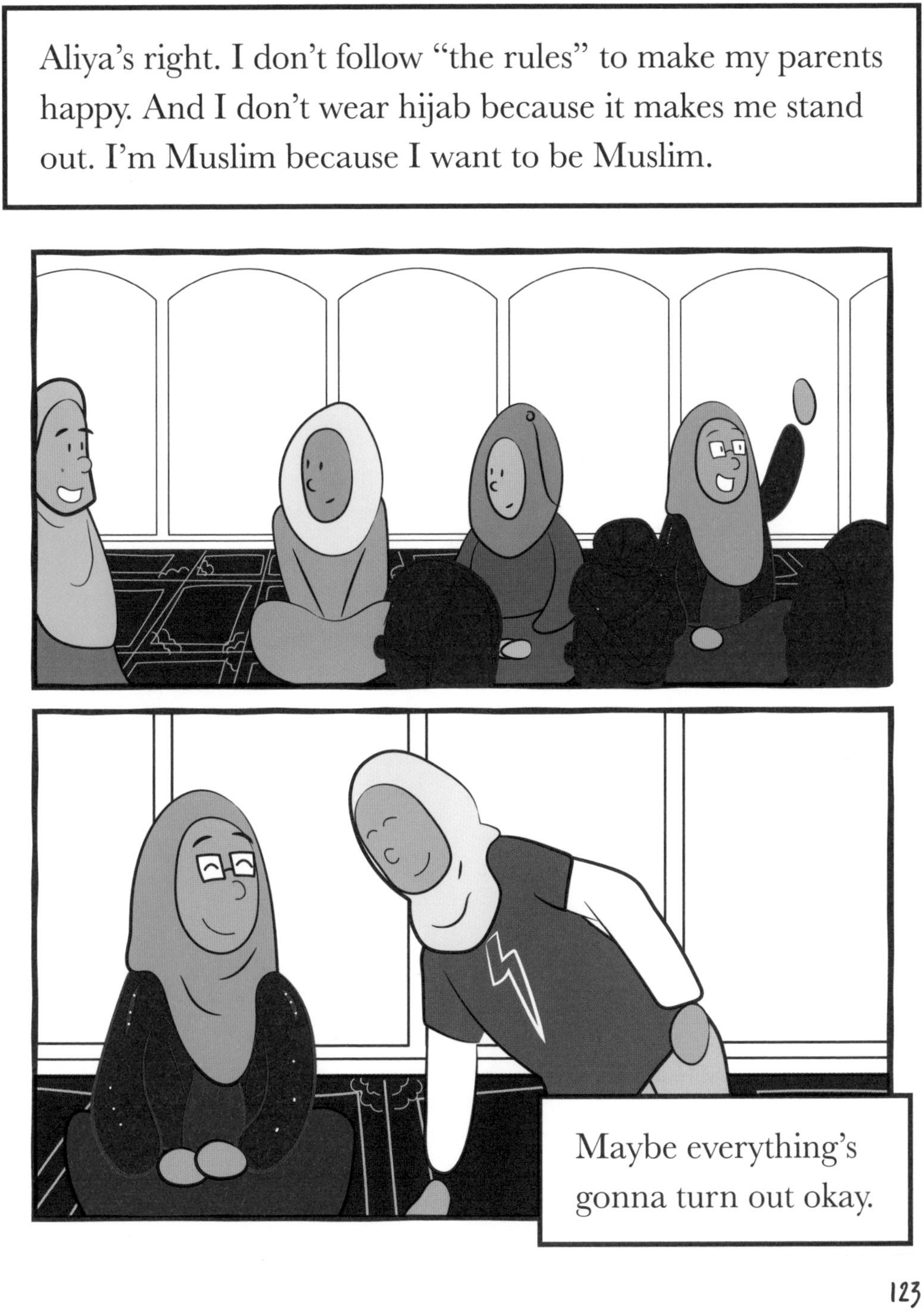
Aliya's right. I don't follow "the rules" to make my parents happy. And I don't wear hijab because it makes me stand out. I'm Muslim because I want to be Muslim.
Maybe everything's gonna turn out okay.

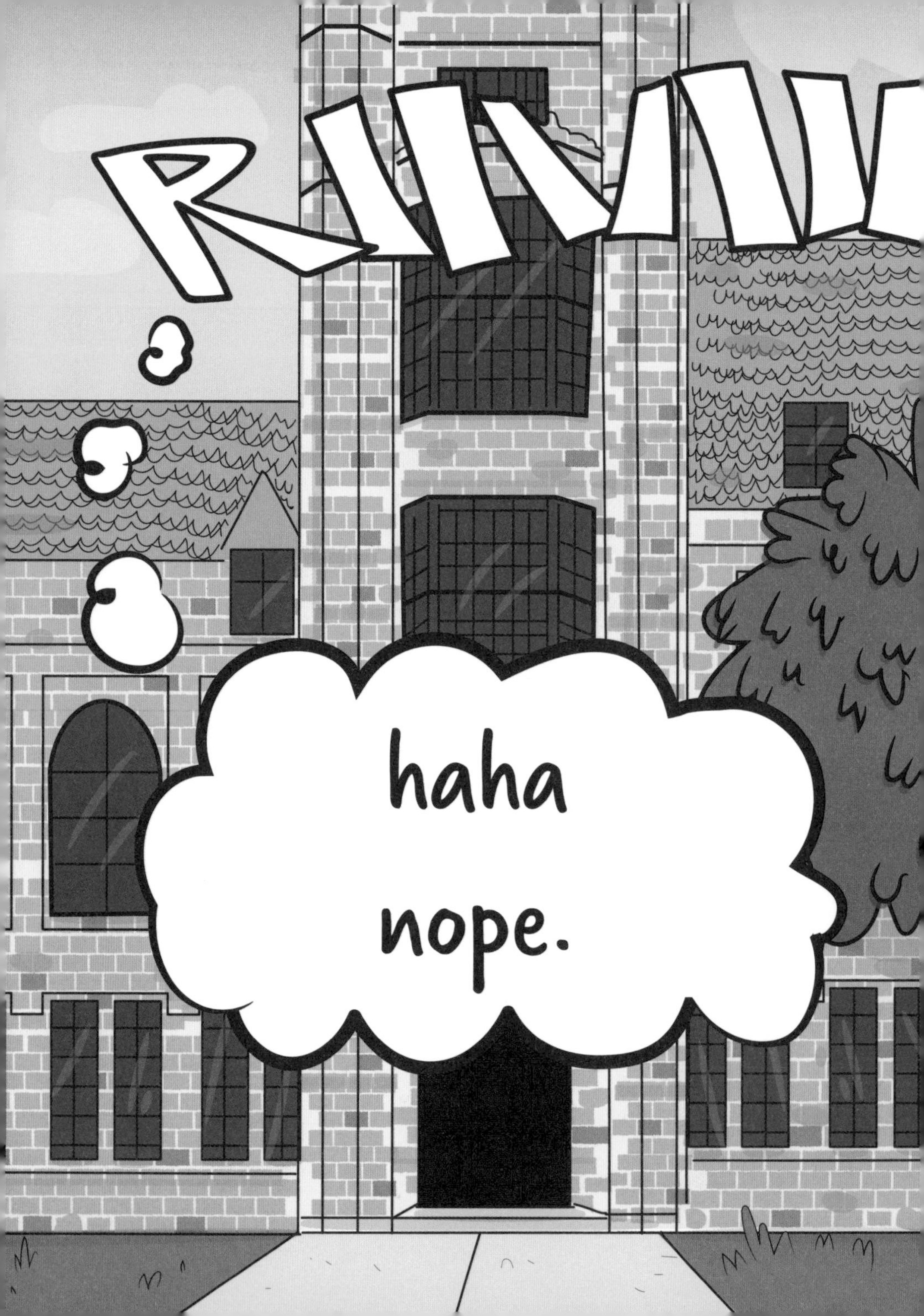
haha
nope.

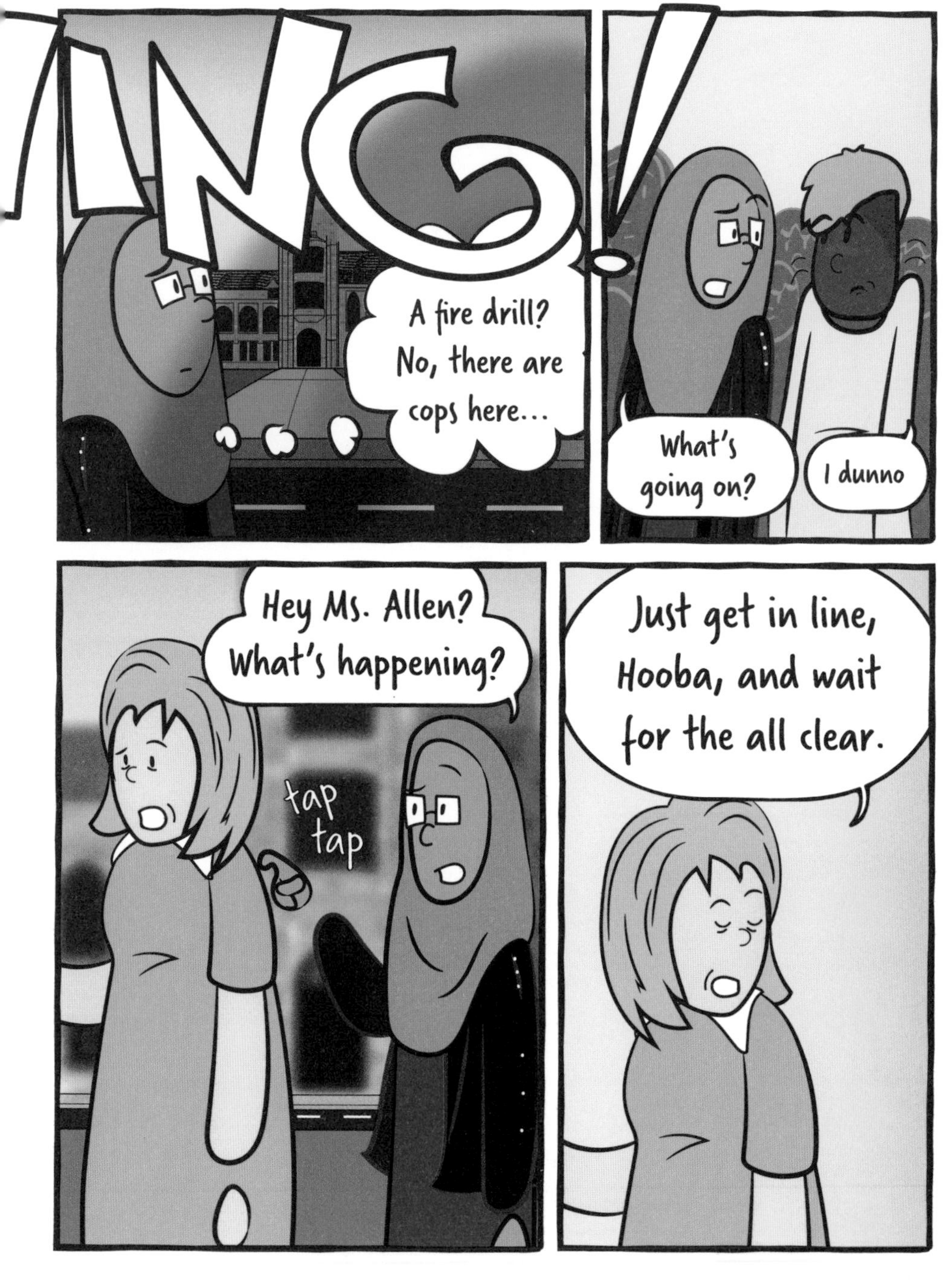
ING!
A fire drill? No, there are cops here...
What's going on?
I dunno
Hey Ms. Allen? What's happening?
tap tap
Just get in line, Hooba, and wait for the all clear.

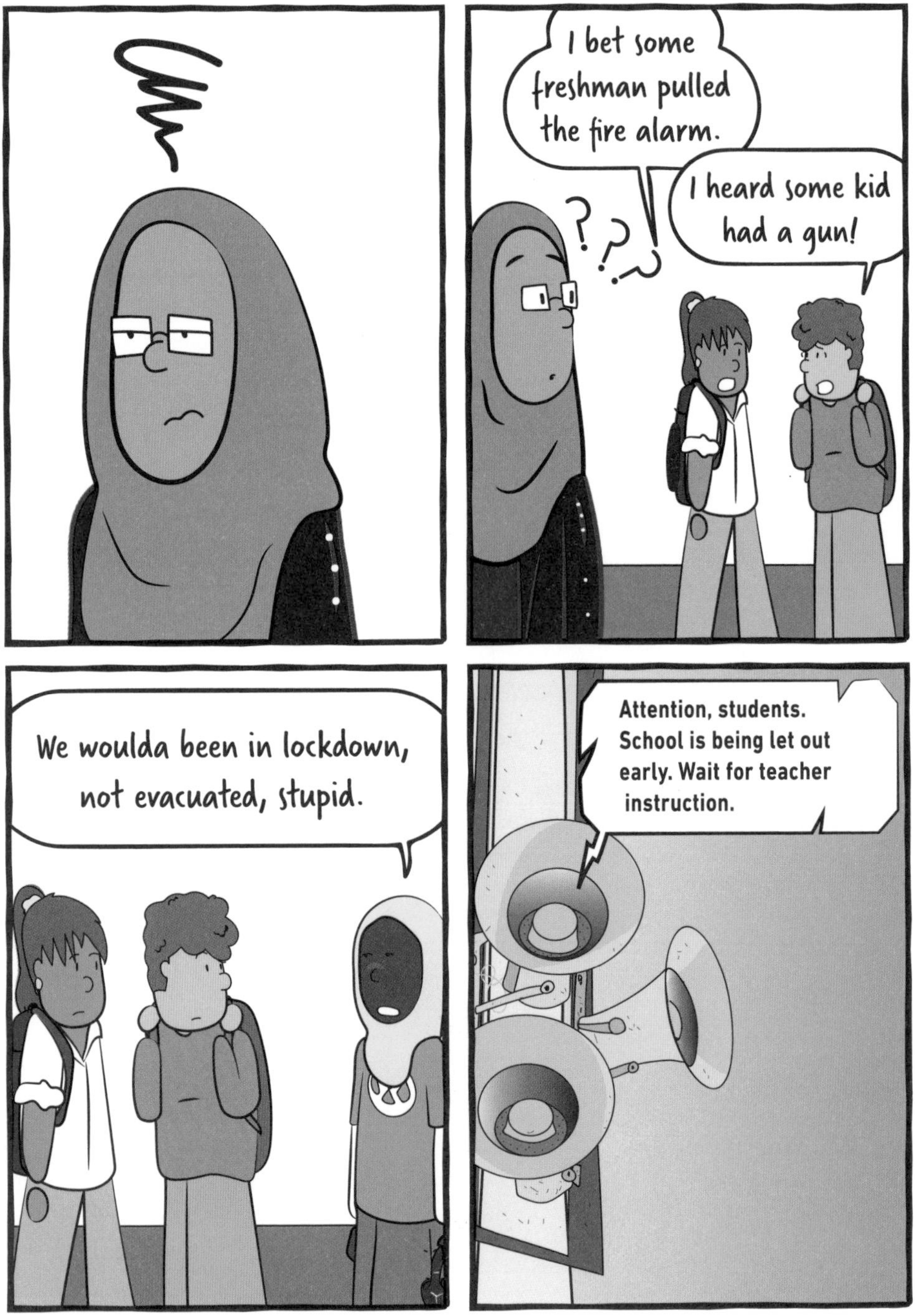
I bet some freshman pulled the fire alarm.
I heard some kid had a gun!
We woulda been in lockdown, not evacuated, stupid.
Attention, students. School is being let out early. Wait for teacher instruction.

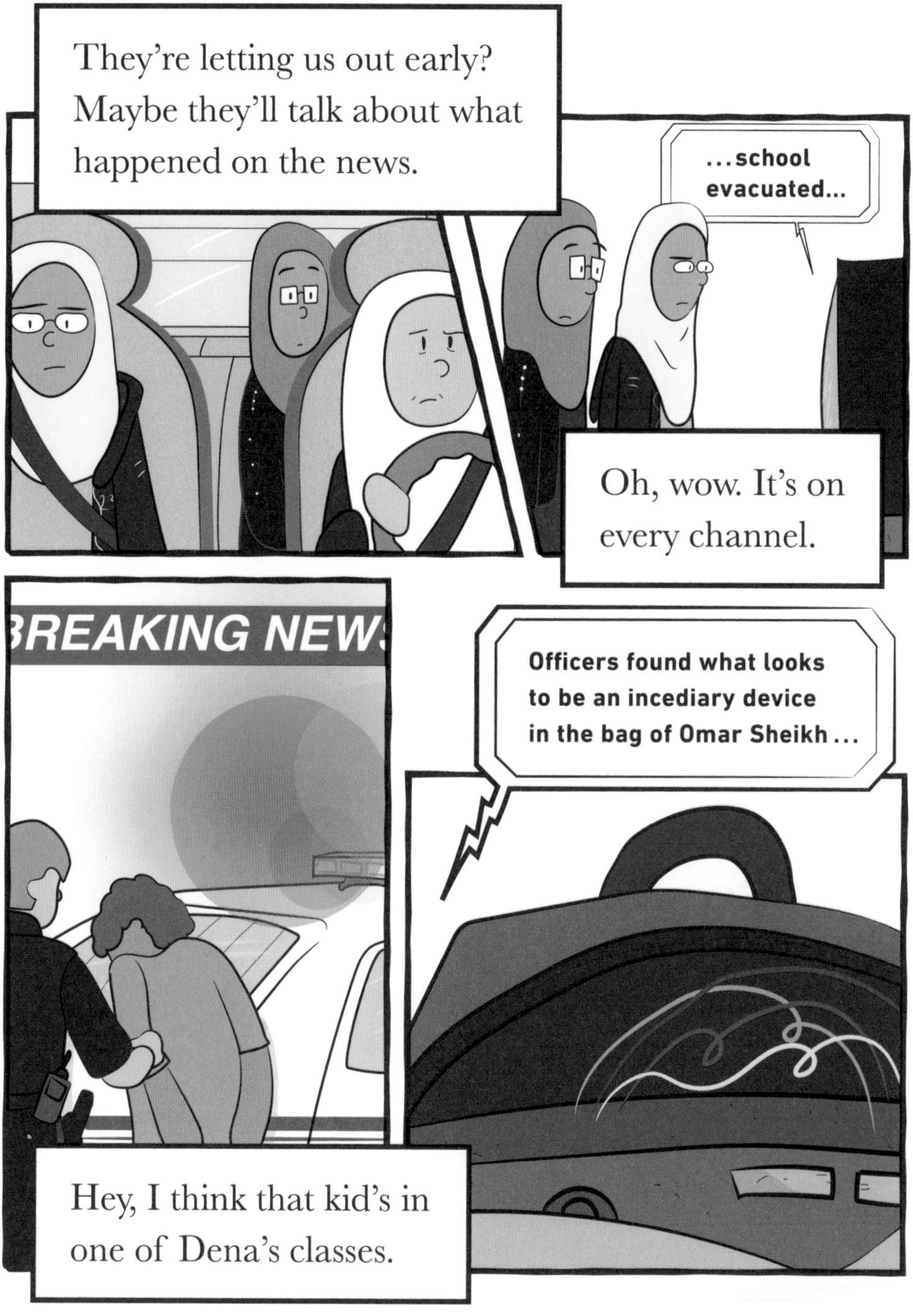

They're letting us out early? Maybe they'll talk about what happened on the news.
...school evacuated...
Oh, wow. It's on every channel.
BREAKING NEWS
Officers found what looks to be an incediary device in the bag of Omar Sheikh...
Hey, I think that kid's in one of Dena's classes.

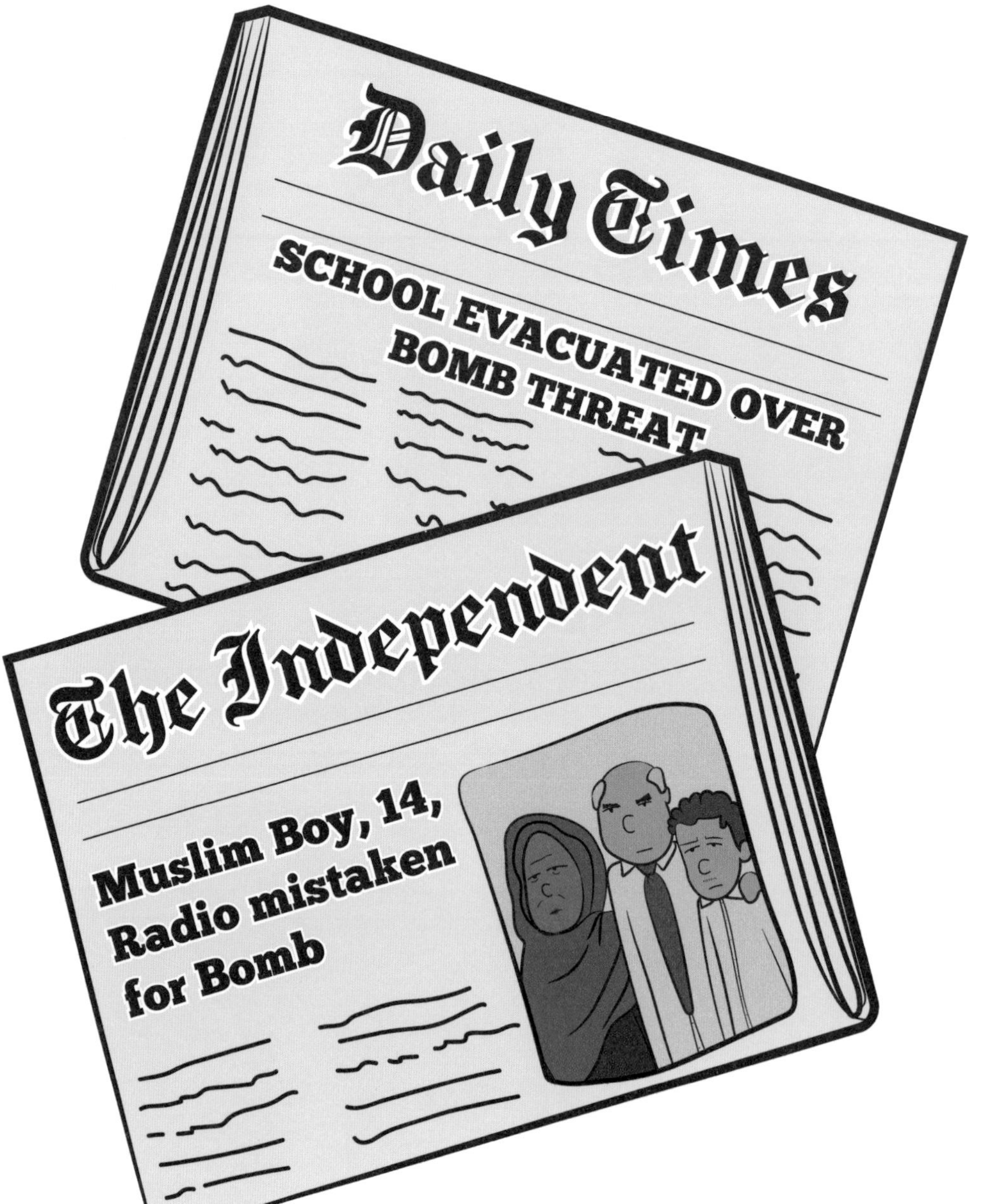
Daily Times
SCHOOL EVACUATED OVER BOMB THREAT
The Independent
Muslim Boy, 14, Radio mistaken for Bomb

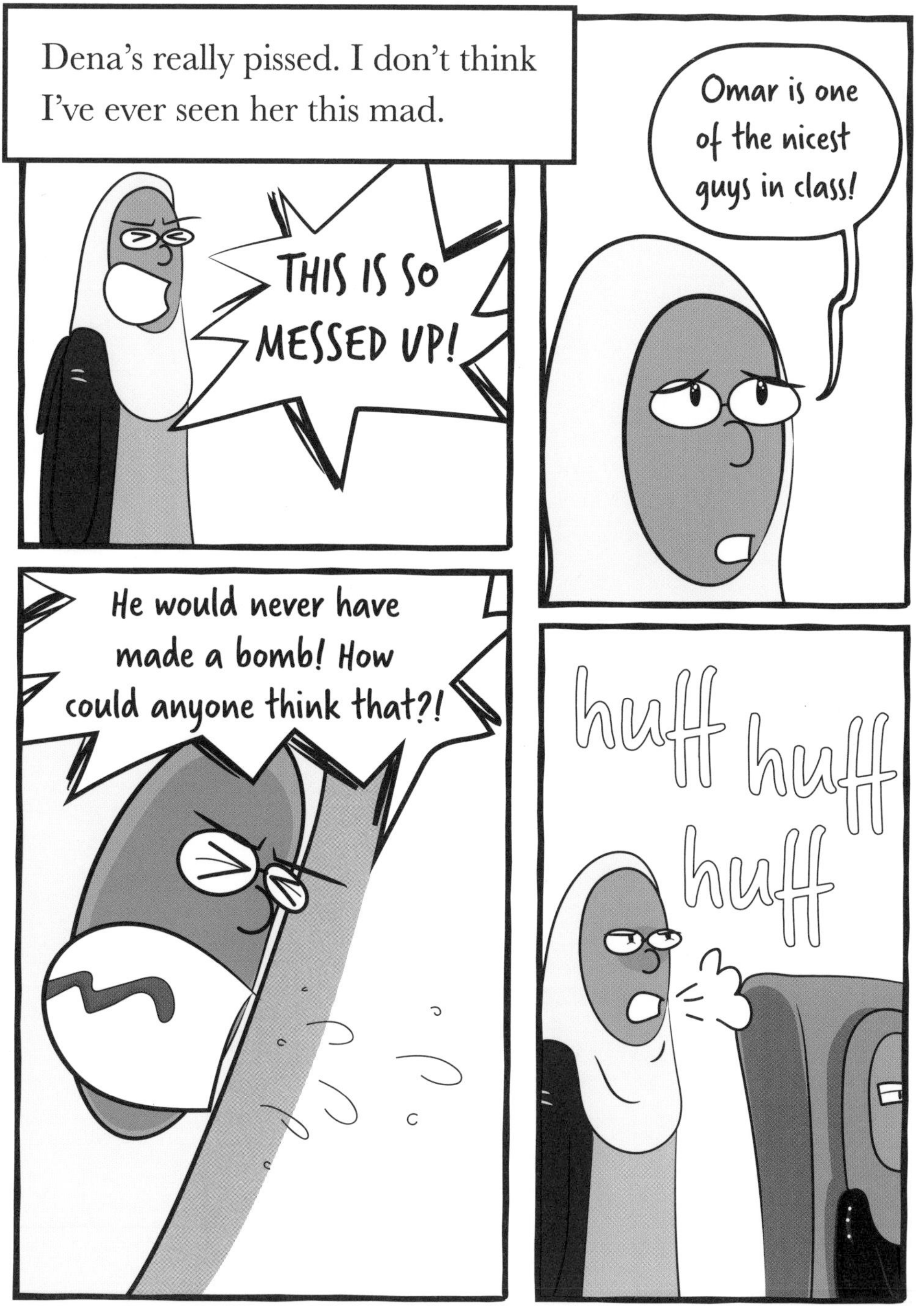
Dena's really pissed. I don't think I've ever seen her this mad.
THIS IS SO MESSED UP!
Omar is one of the nicest guys in class!
He would never have made a bomb! How could anyone think that?!
huff huff huff

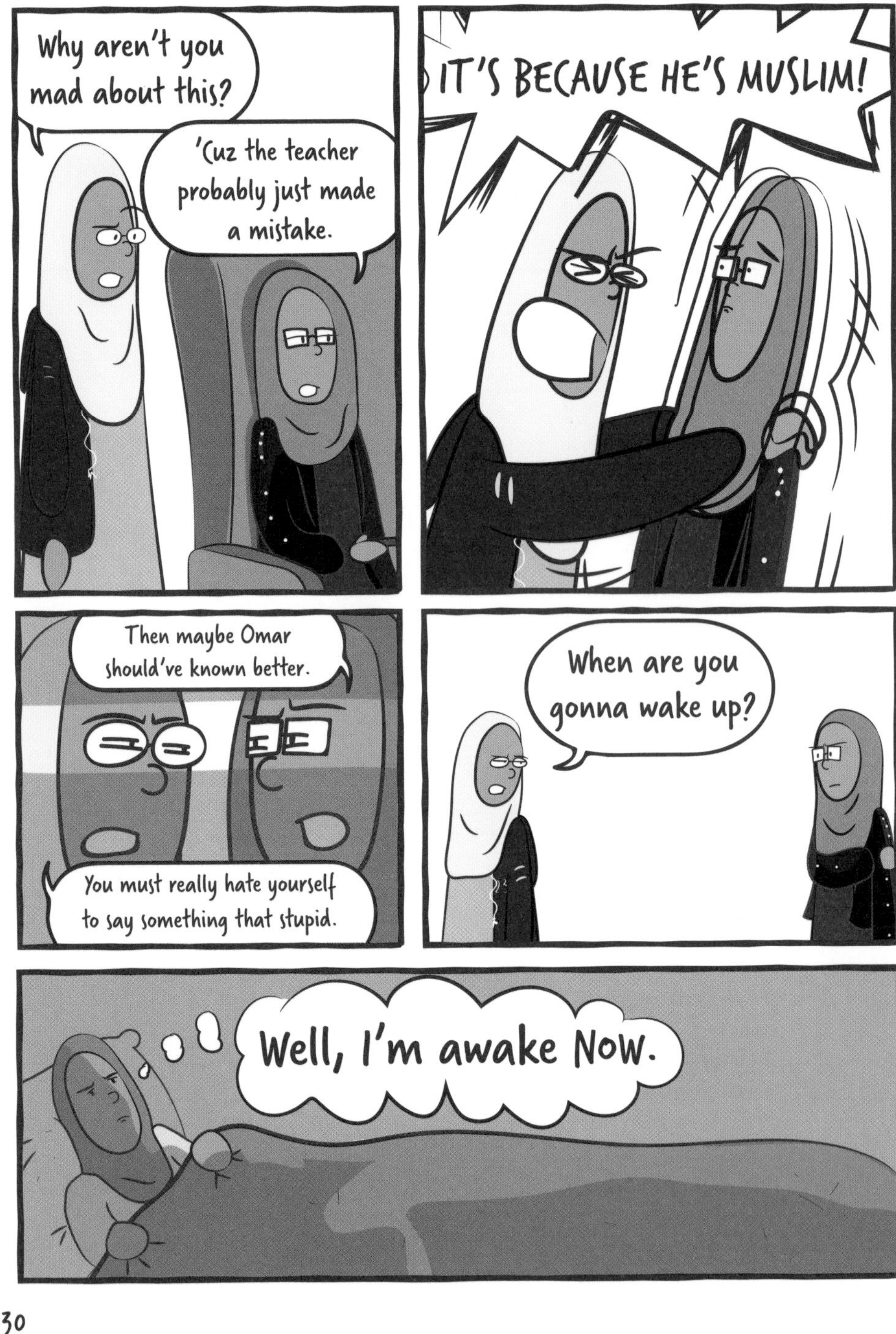
Why aren't you mad about this?
'Cuz the teacher probably just made a mistake.
IT'S BECAUSE HE'S MUSLIM!
Then maybe Omar should've known better.
You must really hate yourself to say something that stupid.
When are you gonna wake up?
Well, I'm awake Now.

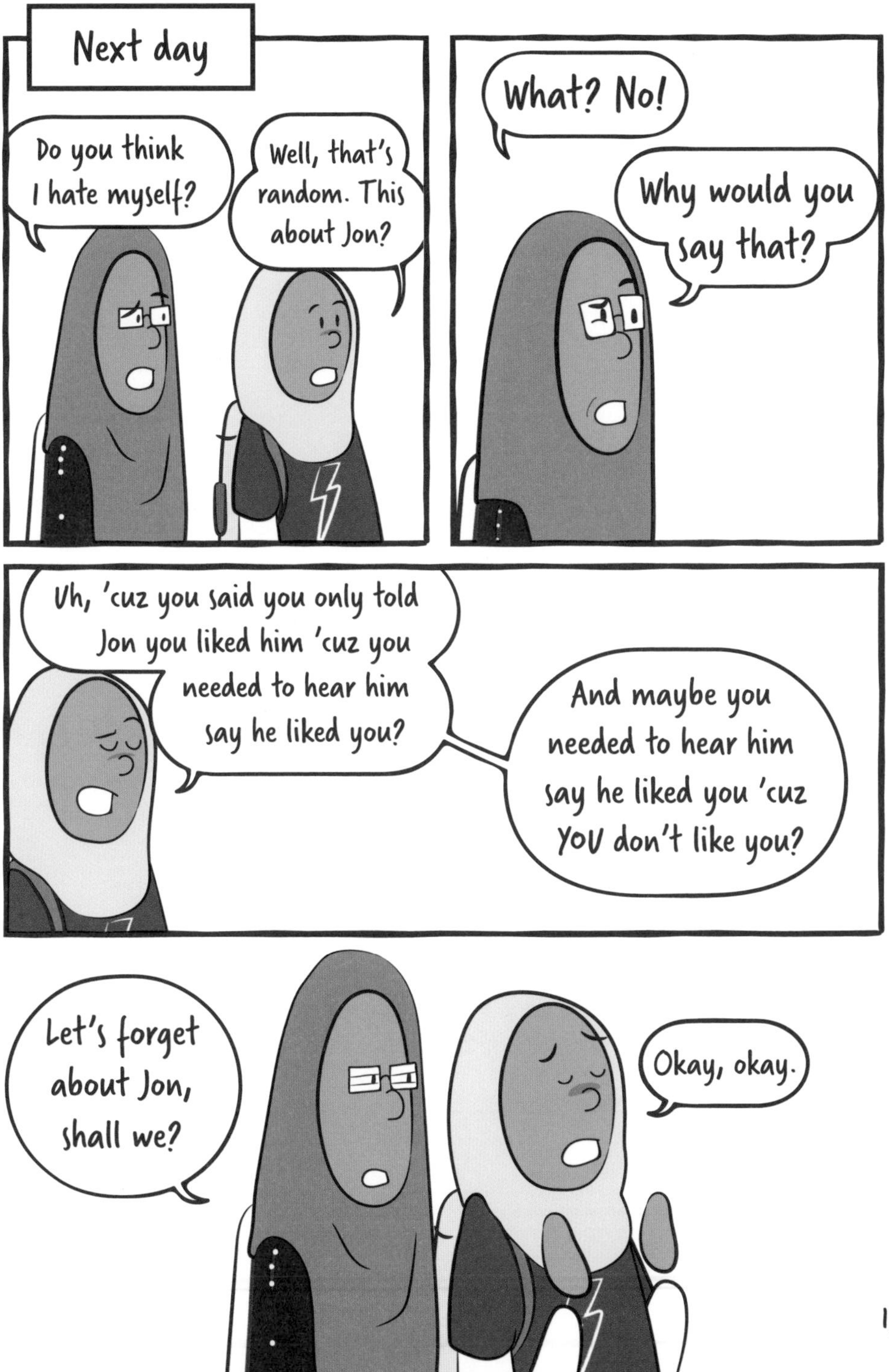
Next day
Do you think I hate myself?
Well, that's random. This about Jon?
What? No!
Why would you say that?
Uh, 'cuz you said you only told Jon you liked him 'cuz you needed to hear him say he liked you?
And maybe you needed to hear him say he liked you 'cuz YOU don't like you?
Let's forget about Jon, shall we?
Okay, okay.

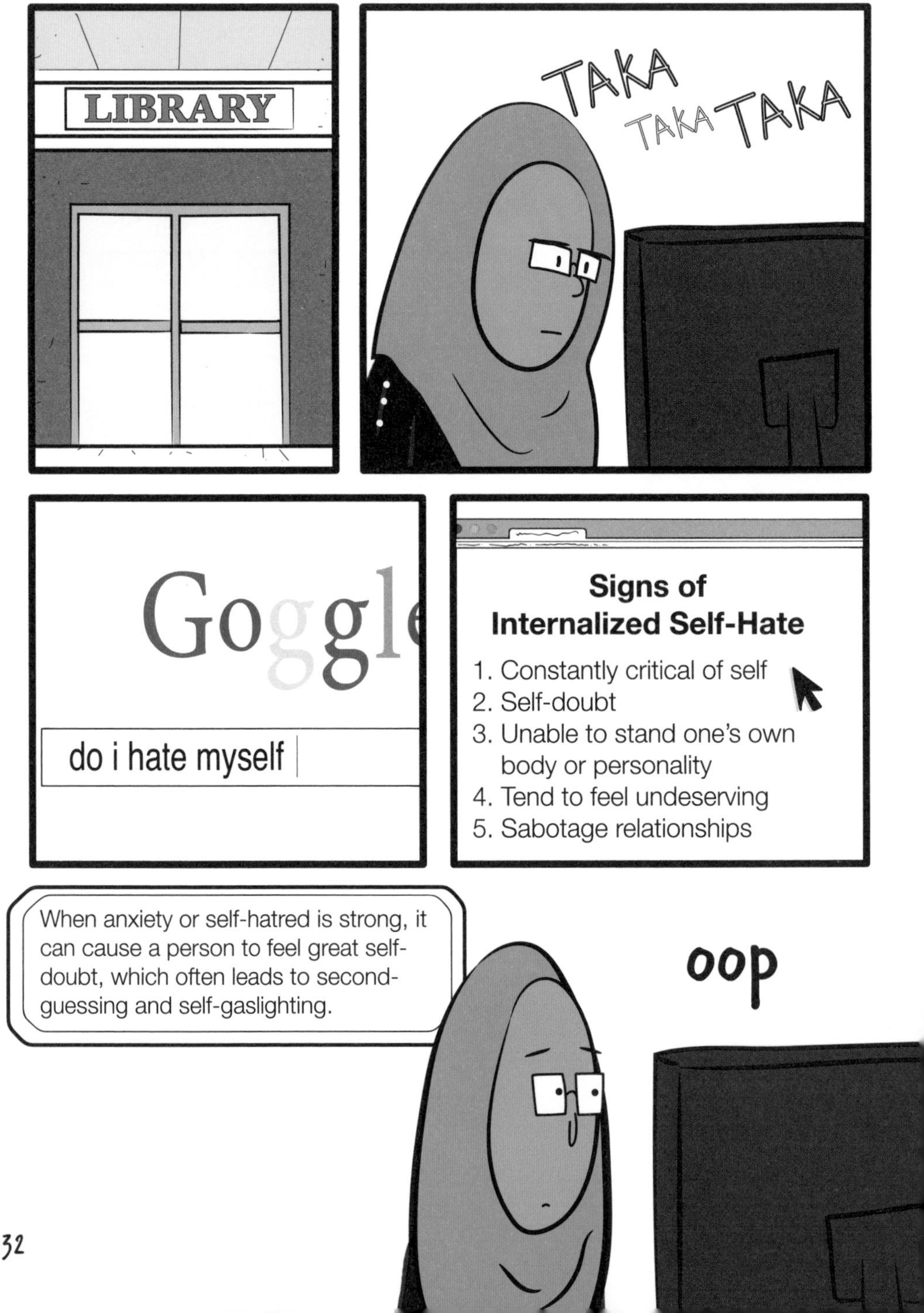
LIBRARY
TAKA TAKA TAKA
Goggle
do i hate myself
Signs of Internalized Self-Hate
1. Constantly critical of self
2. Self-doubt
3. Unable to stand one's own body or personality
4. Tend to feel undeserving
5. Sabotage relationships
When anxiety or self-hatred is strong, it can cause a person to feel great self-doubt, which often leads to second-guessing and self-gaslighting.
oop

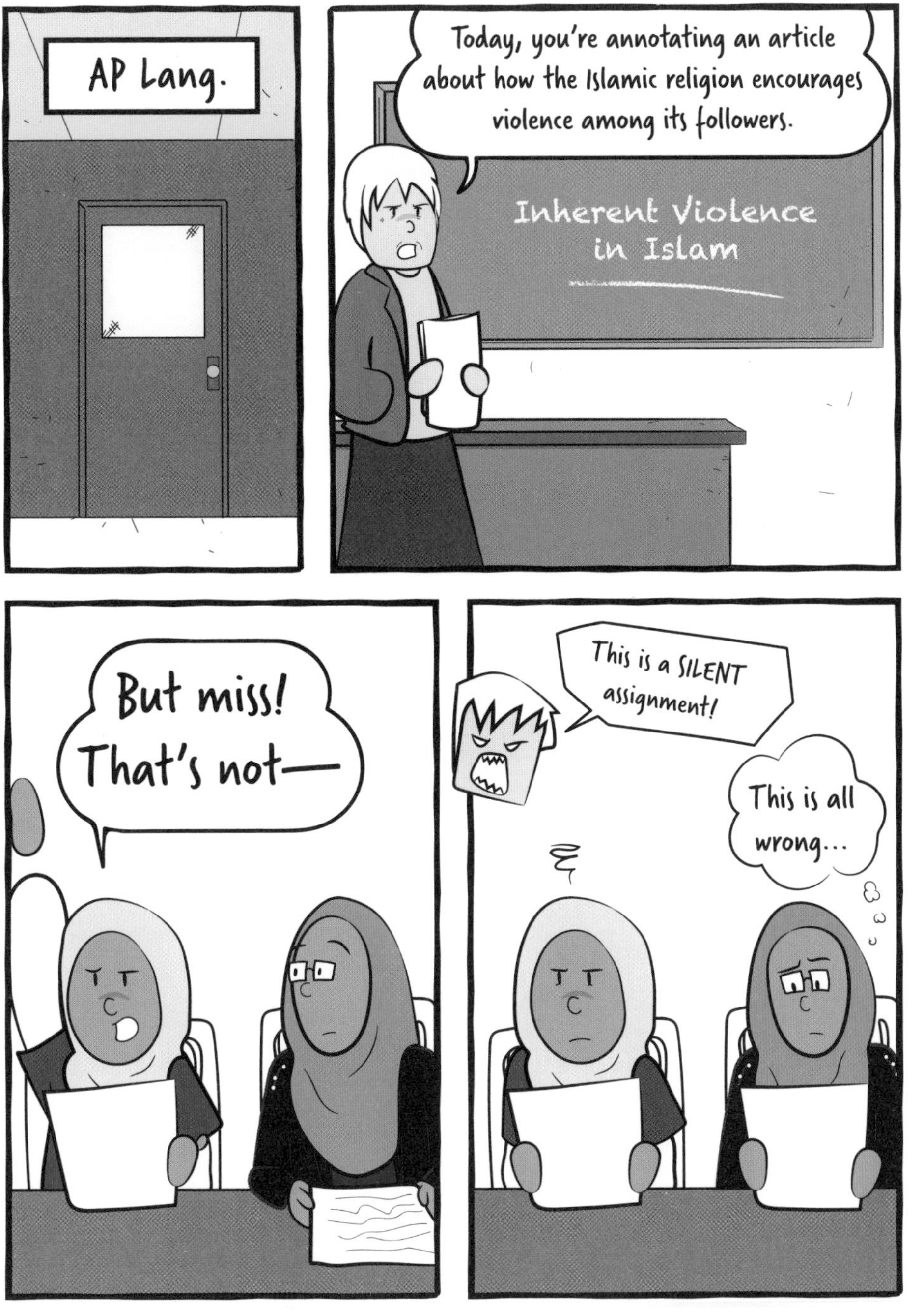
AP Lang.
Today, you're annotating an article about how the Islamic religion encourages violence among its followers.
Inherent Violence in Islam
But miss! That's not—
This is a SILENT assignment!
This is all wrong...

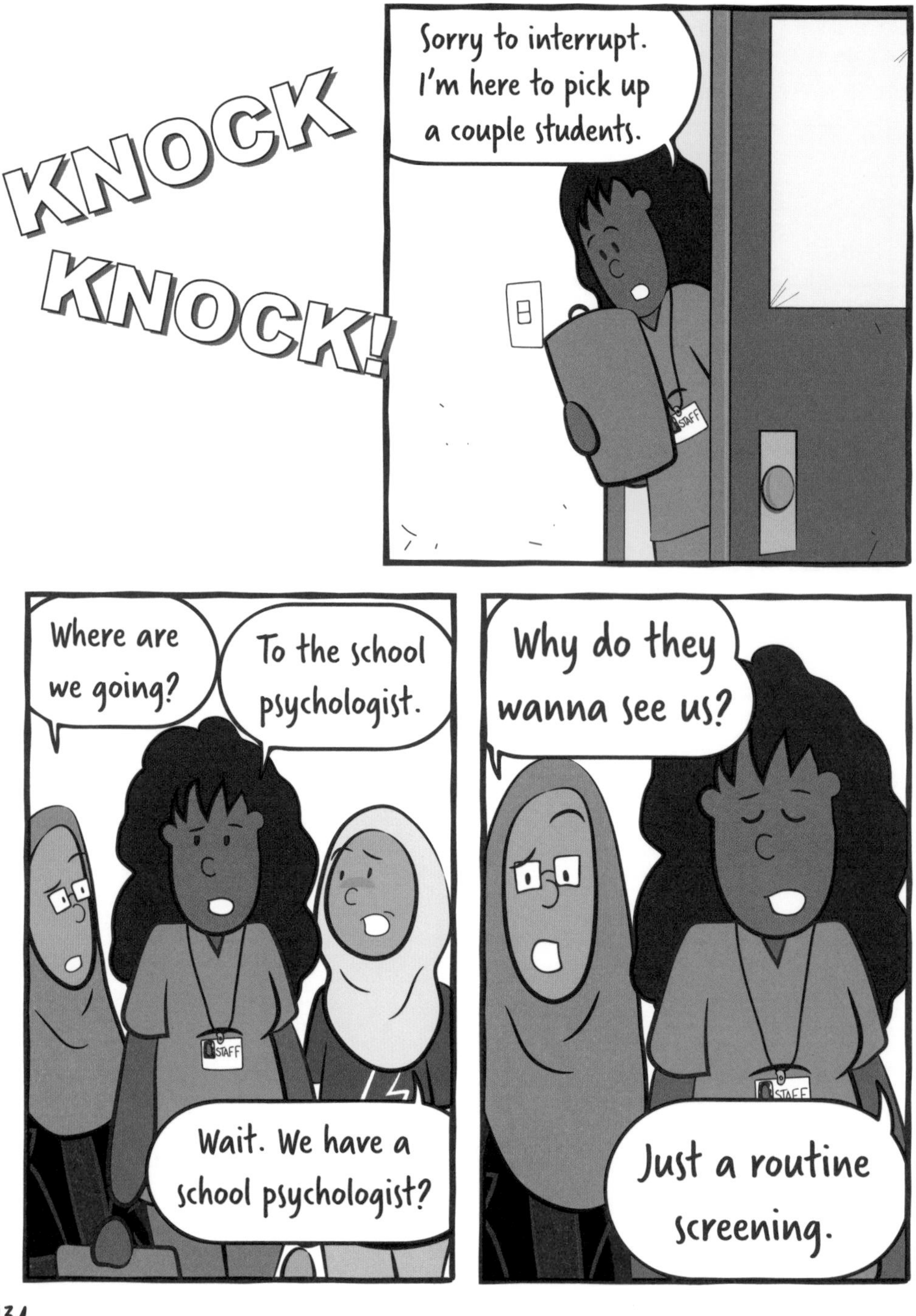
KNOCK
KNOCK!
Sorry to interrupt. I'm here to pick up a couple students.
STAFF
Where are we going?
To the school psychologist.
STAFF
Wait. We have a school psychologist?
Why do they wanna see us?
Just a routine screening.

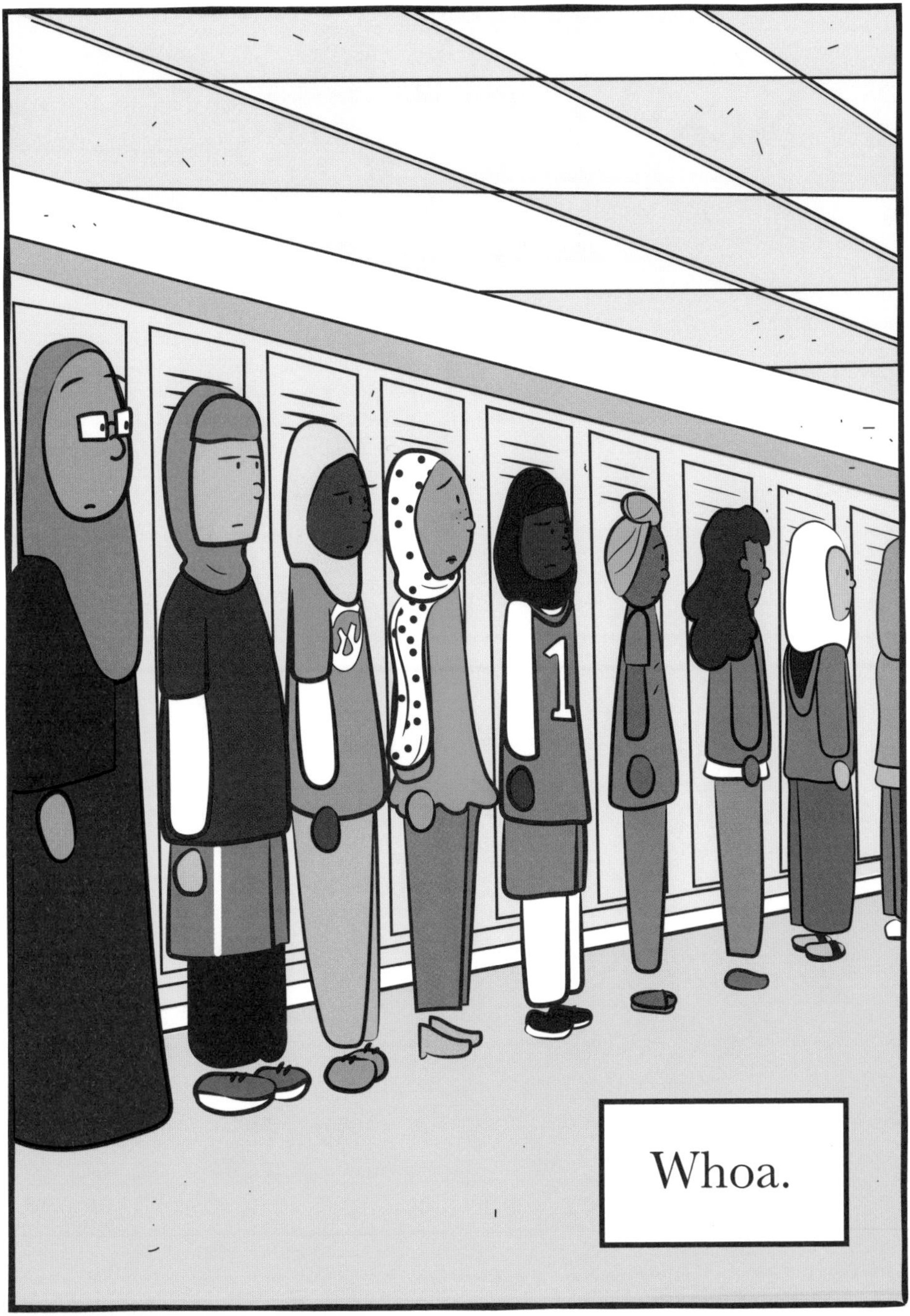
1
Whoa.

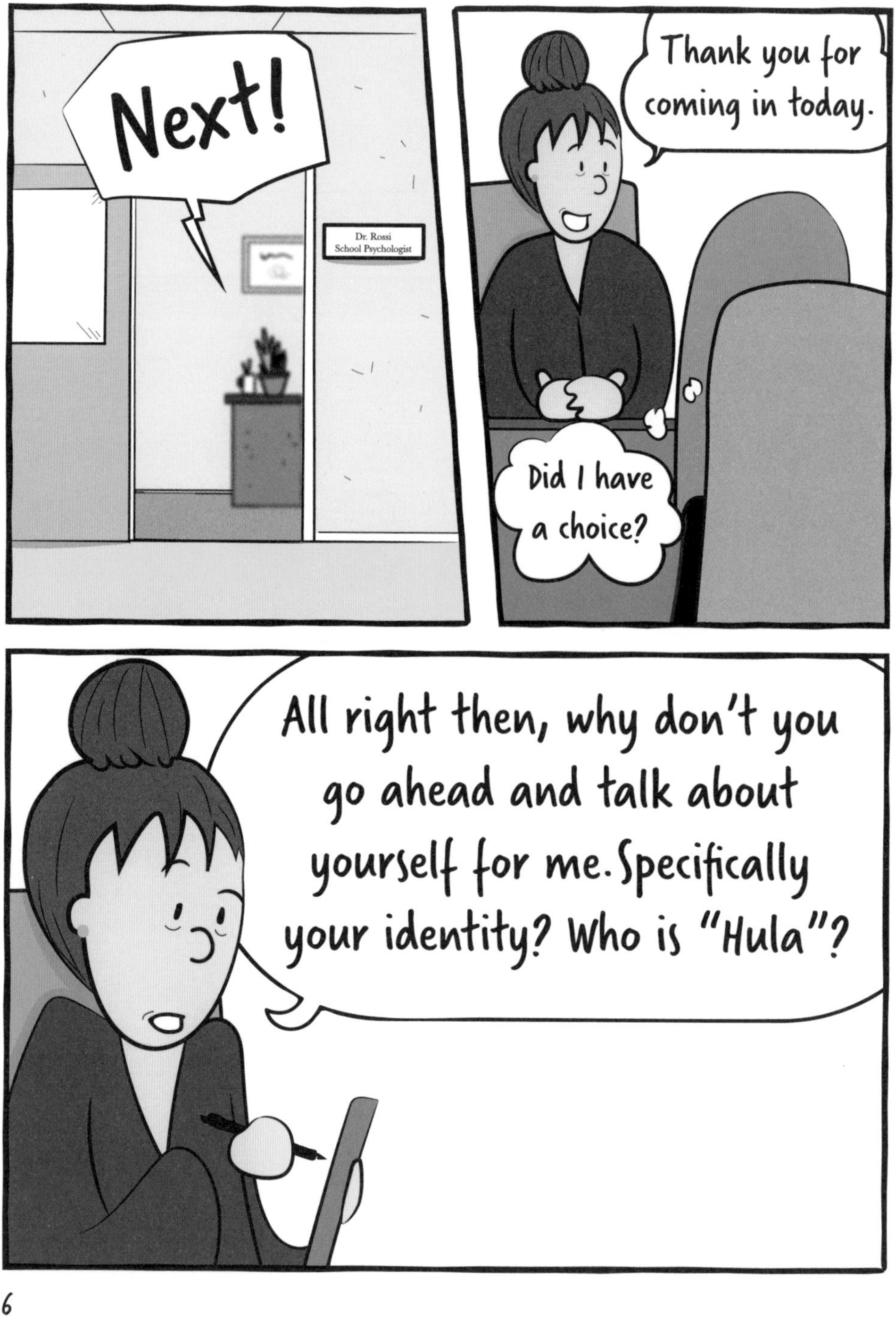
Next!
Dr. Rossi
School Psychologist
Thank you for coming in today.
Did I have a choice?
All right then, why don't you go ahead and talk about yourself for me. Specifically your identity? Who is "Hula"?

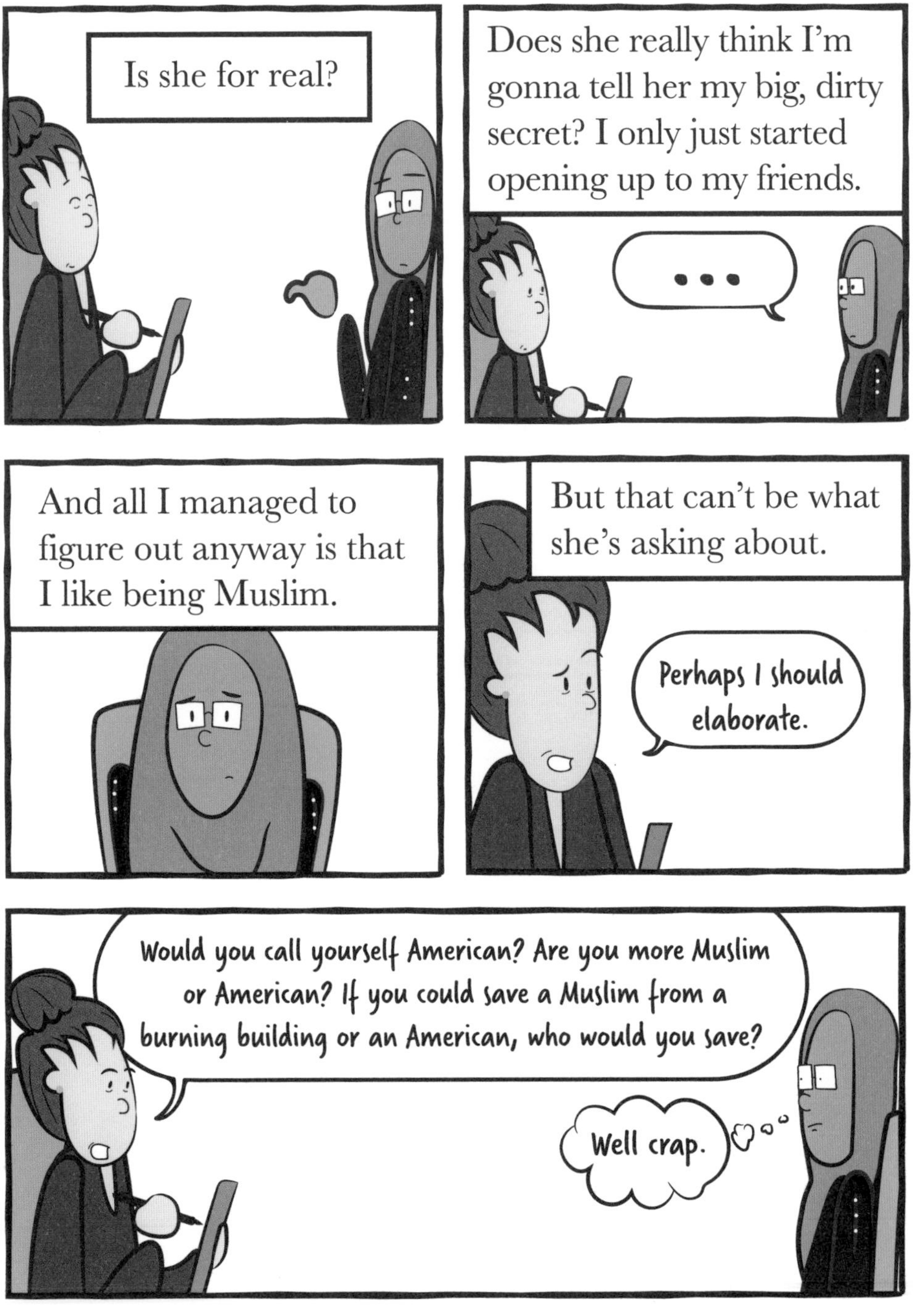
Is she for real?
Does she really think I'm gonna tell her my big, dirty secret? I only just started opening up to my friends.
...
And all I managed to figure out anyway is that I like being Muslim.
But that can't be what she's asking about.
Perhaps I should elaborate.
Would you call yourself American? Are you more Muslim or American? If you could save a Muslim from a burning building or an American, who would you save?
Well crap.

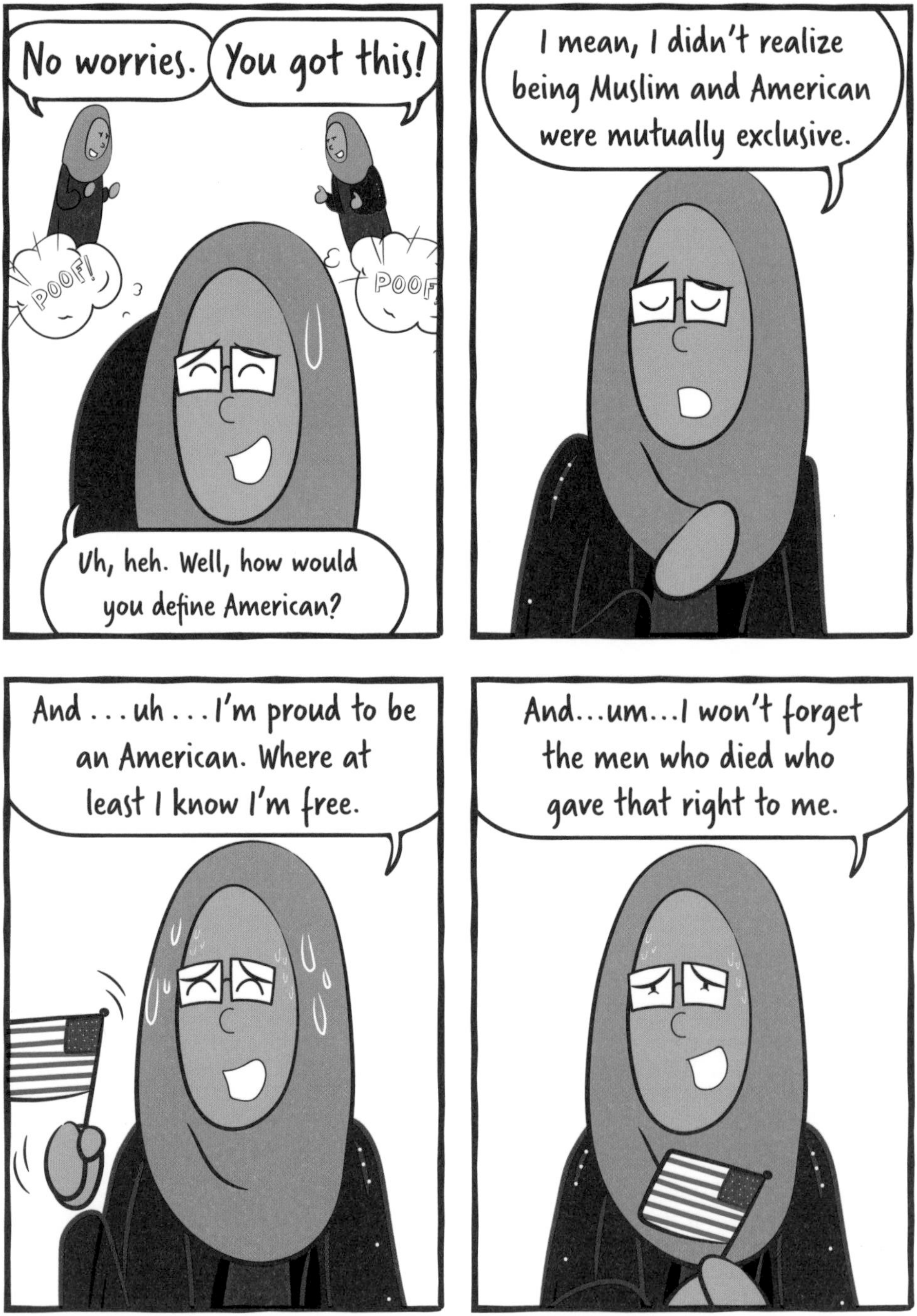
No worries.
You got this!
POOF!
POOF!
Uh, heh. Well, how would you define American?
I mean, I didn't realize being Muslim and American were mutually exclusive.
And . . . uh . . . I'm proud to be an American. Where at least I know I'm free.
And...um...I won't forget the men who died who gave that right to me.

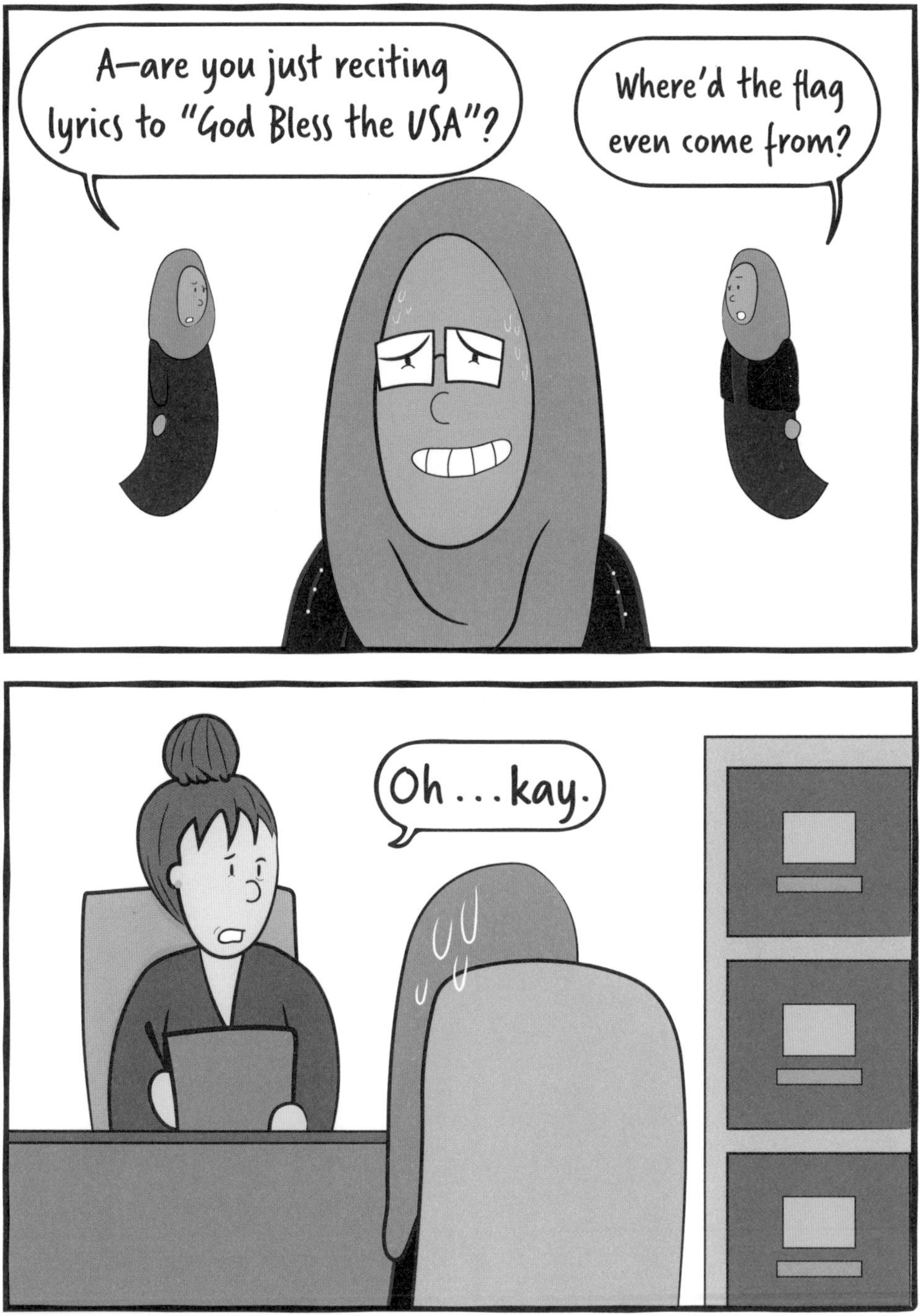
A—are you just reciting lyrics to "God Bless the USA"?
Where'd the flag even come from?
Oh . . . kay.

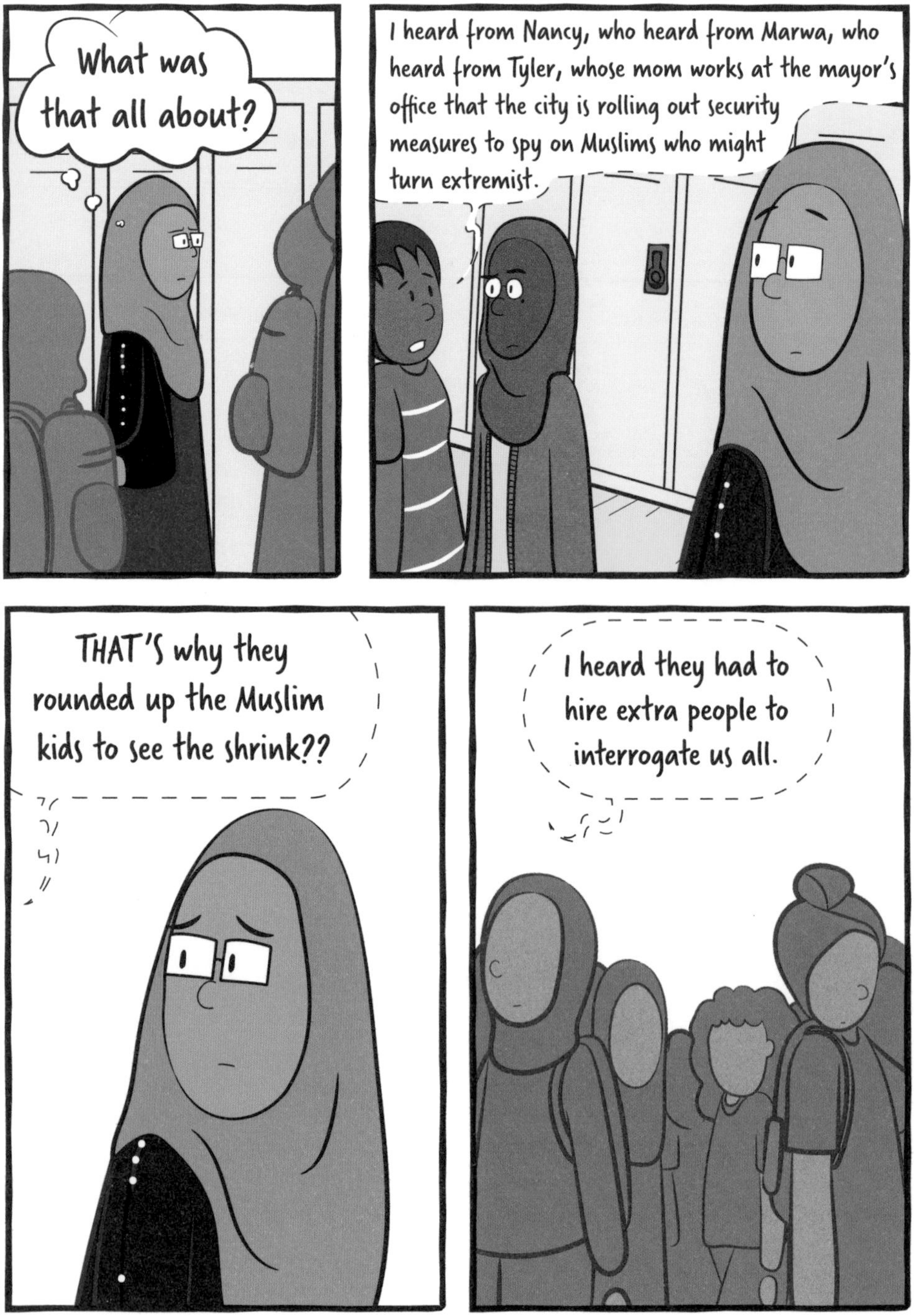
What was that all about?
I heard from Nancy, who heard from Marwa, who heard from Tyler, whose mom works at the mayor's office that the city is rolling out security measures to spy on Muslims who might turn extremist.
THAT'S why they rounded up the Muslim kids to see the shrink??
I heard they had to hire extra people to interrogate us all.

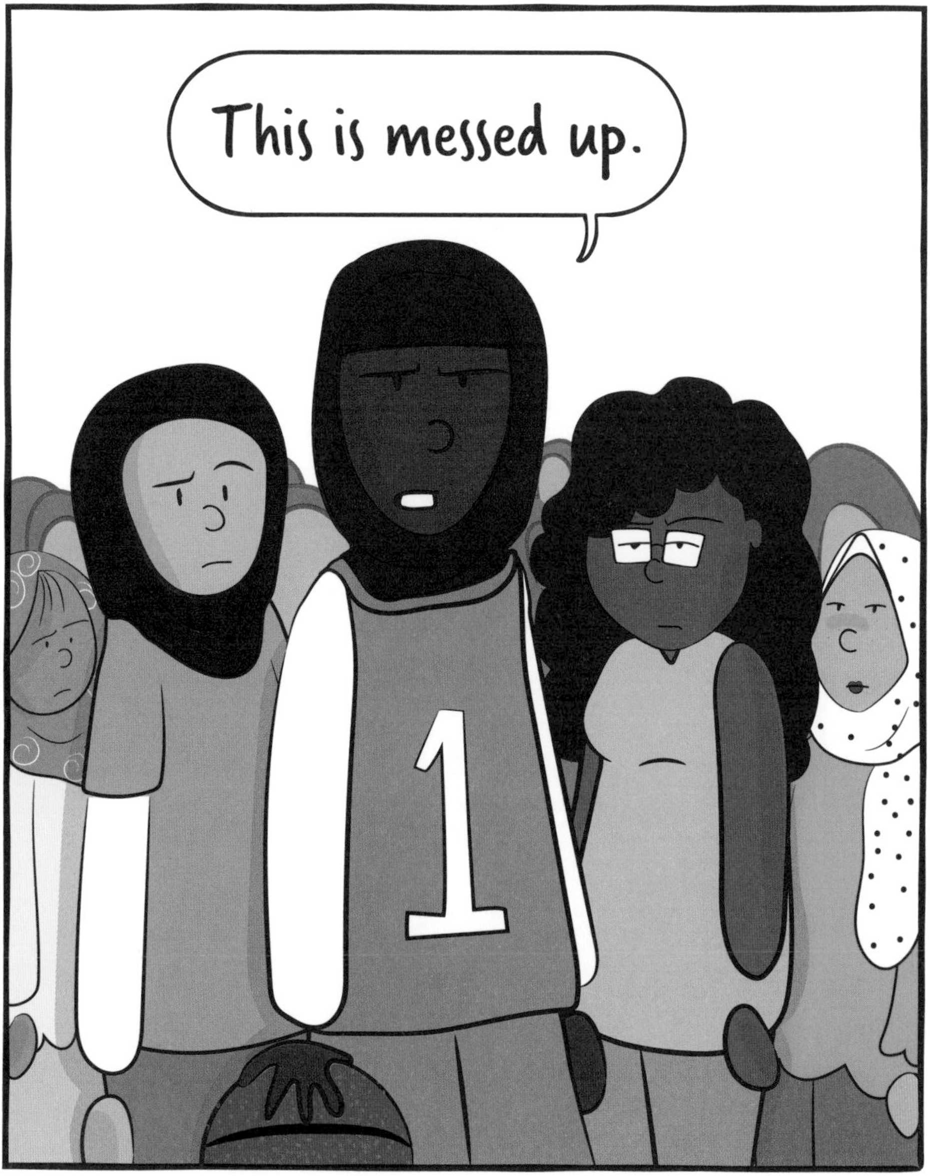
This is messed up.
1

"The Enemy"

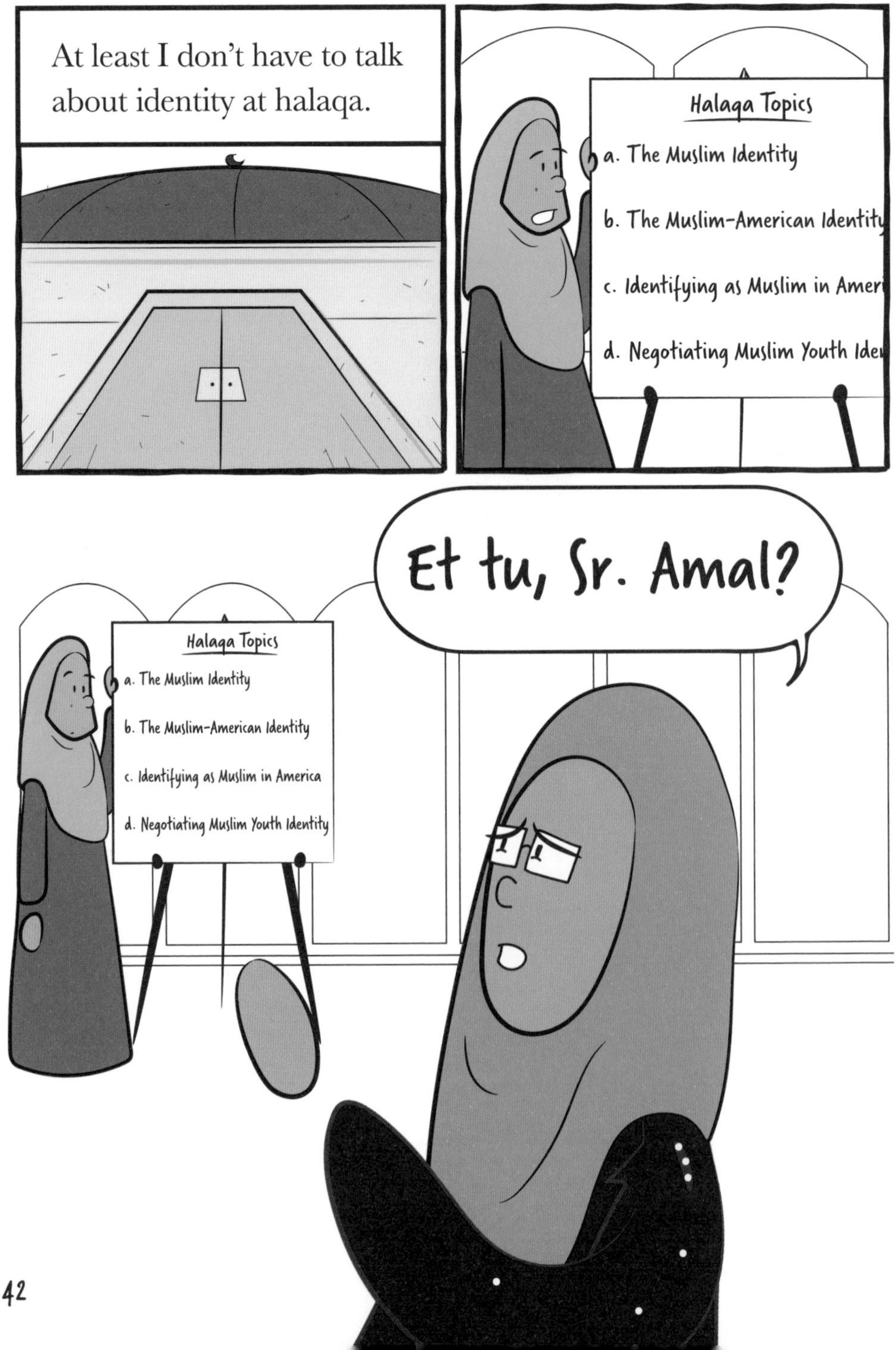
At least I don't have to talk about identity at halaqa.
Halaqa Topics
a. The Muslim Identity
b. The Muslim-American Identity
c. Identifying as Muslim in America
d. Negotiating Muslim Youth Identity
Et tu, Sr. Amal?

Huda F Is Lost

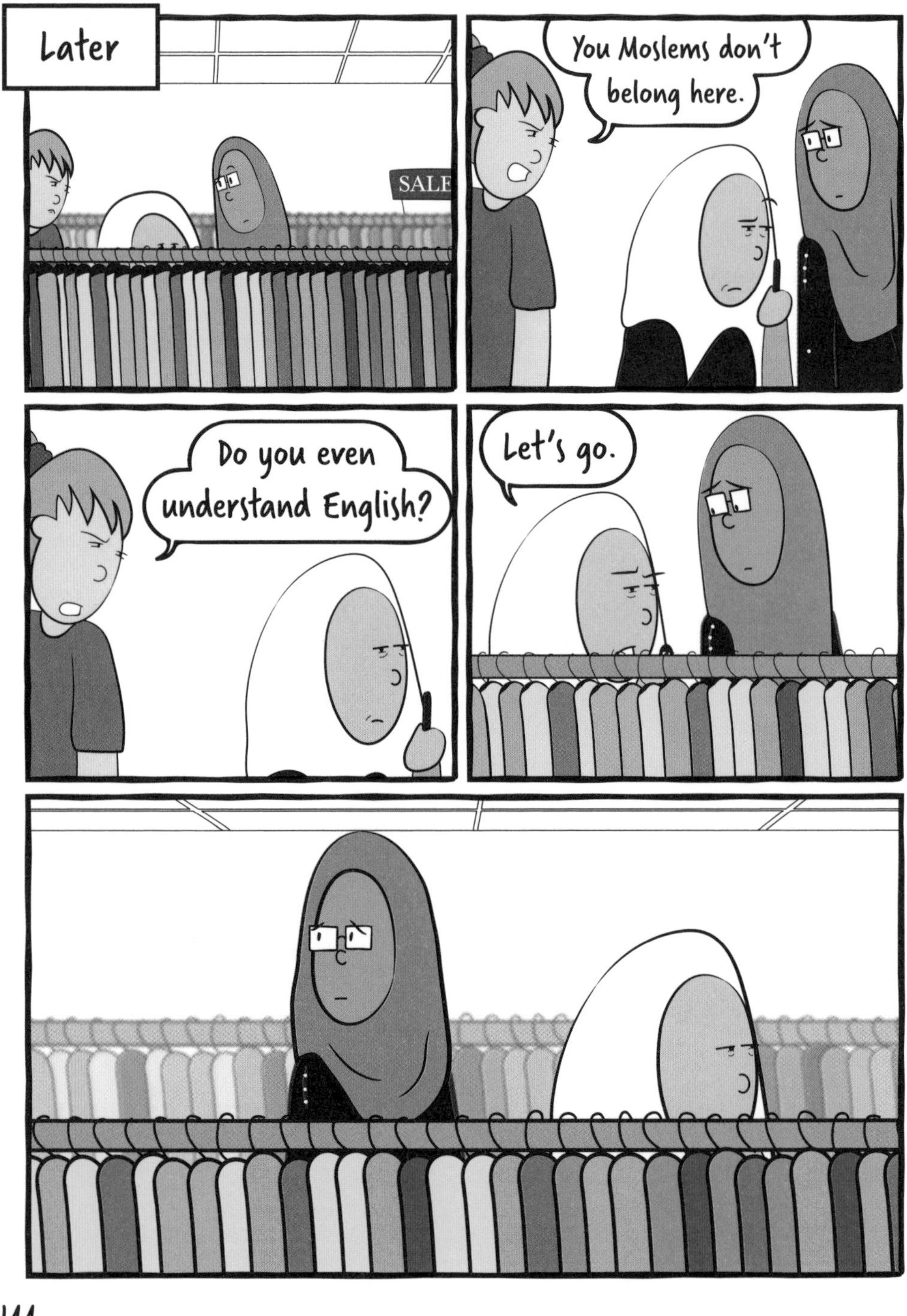
Later
SALE
You Moslems don't belong here.
Do you even understand English?
Let's go.

Did people always stare at me like this? Is it because I'm an Arab-Muslim hijab-wearing American what-ever? Was I always this tense? Did I just ignore it? I—I can't be sure.

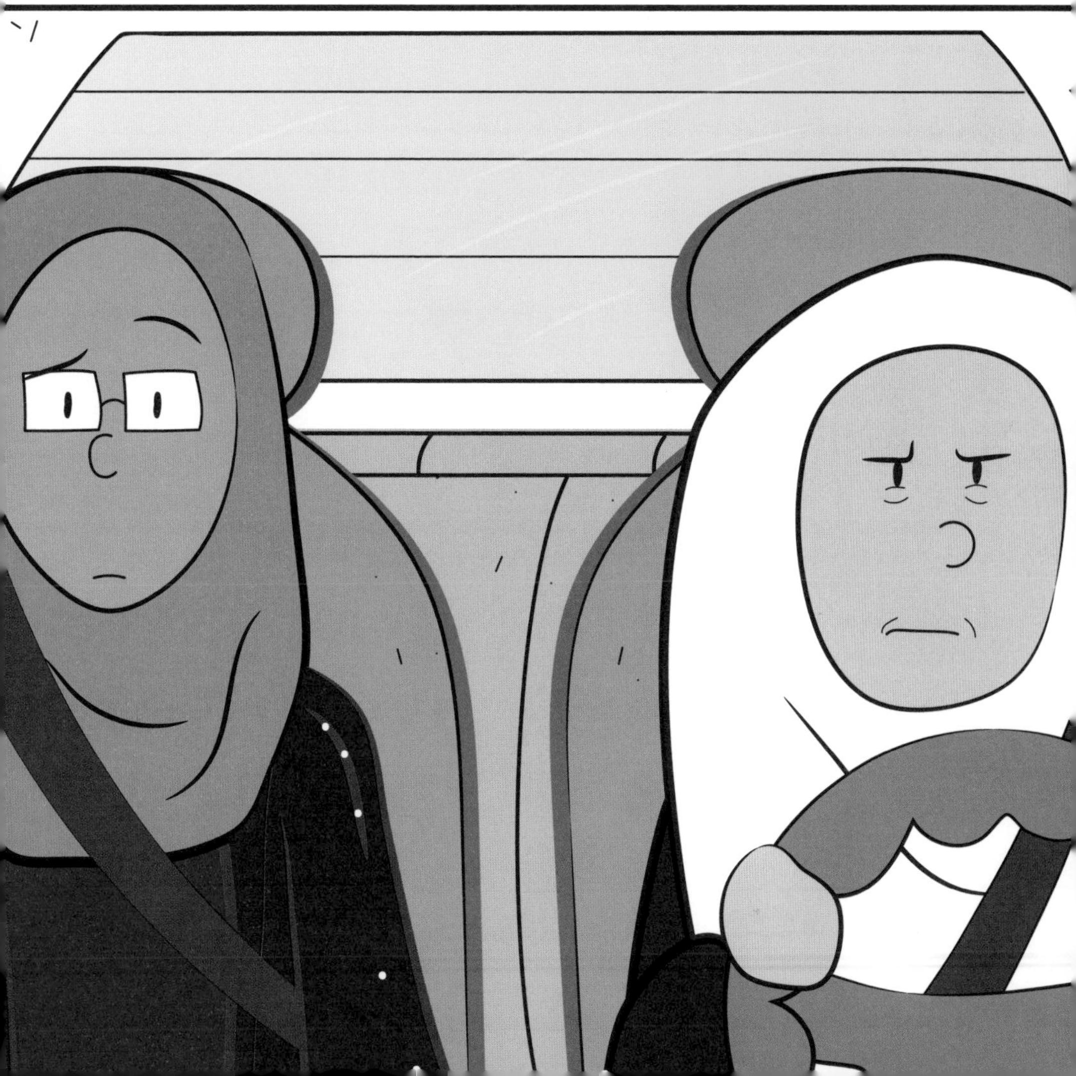

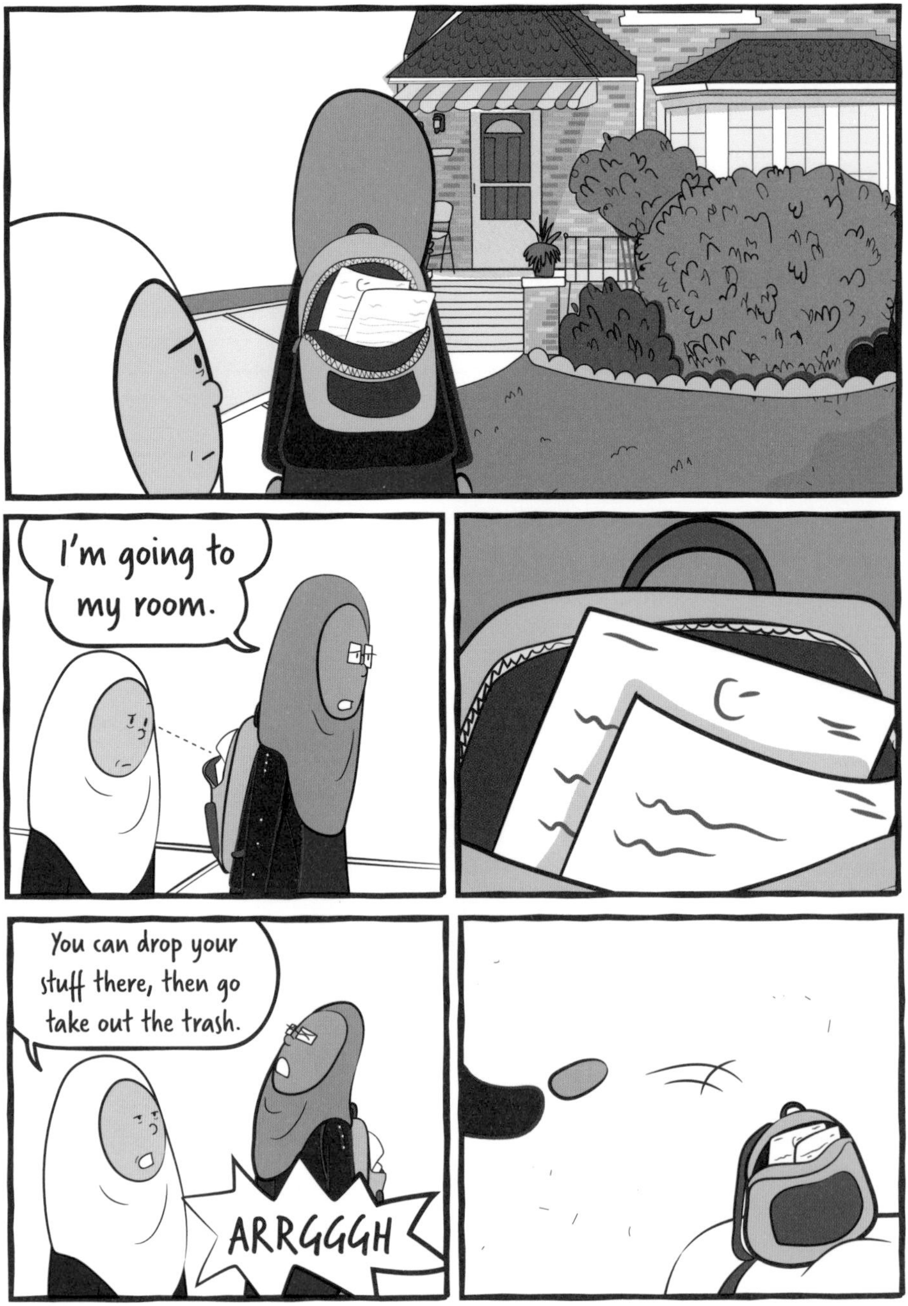
I'm going to my room.
You can drop your stuff there, then go take out the trash.
ARRGGGH

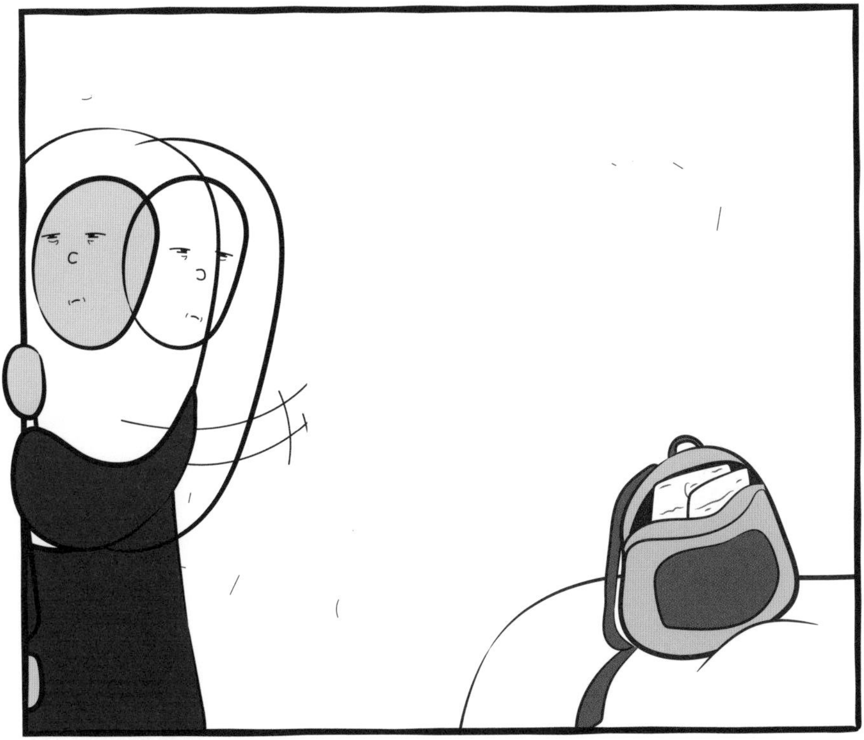

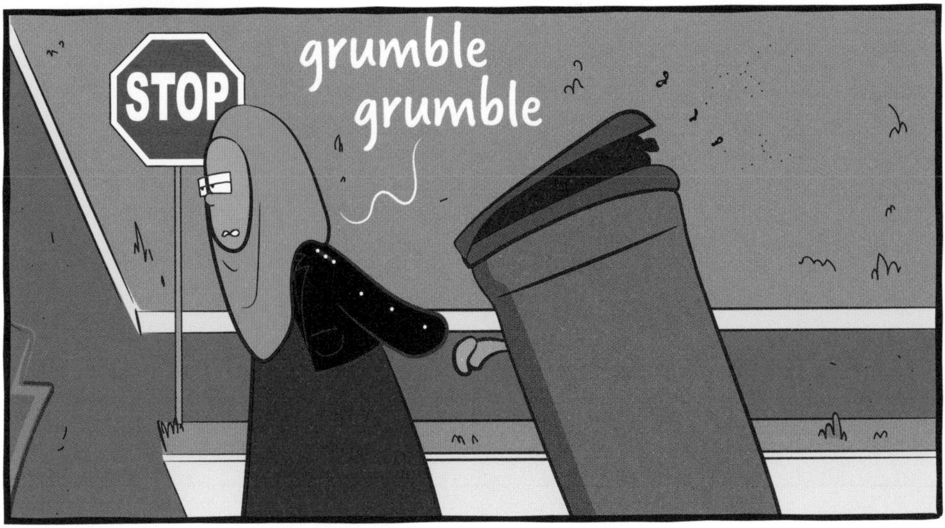
STOP
grumble
grumble

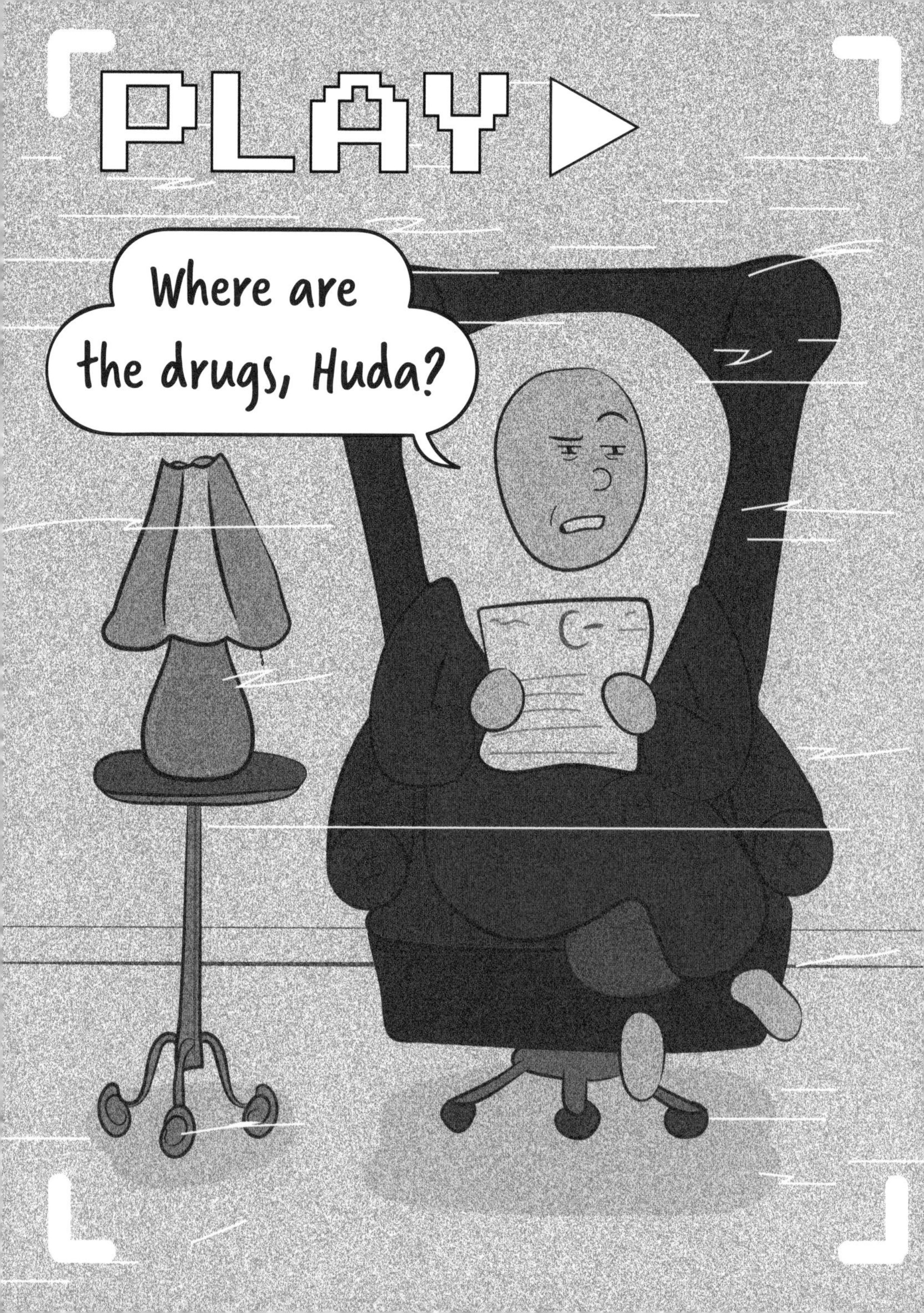
PLAY
Where are the drugs, Huda?

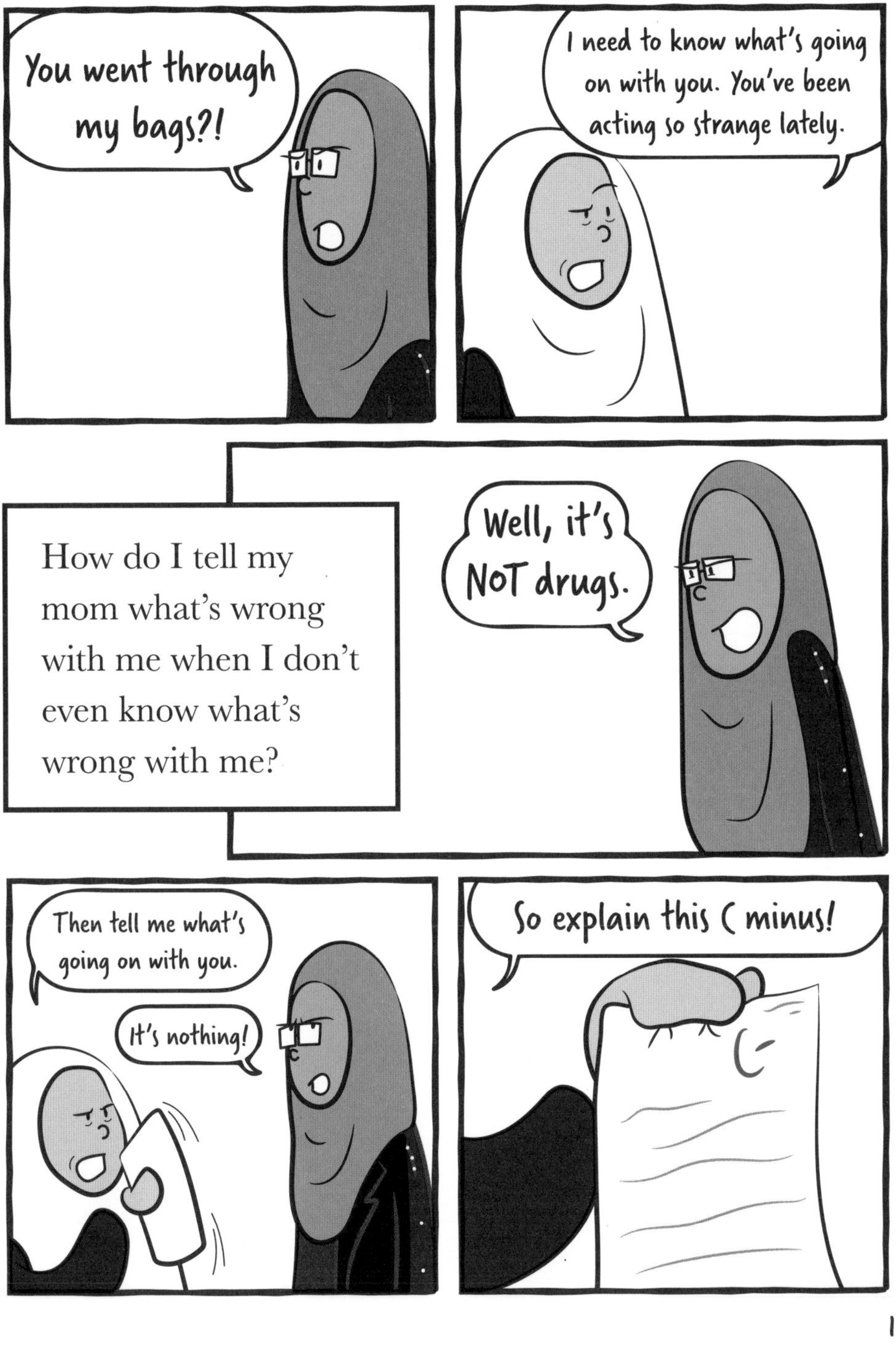
You went through my bags?!
I need to know what's going on with you. You've been acting so strange lately.
How do I tell my mom what's wrong with me when I don't even know what's wrong with me?
Well, it's NOT drugs.
Then tell me what's going on with you.
It's nothing!
So explain this C minus!
C-

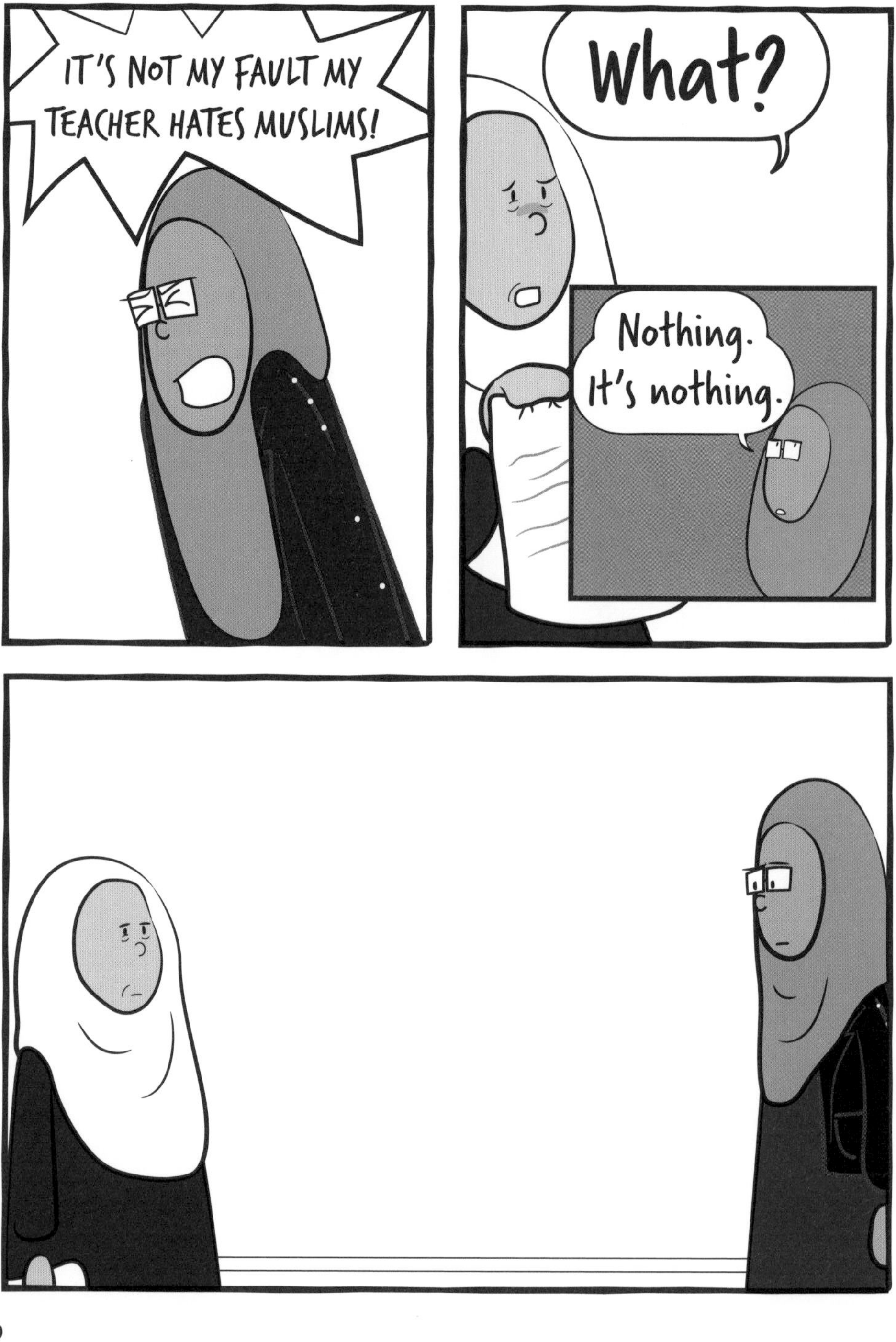
IT'S NOT MY FAULT MY TEACHER HATES MUSLIMS!
What?
Nothing. It's nothing.

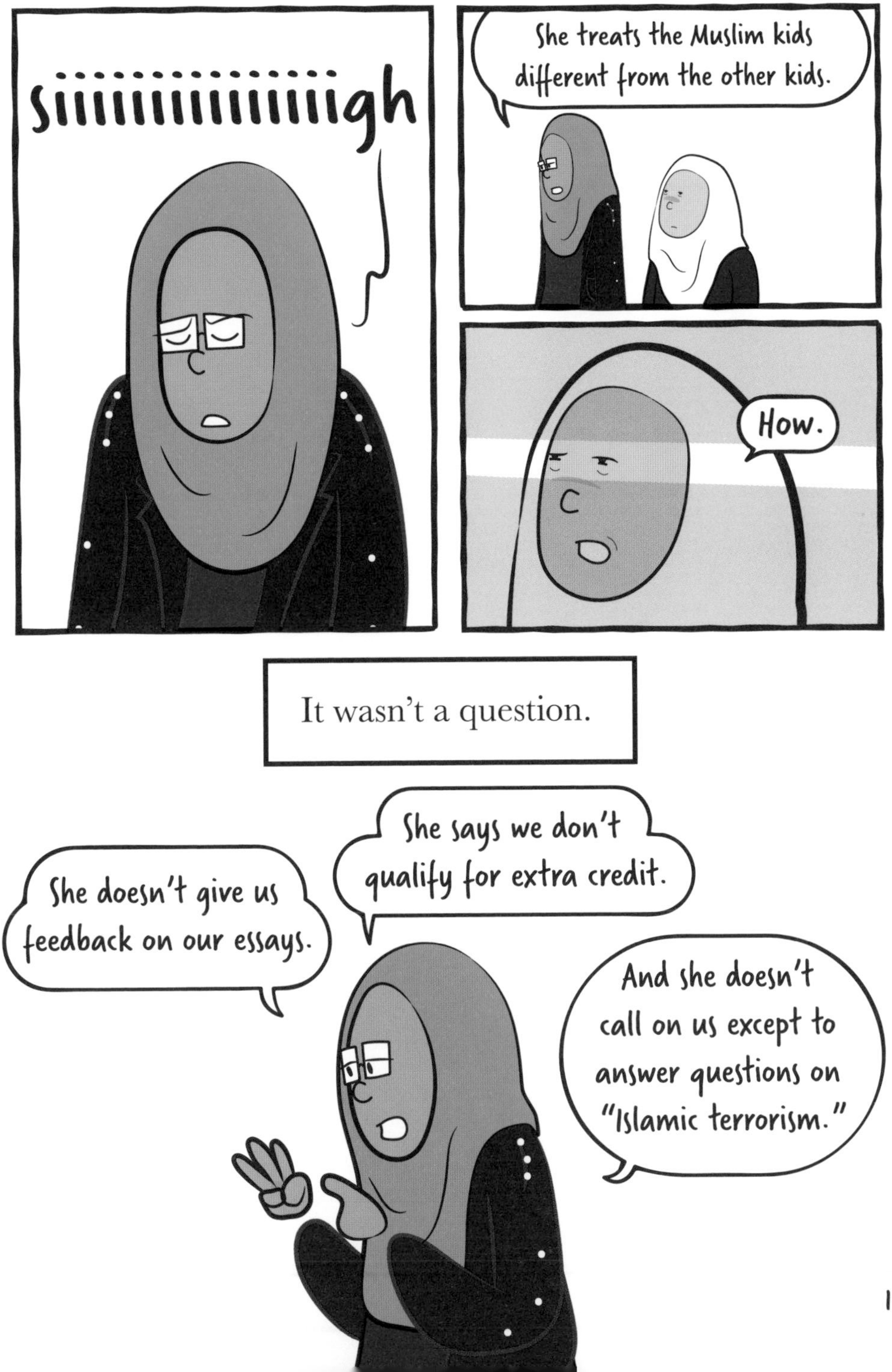
siiiiiiiiiiiiiiiigh
She treats the Muslim kids different from the other kids.
How.
It wasn't a question.
She doesn't give us feedback on our essays.
She says we don't qualify for extra credit.
And she doesn't call on us except to answer questions on "Islamic terrorism."

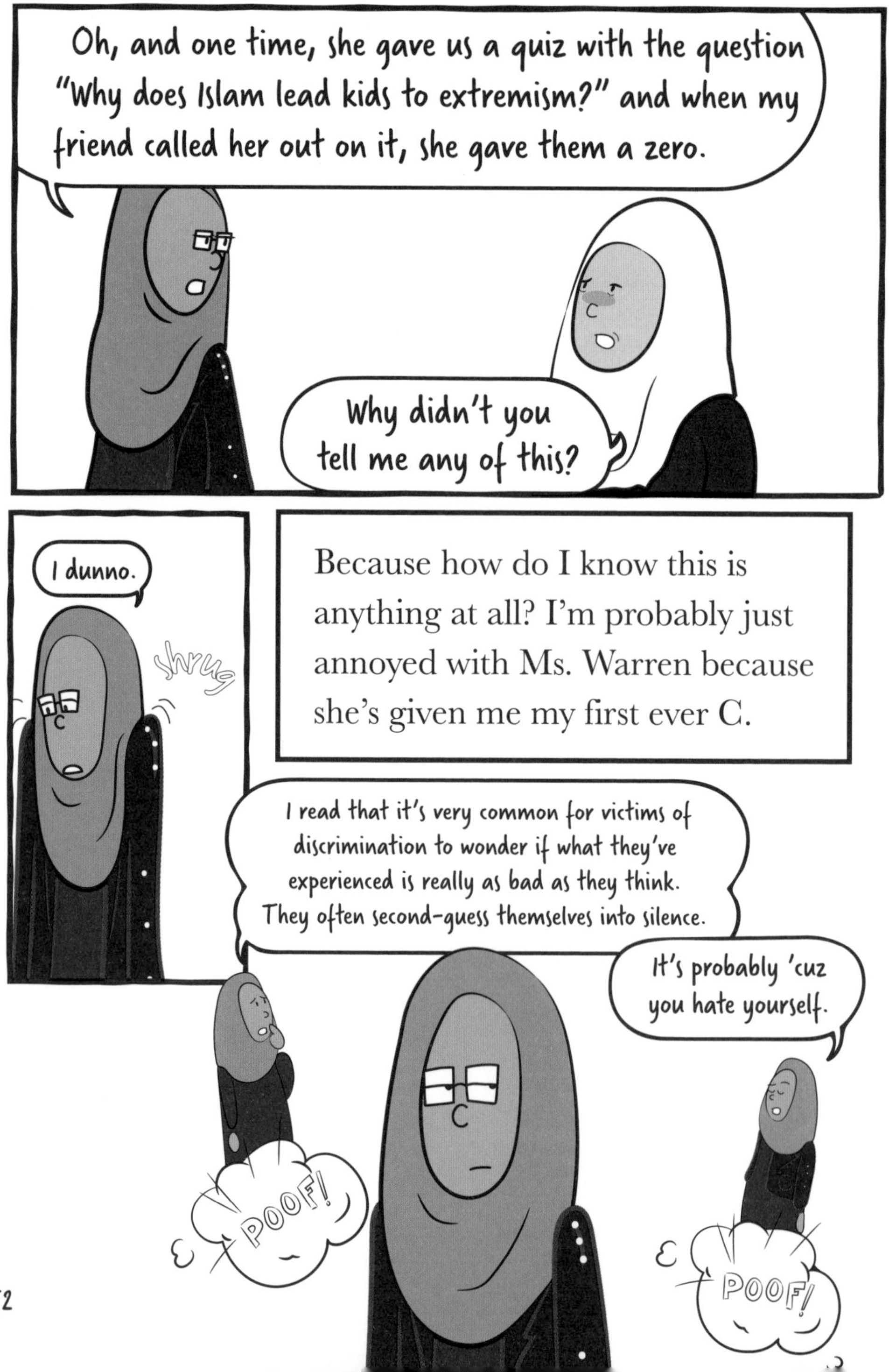
Oh, and one time, she gave us a quiz with the question "Why does Islam lead kids to extremism?" and when my friend called her out on it, she gave them a zero.
Why didn't you tell me any of this?
I dunno.
shrug
Because how do I know this is anything at all? I'm probably just annoyed with Ms. Warren because she's given me my first ever C.
I read that it's very common for victims of discrimination to wonder if what they've experienced is really as bad as they think. They often second-guess themselves into silence.
It's probably 'cuz you hate yourself.
POOF!
POOF!

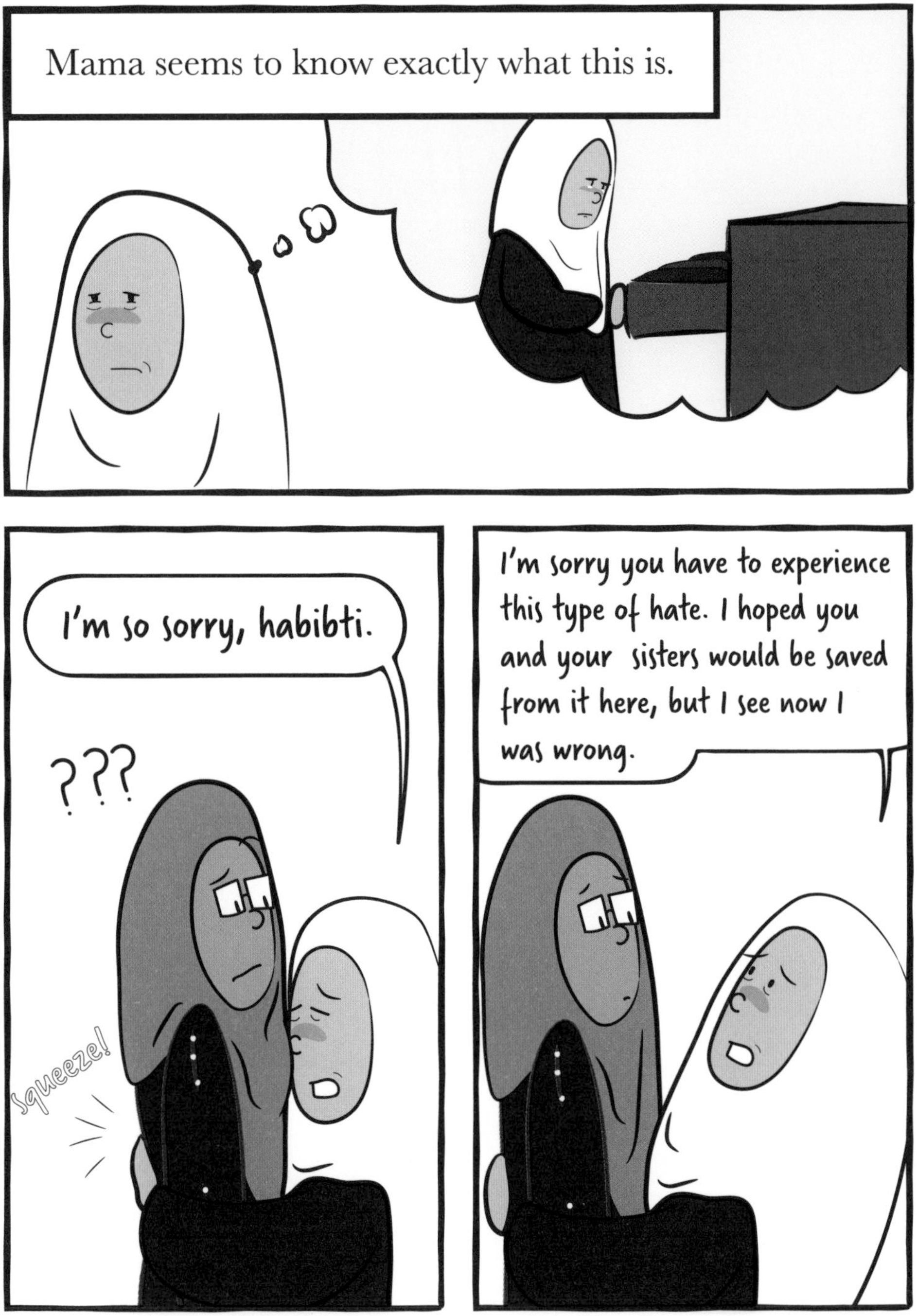
Mama seems to know exactly what this is.
I'm so sorry, habibti.
???
Squeeze!
I'm sorry you have to experience this type of hate. I hoped you and your sisters would be saved from it here, but I see now I was wrong.

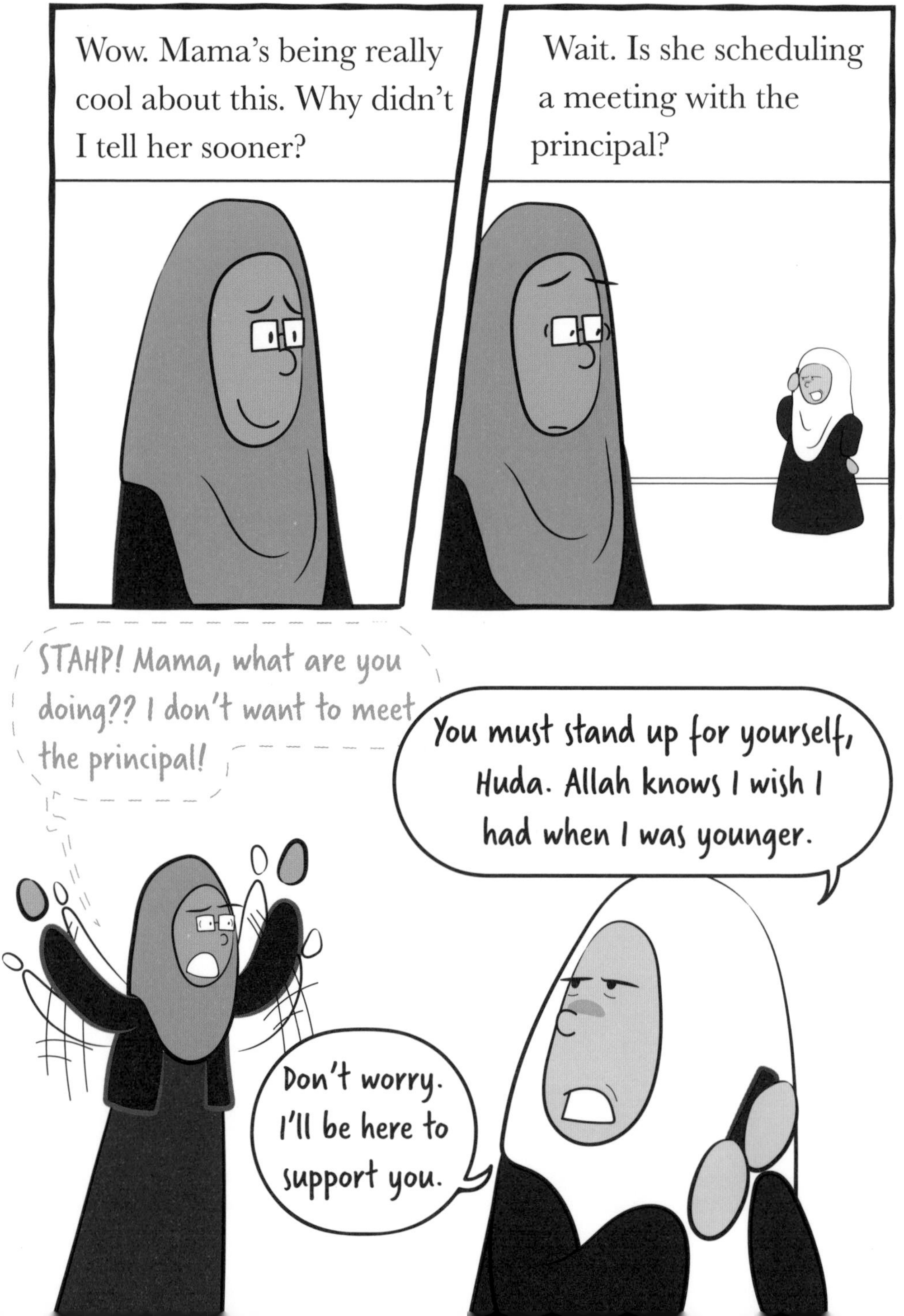

Wow. Mama's being really cool about this. Why didn't I tell her sooner?
Wait. Is she scheduling a meeting with the principal?
STAHP! Mama, what are you doing?? I don't want to meet the principal!
You must stand up for yourself, Huda. Allah knows I wish I had when I was younger.
Don't worry. I'll be here to support you.

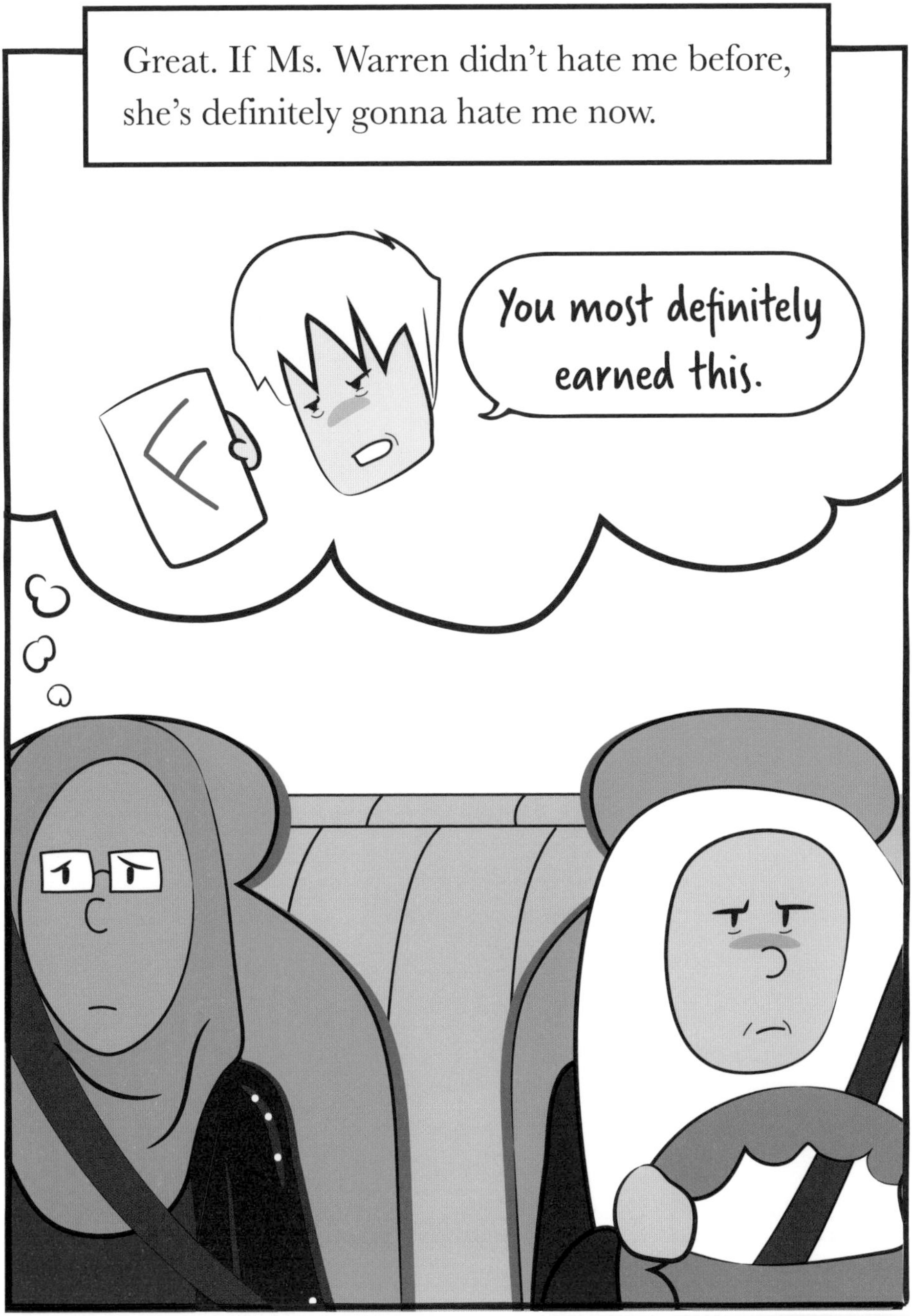
Great. If Ms. Warren didn't hate me before, she's definitely gonna hate me now.
You most definitely earned this.
F

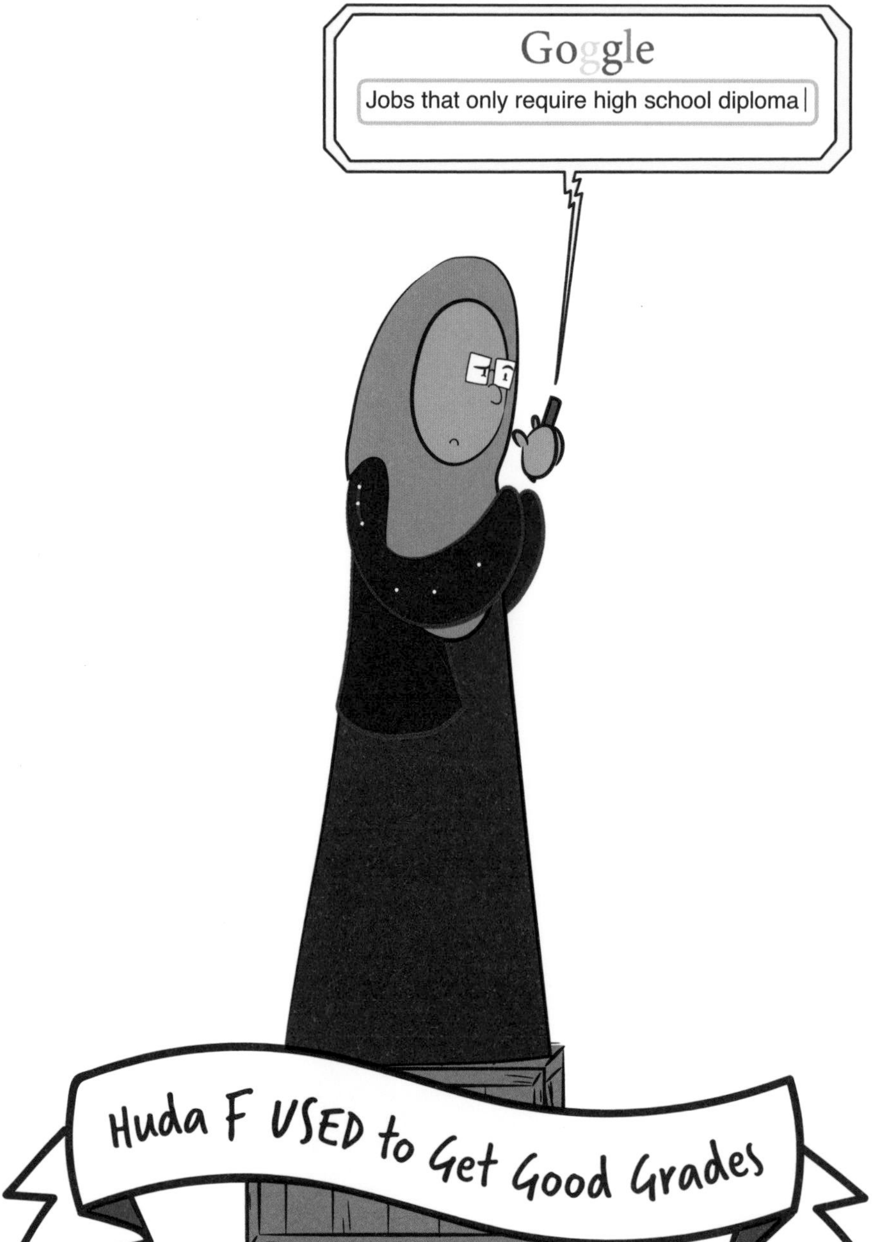

Goggle
Jobs that only require high school diploma
Huda F USED to Get Good Grades

Am I really gonna jeopardize my grade—the ONE thing I have going for me—over what may very well be imagined slights? The teeniest, tiniest of microagressions?

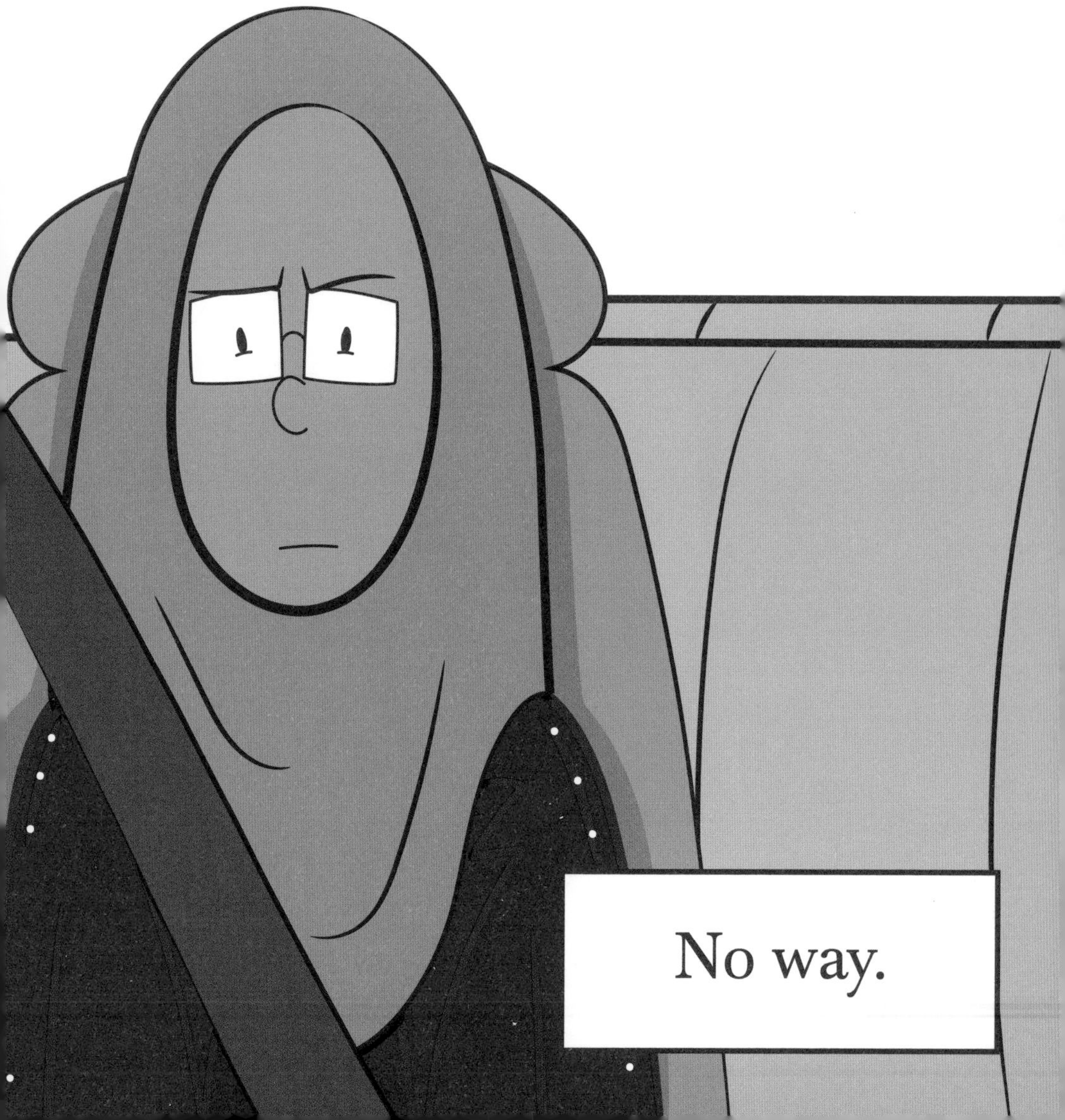
No way.

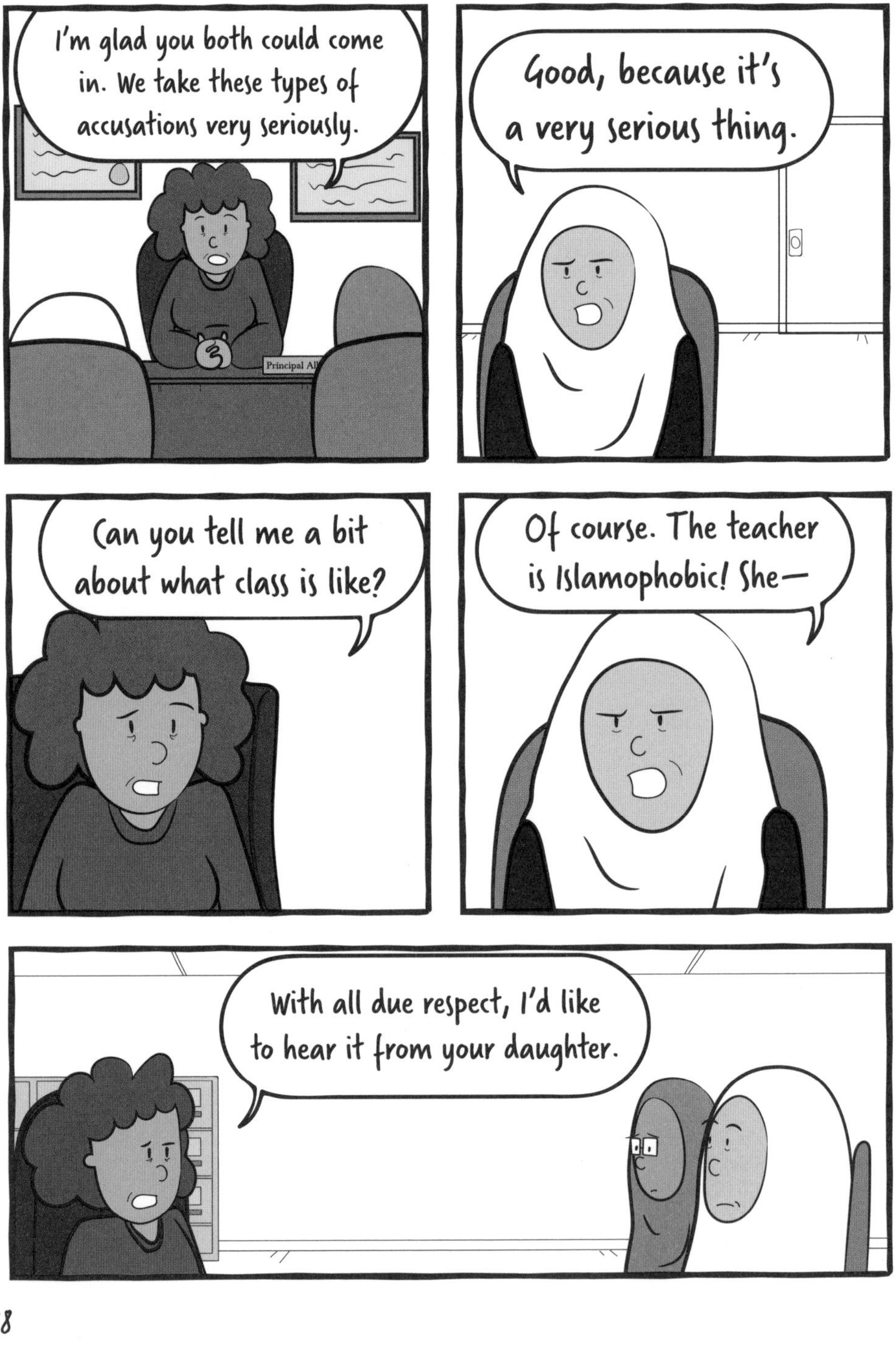
I'm glad you both could come in. We take these types of accusations very seriously.
Good, because it's a very serious thing.
Can you tell me a bit about what class is like?
Of course. The teacher is Islamophobic! She—
With all due respect, I'd like to hear it from your daughter.

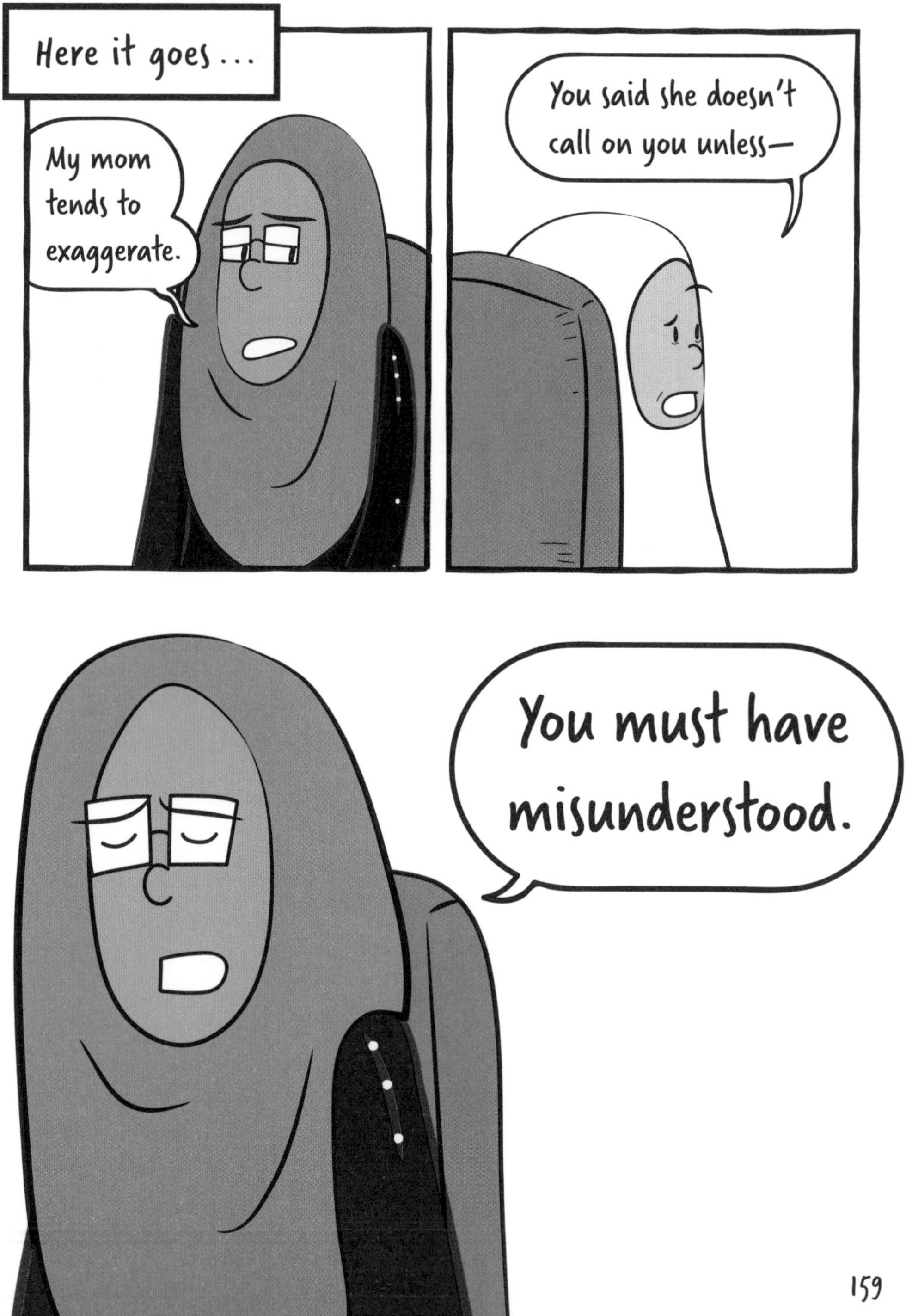
Here it goes . . .
My mom tends to exaggerate.
You said she doesn't call on you unless—
You must have misunderstood.

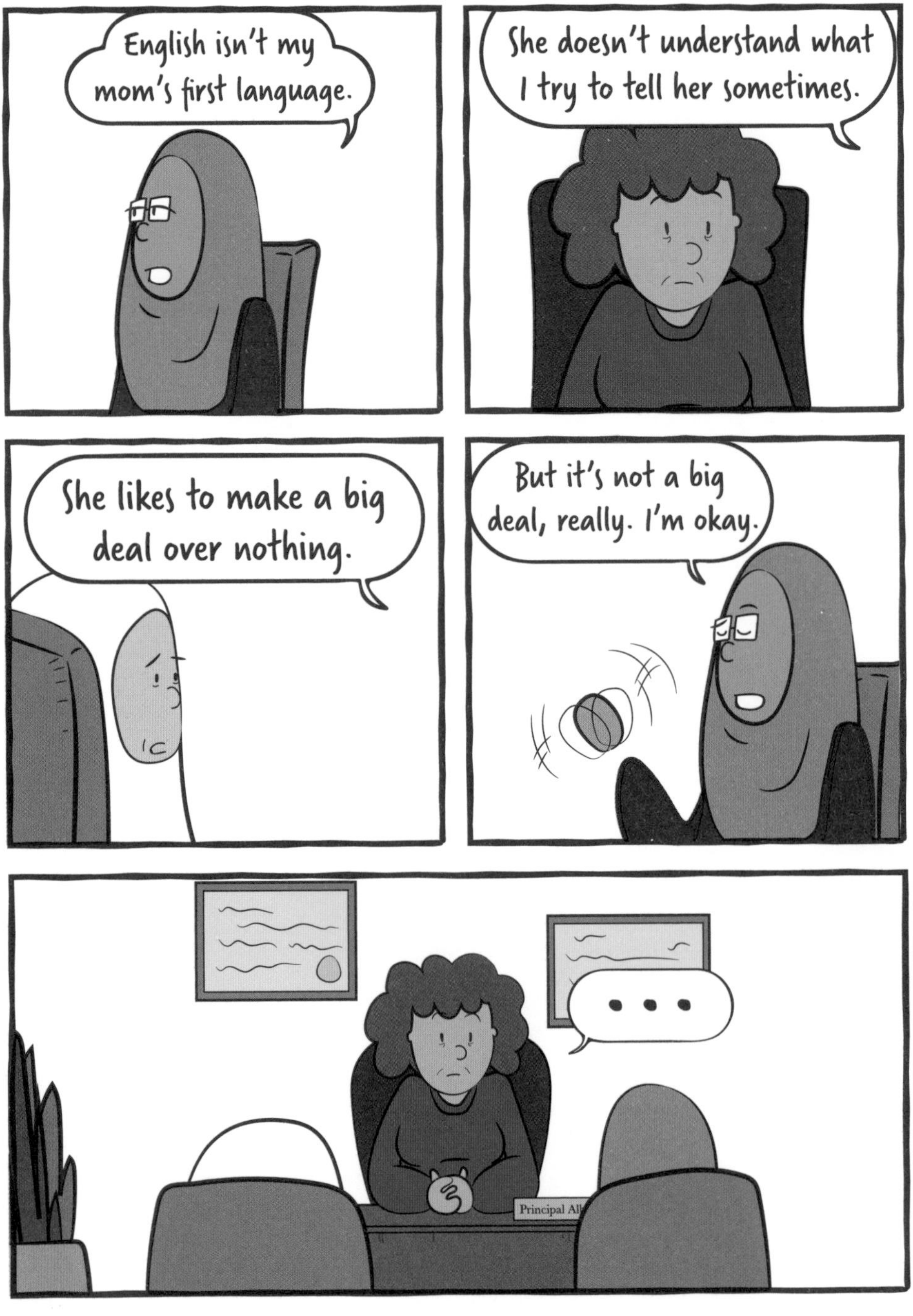
English isn't my mom's first language.
She doesn't understand what I try to tell her sometimes.
She likes to make a big deal over nothing.
But it's not a big deal, really. I'm okay.
...
Principal Al

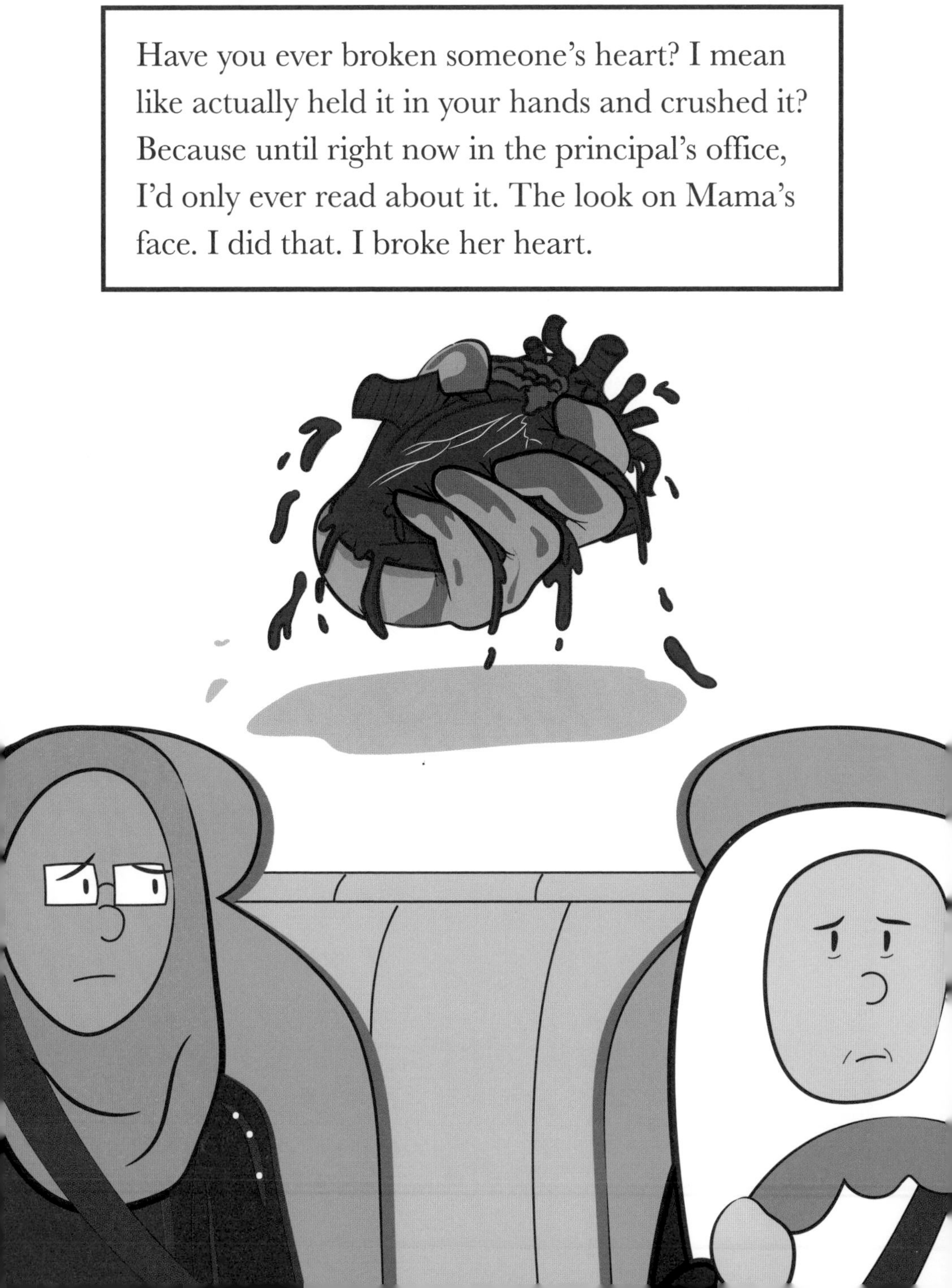
Have you ever broken someone's heart? I mean like actually held it in your hands and crushed it? Because until right now in the principal's office, I'd only ever read about it. The look on Mama's face. I did that. I broke her heart.

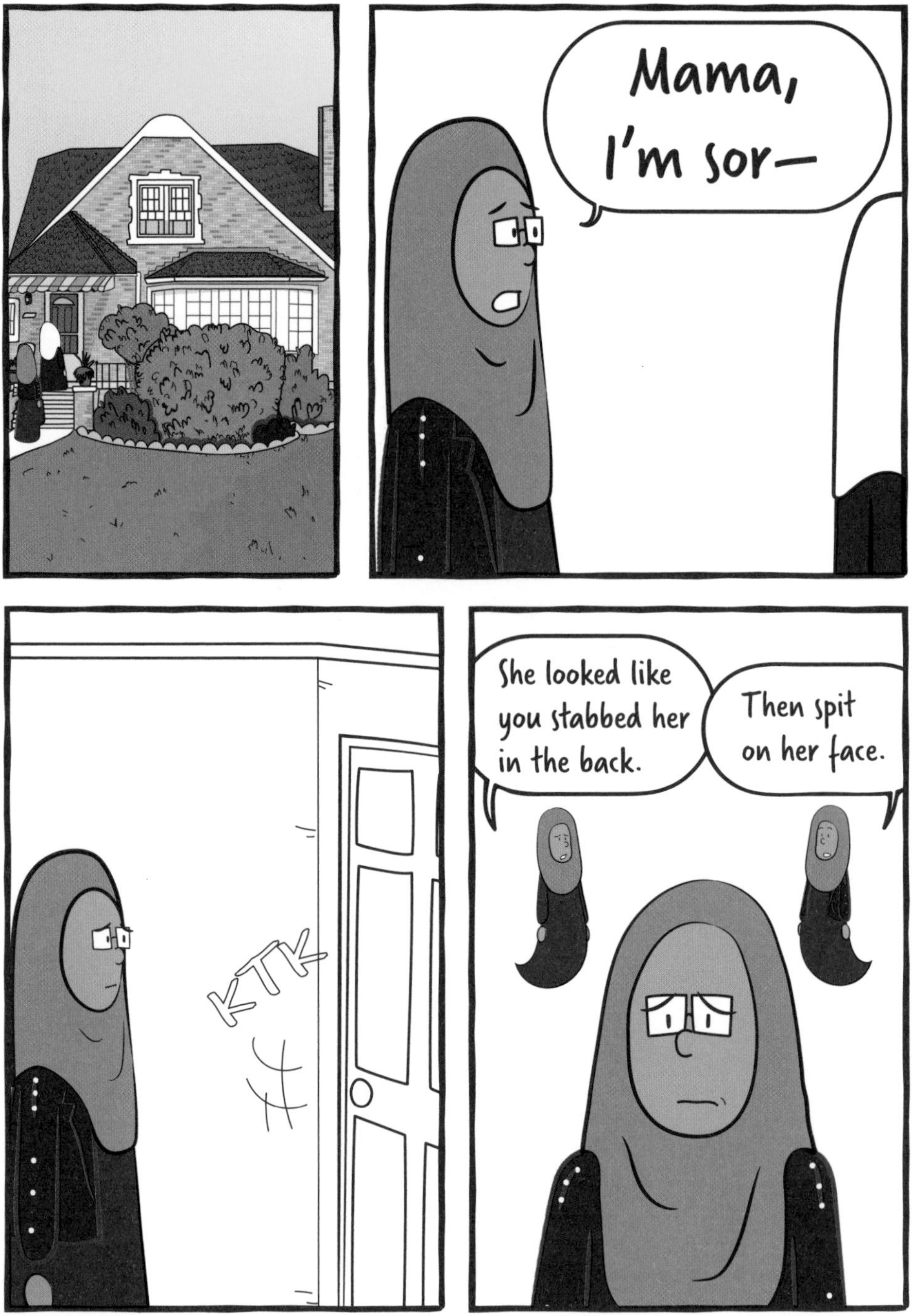
Mama, I'm sor—
KTK
She looked like you stabbed her in the back.
Then spit on her face.

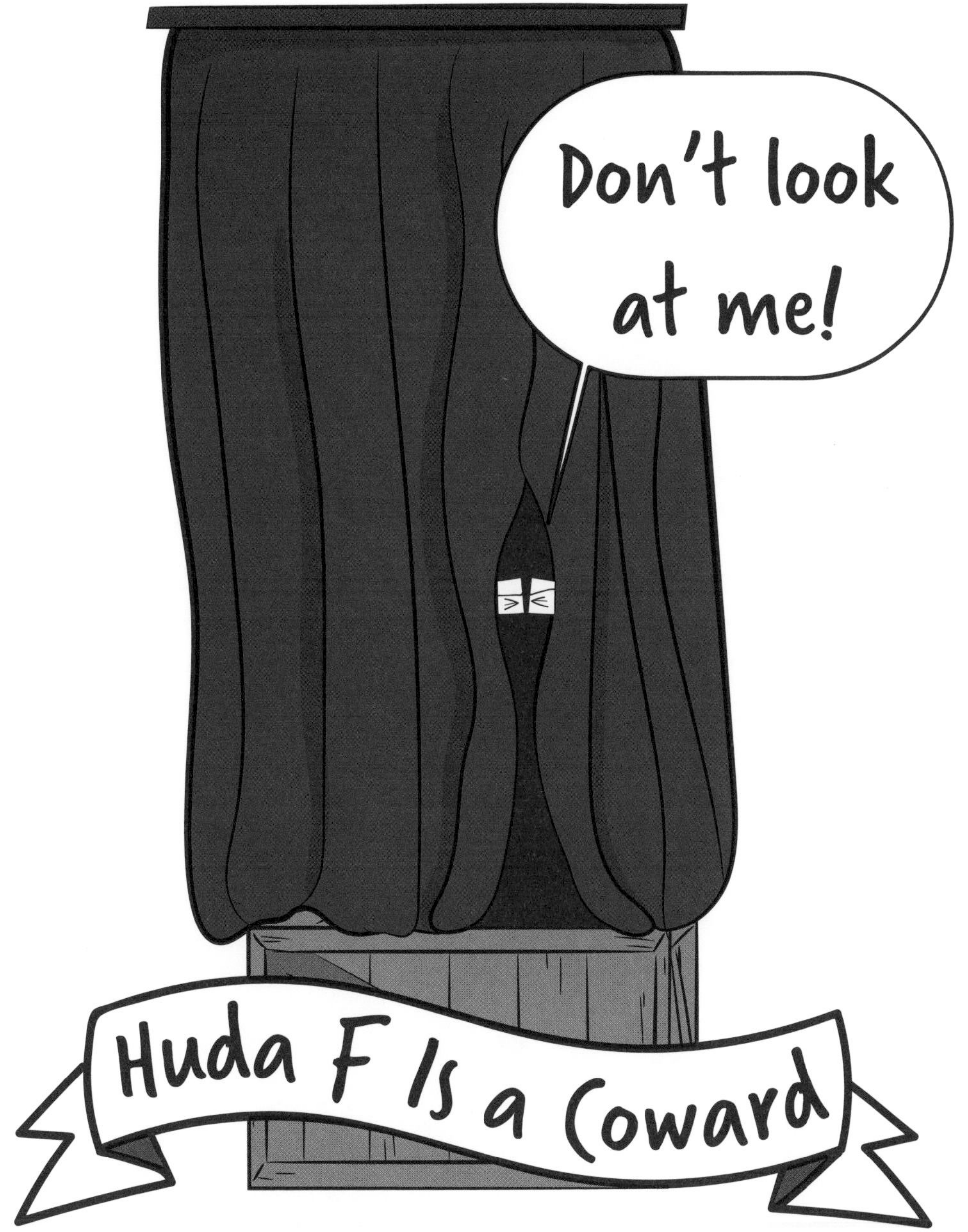
Don't look at me!
Huda F Is a Coward

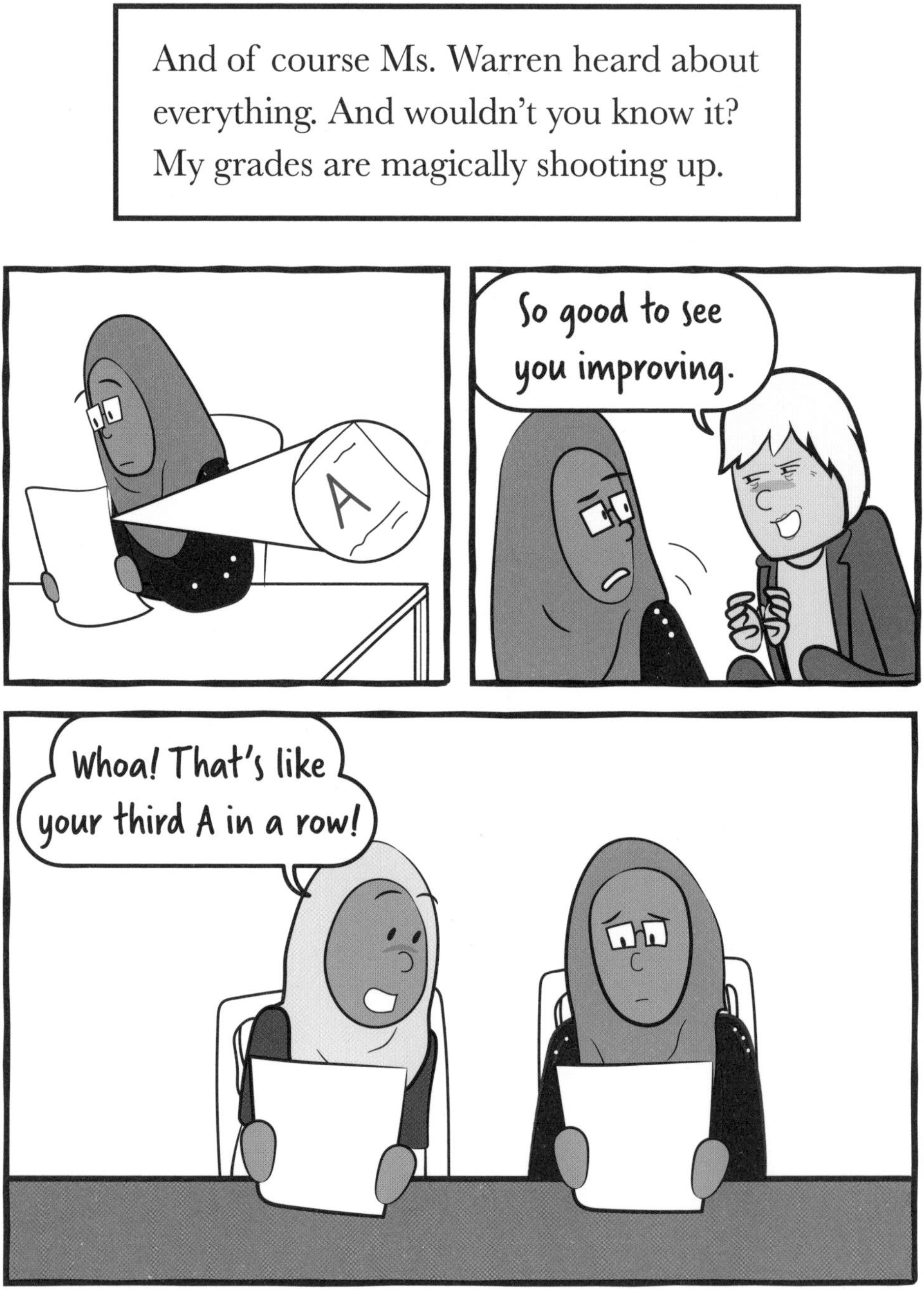
And of course Ms. Warren heard about everything. And wouldn't you know it? My grades are magically shooting up.
A
So good to see you improving.
Whoa! That's like your third A in a row!

I feel sick.

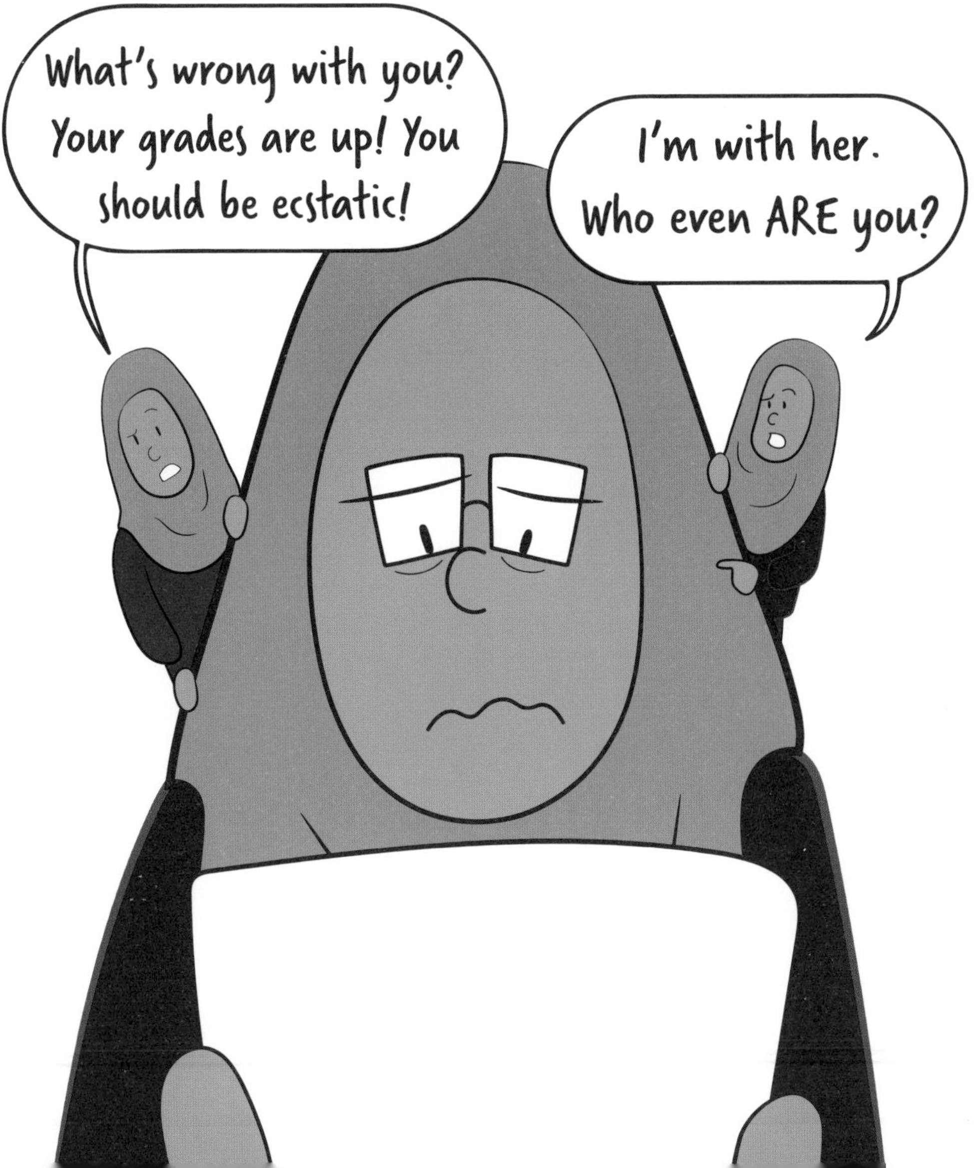
What's wrong with you? Your grades are up! You should be ecstatic!
I'm with her. Who even ARE you?

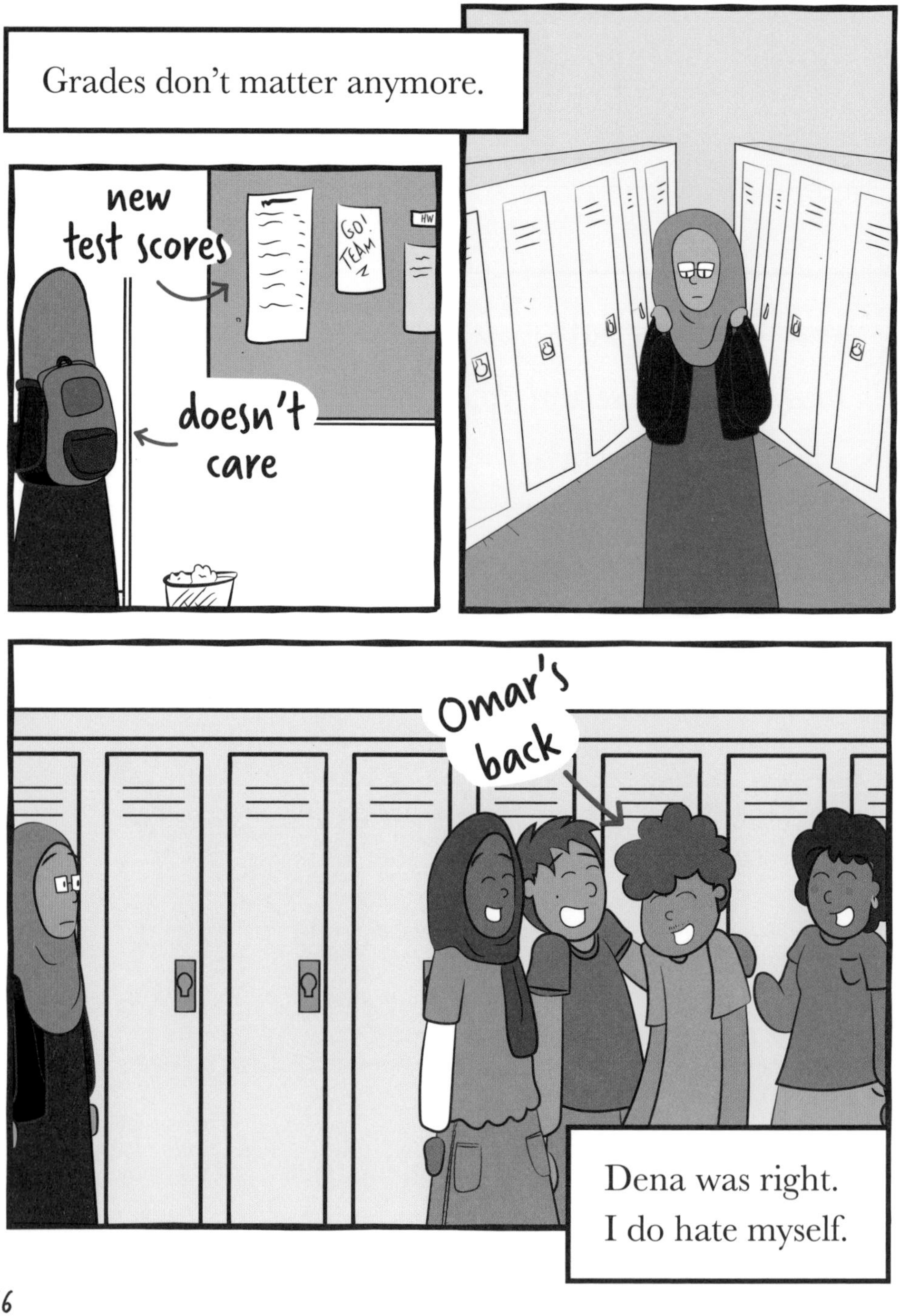
Grades don't matter anymore.
new test scores
doesn't care
GO! TEAM
HW
Omar's back
Dena was right.
I do hate myself.

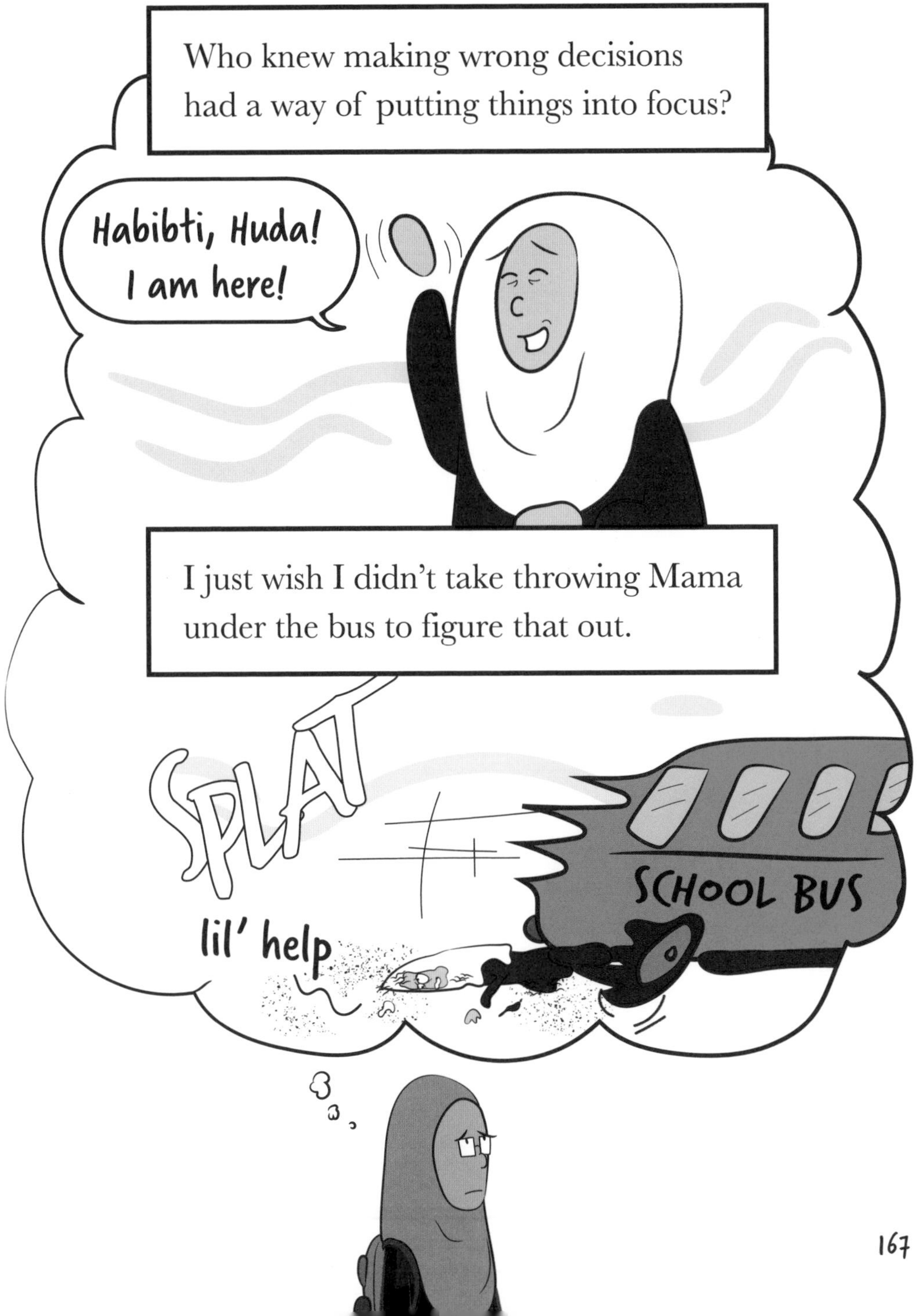
Who knew making wrong decisions had a way of putting things into focus?
Habibti, Huda! I am here!
I just wish I didn't take throwing Mama under the bus to figure that out.
SPLAT
SCHOOL BUS
lil' help

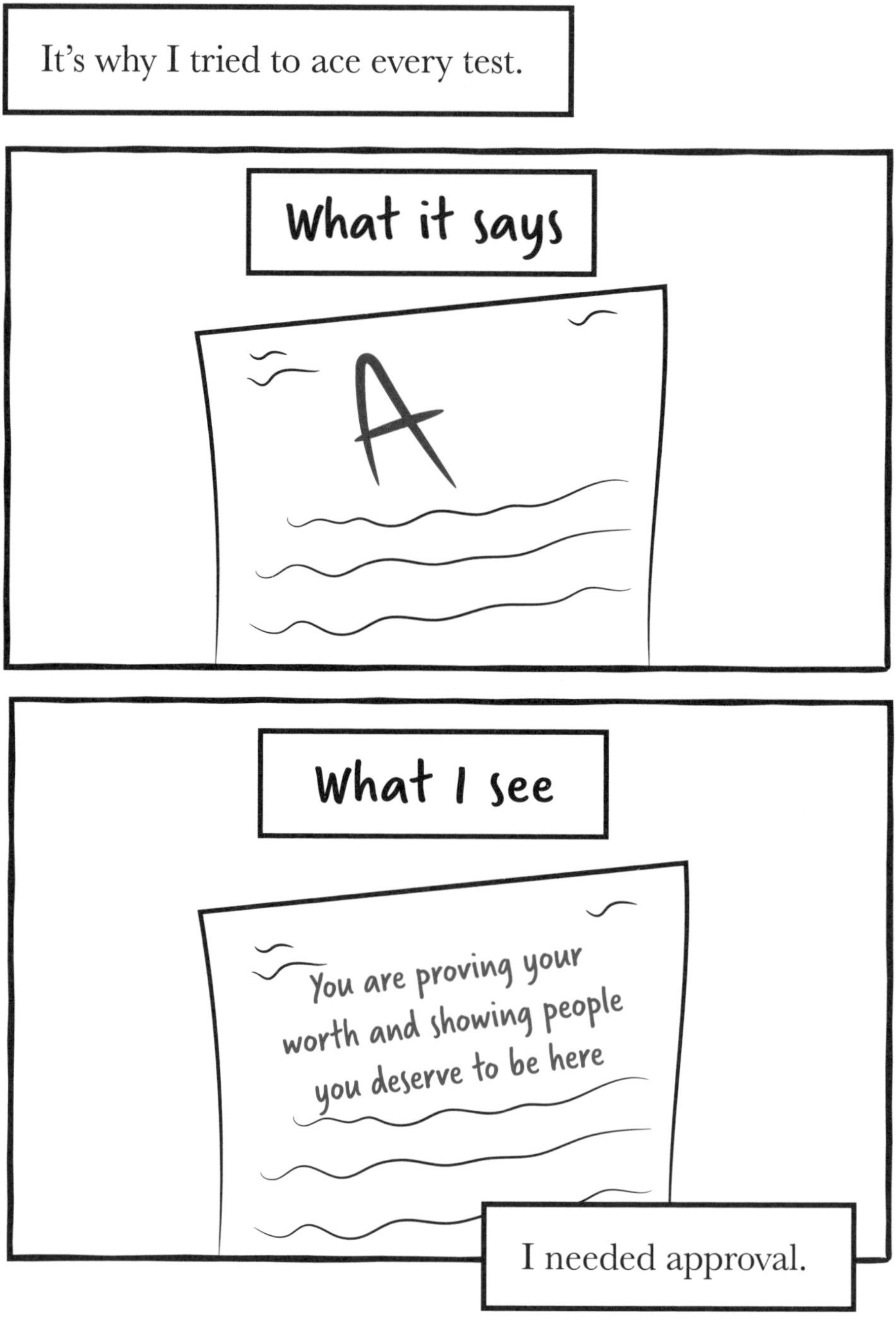
It's why I tried to ace every test.
What it says
A
What I see
You are proving your worth and showing people you deserve to be here
I needed approval.

It's why I faked personalities so people would like me.

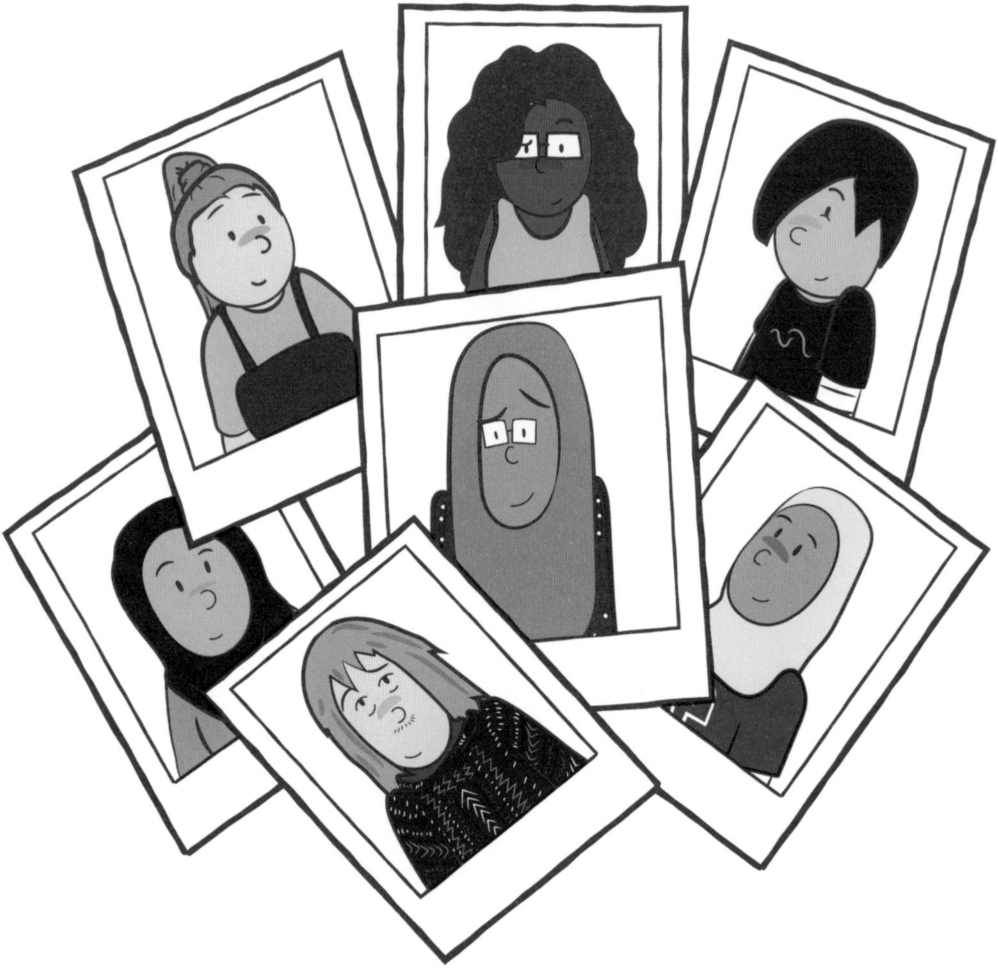

I needed acceptance.

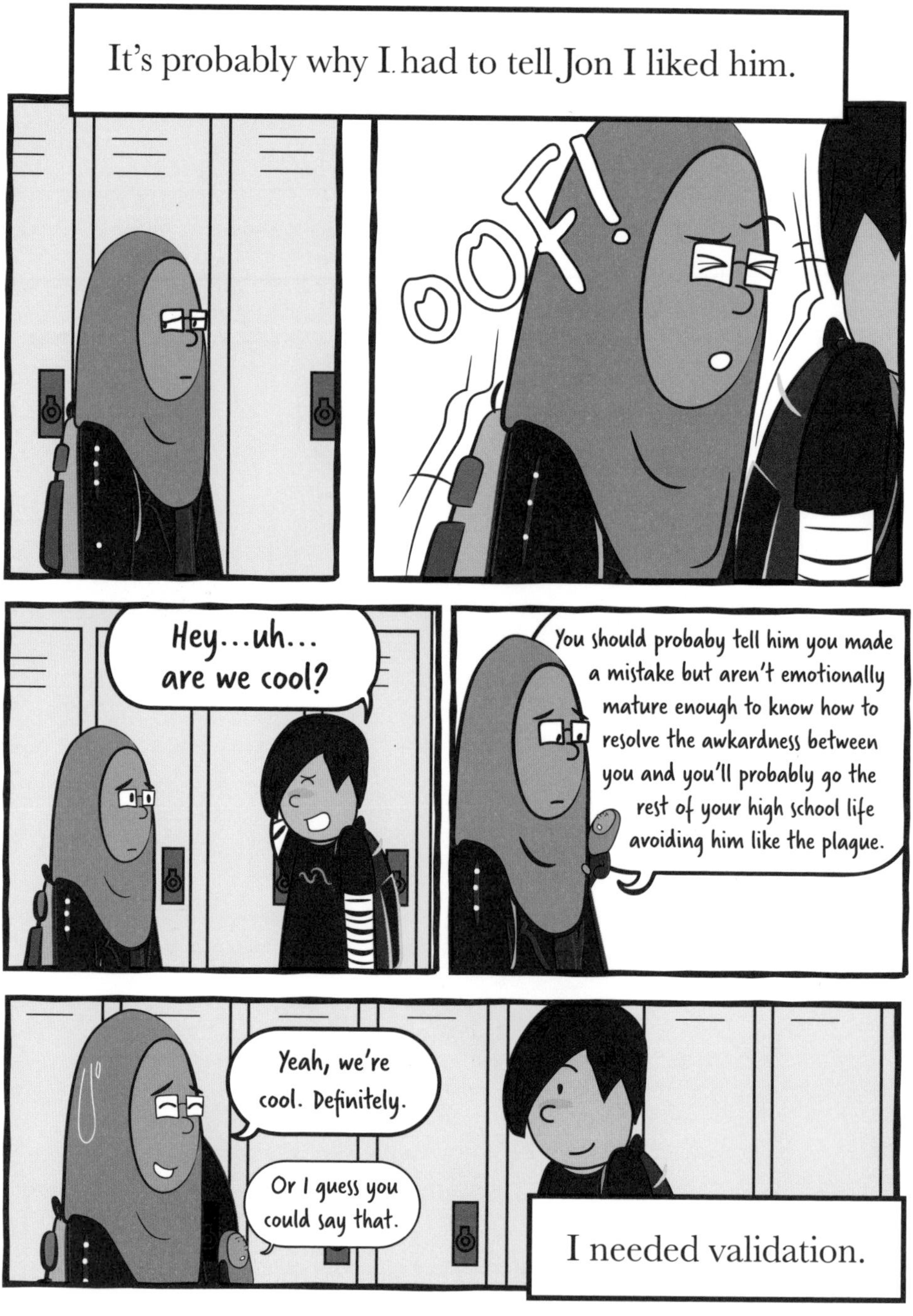
It's probably why I had to tell Jon I liked him.
OOF!
Hey...uh... are we cool?
You should probaby tell him you made a mistake but aren't emotionally mature enough to know how to resolve the awkardness between you and you'll probably go the rest of your high school life avoiding him like the plague.
Yeah, we're cool. Definitely.
Or I guess you could say that.
I needed validation.

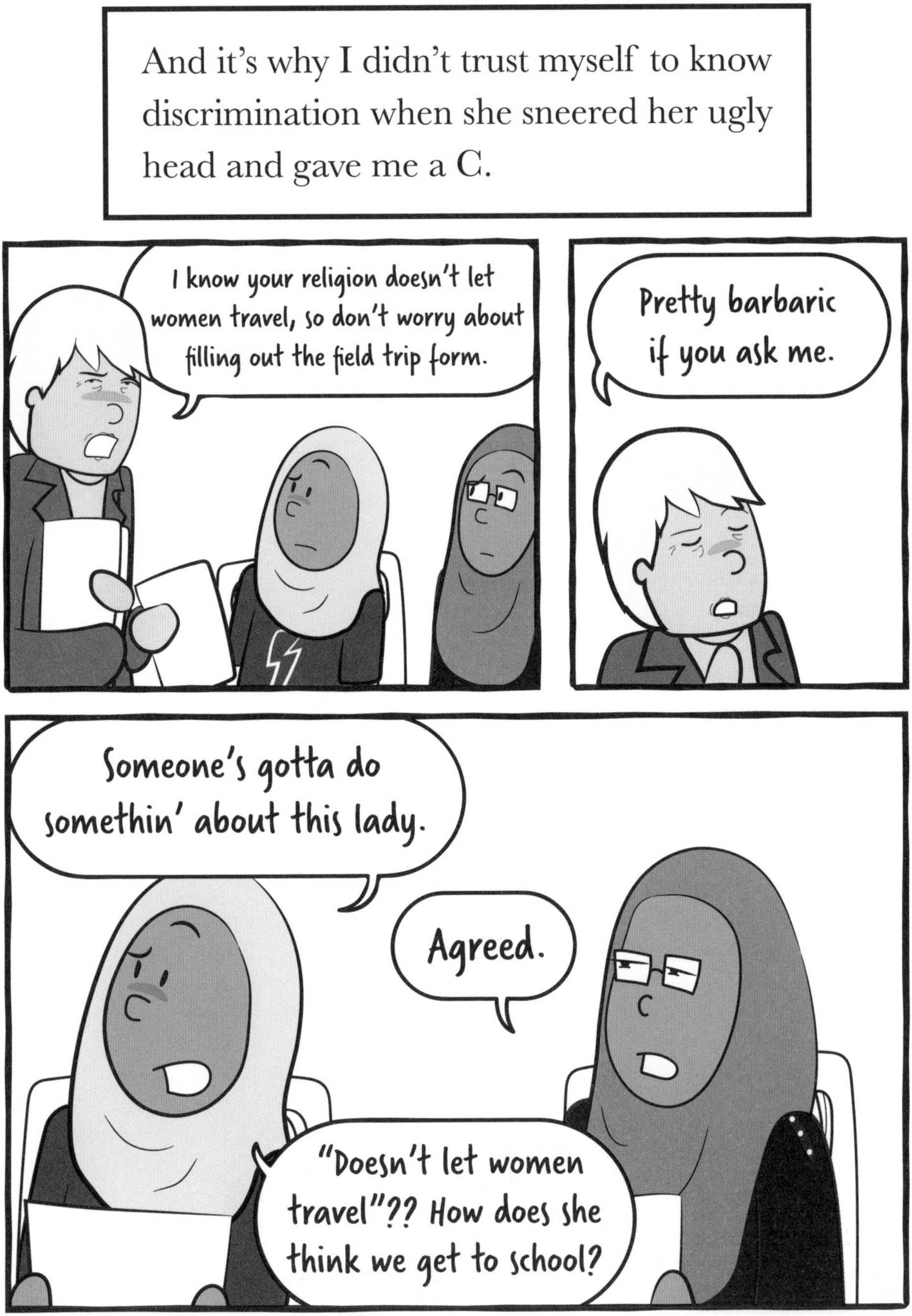
And it’s why I didn’t trust myself to know discrimination when she sneered her ugly head and gave me a C.
I know your religion doesn’t let women travel, so don’t worry about filling out the field trip form.
Pretty barbaric if you ask me.
Someone’s gotta do somethin’ about this lady.
Agreed.
“Doesn’t let women travel”?? How does she think we get to school?

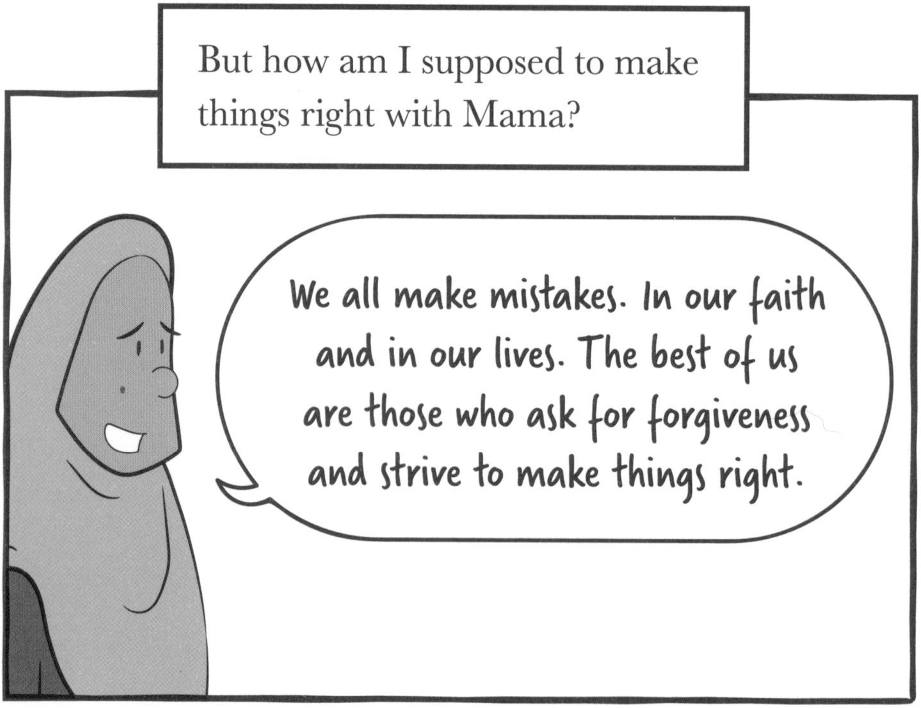
But how am I supposed to make things right with Mama?
We all make mistakes. In our faith and in our lives. The best of us are those who ask for forgiveness and strive to make things right.

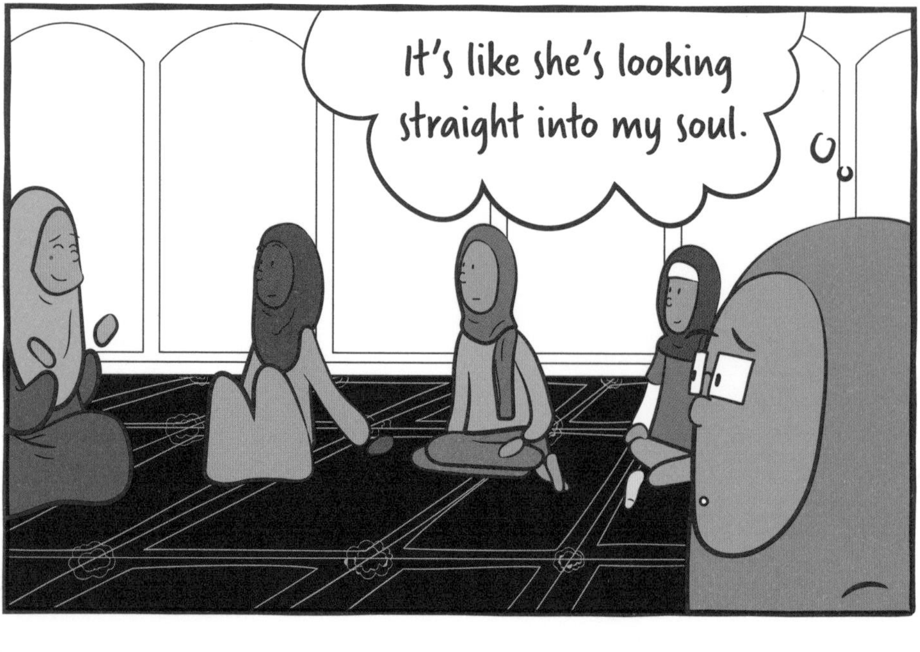
It's like she's looking straight into my soul.

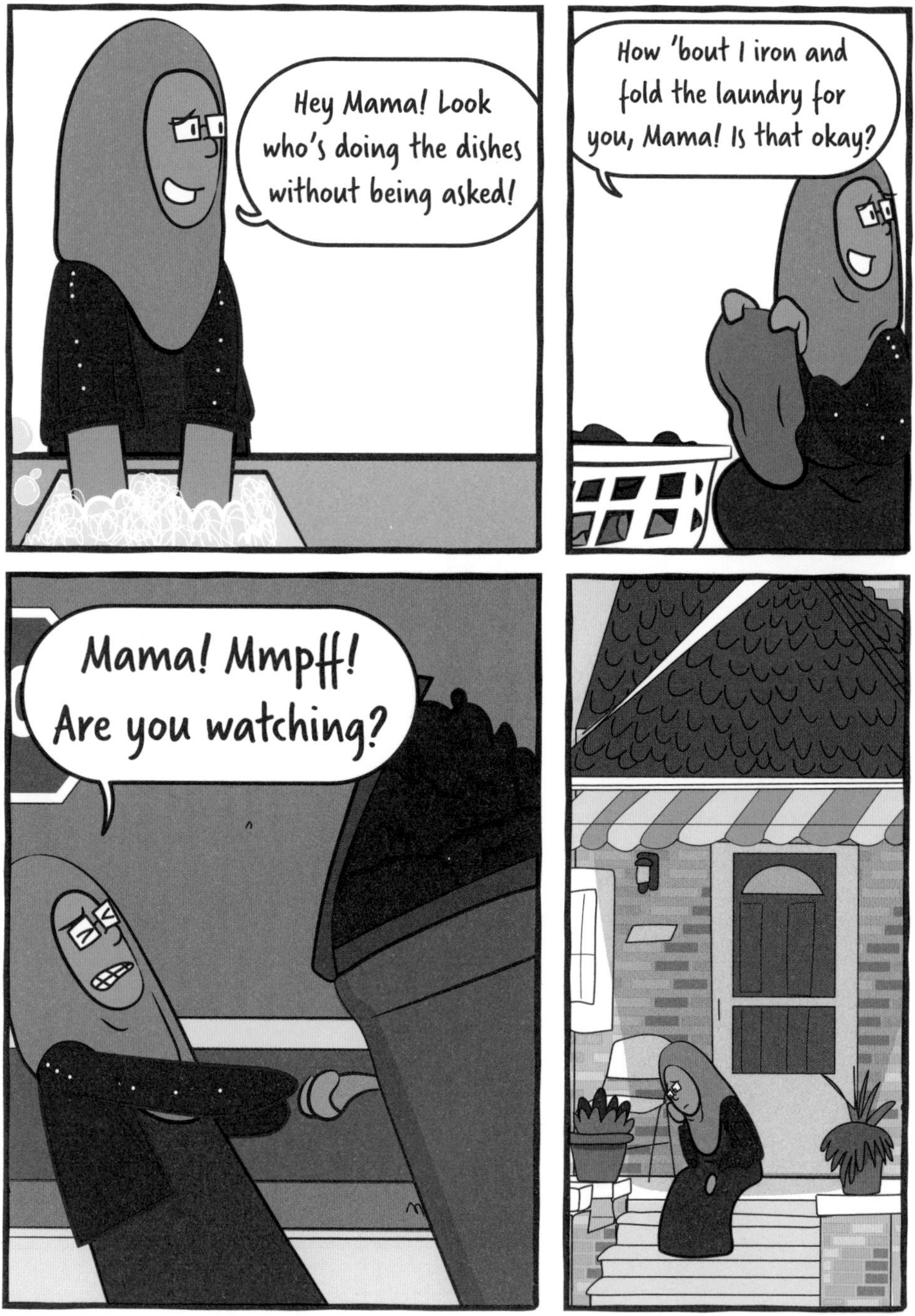
Hey Mama! Look who's doing the dishes without being asked!
How 'bout I iron and fold the laundry for you, Mama! Is that okay?
Mama! Mmpff! Are you watching?

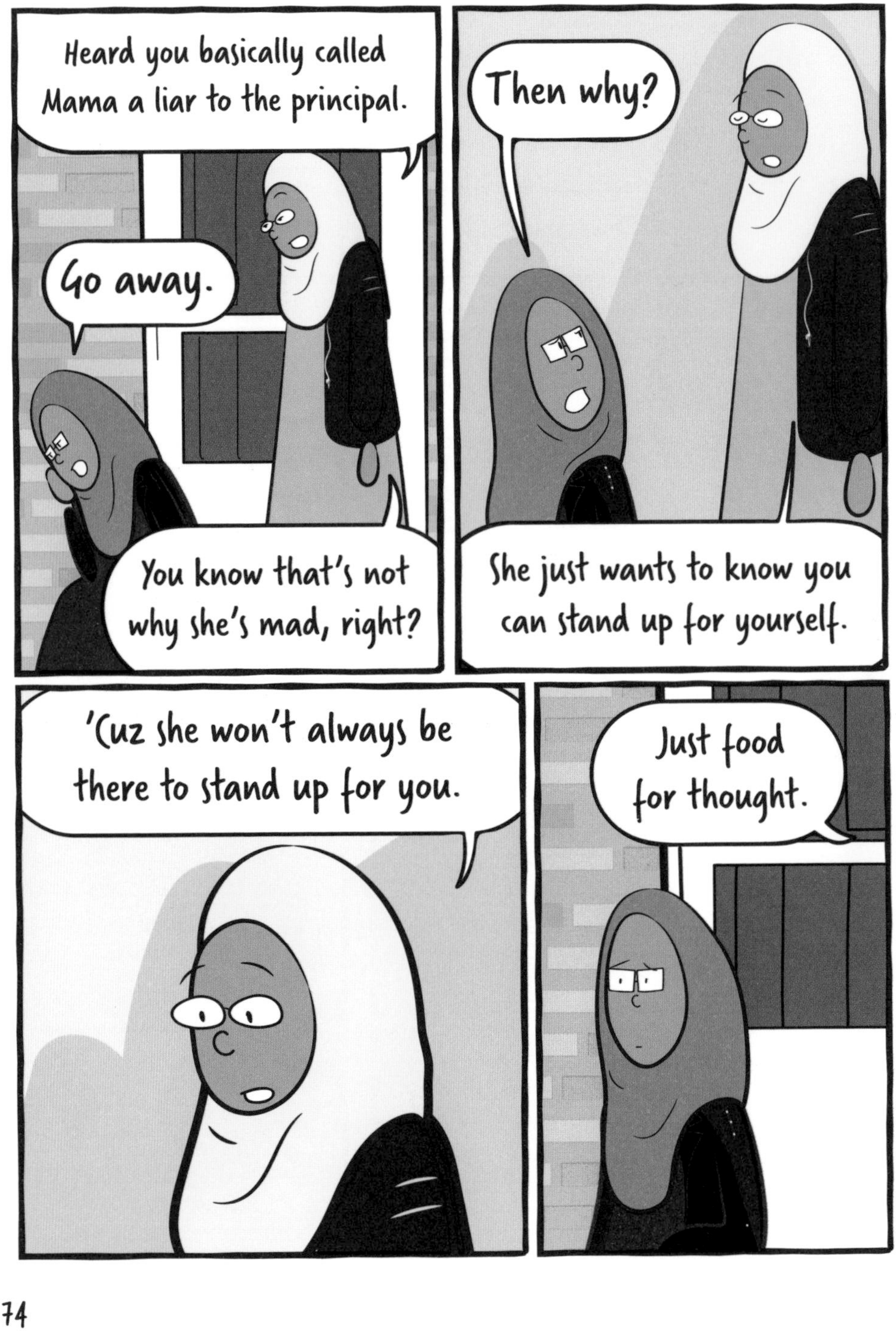
Heard you basically called Mama a liar to the principal.
Go away.
You know that's not why she's mad, right?
Then why?
She just wants to know you can stand up for yourself.
'Cuz she won't always be there to stand up for you.
Just food for thought.

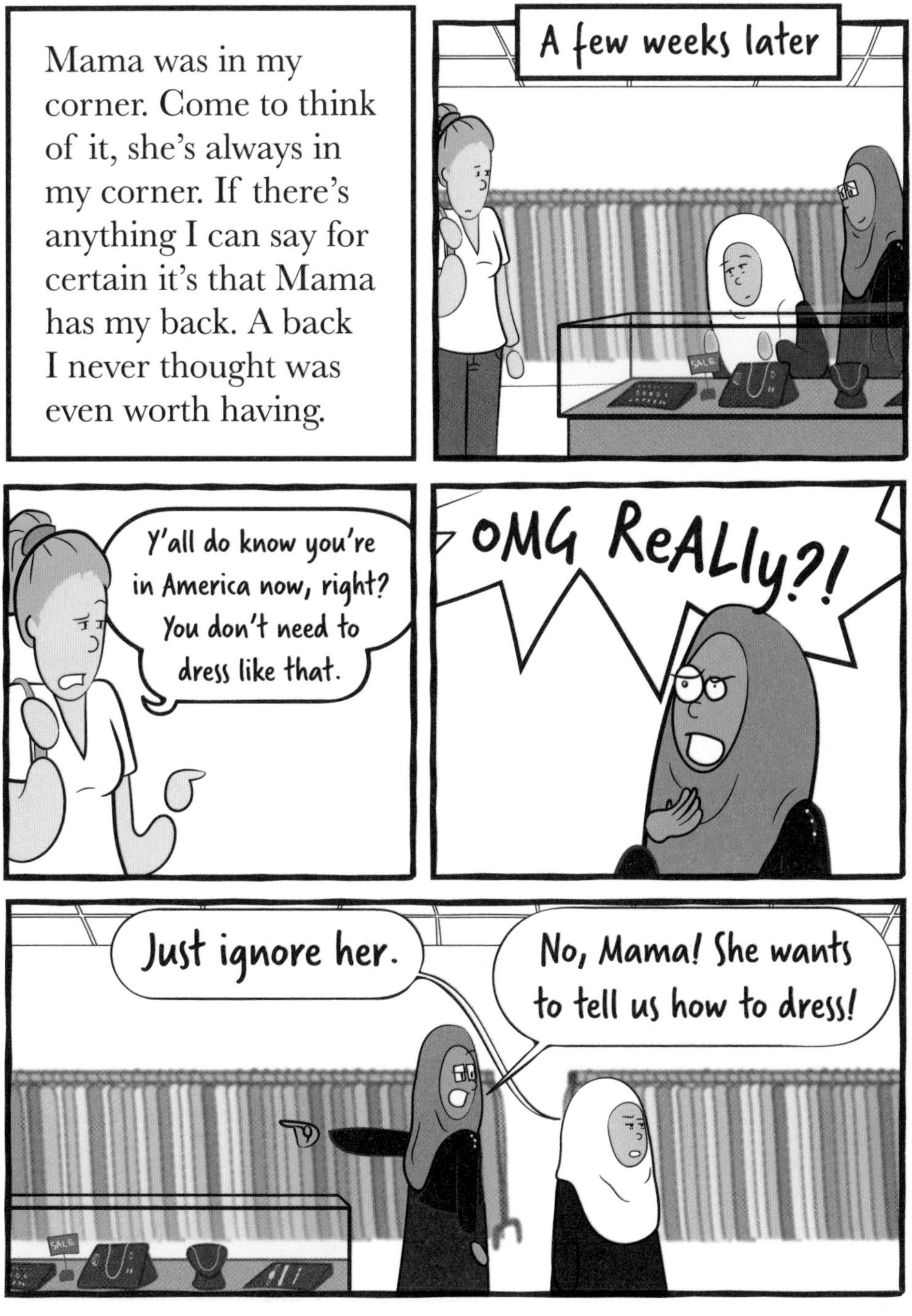
Mama was in my corner. Come to think of it, she's always in my corner. If there's anything I can say for certain it's that Mama has my back. A back I never thought was even worth having.
A few weeks later
Y'all do know you're in America now, right? You don't need to dress like that.
OMG ReALly?!
Just ignore her.
No, Mama! She wants to tell us how to dress!
SALE
SALE

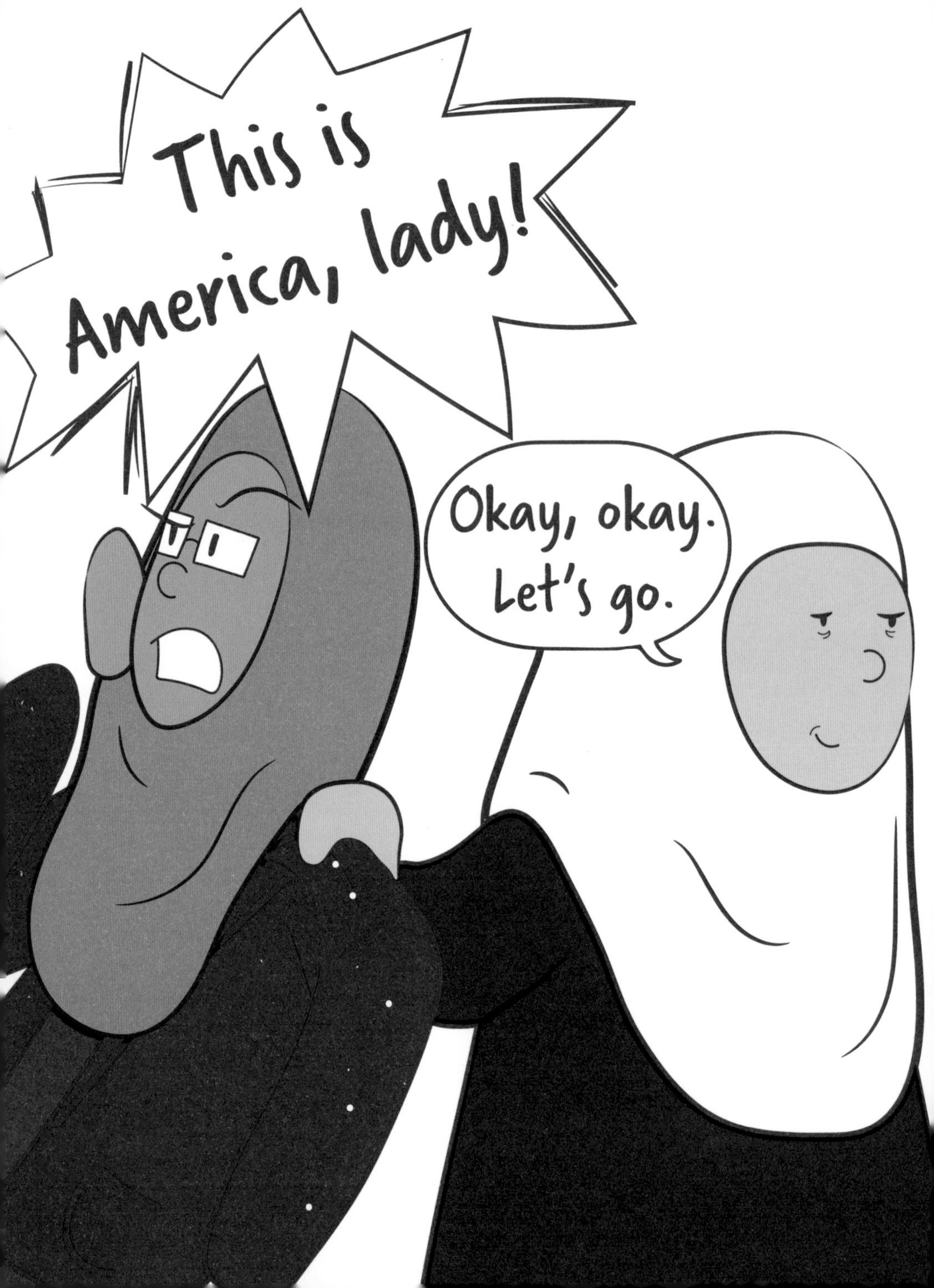
This is America, lady!
Okay, okay. Let's go.

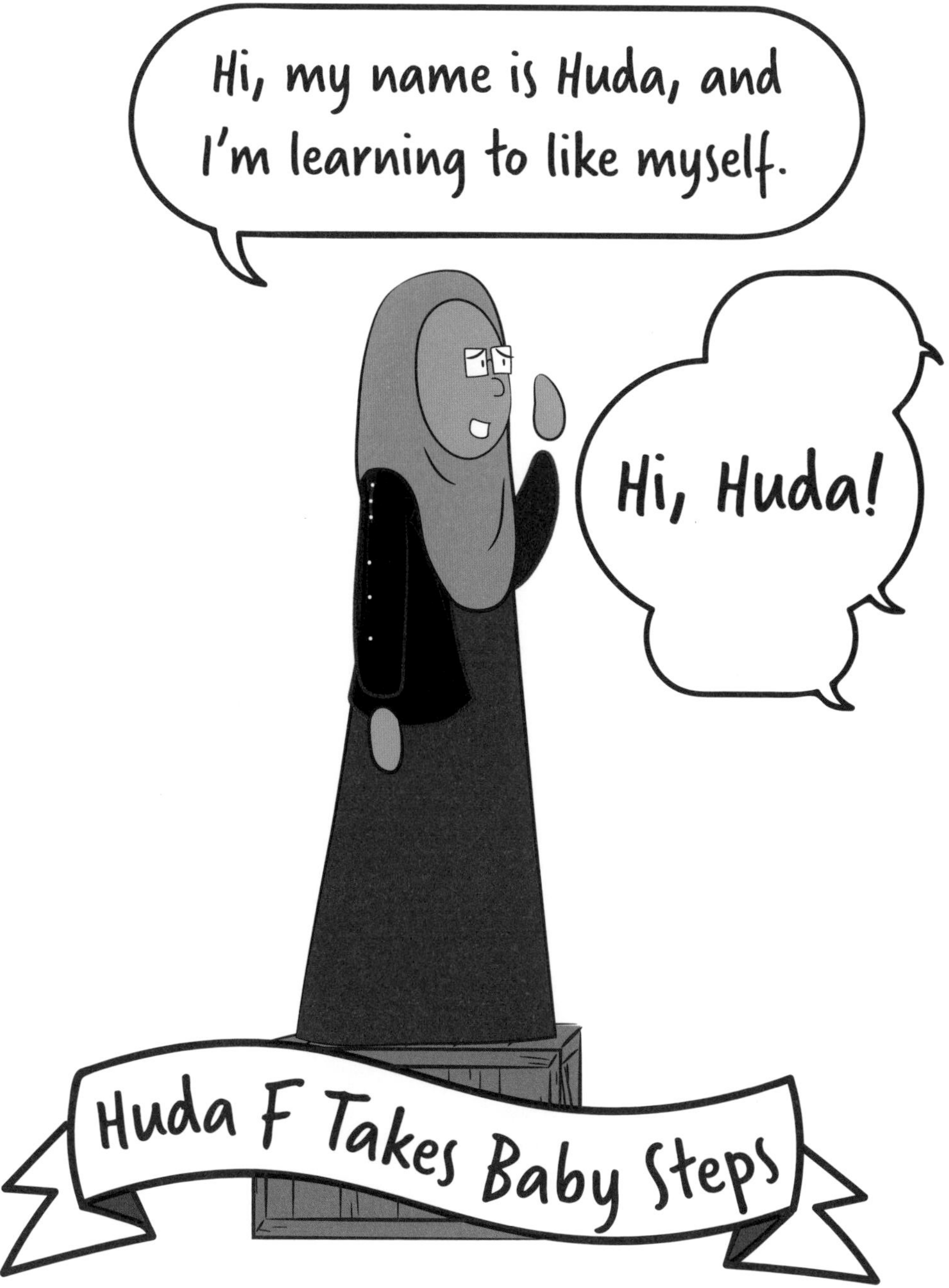
Hi, my name is Huda, and I'm learning to like myself.
Hi, Huda!
Huda F Takes Baby Steps

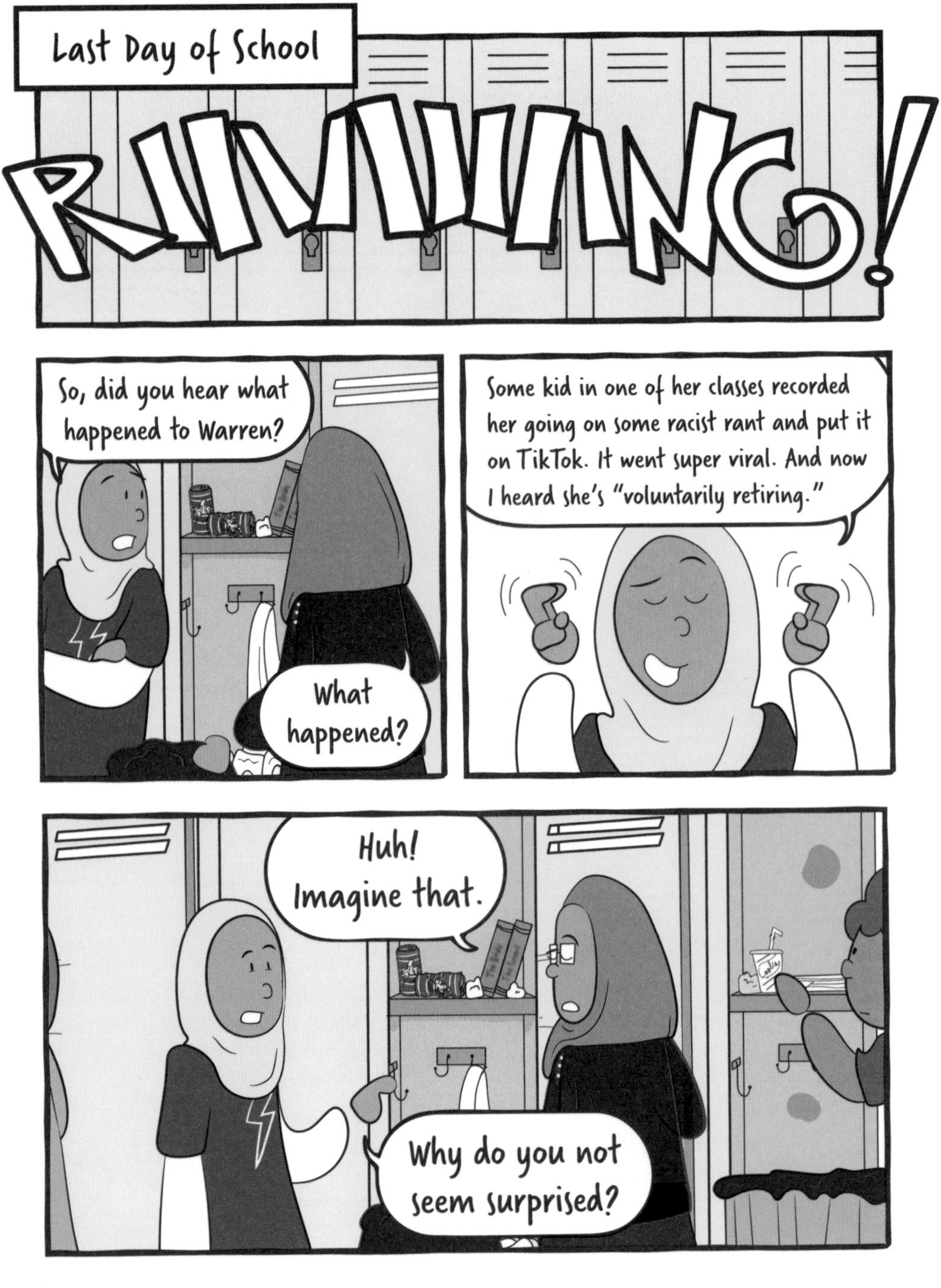
Last Day of School
RIIIIIIIING!
So, did you hear what happened to Warren?
What happened?
Some kid in one of her classes recorded her going on some racist rant and put it on TikTok. It went super viral. And now I heard she's "voluntarily retiring."
Huh! Imagine that.
Why do you not seem surprised?

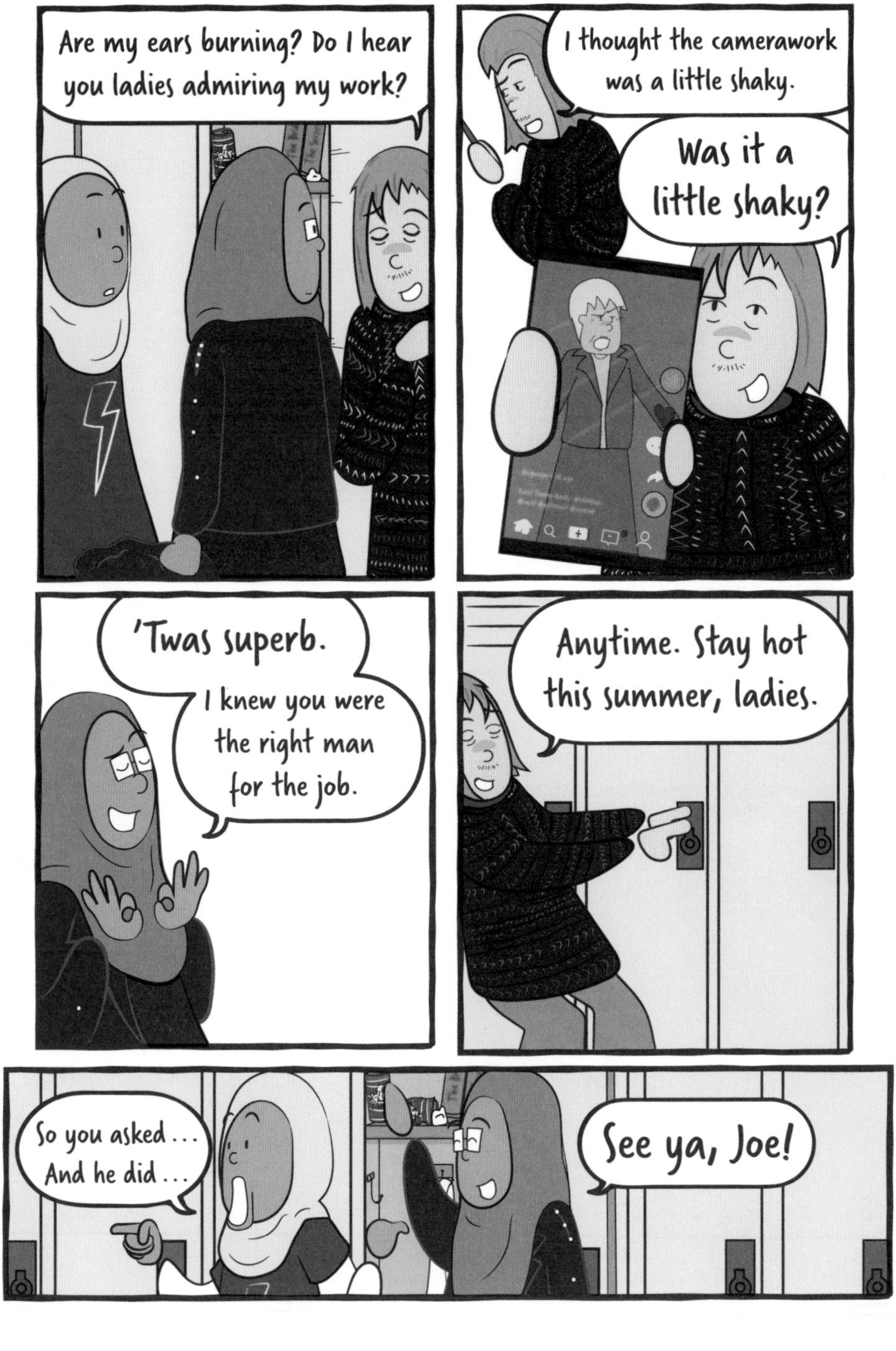
Are my ears burning? Do I hear you ladies admiring my work?
I thought the camerawork was a little shaky.
Was it a little shaky?
'Twas superb.
I knew you were the right man for the job.
Anytime. Stay hot this summer, ladies.
So you asked . . . And he did . . .
See ya, Joe!

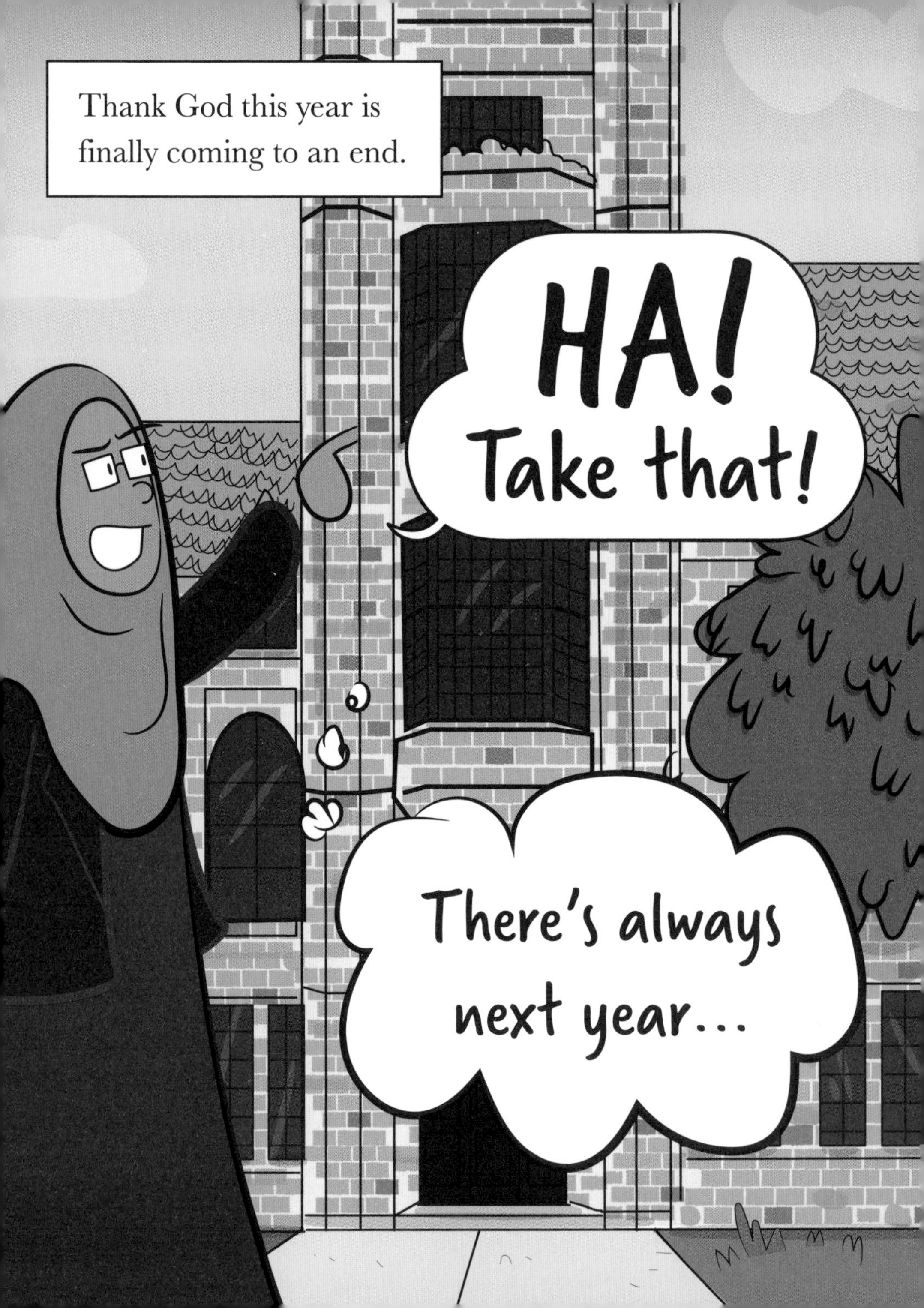
Thank God this year is finally coming to an end.
HA! Take that!
There's always next year...

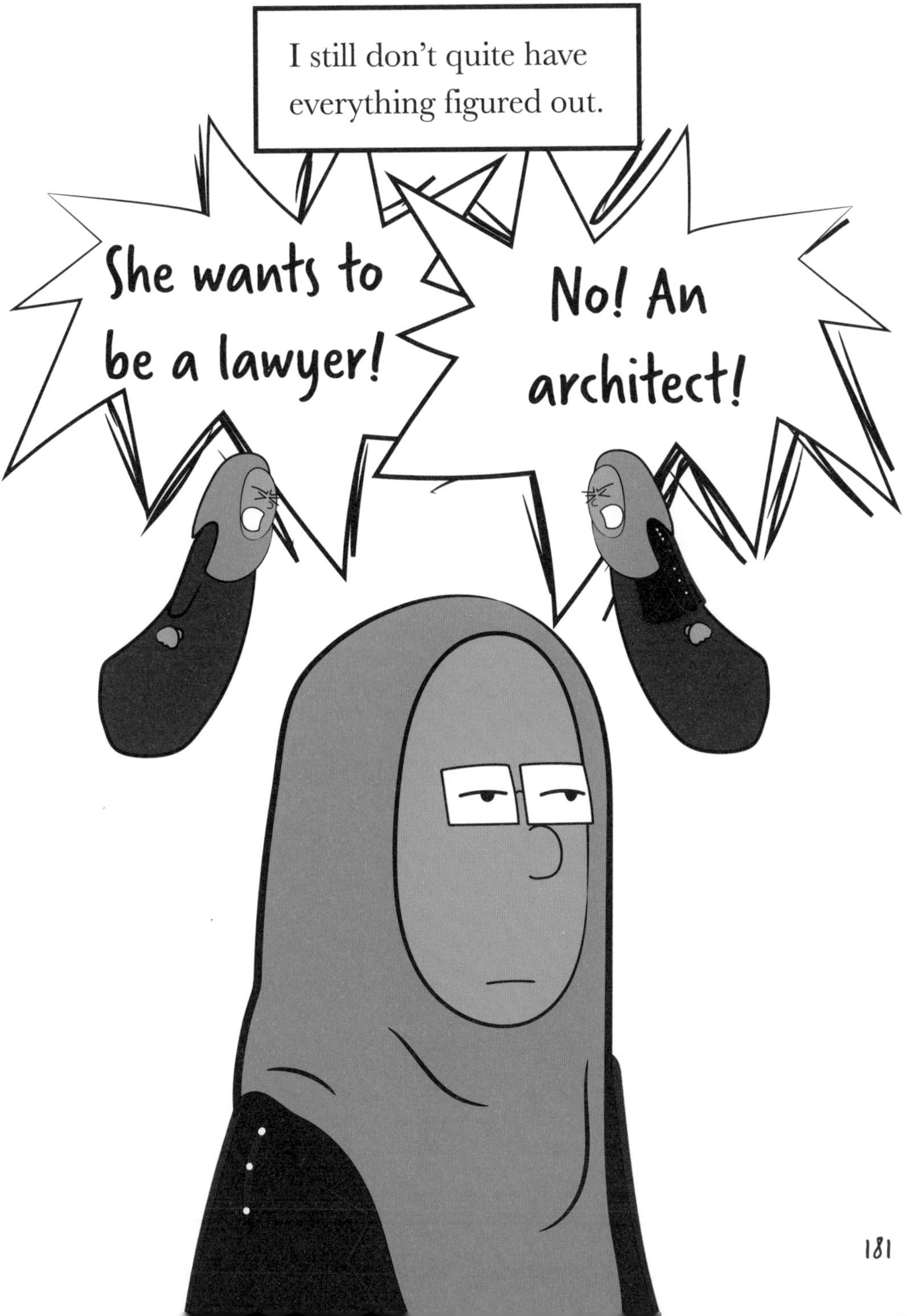
I still don't quite have everything figured out.
She wants to be a lawyer!
No! An architect!

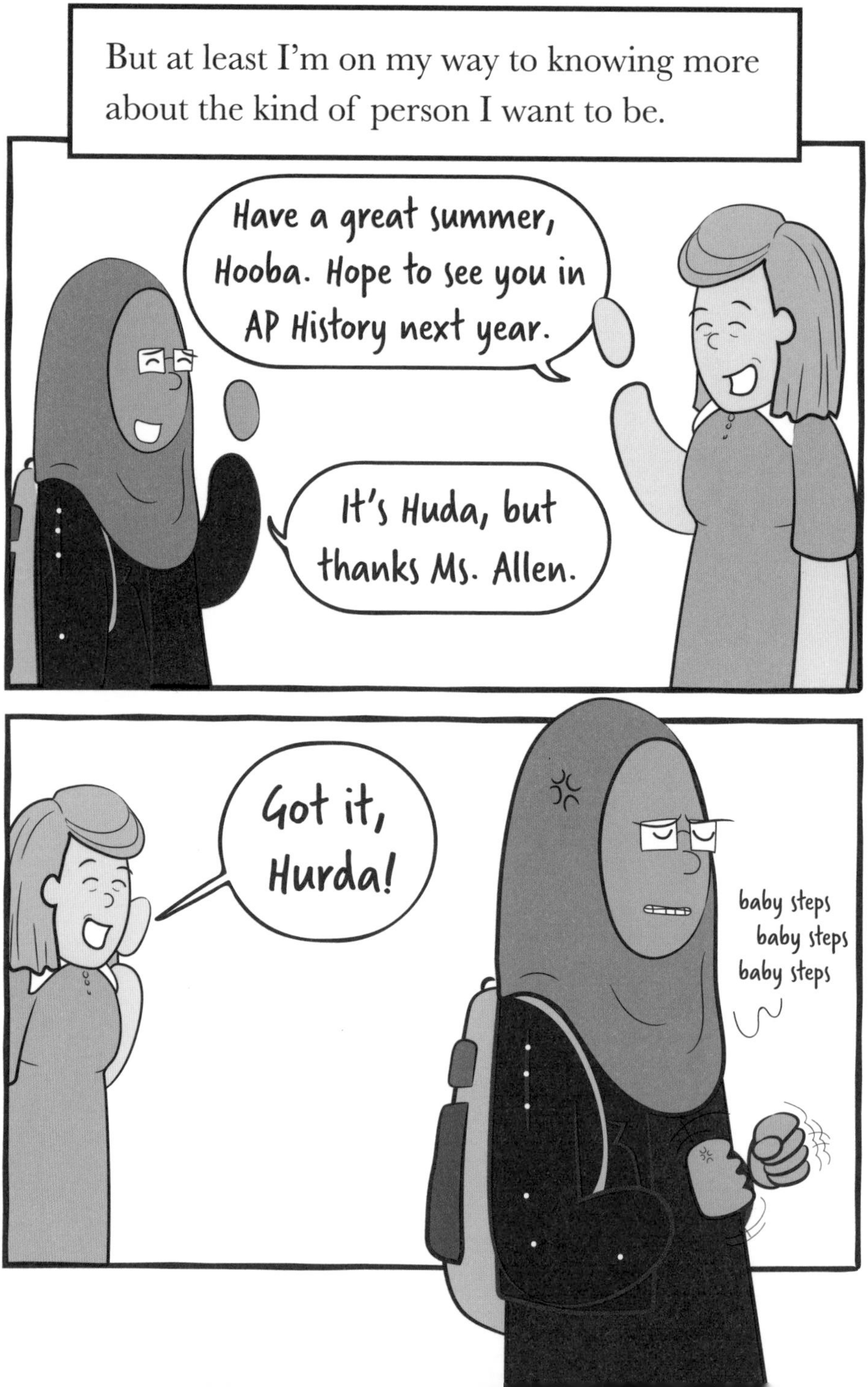
But at least I'm on my way to knowing more about the kind of person I want to be.
Have a great summer, Hooba. Hope to see you in AP History next year.
It's Huda, but thanks Ms. Allen.
Got it, Hurda!
baby steps
baby steps
baby steps

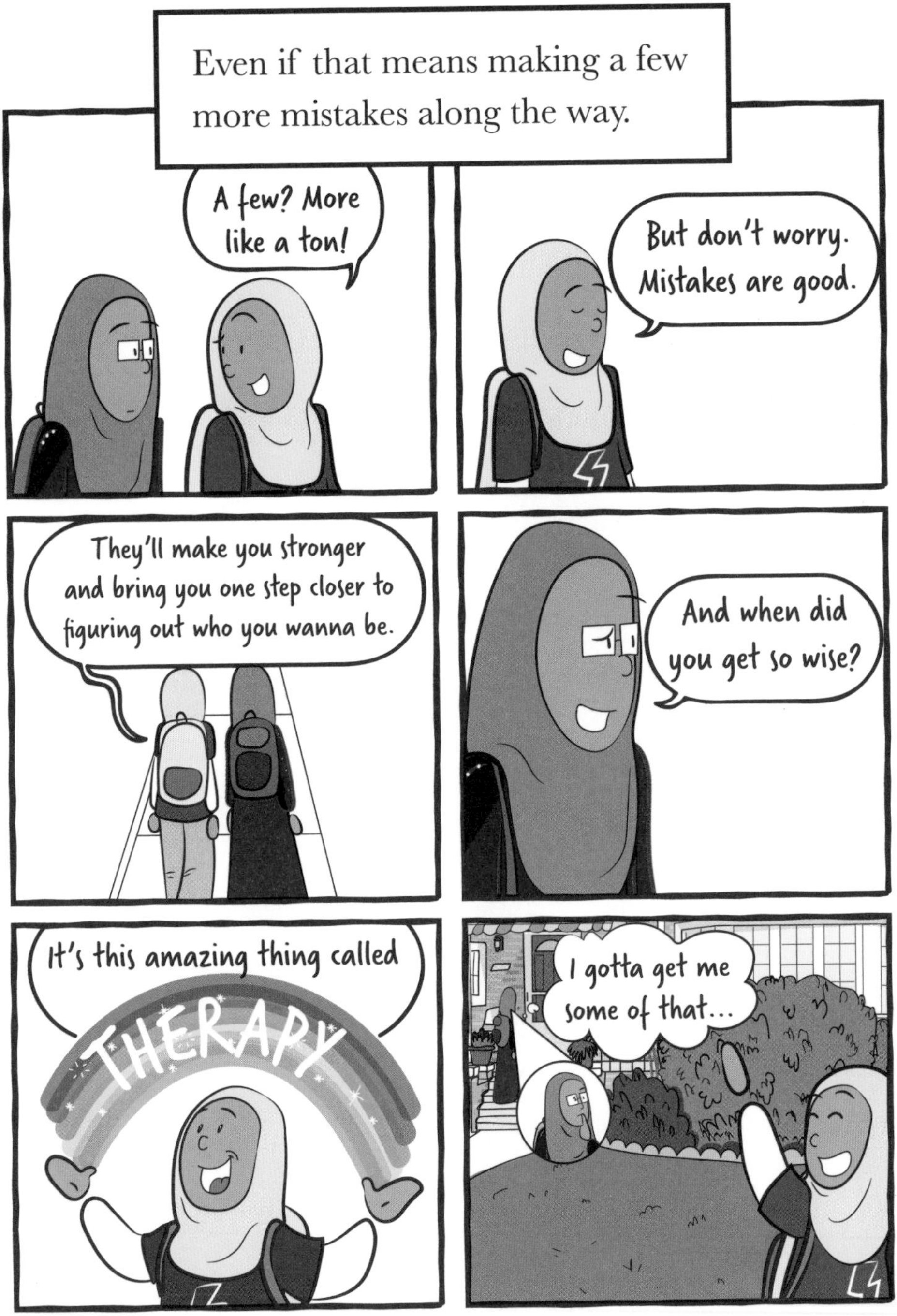
Even if that means making a few more mistakes along the way.
A few? More like a ton!
But don't worry. Mistakes are good.
They'll make you stronger and bring you one step closer to figuring out who you wanna be.
And when did you get so wise?
It's this amazing thing called
THERAPY
I gotta get me some of that...

In the meantime, I just need to make it through the summer.

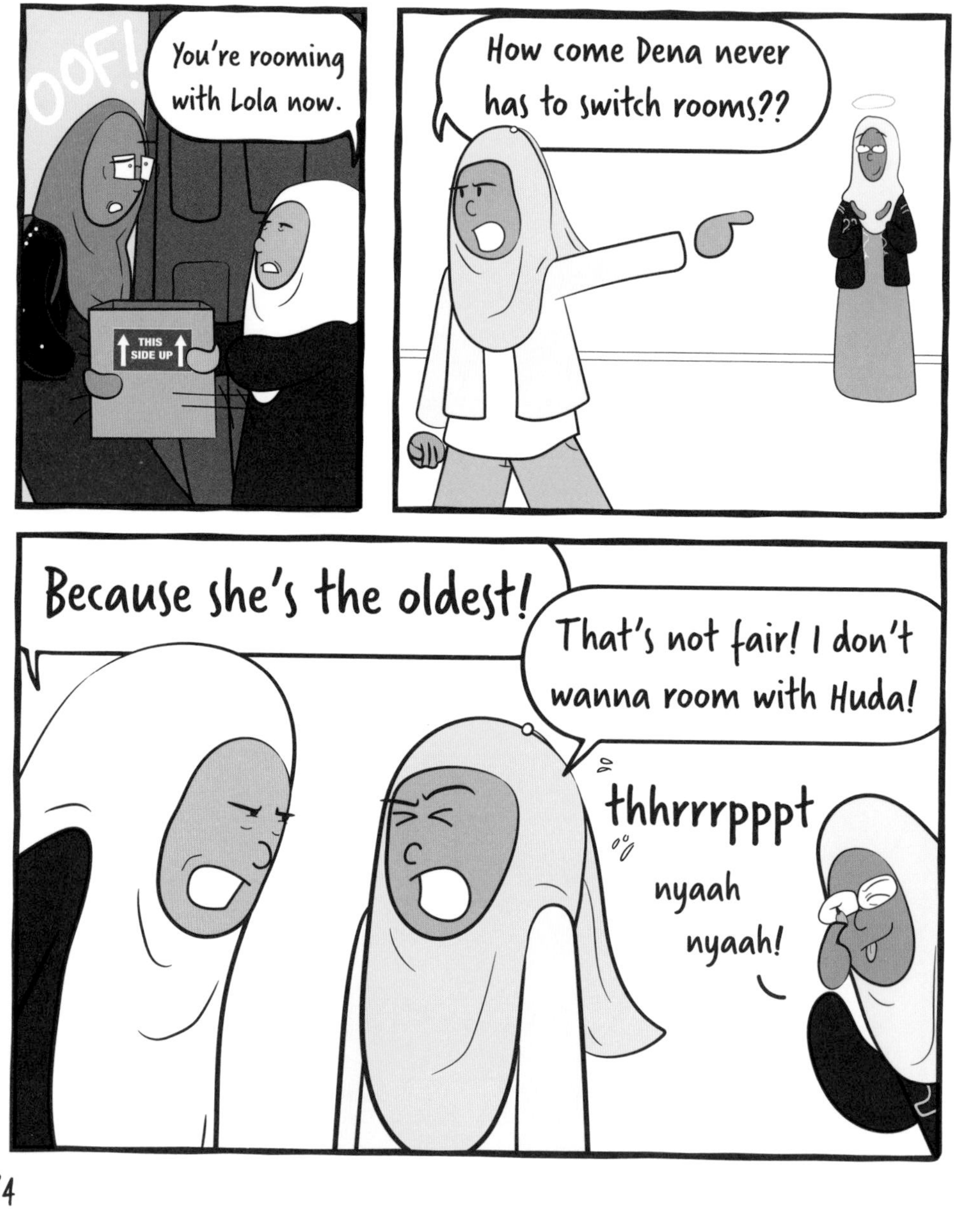
OOF!
You're rooming with Lola now.
THIS SIDE UP
How come Dena never has to switch rooms??
Because she's the oldest!
That's not fair! I don't wanna room with Huda!
thhrrrpppt
nyaah nyaah!

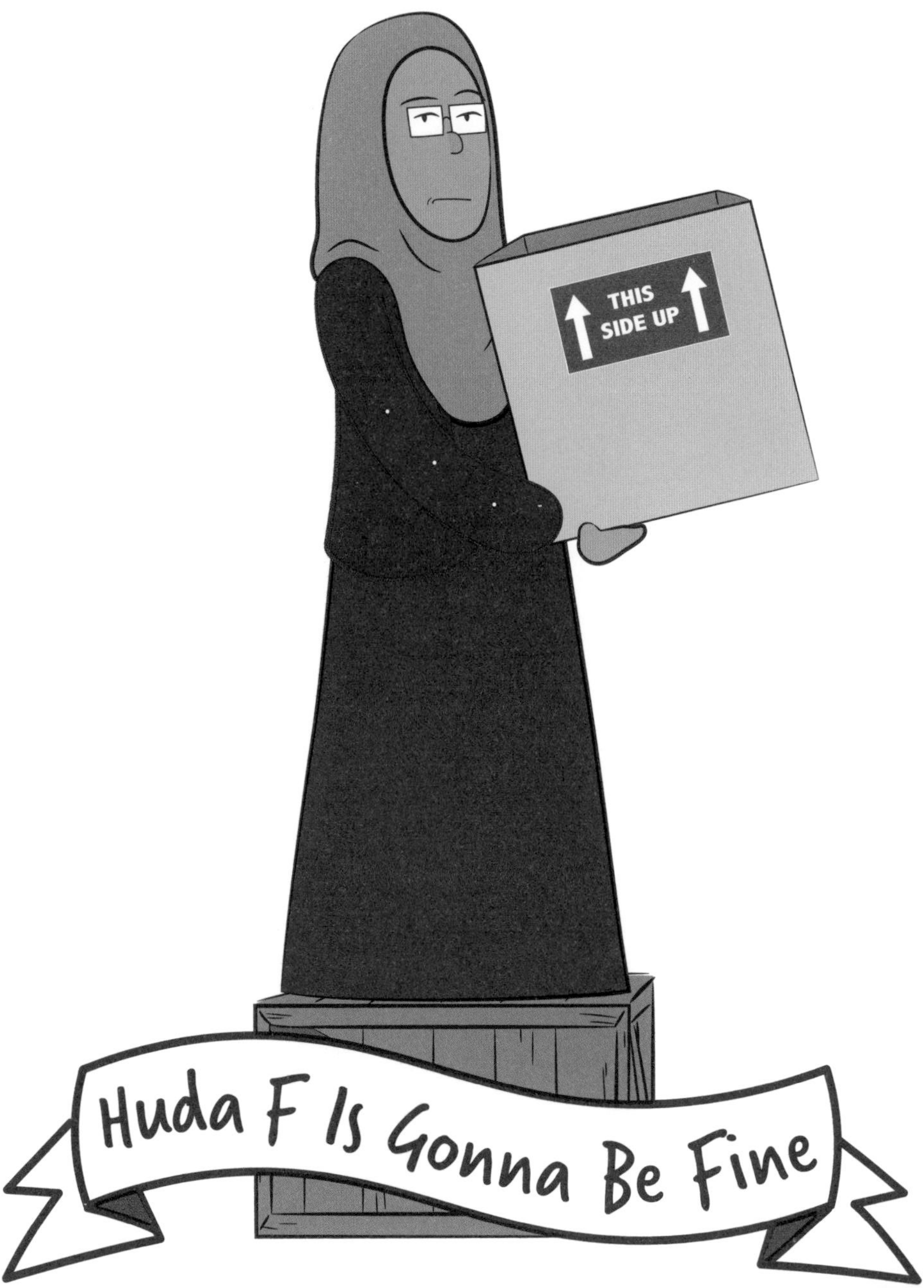
THIS SIDE UP
Huda F Is Gonna Be Fine

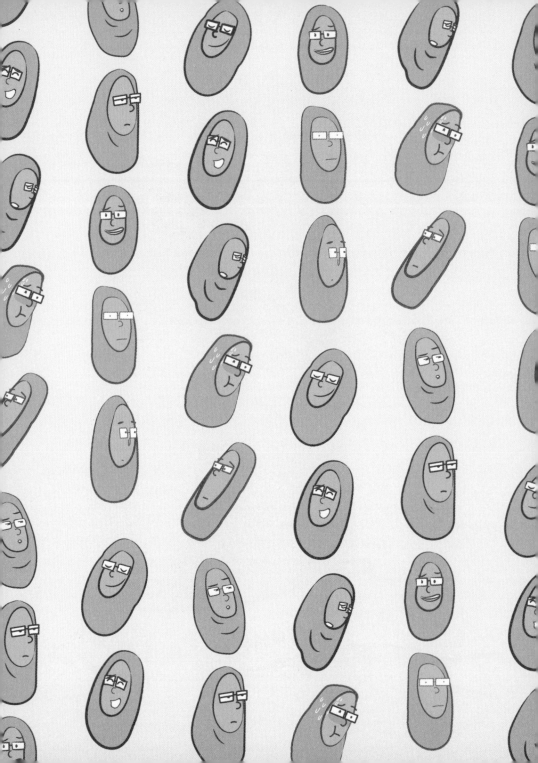

In the name of God,
the Most Gracious the Most Merciful

Acknowledgments

Phew! You made it to the end! This is the best part because now you get to read about all the awesome people who helped bring this book to life.

First, I cannot express enough my gratitude to my husband, who thankfully did not know me in high school and did not have to witness my ridiculous antics and even more ridiculous experiments with different personalities. He was born fully aware and 100 percent sure of who he is, so I know I would have come off as a weirdo and we would probably never have gotten together. But lucky him, here we are! Thank you, babe, for all the weekends spent having fun and making memories with our son while I was holed away trying to finish this book. You are my inspiration and the love of my life.

To my mama and the women of the Muslim community in Dearborn who thought I was never listening during halaqa: I promise I heard every word (some of which even stuck!). Thank you for making dua for me and for teaching me the importance of finding balance and moderation in everything I do.

To Sarah Sultan and S. K. Ali: many MANY thanks for being my sounding boards and helping me get this story just right. Your friendship and guidance will never go unappreciated.

To my editor Dana, my design editor Mina, and the publishing team at Dial: my deepest thanks. Your notes and encouragement for making sure I told my most authentic story are so appreciated. And to know I didn't have to compromise myself to tell this story brought me such relief.

And finally, this book could not have been written without the unwavering support of my agent, Kathleen, and the team at New Leaf Literary. Kathleen, you are so good at everything you do and I am constantly inspired by you. Thank you for believing in me!